TUGBOAT ANNIE

Great Stories from
THE SATURDAY EVENING POST

Other books in this series

GREAT LOVE STORIES
from *The Saturday Evening Post*

MYSTERY & SUSPENSE
Great Stories from *The Saturday Evening Post*

GREAT WESTERNS
from *The Saturday Evening Post*

ALEXANDER BOTTS
Great Stories from *The Saturday Evening Post*

TUGBOAT ANNIE
Great Stories from *The Saturday Evening Post*

TUGBOAT ANNIE

Great Stories from THE SATURDAY EVENING POST

by Norman Reilly Raine

THE CURTIS PUBLISHING COMPANY   INDIANAPOLIS, INDIANA

TUGBOAT ANNIE
GREAT STORIES FROM *THE SATURDAY EVENING POST*

Copyright © 1977 by Elizabeth Raines

Copyright © 1931, 1932, 1934, 1936, 1938
1946, 1947, 1949, 1952, 1953, 1954, 1956, 1957, 1961
by The Curtis Publishing Co.

Printed in the United States of America.
All rights reserved. No part of this book
may be used or reproduced in any manner
whatsoever without written permission
except in the case of brief quotations
embodied in critical articles and reviews.

For information address
The Curtis Publishing Company,
1100 Waterway Boulevard,
Indianapolis, Indiana 46202

Library of Congress Catalog Card Number 77-78985
I.S.B.N. 0-89387-010-Z

CONTENTS

Tugboat Annie	1
Passage to Secoma	18
Spareribs and Sauerkraut	36
Iron John	56
Mr. Bullwinkle Earns His Pay	75
A Matter of Business	96
"If the Cap Fits"	116
Tugboat Annie Sails Again	132
Tugboat Annie Saws Off a Leg	150
Tugboat Annie Wins Her Medal	167
The Framing of Tugboat Annie	184
Tugboat Annie Burns a Bridge	217
Tugboat Annie's Secret	203
Tugboat Annie Loses a Tow	233
Tugboat Annie's Long Shot	248
Tugboat Annie Loses Command	261
Tugboat Annie and the Dangerous Cheapskate	285
Tugboat Annie and the Sunken Gold	298

INTRODUCTION

Tugboat Annie is a character, and in Norman Reilly Raine's stories we see how much a character depends on character, on principles, on honesty, on forthrightness, on consistency. Annie is not above ordering her engineer, Big Sam, to slacken the nuts on the connecting-rod crank bearing on her rival Horatio Bullwinkle's tug, the Salamander. And Bullwinkle is quick to retaliate. It is all give and take dock work. But Annie's character, her knowledge of the sea, of the hazards of shoals and straits and capes around the Washington coast, and her persistence, her daring and ability to enlist maritime law on her side triumph over the pettiness of loosened nuts and bolts and win the day for the Narcissus. Bullwinkle's character is mean while Annie's is purposeful. He is not above calling Annie simple. When a possible contract says about Annie, "She's got a pretty good argument, and she seems to have a head on her," Bullwinkle replies, "So's a glass o' beer but that don't mean nothin'." Annie, who is as good at give and take as a situation-comedy fast man, can be soothingly silent when occasion demands. She is also likable, while her rival Bullwinkle is merely obsequious.

Not everybody takes a liking to Tugboat Annie. They berate her because she is a woman, because she is uncouth, because she persists. "Will you get the hell away from here, you lunatic!" shouts an exasperated shipmaster she is trying to rescue, though she knows the ship is waiting to be saved by Bullwinkle, who has a contract for the job. Undaunted, Annie offers the shipmaster advice which he takes and which later entitles her to salvage rights since it keeps the ship from running afoul.

INTRODUCTION

Annie has a contradictory side to her which endears her to us as firmly in our emotional moorings as her rough language and bravery. For example, Annie has named the other tugs of the Deep-Sea Towing and Salvage Company, and she has chosen monikers for the snub-nosed ruffians that contradict what Raine calls her "hard-bitten soul": Orchid, Pansy, Honeysuckle, Daffodil. When she kicks somebody, her shoe is usually off and she blunts her "Git that long back o' yours out o' the galley, Shif'less, and keep it out! Every time me back's turned, ye snuffle around in here pinchin' grub. Get away aft, ye lazy bag o' bones, and overhaul that line, like I told ye! Go, hump yerself! And darn that hard carcass o' yours!" with her comments about the crew's anatomy. She is like them, she is one of them. But she is smarter, more resourceful, and she has none of their weaknesses—her late husband's drinking, or her crew's laziness, or anybody else's loose thinking—none are part of Annie's makeup.

She wears none. There is nothing behind her homely and honest face except an I.Q. that would do Horatio Hornblower justice, a caginess that puts the devious Bullwinkle to rout in every combat, and a stubbornness and unhypocritical morality that makes her the queen of the waves and an undoubted commercial success as a tugboat master. She changes her hat through the years—at first she wears a battered bonnet with a battle-scarred feather, then switches it for a felt man's hat, but she never changes her good sense and industriousness.

Raine was a first-class writer: "At sunset the wind increased, blowing the smoke of steamers in indigo veils over the white-capped harbor, and when darkness fell, it had increased to a half gale. The fleet of weather-beaten tugs alongside the wharf moved and chafed restlessly as the wind and tide tugged at them, and small craft on the sound fled for the winking harbor lights."

"It was one of those leaping mornings when the world seems to have been sluiced in a bath of rarefied sunlight, then hung on a celestial clothesline to dry. The brilliant day, the sharp invigorating breeze, gave to the Secoma waterfront a staccato air, so that harbor shipping appeared to move with greater alacrity, the ferries shuttling across Puget Sound tootled with a shriller exhilaration, and even the shabby dockside loungers seemed to loaf at a quickened tempo." But Raine, like his heroine, never loses himself in purple prose. The action, the plot catch you, not the words.

What happens next drives the reader along with the relentless pleasure Annie herself feels when the Narcissus is at work, earning her keep, outwitting her antagonists in the eternal struggle to win the waves.

INTRODUCTION

Great *Post* illustrators, Anton Otto Fischer, who specialized in seascapes, and Harold Von Schmidt, completed the handsome Tugboat Annie stories with paintings that left readers clamoring for more. Raine turned out an incredible 75. But it was never enough. The Marie Dressler and Marjorie Rambeau movies helped fill some of the gap but the appetite for the elephantine Annie seemed insatiable. Here then are 18 of Raine's classics, agonizingly selected from the 75, all of which cried to be included.

TUGBOAT ANNIE
Great Stories from
THE SATURDAY EVENING POST

TUGBOAT ANNIE

"I'm fired? Who says I'm fired?" Tugboat Annie Brennan leaned across the desk of the president of the Deep-Sea Towing and Salvage Company, and thrust her formidable jowls into his red, embarrassed face. She repeated, with husky emphasis: "Who says so?"

"Now, Annie! Please——"

"Don't you 'Now, Annie' me, Alec Severn! And answer my question!"

"Why——" Mr. Severn coughed, and mopped his perspiring brow. "Well—hrrmph! It's Mr. Conroy. The business needs money, and he's putting it in—a lot of it. Enough to buy that new tugboat we want so badly. He's an absolute godsend. But he's got ideas—about women, I mean."

"Huh! What man hasn't? And what is these fool ideas?"

"Well, he—he thinks that managing a towing and salvage company is a man's job. He has the notion that women lack the—well, intelligence was the word he used—to handle the active side of the business. Says men won't do their maximum of efficient work under a woman chief. They resent her."

Tugboat Annie snorted, "I'd like to see any o' the boys on the Narcissus resent me. I'd heave 'em——"

"I know—I know! But Mr. Conroy doesn't understand. You and I belong to the old school, Annie, and our ways don't seem to fit these days somehow. Mr Conroy, now, he's modern. He's efficient and understands modern business methods." He hesitated and lowered his voice: "Tell you the truth, Annie, I don't just fancy the man. There's something about him—cold. If there was any other way of getting the money I'd see him in——I mean, I wouldn't have him! But

1

there isn't. And he thinks that——Wait a minute. Here he comes up the stairs. He can tell you himself—thank the Lord!" he concluded.

Tugboat Annie drew herself up and glared, first out the window, to the crowded shipping of the harbor and the busy wharves, and then at the office door. She was large-framed, solidly built, with rugged, almost masculine features, and shrewd, quick, blue eyes, and her movements had an elephantine energy that galvanized everyone with whom she came in contact. When she passed through a room, dust and odd bits of paper danced in her wake. And when she stood, as now, with beetling brows and sturdy legs apart, the feather in her antiquated bonnet nodding raffish defiance, she looked not unlike a blowzy but exceedingly combative bulldog.

The door opened and Severn held his breath. Mr. Conroy entered, a businessman from his crisp, graying hair, precisely parted, to his efficiently polished English oxfords. Mr. Conroy liked to convey the impression of a micrometrically functioning, hard-glazed piece of steel mechanism; and his impersonation was highly successful.

"Morning, Severn," he said crisply; but Tugboat Annie heaved herself forward.

"Say!" she demanded. "Are you the lallapaloosa that says I'm fired?"

Mr. Conroy drew back, hastily adjusting his glasses. "Why, I'm afraid I don't understand."

"Neither do I. Neither does Alec. So who does?"

Severn said, placatingly, "This is Mrs. Brennan, Mr. Conroy. You remember we discussed her——"

"Tugboat Annie Brennan! That's what the waterfront calls me. And I didn't get the name pushin' toy boats around the bathtub, either! Now, what you firin' me for?"

Severn interposed again: "You see, Conroy, Mrs. Brennan's husband, Terry, was senior captain of the company for a good many years. He was a good tugboat man, but——"

"Terry was a drunken sot. But he was the best husband a woman ever had, Lord rest his soul! And in between his rasslin' bouts with old John——"

"John?" said Conroy, with raised eyebrows.

"Barleycorn!" said Tugboat Annie briefly. "In between bouts I ran his job for him. A year ago he died o'——"

"Syncope," Severn hastily interpolated.

"Water poisonin'!" Tugboat Annie corrected grimly. "Drank a glass o' water, thinkin' it was gin, and his stomach couldn't stand the shock. Alec let me stay in his place, and I done a good job of it too. Ain't I, Alec?"

"Yes, you have, Annie," Severn assented. "Mrs. Brennan knows her work and this coast, Conroy, as few men do. She's been at it for twenty years or more, and I've full confidence in her. Don't you think——"

During the recital Conroy's thin lips had tightened to an obdurate line.

"The opinion I expressed to you yesterday, Severn, has not altered. It has been strengthened. To be quite frank, Mrs.—er—Brennan does not impress me. She is too—shall we say, informal? I propose, if I enter this company, to make it the strongest on the seaboard, and the position of senior captain will be one of responsibility, dignity. No doubt she knows something about the work. But she is a woman, and—in this business particularly—that is not a good thing."

Tugboat Annie choked, was ready with a stormy interruption, but Conroy held up a peremptory hand.

"Her influence, in what essentially is a man's sphere, is bound to have undesirable results. I think I can see it, even now, in small things. The names of your present vessels, for instance."

"I named them tugs! What's the matter with 'em?" Annie demanded furiously.

Conroy shrugged. "Tugs connote strength; rude but efficient power. And instead of calling them appropriate names, such as, say, Trojan, Titan, Atlas, Hercules, they are called"—he smiled acridly—"Daffodil, Asphodel, Pansy and Narcissus."

"What of it? Can't a person like posies?"

"May I remind you that I am not deaf?"

"Mebbe you're not, but you're awful dumb! Here I've give twenty years of my life to the company, and you come along and I'm throwed out like an old sweat rag. Didn't it ever occur to you, Mr. Conman, or whatever your name is, that loyalty and hard work's worth something to business, as well as a lot o' fancy names? Huh? . . . Oh, well! What's the good o' spinnin' me jaw? When do I go, Alec?"

Conroy said magnanimously: "I have no objection to your carrying on until we get a man to fill the place, Mrs. Brennan."

"You have no objection, ye cold-blooded haddock! What have you got to say about it? You ain't even in the company yet. I'll take my sailin' orders from Alec here, if he ain't lost his tongue."

"Go back to the Narcissus, Annie," said Severn unhappily. "I'll let you know. I'm sorry——"

Conroy moved apprehensively aside as Tugboat Annie barged toward him, but she passed without a word and went down the stairs to the bright, dust-hazed sunlight of the busy waterfront street. Trucks rumbled and bumped over the pavement, motor traffic roared past, a long line of box cars was shunted by, and from the harbor beyond the sheds came a sonorous chorus of whistles—tugs, liners and deep-water tramps. Blind and deaf to it all, her hat feather bobbing deliriously, she fussed through the traffic and was nearly run down by a three-horse dray. She looked up at the grinning driver and stopped, inclined for battle.

"Don't ye know the rules o' the road, ye cock-eyed baboon?" she roared.

Crossing the railroad tracks, she got one shoe half full of gravel, which did not improve her temper. She limped painfully out on the long, dingy wharf alongside which were berthed the tugs of the Deep-Sea Towing and Salvage Company, and, part way, stopped to remove the gravel from her shoe. She shook the shoe irascibly, and it flew from her grasp and disappeared with a splash into the dock. Tugboat Annie watched it sink, her lips moving wordlessly, then limped on her stockinged foot, great toe protruding, the length of the wharf.

The Narcissus, biggest of the fleet, was moored at the end; and when she saw the familiar, powerful snub bow with its great collision mat of woven hemp, bleached by hard service in sun and rain and salt water, the glass-enclosed pilothouse, the heavy towing bitts on the fantail, and the grimy red and white and black of the house, she forgot for a moment that it was no longer her home.

"Ain't she the dirty old tramp?" she muttered pridefully to herself. "Got to get a new sta'board fender, though."

She stepped heavily from the stringpiece to the narrow deck, and crossed through, over the engine-room grating, to the port side. A gangling man in stained dungarees, with a prominent Adam's apple, a stubble of beard and amiable, washed-out eyes, was seated on the pilothouse steps, his neglected paint pot beside him, while he sucked on a cigarette. He looked up at her approach, flung the butt hastily over the side and commenced furiously to slap paint on the house. Tugboat Annie bellowed at him:

"Shiftless, you been poundin' your ear all mornin' while I been ashore? Ye have, ye lazy numskull! Look at that house! Hardly a dab on it! Come here!"

With an uncertain grin, Shiftless approached, an elbow raised to protect his ear. "Aw, now, Annie——" he protested.

She gave him a hearty cuff. "You been drinkin' some o' Rosinski's snake blood again, too, ye worthless hound! You lemme sniff that stuff on ye again and I'll skin ye alive. D'ye hear?"

"Yes, Annie."

"Don't forget it! Where's Sam—in the engine room?"

"Yes'm."

"Go below, then, and tell him I want a complete list of engine-room stores by six o'clock tonight. And stop in the galley and tell Pinto I want a list o' grub on hand from him." She noticed his startled stare. "What's the matter—you paralyzed? . . . Well, move!"

She watched, grimly, as he dropped his brush and ran. "They won't say I didn't turn the old hooker over to 'em shipshape," she grunted. "Frozen-faced old sculpin!"

She went into her cabin and flung her bonnet, with its agitated feather, on the settee. Then she commenced to change, her gaze roving around the familiar, cluttered room that had been her only home for so many years. Her glance rested finally, after purposely avoiding it, upon a large tinted chromo of the late Captain Brennan, in a plush-and-gold oval frame. The departed's face was round and beefily good-natured, with a half grin under the large, black, bartender's mustache, a lock of glossy hair plastered down his forehead, and the humorous, dark eyes of Erin.

Tugboat Annie stood motionless, regarding it. "You certainly was a soak, Terry," she muttered huskily, "but— Oh, go on, you big louse! What are ye starin' at?" She turned the picture to the wall and rubbed her nose hard with her knuckles. "Sentimental old fool I'm growin' to be! Where the devil'd I put me other shoe?"

They were at supper—the small ship's company of the Narcissus, with Pinto, the cook—when the telephone on the wharf rang sharply. It was for Tugboat Annie. She lumbered out onto the quay, her capacious mouth full of steak and potatoes, and with a slice of bread and butter in her fist.

"Hello," she said, gulping hastily. "Wha'—what's that? . . . A ship ashore? Where? . . . All right, Alec. I'll take the Pansy along, too, huh? . . . What's that? Conroy coming? . . . No—no! I wasn't swearin'—just swallerin' me supper. Tell him to shake a leg, then. If he shakes it hard enough mebbe it'll break. Wants to l'arn something about the work, huh? Hmmph! . . . All right, Alec. Same to you, wi' knobs on it, you old gafoozeler!"

She waddled hastily back to the Narcissus, cramming her face with bread and butter as she went, and burst into the tiny saloon.

"Git below, Sam, and you, too, Shiftless. One of you other boys stand by to cast off. Somebody tell Pinto to keep supper warm."

"What's all the excitement, Annie?" asked Sam, a slow-speaking, slow-moving mountain of mechanical competency.

"There's a ship—the Barracuda—beached and on fire in Juan de

Fuca Strait, near Neah Bay. You know her—the one that runs to California and Mexican ports, with old Skinflint Crabtree in command. Look alive, now! The Puget Sound Towing Company'll be sending a tug; so will the Secoma Salvage crowd; so it'll be a race. Oh, cuss it!" She stopped suddenly. "We've got to wait for a passenger. Feller called Conroy, who's goin' to be Severn's partner in the company. Well, go on, all of you; don't stand there goggle-eyed! Alec can have a partner if he wants, I guess!"

She went to the pilothouse and looked out the door. Conroy was proceeding sedately along the wharf. Tugboat Annie bawled:

"Get a move on, queer feller! A person'd think ye was walkin' on fly paper!"

He came to the rail, jumped down. "What's the hurry?" he inquired crisply. "Don't you know that haste breeds inefficiency?"

"So does a litter o' feathered pigs! . . . All right, Henry; cast off!"

Tugboat Annie spun the wheel over. The engine-room signal jingled and the Narcissus drew away from the wharf and piled up a big bow wave as she headed up Puget Sound. The fresh breeze of the afternoon had dropped, and the night was calm and almost sultry; and as darkness came and Secoma fell astern, the lights of the towns scattered along the sound danced with jeweled brilliance over the water that spread like a sheet of rippling orchid silk to the far, island-dotted shore. Two hundred yards astern, the riding lights of the Pansy glowed, ruby and emerald and topaz, in the velvet dusk.

For a time Tugboat Annie steered in silence, with Conroy standing on deck outside the pilothouse. Suddenly she addressed him:

"You had your supper yet?"

"No"—testily.

"Ain't that just too bad?" Tugboat Annie gave her attention to her steering. Then she shook herself in a burst of exasperation and ripped out: "Darn me, anyway! . . . I never give meself no peace! Go on along to the cabin, then! The boys'll be finishin' their supper presently, and I'll have Pinto set a place for ye."

Conroy eyed her coldly. "You mean I'm to eat with the crew?"

"Why not?" Tugboat Annie snapped. "It won't poison 'em, mebbe."

"I'll have mine alone," Conroy said firmly. "I'm practically a member of the firm now, you know. Mr. Severn and I came to an agreement this afternoon."

"That was clever of Alec," Tugboat Annie grunted.

"What was?"

"Comin' to an agreement wi' you." She put her head out the door. "Pinto! Pinto!"

A voice hailed back, "Yaas, ma'am?"

"Set a place for the queer feller in the cabin. If he don't come for it, he don't eat."

"Yaas, ma'am!"

Conroy was no fool. He went aft to his meal.

The night passed, and at daybreak Tugboat Annie was again at the wheel, relieving the yawning mate. The Narcissus was forging steadily through the wind-ruffled blueness of Juan de Fuca Strait, with the snowy peaks of the Olympic Peninsula far off to port, making a glory of the morning sky. The Pansy was a mile astern; and to starboard, one slightly ahead, the other abeam, were the big wrecking tugs of the rival companies. Conroy, who had been forced to sleep on the pilothouse settee, was also up and about, stretching his limbs after an uncomfortable night.

He stood on the sloping forward deck of the Narcissus, drinking in the sharp, salt-laden air, when Tugboat Annie hailed him.

"Ye came aboard to l'arn things, didn't ye, mister?"

"To observe things, Mrs. Brennan."

"Aye? Well there's Lesson No. 1 in the tugboat business, or any other kind o' business."

"What is that?"

"Not to let your competitors beat ye to a job," she elaborated. "See them tugs over there? One's the Firefly and the other's the General Mason, both belongin' to rival companies. And see that point o' land ahead? That's Cape Flattery. That's where the Barracuda's piled up. Look at them tugs pushin' the water away. Whoops! Go along and tell Sam to make her give everything she's got!"

Caught against his will in the current of rivalry, Conroy obeyed. Black smoke poured from the Narcissus's funnel crown, and there was a slight access of speed. But the competing tugs also cracked on their ultimate ounce of pressure and the positions of the three remained unchanged. The nearest tug—the Firefly—edged close, and a red-whiskered giant in her pilothouse leaned out.

"Hey there, Annie!" he bawled. "What'll ye give me to go home?"

"Hello, Red!" Tugboat Annie boomed. "I'll tell your wife where I seen ye night afore last, if ye don't. Go on now; beat it, afore that face o' yours turns me breakfast!"

Red Whiskers chortled delightedly. They exchanged further rough persiflage, in which Tugboat Annie more than held her own, and he sheered away.

They surged around the point almost abreast, and their quarry lay before them: a big five-thousand-ton steamer, with rusty, red-lead-patched hull, dun-colored houses and an orange funnel. She was lying with a slight list to starboard, her forefoot on a shelving rock and her stern afloat in deep water. Some distance off her stern the flooding tide boiled and receded over the hidden reefs through which she had made her course the previous day. A pale streamer of smoke still spiraled upward in the quiet air from one of the forward holds. Simultaneously the racing tugs whistled, and figures waved in response from the stranded vessel's deck.

Tugboat Annie signaled the engine room and the Narcissus threaded skillfully through the reefs and came to rest in the clear water almost under the vessel's stern, with the words on her counter—Barracuda, San Pedro—looming above. A short distance off, the other tugs rounded to, rolling lazily in the long swell.

There was confused shouting on the Barracuda's deck, and a seaman ran aft and leaned over the poop rail. He addressed the Narcissus: "Captain Crabtree says, will you come abreast o' the gangway? There's clear water there."

Tugboat Annie looked faintly puzzled. Then she set her massive jaw, and calling Henry to the wheel, walked casually along the port side to the fantail, inspecting the stranded tramp's position. She halted and looked over the side for a moment, as though gauging the depth of water and the position of the rocks under the steamer's stern; then returned to the pilothouse. The Narcissus sloshed around and nosed into line with the other two, abreast of the partly lowered gangway.

A thin, walnut-faced man with prim lips and a small nose, slightly drooping at the end, stood in the waist at the head of the gangway. His calculating eyes surveyed the three tugs, waiting on the other side of the reef like dogs about to scramble for a bone, with the Pansy coming rapidly up astern. He raised a megaphone and shouted, with a slightly nasal twang:

"This is just a towing job, boys, for we'll float off at high tide, or kedge off; and we can proceed ourselves in a pinch. But we've a list, and water in No. 1 Hold, and our steering gear's jammed through runnin' in here among the rocks. So I'd rather be towed in. Now, what's your price to Secoma?"

Conroy turned impatiently to Tugboat Annie. "Get a bid in quick."

Tugboat Annie croaked: "Quit your brayin' and shut up! I'll handle this!"

"By the way," resumed the Barracuda's master, "you boats all belong to the same company?"

"Yes!" shouted the red-whiskered one.

"No!" replied the master of the General Mason.

Tugboat Annie did not speak.

"The 'no's' have it," shouted Captain Crabtree with a sly grin. "So ye'll have to bid for it."

Red Whiskers exchanged a few lurid compliments with his rival, and it was a minute or two before they got back to business.

"Come on, boys! We haven't got all week!" the Barracuda's master reminded them. "What's your price?"

"Six hundred dollars, includin' haulin' you off the rocks!" bellowed Red.

"Five hundred and fifty!" countered the General Mason.

"Why the deuce don't you say something?" Conroy demanded angrily of Tugboat Annie.

"Will you close your jaw, horseface?" Annie demanded. She stuck her massive head, adorned with a disreputable felt hat of the late Captain Brennan, out of the door and stared up at the master of the Barracuda.

"What about you?" he called. "You goin' to quote me foolish prices too?"

"What's your cargo?" she bellowed.

Captain Crabtree appeared to hesitate. He said reluctantly: "Fish oils, turpentine, paint——"

"——alcohol, glycerin and tar paper!" she finished for him. "From San Francisco, for Secoma. I know the stuff you generally carry." She left the pilothouse and lumbered out on deck.

The master of the Barracuda registered astonishment, "Sa-ay, you're a woman!"

"They ain't no law against that!" Tugboat Annie shot back. "What did ye think I was—a giraffe?"

"But it's kind of unusual——"

"So's elephant's eggs! ... Come on, Crabtree; get down to business! A ship on fire and an inflammable cargo—my price is eight hundred dollars!"

"So's mine!" the competing captains amended hastily.

"You're a bunch o' pirates!" Crabtree yelled. "The usual price is about three hundred dollars. Ye'll have to bring that bid down."

"You're a skinflint," Tugboat Annie informed him, "but I'm bringin' it down. Seven hundred and fifty."

"Seven twenty-five!" shouted the General Mason.

"Seven hundred!" Red countered.

"Six hundred and seventy-five!"

"Six hundred and fifty!" Tugboat Annie bawled. "I got two

tugs—that little Pansy there, and this one. Two tugs to haul ye off and into Secoma for only six-fifty! And I'll stand ye a gallon o' beer when we git in!"

"Six hundred flat!" howled the General Mason's skipper. "Cuss you, Annie! You tryin' to ruin the job?"

For half an hour the battle raged. The General Mason dropped out at five hundred, and her disgruntled master stood off and listened. "You're a fool, Red," he volunteered bitterly, "lettin' Annie suck ye into this! Can't you see she's gone off her nut?"

But the Firefly's master was of tougher metal, and the price was hammered down to three hundred and fifty dollars. And there, face and whiskers flaming, and streaming with sweat, he stuck.

"That's my final word, and not a cent less. It ain't worth it." He was dancing with disappointed chagrin. "I wouldn't have run the price that far down, Annie, only ye got me so mad——"

"Take a runnin' jump over the side afore ye catch afire, Red!" she counseled. She looked up at Crabtree, hugely enjoying himself at the head of his vessel's gangway.

"You're sure the fire's under? And what other damage is there beyond the jammed steerin' gear and water in the hold?"

"That's all, missus. Come on; beat the captain's bid! It'll be a bargain for you at three hundred."

Tugboat Annie seemed perplexed, unsure of herself. Her brow was corrugated, her large mouth set in a grim line. She rubbed her nose with her knuckles, then turned abruptly to Conroy.

"Well, fish ears, what would you say?"

Conroy had lost his cool self-possession. He was white with temper.

"Say? I'd say you're the world's colossal ass, woman! You heard what those two captains said, didn't you? You get yourself in a jam, then have to have a man to solve your problem for you. That's woman's business efficiency! If you take that job on now, I stay out of the company!"

Tugboat Annie looked up at the grinning master of the Barracuda. "Three hundred it is, captain!" she said promptly. "We'll stand by to take your line and drag you off."

But Captain Crabtree shook his head. "Oh, no. You're doing the towing, so we'll use your line. And if our steerin' gear's repaired before we git in, I won't need your small tug; so I want a deduction of 30 percent per land mile off the towin' price from the point of repair to Secoma."

"You see? You're properly hooked!" Conroy snarled. "Probably there's nothing much wrong with his steering gear. He'll have it fixed by the time you get underway, and with 30 percent off, you'll have to tow him to Secoma for two hundred and ten dollars! Hah! Woman's clear brain! Woman's business intuition!"

"Let's get going!" Captain Crabtree hailed. "What do you say, there, missus?"

The Firefly surged past, close to the Narcissus's bulwark, with only the lift of a sea between, and her bewhiskered master called across:

"Tell him to go to hell, Annie! I sure would hate to see you stuck like this. We'll all go home and leave him here to rot!"

"You go play parchisi wi' your grandma, Red. I know what I'm doing!" But Tugboat Annie's rugged face was grim as she again turned to the Barracuda. "There's weather comin' up; so when we get ye off and it comes on to blow, use your own power to ease the strain off the towline."

"What? Use my own coal when I'm paying you to tow me? Ha-ha-ha! Not a chance!"

"All right, Captain Shylock!" Tugboat Annie shouted in a sudden rage. "Have it all your own way!"

The wind was blowing along the strait. With the flood tide and the terrific hauling strength of the Narcissus and the Pansy, the Barracuda slowly was snaked off the rock shelf, through the reef, and into deep water beyond. She was down by the head, with the water in the forward hold, but not seriously so. It was nearing dark, with an overcast sky, and sudden squalls spattered the deck with rain. The Narcissus took up the pull of the heavy hawser; the Pansy, with a line aboard, did her bit; and the Barracuda began slowly to forge ahead.

Tugboat Annie stood at the wheel with a huge bean sandwich in one fist and a blue-granite mug of steaming coffee nearby, dividing her time between eating, steering and watching speculatively the head of Conroy, who stood on the forward deck, his hostile face turned toward the stormy waters of the strait ahead. She hailed him:

"Foul-weather Jack's abroad, so if ye like fresh air ye'll get plenty before the night's out."

He rounded on her, his eyes hard as flint through his glasses, his clothes wrinkled and spattered with salt spray. But before he could deliver the spiteful comment that rose to his lips, one of the deck hands appeared in the pilothouse.

He said, "Annie, Sam sent me to tell you that Shiftless is drunk as a fiddler's dog. He can't go on watch."

"What's that?" Tugboat Annie roared. "Here! Take the wheel.... Look out, ye clumsy ox!... There now. Keep her as she is."

She lumbered hastily aft and disappeared down the engine-room housing. For a few minutes there was the sound of a minor hurricane below, dominated by her vigorous bellow. She reappeared, breathless and disheveled, followed by the oil-grimed figure of Sam, the engineer.

"That'll l'arn him, eh?" she threw over her shoulder. The big man grinned.

Conroy turned on her.

"Another sample of feminine muddleheadedness, eh, Mrs. Brennan?" he snapped sarcastically. "No extra fireman. Do you know what you're going to do now?"

"Yes," she wheezed, "I know. It's one problem you're going to answer for me."

"Don't be humorous," he told her shortly, but the expression on her face, heavy and lowering, like an angry mastiff, was anything but that. She balanced easily on the heaving deck and spoke, her voice strident over the rising wind:

"Mebbe you'll think it's funny! But I've something to say to you. The other day ye had me fired, ye cold-blooded squid! Why? Because I was a woman! Then ye came aboard here to snoop; get something on me to feed your mean little ideas about women who do a man's job for a livin', huh? Wanted to see how a fool woman did things. Well, you're goin' to find out. I was kind o' hopin' that mebbe ye'd forget yourself and get a little human, but I see it ain't in ye. But ye've the outward carcass of a man, and I'm goin' to put it to work."

"What do you mean?" Alarmed, Conroy stepped back before her menacing advance.

"Mean?" she erupted. "I'm goin' to let ye practice some of that efficiency you're always gassin' about. A bent tool is better than none—so get ye below to the stokehold. You're goin' to spell the other fireman and help keep the steam pressure up till we git in. It'll mebbe sweat some of the conceit out of ye; and even if it don't, ye'll have something to remember Tugboat Annie by!"

Conroy felt the wind in his hot face, looked out at the driving whitecaps overside.

"Don't be ridiculous! I'm practically part owner——"

"You're part owner of a coal scoop from now on.... Sam——"

The big engineer brought his hulking frame into the foreground and jerked his thumb.

"That way," he growled.

Conroy clung to the rail, half crying with humiliation, but Sam grasped him from behind with sinewy hands and frog-marched him along the narrow deck. They disappeared into the housing. There was a clatter, a couple of sharp smacks, and a cry abruptly silenced.

"And that," mused Tugboat Annie in her cabin sometime later, to the appreciative chromo of the late Captain Brennan, "was that!"

Shortly after dark, with a half gale blowing, and the seas, white-crested and angry, catapulting past the rail, the lights of a moving vessel, yawing and dipping, came swiftly up from astern and swung as close to the Narcissus as safety would permit. It was the Pansy. Her master megaphoned across:

"The Barracuda's got her steering gear repaired and Crabtree cut us adrift. That's something off his towing bill."

"The dirty old curmudgeon," Tugboat Annie growled. She shouted back: "All right! Don't worry! Just stand by in case we need you!"

Shortly after midnight the towline parted with a crack, and the Narcissus lurched away on the crest of a sea. She picked up the Barracuda's lights, but in a darkness intensified by driving rain squalls, and battered by wildly mounting seas, it was impossible to get another line aboard, and an anxious vigil ensued which lasted until daybreak. Dawn spread over a green and tumbling waste, and the Barracuda, drifting with wind and current, and with the seas spouting up her rusty side, was rounded up. It was nearly noon, however, before Tugboat Annie's superb seamanship was effective and a line again was taken on board.

Red-eyed with lack of sleep, but indomitable, she stood at the wheel as the slow, heartbreaking voyage was resumed, gauging each charging comber, easing off, bringing up the head, inching down the coast that was almost obscured by driving spindrift. Conroy, who had come off watch, stood in the lee of the house, dividing his attention between cruelly blistered palms and the smoking combers that thundered up from astern, swooped under the fantail and roared away into the maelstrom ahead. He was quiet now, outwardly subdued, but he had watched with angry concentration the battle to pick up the drifting Barracuda, and he promised himself his full innings when and if the voyage was done. Once he ventured near the wheelhouse, like a scorched moth which cannot resist the flame.

"What if the Barracuda breaks adrift again and piles up on the beach?" he said in surly tones.

Tugboat Annie did not turn her head. "If that happens, queer feller," she rasped, "you'd better say your prayers, if ye know any, for I'll go after her. I'm goin' to get that vessel to port if I have to chase her ashore and put wheels under her. Now get away from the pilothouse before I forget I'm a lady."

The gale had blown itself out by dark, and although the seas still were menacing, Tugboat Annie's expert knowledge of Puget Sound waters enabled her to take the leeward of every available point of land. The sky had cleared and the light-spangled hills of Secoma blazed like a heavenly galaxy ahead. Slowly they moved up the harbor to a vacant berth and the Barracuda was made fast.

Tugboat Annie, coming from the pilothouse to the deck, encountered Conroy as he emerged from the engine room.

"I'm going ashore now——" he began, but Tugboat Annie's rough croak interrupted him:

"And who cares? I hope ye've l'arned something of a woman's ways on a deep-water tug. Good night and bad luck!"

She turned in to her bunk as she was. But at nine o'clock the next morning with her feathered shore-going bonnet perched defiantly on her tousled head she sat in her cabin awaiting the arrival of Alec Severn and Captain Crabtree. Severn arrived first. His red face was depressed and unhappy.

"Hello, Annie," he said tonelessly.

"Hello, Alec. What are you looking so glum about?" she rumbled. "It'd give a body the bellyache to look at ye."

For a moment he did not answer. Then he looked up and met her bovine gaze.

"I fought your battle for you with Conroy all the rest of that day, Annie. And I told him, finally, that rather than let you go I'd see him and his money some other place. Then he came around a bit, for he's really keen about taking over the company. And he's got a reputation——"

"Hmmph! What kind? There's several, ye know!"

"It's the right business kind, it happens. Finally I persuaded him to go out with the Narcissus that night and see for himself how efficiently you really could handle a difficult job. . . . Well, no use going into the horrible mess you made of it. He telephoned me last night after you got in."

"He would," Tugboat Annie rasped, but Severn continued without heeding her:

"The job was worth five hundred dollars at the least, considering we had two tugs and had to pull him off the rocks and all. But you let your stubborn dislike of Conroy override the interests of the company, and you got well hooked by the Barracuda's master as a result. What got into you, Annie? You never let me down before!"

"It must be the tie ye're wearin', Alec," said Tugboat Annie. "It's kind of a bilious color. Is Sweet Forget-Me-Not comin' along here this mornin'?"

"Yes, he's due any time now—him and the master of the Barracuda."

The two men arrived together—Conroy again the cold, immaculate machine, and Captain Crabtree looking, in his shore-going clothes, like an apple that had hung too long on the tree. Conroy bowed stiffly to Severn, ignoring Tugboat Annie.

"Had your lemon juice this morning?" she asked solicitously.

Severn motioned her to silence. He came abruptly to the point:

"Don't you think, Captain Crabtree, that in consideration of what the Narcissus pulled you through last night, it only would be fair if you paid the full towing fee of three hundred dollars, as originally agreed?"

"No, I don't," said Captain Crabtree with a grin.

"But you might have lost your ship."

" 'Might' is a chancy word, sir. And an agreement's an agreement. I can't afford to be kind-hearted. With the 30 percent reduction which became effective when we repaired our steering gear breakdown, I figger I owe you two hundred and forty dollars."

"No, ye don't," grunted Tugboat Annie.

"Don't what?"

"Ye don't owe us one cent on the agreement we made."

Captain Crabtree stared at her with gratified surprise. "Well, that's very nice. You haven't took leave of your senses, though, have you, missus?"

"I leave that to shipmasters o' vessels in distress," Tugboat Annie replied.

Severn interfered, his face pink with vexation.

"Now, look here, Annie; you keep out of this. You've done damage enough."

"Sure. I forgot!" Tugboat Annie rumbled. "It's the men that's the smart ones! You, and Crabtree, and Frog-Face there! I'm just a dumb tugboat skipper. Is that it? All right! Now you hold your jaws, all of ye, till I tell ye something. Crabtree, here, took me for a sucker yesterday. Well, I was! I let 'em beat me at every turn—steerin'-gear business and all!" She snorted contemptuously. "Why, I'd have towed him home for nothin', knowin' what I did! See? He knows already what I'm gettin' at, the wizened little rascal!" She pointed a horny, accusing finger at Captain Crabtree, who twisted his head in his over-large collar and looked remarkably uncomfortable.

"What do you mean?"

"I'll make it plain enough. I tumbled to his game the minute he told his man to order the tugs abreast of the gangway, where he had to talk with a megaphone, instead of over the Barracuda's poop, where it would ha' been much easier. There was something around the stern of his ship he wanted to hide. . . . That right, Crabtree?"

The shipmaster essayed a nonchalant smile. It was not successful. Tugboat Annie continued:

"I had a good look for meself, found out what I wanted, and moved up alongside the others. The bidding was most interesting, though our passenger didn't seem to enjoy it overmuch. Crabtree could make all the stipulations he liked, after he'd answered one question I'd put him. Remember it, captain? You bet your Sunday tights ye do! I asked him if his vessel had sustained any damage beyond the fire, water in the hold and jammed steering gear. He said no, as there's witnesses to prove; and on that basis we entered into an agreement which covered towage alone. But the book says— Wait a minute—"

Tugboat Annie went to a shelf and took down a dog-eared manual of maritime law, wet her thumb lavishly and turned over to the required page.

"Ah! Here it is, as plain as the cast in yon queer feller's eye." She read:

"Where a towage service is entered into on the assumption that the tow is in a seaworthy condition, and she conceals from the tug any material fact which would tend, if known, to increase the amount of remuneration agreed upon, the tug is not prevented by the fact of prior agreement from claiming further reward; for in such case the towage may cease to be towage and become, in effect, salvage."

"Well," said Conroy sharply, "what are ye getting at?"

"Just this, Mr. Great Thinker—that because he concealed from me the fact that the Barracuda had stripped her propeller in among the rocks, our towing agreement didn't mean a thing, and we've got an unbeatable claim for salvage. If I'd left him piled up on the rocks, the Barracuda would have been pounded to pieces in the gale. But bein' just a stupid, mutton-hearted female, I yanked her home. So instead of a lousy towin' fee of two hundred and forty dollars, we'll get a salvage award of about a third the value of the ship and cargo." Tugboat Annie halted and blew her nose with an elephantine flourish. "And now, if ye can see clear to lend me sixty cents till payday, Alec, I'd like to go ashore and telegraph me daughter."

Captain Crabtree was on his feet, shouting profane defiance, but Tugboat Annie soon reduced his bluster.

"Go outside before ye explode, ye nasty little feller!" she trumpeted. "And as for denials, ye can save 'em up for the marine surveyor. Now, go on; get out o' here afore I fetch ye a kick in the rear!"

The chastened and badly frightened Captain Crabtree having hastily departed, Tugboat Annie stood with rugged, flushed face at the head of her bunk, her eyes resting on the hand-tinted features of the late Captain Brennan in their plush-and-gold oval frame. She was queerly silent for a time, and so were the two men before her. Then she puffed her lips, blew a vast, irritable breath, and addressed Severn:

"Well, Alec! What about that sixty cents?"

"What are you going to say to your daughter, Annie?"

"Her home's in Vancouver. I'm goin' to ask her if she's got room for her ma, since there's no room for me here."

Severn's florid face went deeper red than usual with embarrassment. He said, "You'll do nothing of the kind, Annie. Your place is here, and I'm not letting you go on anybody's terms. Maybe I can't find the right words to tell you——"

"Perhaps I can," said Conroy, rising briskly. "Mrs. Brennan, I'm sorry. I apologize for misjudging you. You're clever—and you've taught me something about women. And, Severn, I'd like very much to put through our agreement of the other day and buy an interest in the company. As for Mrs. Brennan, I'd be proud and delighted——"

Severn looked up swiftly and met Tugboat Annie's eyes, and an almost imperceptible signal was exchanged. Tugboat Annie favored the departed Terry with a wink. Then she faced Conroy with booming voice:

"So ye discovered that a woman could be clever, did ye, Columbus? And ye'd like to buy into the company, now it'll be well off without your dirty money? Hmmph! I've no doubt! And ye're sorry—and ye'd be proud and delighted! Well, if ye ain't glued to that chair, I'll be proud and delighted if ye'll take yourself and your sorrow and drop 'em both in the dock. It'll be hard on the fishes, but they can stomach ye a sight easier than I can. And the sooner ye do it, the better!"

As Conroy moved toward the door she pulled off her dilapidated, shore-going bonnet and flung it on the settee. She grinned at Severn. "I feel more like meself now," she puffed, and her small, roving eyes once more met the framed, ingratiating smirk of the late Captain Brennan.

"What's that ye said, ye wicked man?" she asked huskily; and to ears and eyes that understood his kind of language, the smiling defunct made adequate reply.

PASSAGE TO SECOMA

The traffic agent of Pacific Cargo Carriers, Inc., looked dubious and the least bit frightened. He twiddled his pencil, stroked his chin and looked up across the counter into the massive, bulldog features of his prospective passenger; and noting further the beetling brows, square chin and heavy, middle-aged frame of her, his inclination to be curt died.

Instead, he frowned judicially and hedged:

"Well, ma'am, I don't know if we can give you a passage in the Mercurio or not. You see——"

The would-be passenger's formidable jaw bulged. She shifted on solid feet and the feather in her dilapidated bonnet lolloped menacingly.

"Ye don't know? The vessel carries passengers, don't she?"

"Not as a rule. Only now and again. She is primarily a cargo carrier, you see, and has no stewardess. So we can't take lady passengers in any case."

The applicant blew a sigh of relief. "That's all right, then," she said. "I ain't no lady. So make out a coupla tickets fer me and Sam here." She turned to a big man, solemnly masticating a toothpick behind her, and winked.

The agent was stumped. He muttered, "By George, ma'am, you are a most extraordinary woman!"

"I come here fer steamboat tickets; not to have me character discussed," she boomed. "Do I get 'em, or don't I?"

The agent said feebly: "You may not find things to your liking on board. After all, she's not a liner."

"I know that. I've sailed in tramps afore."

"And Captain Nelssen won't like the idea of a woman passenger."

"I won't eat him!"

The agent seemed not so sure. But he reluctantly produced passenger-transportation forms. He said: "This gentleman your husband?"

The lady indulged in resounding mirth. "Who—him? Lordy, no! He's me chief engineer. Big Sam Doolittle. Name fits, too; eh, Sam?"

Big Sam grinned uneasily and regarded the frayed end of his toothpick. "Sure," he said.

The agent stared. "Your chief engineer, you said?"

"I ain't never been pinched fer lyin'."

"What is your name?"

"Captain Annie Brennan."

The agent's manner underwent swift change. He cried: "What? Not the senior captain of the Secoma Deep-Sea Towing and Salvage Company—the woman they call Tugboat Annie?"

Tugboat Annie beamed. "That's me moniker around Puget Sound."

"Why didn't you mention that before, Mrs. Brennan? If I'd known——"

"Ye didn't ax me."

"What brought you to Los Angeles?"

"Me company sold a tug—the Lilac—to the Red Stack people at San Pedro, and Sam and me delivered her, wi' a Red Stack crew. The weather was bad comin' down, and we had quite a time. So I thought we'd go back slow on a tramp and rest up wi' nothin' to worry about. Besides, it's cheaper. Where's the Mercurio lyin'?"

"At San Pedro. She is discharging an Antwerp cargo, and is due to load for Sound ports. Just five hundred tons. But we're after another, larger cargo—— Just a minute"—as the door opened. "Here's Captain Nelssen, of the Mercurio, now. I'd like you to meet him."

Captain Nelssen was tall and erect, with wide, lean shoulders and springy legs; the shrewd, thin-lipped type, with hard, gray, overbearing eyes. His well-fitting blue-serge suit could not conceal that he was a seaman. He nodded to the agent briefly, and was about to pass through to an office beyond.

The agent halted him: "Hold on a moment, captain. I want you to meet your two passengers on the northern trip."

Captain Nelssen's mouth became a hair line. He favored Sam with a glance and Tugboat Annie with a disapproving stare. "Passengers?" he rasped. "Nothing doing! There's grief enough at sea, without a woman in a ship." He addressed Annie: "What's the matter with passenger vessels? There's plenty of 'em."

Tugboat Annie's bonnet feather quivered. "I preferred a tramp—but now I've seed you, I'm more pa'tickler!"

Captain Nelssen's weather-beaten face deepened. He was about to make angry reply, when the agent intervened.

"You don't understand, captain," he said placatingly. "This lady is Tugboat Annie Brennan—you remember, the tugboat master who outwitted Captain Crabtree, of the Barracuda."

Annie waved a large and deprecatory hand. "'Twas nothin'," she disclaimed. "Crabtree dug a hole fer me and fell in it hisself."

The Mercurio's master fixed her with an unwinking stare. "Captain Crabtree is a friend of mine."

Annie nodded soberly. "He would be. Well, never mind. I guess that me and Sam can manage to stomach ye fer one v'yage."

"I'm not taking you," Nelssen told her brusquely. He said, to the agent's protests, "We'll need the passenger space for cargo if we get that extra consignment."

He went on into the inner office, and the agent turned to Tugboat Annie with a shrug.

"I'm sorry, Mrs. Brennan. He's one of our best shipmasters, and we wouldn't like to force the point."

Tugboat Annie struggled with her temper. "That's all right, friend," she said. "If we don't sail wi' old froze-face, it'll prob'ly save wear and tear on our feelin's."

"The Green Stripe Line has a Puget Sound service. Why don't you try there?" the agent said.

Annie grunted a "Thank ye," and with defiant feather, and Sam in her wake, she barged through the doorway to the street. In the office of the Green Stripe Line they had no difficulty. A clerk with prominent eyes and a scuffed tie attended to them.

"Our Bandora's got two extra cabins," he told them. "She's commencing to discharge alongside at San Pedro this afternoon. Then she's to load four thousand tons of citrus fruits for the Northwest and B.C., and she'll sail on Thursday afternoon. I hope that will suit you."

"Sure her captain won't object to us on grounds o' spavins, Charley horse or general principles?" Tugboat Annie asked grimly.

The clerk smiled. "Captain Neap is hardly the objecting type."

"He'd never rate a job wi' the Pacific Cargo crowd, then." Annie inspected her watch. "Time we was humpin' along. Come on, agile."

Together they went down the busy street toward the suburban car terminus. Tugboat Annie was her cheerful, observant self again, and as they rolled along, her adamant bulk caroming passersby, she commented in lively fashion on everything she saw.

PASSAGE TO SECOMA

At San Pedro, the port for Los Angeles, they located the S.S. Bandora, an uninspiring cargo carrier with a band of dirty green around her funnel and along her rusty, red-lead-patched hull. Groups of stevedores were about her decks, but, although steam hissed in her winches and two great packing cases had been lifted from her hold to the wharf, there was about her an atmosphere of suspended animation.

"Hmph!" grunted Annie. "Goggle-eyes at the office said she was workin' cargo. I wonder——"

They climbed the accommodation ladder. At the top Tugboat Annie addressed a beery-looking man in soiled dungarees who was amusing himself by spitting on the wharf.

"Where's the master's cabin?"

He turned and grinned, showing a toothless cavern redolent of pierhead whisky, and jerked his thumb.

"Up there, missus."

Tugboat Annie looked where he indicated. "Blessed wi' wings, is he? Have another guess."

His thumb became more definite, and they climbed the ladder to the navigating bridge; and seeing above a cabin door abaft the chart room a painted-over brass plate with "Captain" faintly etched thereon, Tugboat Annie knocked.

"Come in," a voice replied.

Entering, they found themselves confronting a rabbit-faced little man with mild blue eyes, a weak chin and thin spirals of hair on a nearly bald head. His sudden agitation, on seeing them, was explained by the fact that his rather shabby uniform was hung about the furniture while he was in the midst of dressing in a shore suit.

Tugboat Annie planted herself solidly inside the doorway.

"You Captain Neap?" she asked.

"Get out of here!" the little captain squeaked. "Go on! I didn't know females was about! Get out, quick, and wait outside!"

"Shucks," said Tugboat Annie, "no need to git your tongue in an uproar. 'Tain't the fust time I seen a man outside his jeans. And you ain't no Cleopatria."

"Will you get out?"

"Oh, all right! . . . Come on, Sam. Pernickety old nanny goat!"

They retired while Captain Neap completed his toilet. At his peevish summons they reentered.

"What do you want?" he demanded. "I got a lot of troubles today, so make it short."

Tugboat Annie eyed him for half a minute without speaking, and under her steady stare some of the starch went out of him. She noted the vacillating chin, the amiable but weak mouth, the timid kindliness of his eyes that sought to hide behind bluster. Again he demanded their business; but his bark had lost its threat, had taken on a faintly defensive note, and Annie completed his rout by calmly pointing out a segment of shirt tail which somehow had managed to escape the custody of his trousers top.

"Better take a reef in yer mains'l there, cap'n," she said.

Captain Neap turned quick scarlet and stowed the offending canvas out of sight. He said: "I presume you're the passengers the agent telephoned about."

"Ye presume right. We're goin' to Secoma wi' ye."

He shook his head. "No, you're not. We're not going to Secoma; so I'll bid you a good day."

Tugboat Annie became annoyed.

"Hell and hardtack!" she roared. "Does a pusson have to be royalty to get a passage to Secoma in a tramp? Fust the master o' the Mercurio, and now you! What's wrong wi' us—are we catchin', or something?"

The master of the Bandora became suddenly intent. "What was that you said about Captain Nelssen?"

"Never mind. What I'm askin' is, what's wrong wi' us?"

Captain Neap swallowed rapidly. "It isn't that. It's——"

"I don't care what it is. Here's our tickets"—Annie flourished them—"and here we stop! So pacify that Adam's apple o' yours and talk sense!"

"I've told you. This vessel isn't going to Secoma."

"But the agent sold us——"

"I know," Captain Neap interrupted testily, "but since then he phoned me. Something's happened." His little face went Turkey red with rage. "And it's all the doing o' that seagoing polecat you mentioned a minute ago. We were supposed to discharge here and load four thousand ton of citrus fruits for the north——"

"Well, what about it?"

"There's this about it: The cargo we got below now for discharge belongs to a subsidiary of Pacific Cargo Carriers, which had none of its own ships available to carry it. Contract read: 'Delivery at San Pedro here, or San Diego, at option of consignees.' Hearing nothing to the contrary, I put in here for discharge, and now, with everything set, the consignees demand delivery in San Diego."

"I see," said Annie. "And by so doin', ye'd lose that four thousand tons for the north, which Nelssen would pick up. 'Tis kind of aggravatin'."

"Aggravating?" Captain Neap leaped to a port and jabbed a quivering forefinger. "There's Nelssen's Mercurio lying across there! He's cute as a fox and cold as a snake, and 'twas him put his company up to this, sure as hell—begging your——"

"That's all right; I've heerd the word afore. Go on."

"You understand what I'm getting at?"

"Sure. It sticks out as plain as Sam's ears."

Captain Neap eyed her with dawning respect. "Say, you can figure things out like a man, almost."

"No, no!" said Tugboat Annie hastily. "I don't, thank God. I figger accordin' to common sense. You goin' to let Nelssen git away wi' it?"

"I got no choice. The charter party reads——"

Tugboat Annie waved her hand. "It ain't for me to tell ye yer business, cap'n," she said slowly, "but, seems to me, I noticed two big cases out on the wharf. They come out o' this ship?"

"Yes. They're part of that cargo. That's as far as the discharge got when the consignees stopped us."

"Did the consignees' agent check 'em off the bill o' lading?"

"Yes."

"There ye are, then!" cried Annie triumphantly. "By acceptin' one passel o' this cargo they've legally taken delivery in San Pedro."

The light of comprehension enlivened the timid eyes of Captain Neap. "Then I don't have to go to San Diego? I can——"

"Discharge the rest right on the dock."

"But if they won't accept it?"

"Then charge 'em a thumpin' big demurrage fee for every day your vessel's held up. And if their delay prevents ye from shippin' that other big cargo"—Tugboat Annie grinned widely—"sue 'em——"

"For the freight I'll lose thereby! Gosh, that's great! I'm glad I thought of it!"

"You're wonderful!" said Tugboat Annie.

The little captain inflated his chest. "I'll show Nelssen he can't monkey with Hannibal Neap! I'll show him!"

"Sure! You show him. And give him a boot fer me while ye're at it. Now, where's our cabins?"

"Cabins?" said Captain Neap vaguely, still in the clouds. He came back to earth: "Cabins! Oh, yes; I see!"

He rang for a steward, and when the man—a loutish-looking fellow—appeared, instructed him to show the passengers to their rooms.

"Show the what?" said the steward truculently.

PASSAGE TO SECOMA

Captain Neap gave him an uncertain look. "The passengers," he said weakly. "This lady and gent."

The steward indulged in a scowl. He grumbled: "What does the owners think this is—Noah's Ark?"

"Now, now, that'll do," reproved the master, when Tugboat Annie looked to him to administer swift discipline.

"Hmph!" said the steward. "There ain't enough slavery on this hooker already."

"Orders is orders, steward," said Captain Neap. "Go along, now."

"And git a move on!" Tugboat Annie supplemented suddenly, in a hurricane roar that blasted the astonished man into movement and through the door.

"Who the haitch do you think you are?" he inquired nastily when he had recovered from his surprise. "I don't take no orders——"

"On yer way, fish-ears," bellowed Annie, "afore I make ye a present of a kick in the pants!"

Having stowed her things in the small but comfortable cabin assigned to her, Tugboat Annie doffed her single sartorial pride, the ancient feathered bonnet which she always wore ashore, and broke out her seagoing headgear—a dilapidated felt hat which had once belonged to her husband, Captain Terry, now defunct. Then she went out on deck and joined Big Sam at the rail of the lower bridge. Discharge had been recommenced, and the vessel was loud with the rattle of winches, stevedores' prayers and the thunder of steam. Annie, humorously observing this busy fruit of her suggestion, presently became aware of a hard, erect figure surveying them grimly from the nearby Mercurio's bridge.

"Pipe old starch-neck wearin' his eyeballs out on us," she grinned. "I'd like to tell him 'twas me put the flea in his lug. Just the same, he's got a handsome ship—especially compared wi' this untidy trollop. Look at her; dirty brass, dirty decks, loose gear lyin' around like a hoorah's nest! All it needs is a litter o' pigs—and I ain't sure if ye called the crew by name they wouldn't squeal! Either little Captain Queer-feller ain't got a grip on things or her owner keeps her parish rigged. Shame, ain't it?"

"What is?" said Big Sam.

Tugboat Annie gave up. "Why don't ye try sleepin' horizontal fer a change?" she advised. "It'd be easier on yer feet."

That the Bandora was parish rigged—that ancient sea term to describe a poorly found ship—was evident when she had completed loading her citrus-fruit cargo and put to sea. Food and stores were the cheapest to be obtained, and, in quantity, conformed exactly to legal requirements, with no extras; and officers and men, of both deck and engine room, paid the minimum wages, were, as was natural, shiftless, untidy and slack on their jobs.

"Look at 'em," Annie commented to Sam. "Creepin' around the decks like a flock o' dejected tomcats. I'd give 'em some spit and polish if I was commandin' this tub!"

Nevertheless, she was enjoying the voyage. The Bandora snored along at a steady nine knots across the flat blue Pacific floor, and when Cape Blanco was passed the gold of the California coastal hills melted into the distant emerald of the Oregon Coast Range. Relaxed in the sunshine of slow, lazy days, Tugboat Annie was hugely content. She saw little of Sam, for he had tacked together a monosyllabic intimacy with the beery man whom Annie had addressed on first coming on board and who, it developed, was the chief engineer. So for much of the time she was alone, reading or, preferably, idling on the bridge. Occasionally, when she was stretched out in a chair on the lower bridge, Captain Neap, with an apologetic air, would seat himself gingerly in a neighboring chair and exchange views across a space of five or six feet.

They were talking thus, one day of brilliant sunlight, with the ultramarine of the Pacific lifting the vessel's forefoot and the lacy brine bubbling musically along her side.

"Pull yer chair over closer," Tugboat Annie told him irascibly. "Land sakes! Afraid I'll vamp ye, or somethin'? Eh? Well, ye needn't be. My passion's tugboats. And I got a gullet like a nutmeg grater, talkin' long distance to ye! You married?"

Instantly she regretted the question, for Captain Neap's mild blue eyes unexpectedly filled.

"Was," he said shortly. Then, seeing Annie's heavy face turned to seaward, the urge to confide led him on: "Till voyage before last. She was with me for a holiday, and malaria took her at Essequibo. I guess I've let things slip a bit, here and there, since." He gulped and straightened his narrow shoulders. "But—but she always used to say I was great," he added shyly.

Tugboat Annie swung around; answered with uncalled-for heartiness: "Great? O' course, you're great! You keep on thinkin' that, jest like she told ye, cap'n! Ain't nobody knows a man as well as his wife does! Durn me!" she sparred huskily. "Must 'a' ketched cold—blowin' me beezer on a nice day like this!"

They sat in understanding silence for a few minutes.

"Your husband living?" asked Captain Neap.

"No, I'm a whisky widder. Me husband was a soak, God rest him! But I'll say this fer him: He was the best soak in the Northwest. Whatever my Terry done, he done good—the big tramp!"

Thus, having established a bond of friendly interest, they got on well thereafter, under a veneer of short comments and tart replies, and Annie learned much of the little man.

Abreast of the Columbia River the weather thickened abruptly, with a dense fog blowing in straight from seaward and blotting out the sun. The wind rose, and soon cold gray seas lifted out of the mist and dolloped their crests on the Bandora's forecastle head. The old steamer groaned and strained, and the long-drawn, mournful "whoo-oo-oop!" of her whistle sounded at steady minute intervals. The crew moved about the decks like moisture-beaded ghosts, and occasionally through the fog came the deadened warnings of other vessels. Captain Neap did not leave the bridge that night. The following morning he appeared in the saloon for a brief breakfast, red-eyed and weary, but uncomplaining. He ate his meal hurriedly and returned to his post.

"That little wart's a seaman, even if he is pint size and slack in the chin," Tugboat Annie told Big Sam. "And as a human bein' he's wuth ten such bridge ornaments as that Nelssen carbuncle. Wonder where he is now, by the way. He had a small cargo for Sound ports, didn't his agent say?"

Big Sam cleverly balanced the liberal remainder of his bacon and potatoes on his knife and conveyed it expertly to its destination. He washed it down with three-quarters of a mug of coffee and wiped his mouth with the back of a hairy paw. "Huh?" he said.

Tugboat Annie shrugged. "It's jest me girlish optimism, Sam, expectin' that skull o' yours to hold grub and thoughts at the same time."

By noon, with the wind blowing half a gale, they were well to the north of Cape Alava. The fog remained thick, and it was impossible to see for more than half a ship's length away. At nerve-shattering intervals the fog signal boomed forth, and in the times between, the world was filled with the sound of the wind and the angry seas. On the bridge Tugboat Annie looked out over the milky-green water within vision's radius. The whistle blared again, scattering hot drops on the deck; and as the noise ceased she perked up her head and listened intently. Out of the density to port came the deep, answering note of another steamer.

"That's not far off," she commented to Captain Neap. "Sounds like a big vessel too. Don't ye think it'd be wise——"

"My idea exactly," he replied with asperity. He went to the engine-room telegraph and signaled "Slow," then again pulled the whistle cord. The answer was close—too close. The Bandora's master stuck his head into the wind and listened. "I hope that fellow knows what he's doing," he said nervously. "Seems to me he's traveling pretty fast. And this fog's like a blanket."

"Perhaps ye'd better——" Tugboat Annie began.

"I was going to!" snapped Captain Neap, and rang the telegraph for "Stop."

The tremor of the propeller shaft ceased, and as the vessel lost way she rolled widely in the grip of the sea. In the moment of sharp tension they could hear, over the noise of wind and water, the excited yapping of a puppy in the firemen's forecastle.

Captain Neap again raised his hand to the whistle cord, and as the steam plumed forth, a huge black shape loomed out of the fog with towering steel sides, lines of brass-rimmed ports, high superstructure of white houses and lofty bridge, and a wide swell of roaring white pushed before the great, knifelike stem. Someone shouted and waved from her high bridge; then, with terrific impact, she struck and there was the thunder of shearing steel and the scrape and shriek of tearing plates as the stranger rammed the Bandora's port bow, pushed her aside until the water boiled through the starboard hawsepipe, and ghosted past in a long, blurring rush.

The Bandora, shuddering in every bolt, listed madly to starboard, hung motionless, then rolled slowly back to an even keel. Tugboat Annie regained her feet and lumbered to the rail. "Ajaxia, Melbourne," she read on the great stern before the liner slid into the curtain of fog.

She turned to Captain Neap. Blood streaming from a cut brow where he had been thrown against a corner of the wheelhouse, he was blowing several sharp blasts on his whistle, but the man on stand-by did not respond. Instead, the crew, pouring up from below, made a rush for the boats.

"Get them ash cats out o' that!" Tugboat Annie bellowed; and after a sharp struggle, aided by the master and the mate, order was restored and the men stood by to await orders.

Tugboat Annie returned to the bridge, wiping her brow. "Where the devil's Big Sam got to? I never seed him miss a scrap afore!" she snapped. "Why ain't he here?"

"I am here," his voice behind her said.

"Git around in front o' me then, ye big lummox!" she roared. "I ain't got peepers in the back o' me head! Where you been all this while—pickin' daisies?"

"Daisies?" he said slowly. "I didn't see no daisies. I been lookin' at the damage up forward."

"How bad is it?"

"The forepeak's stove in and filled, and Chips says there's water in

No. 1 hold. She's settlin' by the head, but she'll keep afloat awhile if the chief turns the pumps to."

But the chief, it developed, had flown to the bottle to solace his nerves, and his assistants were unstrung incompetents.

"P'r'aps Captain Neap'll let you go below and do what's necessary," Annie said to Sam.

"I was just about to suggest it," said Captain Neap promptly.

After the first excitement had flattened down, a complete survey of the damage was made. The forward part of the vessel was flooded, as Sam had said, and seas were breaking over the partly submerged forecastle head. But unless really bad weather developed, there was no immediate danger of foundering. The radio operator emerged from his cabin with a message from the Ajaxia. As the master read it his face was a mixture of anger and uncertainty.

"What's it say?" asked Tugboat Annie, looking over his shoulder.

"They claim they weren't to blame," he piped indignantly, "but they'll stand by if we need assistance, or tow us into Secoma for five thousand dollars. Dear, dear! When my owners hear about this I'll be out of a job for sure!"

"Don't you work up a sweat," said Tugboat Annie. "They're responsible, you bein' stopped and blowin' yer whistle; and the damage'll be covered by the underwriters, in any case. Furthermore, we don't need their help."

"Then I'll tell 'em——"

"To go take a jump in the ditch!"

"You took the words right out of my mouth!" cried Captain Neap. "Here, give me that message form, Sparks!" He scribbled rapidly, crossed out a couple of words at the end, and thrust the paper into Sparks's hand. "Throw 'em that, and see how they like it!"

"What'd ye say?" asked Tugboat Annie. She took the message from Sparks and scanned it. It read: "No help today," with "Many thanks" determinedly crossed out.

"That's all right, isn't it?" the master asked pridefully. "They can't twist double meanings into that!"

"Ye're comin' on noble," Tugboat Annie said.

"I hope everything will be all right. It—this is my first accident in thirty-five years at sea. I wouldn't want to lose my ticket over it."

"All ye'll lose is a bit o' sleep. Make what repairs ye can, and if the weather behaves itself, as I think it will, ye'll mebbe make port under yer own steam."

But the weather, with its usual perversity, set out to make life exceedingly uncomfortable. The wind freshened, kicking up a fairly heavy sea; and although the fog blew clear and the horizon once more was visible, acute danger lay in the possibility that the belting of the seas would buckle No. 2 hold bulkhead or smash the hatches in.

"I don't know," said Captain Neap hesitantly, in the lee of the wheelhouse. "I kind of wish I'd had the Ajaxia stand by. There's the men's lives to think of. And if anything happens——"

"Don't worry," Tugboat Annie told him. "You done what was right. There's plenty o' shippin' hereabouts if ye do need help, and if I was you I'd hang on a bit longer."

But as the day drew to a close, Captain Neap's nervousness increased, and more and more constantly his bleary little eyes scanned the heaving waters in search of a vessel. And when at length the smoke of an approaching steamer bannered across the sky to southward, he declared his intention of asking her to stand by.

"I'll ask if she'll take us off, and wait about till morning. Then, if the Bandora's still afloat, we'll come back to her and carry on."

"It's your vessel," Annie told him. "If things went wrong, I'd hate to think I'd advised ye against yer judgment. But I know what I'd do."

"What?"

"Never mind. You do what ye think best, and I'll stand behind ye."

As the stranger approached in the gathering dusk it became clear that she had sighted them, for she altered her course to bear down.

Later, in response to signals from the Bandora, she hove to a quarter mile away.

"She looks kind o' familiar to me," began Tugboat Annie.

"She's the Mercurio," said Big Sam behind her. "Sa-ay, ain't it nice it's somebody we know?"

He retreated hastily, rubbing a well-kicked shin. Annie and Captain Neap eyed each other. The little shipmaster was having a struggle.

"Can't be helped," he sighed presently. "I'll have to swallow my pride and take what I can get. But of all the vessels on this coast——"

After further signaling and an explanation of their situation, an understanding with the Mercurio was reached. The Bandora was made as secure for the night as possible, the regulation lights were set, and her big power lifeboat was swung out and manned. It was ticklish work getting all hands away in the near dark and heavy sea, but they got clear without mishap after many bunglings, and lunged over the swinging crests toward the Mercurio. As they neared her, Captain Neap looked back at his own vessel, with the two red lights of distress cutting forlorn arcs across the darkened sky, and his knuckles were white as he gripped the gunwale. It was almost dark as they came alongside the Mercurio's sea ladder, but a cluster light had been rigged on deck, and soon the Bandora's crew was streaming upward to the security of the steamer's deck.

As Tugboat Annie and Captain Neap were about to climb, Annie looked up, then nudged him.

"There he is, waitin' to crow!" she rumbled.

"Who?"

"Why, him! That Nelssen! Look at him, would ye—wi' his snout stuck over the side like a hungry buzzard."

Cordiality was absent from Captain Nelssen's greeting as they climbed over the rail. He stood a little apart, regarding them with a cold and secret triumph. Captain Neap approached.

"I'm much obliged to you for standing by," he said diffidently. "I don't know just what to say——"

"Cheaters never prosper. You got what was coming to you for beating me out o' that citrus cargo," said Nelssen coolly; then his eyes fell on Tugboat Annie in her battered felt hat. "Oh, it's you too, is it?"

"Hello, Capone," said Annie cheerfully. "Had yer arsenic today?"

This exchange of pleasantries did not contribute toward cordial relations, but Nelssen reiterated his willingness to stand by until daybreak. "Your vessel'll probably be foundered by morning," he cheered, "but in any case I'll expect your owners to compensate me for my trouble. Now that we understand that, I'll have the steward fix ye a hot meal and sleeping accommodations." He looked at them for a minute as though indulging in some secret calculation. Then, unexpectedly, he gave a frozen smile. "You'll be glad of some sleep I think, Captain Neap—and you, too, missus."

"Don't sprain yer good nature," Annie told him promptly. "The settee in the saloon'll do me fine."

Captain Neap turned thankfully into a spare bunk, and to him presently went Tugboat Annie. He was already in a doze.

"Never mind. Don't git up," she said, and planted herself in a chair. "I jest wanted to ax ye, did ye notice anythin' queer about yon Nelssen tonight?"

"Queer?" Captain Neap tried to lash his fatigue-numbed wits. "Can't say I did. Why? Did you?"

Annie rubbed her nose irritably with her knuckles. "I dunno, but I got a feelin' that weasel's got somethin' up his sleeve. All that stuff about wantin' to be paid fer his trouble was the bunk. And he's jest too kind. Say, kindness wi' him is as natural as hairs on a turtle.

Mebbe I'm jest a cranky old woman, but I got a hunch. You don't feel that way, huh?"

"No, I don't"—Captain Neap gaped widely—"so don't get to imagining things because you don't like the man. And you'd better get some sleep."

"Well, prob'ly ye're right. I'm sorry I disturbed ye. Better git your shut-eye now."

"I was about to," said Captain Neap, and was asleep almost before she had left the cabin.

But Tugboat Annie, unable to overcome that definite uneasiness, tramped the Mercurio's decks for most of the night, staring over the dark, stormy sea to where the lights of the deserted Bandora glowed and winked their ruby warning. It was near dawn and the storm had almost blown itself out when, compelled at last by overwhelming fatigue, she sought her bunk.

Three hours later she was awakened by Captain Neap, dressed and ready for action. "Come on," he said. "We're going back to the Bandora. She's still afloat, about a mile away." He was fairly dancing with impatience.

Annie was not to be moved. "You git some grub in ye fust," she commanded. "I've a hunch ye'll need to be fortified afore the day's finished."

A steward gave them toast and steaming coffee, and afterward they went into the raw, damp air of the deck. A mile away, the Bandora rolled heavily, her fore part under the tumbling seas. But the wind had slackened, the sky overhead was clear, and a sword blade of light was lashing the white horses on the far horizon.

Captain Nelssen was about, hard, capable, alert, his cold eyes roaming with secret humor from the Bandora's crew, clustered on the forward well deck, to the vessel herself.

"Lookit old shad-belly huggin' a laugh to hisself," worried Annie to Captain Neap. "I'll not feel right till we're back on board the Bandora."

Captain Neap addressed the other shipmaster: "I'll be away now, captain. I'm much obliged."

Nelssen nodded. "I'll not say I can't get along without you."

"Or with us either," chimed in Tugboat Annie pugnaciously. "Well, it's mutual. Don't bother to say good-bye."

"No-o," returned Captain Nelssen, and again that sudden frigid grin twisted his lips. "I'll not say good-bye."

"Now, what the devil did he mean by that—the nasty man?" said Tugboat Annie as she took her place in the stern sheets of the boat.

"What does it matter?" returned Captain Neap happily.

"Everything's jake now; the Bandora still afloat, the weather behaving—gosh!" He breathed deeply and put the tiller over. The power boat surged over the back of a sea and straightened out for the run to the Bandora.

They drew close to the vessel's rusty side as she dipped and rolled forlornly under the defeated petulance of the white-lipped combers. Then Tugboat Annie and Captain Neap, both searching for the sea ladder, crossed startled glances.

"It—it's gone!" said Captain Neap in a frightened squeak. "We left it hanging over the starboard side last night."

Then Tugboat Annie noticed something else. "There's steam up still," she said ominously, and her face was grim.

They circled the vessel; and on the port side, close under the Bandora's side, was a ship's lifeboat. Captain Neap jumped from his seat with a startled imprecation.

"Good morning to ye," a voice hailed from above, and they stared up into the grinning face of the second mate of the Mercurio.

Tugboat Annie roared, "What are you doin' up there, ye big ape? Throw over that ladder!"

The second mate grinned the wider: "You wearin' the skipper's pants today?"

Captain Neap spoke up: "You do as you're bid, mister, and throw that ladder over. I'm coming on board my ship."

"Whose ship?"

"Mine!"

"You're mistaken, captain," said the second mate composedly. "This is our ship. She was an abandoned vessel, and so——"

"I know, ye Port Mahon baboon!" yelled Tugboat Annie. "When Nelssen got us safe on board, he sent you off in the dark to take possession. That it?"

"No," said the Mercurio's second mate, hugely enjoying the joke, "it ain't. He sent me away from the Mercurio's port side last night, as your boat came alongside to sta'board. And so, this being a deserted ship, and the law sayin' 'finders, keepers,' we've took her over in the name o' Pacific Cargo Carriers."

Captain Neap, from a height of futile, squeaky rage, suddenly wilted. "I'll never get another command after this," he groaned. "It's my finish."

Tugboat Annie turned her mastiff face upward to where the second mate had been joined at the rail by his laughing men, then rested for a moment on the pinched, beaten face of Captain Neap. Her big chest filled. She placed a hand on his shoulder and her fingers tightened.

PASSAGE TO SECOMA

"Keep yer tail up, friend; ye ain't finished yet," she said gruffly. "Prob'ly I'm just an old fuss budget what's stickin' me nose where it don't belong, but I got an idee. Git hold o' yerself and talk him into lettin' us on board. Promise him anythin'!"

Captain Neap looked up at the second mate. "I guess I'm licked, mister," he said humbly. "But I'd like to come on board. We've got no gear but what's on us. I'll not dispute your claim."

The second mate regarded him with mistrust; then he signaled the Mercurio. "It's all right," he said, when he returned to the rail. "Ye've Captain Nelssen's permission. But no tricks, mind. Remember, we got plenty o' witnesses that the vessel was abandoned when we took her over."

"I'm not denying it," agreed Captain Neap. "You needn't fear."

A ladder was thrown over, and when they got on board, Captain Neap went forward and stared dejectedly at the seas still breaking over the submerged forecastle head. Tugboat Annie, after a brief but earnest conversation with Big Sam and unobserved instructions to the Bandora's crew, mooned about the decks, listening to the steady pulsation of the pumps as one of the Mercurio's engineers kept the incoming water under control. Big Sam disappeared. An hour passed.

Suddenly a confused uproar burst from below, overtoned by frightened shouts and the stamp of running feet, and from the engine room Big Sam fled, eyes bulging with terror. Yelling wildly, he leaped for the rail and down the sea ladder to the boat. Tugboat Annie stiffened; then she ran to the side. Others, attracted by the commotion, also had gone to the rail.

"What's wrong wi' you, ye big jackass? Come back here!" she roared.

"Not me!" Big Sam shouted back. "The blasted old coffin's goin' under!"

"Good-by, Bandora!" one of the vessel's stokers shouted, and leaped for the rail. Instantly the panic spread, and he was followed by others. The Mercurio's men, milling uncertainly about the deck, hesitated until some of their mates and the engineer appeared through the fiddley from below and added their fears to the confusion, and a mad rush for the boats ensued.

Tugboat Annie raised her voice. "Captain Neap!" she bellowed. "Over the side, quick! She's founderin'!" And spying the Mercurio's second mate running down from the bridge, she supplemented: "You can have her, mister! I hope ye can swim!"

The second mate halted and stood over the fiddley grating, listening. Far below, an angry swash and gurgle of water decided him. "Into your boat, men!" he roared to his crew. "The bulkhead must ha' breached!"

From every direction panicky men appeared, and when the boats were filled and shoved off, the Bandora was again an abandoned derelict.

"Offer him a tow away from her!" Tugboat Annie said to Captain Neap, as the Bandora's stern heaved sluggishly on a big roller, then squattered down in a smother of foam. The Bandora's power boat curved around to the frantically pulling Mercurio's boat, passed the second mate a line, then commenced to make a course for the Mercurio, lying, with gleaming brass and paintwork, on the blue sea a mile away. A thousand yards from the Bandora, the power boat suddenly shot ahead, and before the Mercurio's second mate was aware of what had happened, came about in a quick swirl of foam and headed straight back to the abandoned ship. The Mercurio's boat rose and fell without forward propulsion.

"Hey!" roared the second mate. "We're cut adrift!"

"I know that!" Tugboat Annie trumpeted back. "I done it wi' me little hatchet!"

Too late, the second mate realized he had been tricked; and furiously he ordered his men to break out their oars in vain pursuit. Then, realizing the futility of hoping to overtake the speedy power boat, he came about and returned to his own vessel.

Captain Neap, in the Bandora's boat, was stunned. "But I don't understand," he said. "If she's sinking, what's the sense of going back?"

"Heck, she ain't sinkin'!" Annie told him jubilantly. "Sam there got down into the engine room and mugged around as I told him to; then, when he saw the chance, he monkeyed wi' the main injection valve and started bringin' more water into the ship. It didn't do no harm; and took some o' the strain off o' that for'ard bulkhead. But it sounded dangerous to them not in the know. And I had some o' your crew primed to holler and skin out when Sam jumped fer the boat. 'Twas as easy as blowin' yer nose."

Elation lighted the bloodshot eyes of Captain Neap. "Then that means——"

"It means that as soon as ye step foot on board ye'll be in full and legal possession o' yer vessel again."

They came alongside and climbed once more to the deck. The boat was drawn up to the davits, and Big Sam and the Bandora's chief engineer disappeared below. In a few minutes Sam reappeared.

"O.K.?" Tugboat Annie asked.

"Sure! The pumps is spittin' out the water again."

"That's that, then. And now I suppose we can expect a visit from yon two-legged catfish on the Mercurio."

Captain Nelssen already was on his way across; and twenty minutes later his boat danced alongside, while he balanced, an explosive ramrod of fury, in the stern.

Tugboat Annie stuck her blowzy head over the side. "How do ye like yer eggs fried now?" she grinned.

"You think you're almighty smart!" he stormed. "But wait till this gets into court! I—I'll——"

"Look out! Ye're slobberin' down yer whiskers," she replied. "But excuse me, perhaps ye'd like to do yer bellyachin' to the master. . . . Captain Neap!"

Nelssen's incendiary repartee was cut short by the Bandora's master, who leaned over the bridge above.

"I'll thank you to remember you're addressing a lady, Captain Nelssen," he reproved mildly, his diminutive chest inflated with joy.

"Haw, haw! That's a good one!" Tugboat Annie roared gleefully. "That's tellin' him somethin' he didn't know! Good-bye, ye cross between a door knob and a window shutter! And if ye see a big sea-goin' tug, the Narcissus, comin' around Flattery and headed this way, give it a toot, will ye? It's me own vessel, o' the Secoma Deep-Sea Towin' and Salvage Company, what Captain Neap here jest wirelessed fer, to pull us into Secoma."

The Mercurio's master shot his boat close in and entertained them with a series of hair-curling compliments. Annie grinned appreciatively; then, spying two firemen emerging from the fiddley with a full ash bucket, she clicked her fingers and signaled. Joyfully the men upended the bucket into the chute, and with a roar and a cloud of blinding dust, the heavy contents plumped full into the Mercurio's boat. Choking and spluttering, Nelssen sheered off in a thick gray mantle of ash and clinkers.

Tugboat Annie turned her face upward to Captain Neap. "You got anything to say to him afore he goes back to his knittin'?"

"Yes," replied Captain Neap spiritedly, "I have." He leaned across the bridge rail, quivering with pride and excitement. "If ever you're around Puget Sound again, Captain Nelssen——" he piped, then hesitated.

"Go on," prompted Annie. "Ye're doin' great!"

"——if you're ever around again," he finished, flushed and triumphant—"er—drop in!"

SPARERIBS AND SAUERKRAUT

Tugboat Annie Brennan, senior captain of the Deep-Sea Towing and Salvage Company, sat on the rail of her beloved Narcissus, tilted her sea-going hat of battered felt on the back of her untidy head, took off one shoe and gently kneaded her toes. "Cuss that rheumatiz!" she muttered. "It's give me a foot like a camel." She rubbed her nose with her knuckles, sniffed and looked contentedly about her. Alongside the wharf were moored other tugs of the company's fleet: Pansy, Honeysuckle, Orchid, Daffodil—powerful, snub-nosed ruffians, all named by Tugboat Annie, and the pride of her hard-bitten soul. Shipping was moving on the shining waters of the port of Secoma—tramps, ferries and log rafts, liners; and a heavy barge carrying laden box cars slid past the pier end, guided by the puffing Asphodel, another of the company's tugs.

Annie's deep chest filled. "Happy days is here some more," she hummed inaccurately, and stretched her arms. Then her sharp eyes caught a furtive movement at the Narcissus's galley. She left the rail and moved with elephantine circumspection aft, to where a lank, blue-dungareed stern projected from the doorway. She bestowed upon it a hearty kick.

There was a yelp of pain, and Annie danced around on one foot, with the other in her hand, for she had launched the rheumatic, unshod foot in her enthusiasm, and its goal had been an unexpectedly bony part of the recipient's anatomy. He was a thin, gangling man, and as he indignantly turned his weak, blue, red-rimmed eyes on her, his Adam's apple worked agitatedly.

"Hey, you quit kickin' me around, Annie! I w-w-was on'y—"

"Git that long beak o' yours out o' the galley, Shif'less, and keep it out! Every time me back's turned, ye snuffle around in here pinchin' grub. Get away aft, ye lazy bag o' bones, and overhaul that line, like I told ye! Go on, hump yerself! And darn that hard carcass o' yours!"

Shiftless grinned, sidled past with uplifted elbow, and shuffled aft; and Annie, with interior rumblings, retrieved her shoe, got the morning paper from her cabin, and climbing to the wharf, sat on a spile in the sunlight and began to read.

Engrossed, she did not notice the approach of a stout, red-faced gentleman with shrewd little eyes, who came along the wharf, stood behind her and watched the play of light on the sticks, the orange peel and miscellaneous debris floating on the scummy water of the slip.

"Ho, hum!" Tugboat Annie yawned, browsing over the paper; then she lost herself again, in an account of the city's current crime wave.

The man behind her moved, and as his shadow fell athwart the page, Tugboat Annie jumped like a startled if unwieldy gazelle, and swung around.

"Gosh sakes, Ty Connor!" she snapped. "Ye're enough to scare the dandruff off a pusson, sneakin' up like that!"

Nickel-or-Million Connor, the shipping and lumber magnate of Secoma, smiled faintly. "I didn't know you were nervous, Annie."

"'Tain't nerves; it's caution!" She tapped the paper. "Wid all ye read about these here gunsters and gangmen cavortin' around—" She broke off and eyed him shrewdly. "Ye're not lookin' happy today, Ty. What's wrong?"

Connor gazed at the opposite shed. "Nothing."

"Well, that's a comfort," said Annie—"if true." She stood up. "Now looka here, Ty Connor; you stop actin' so silly—comin' down here wid a face as long as a bum's hard-luck story, then tellin' me nothin's wrong! Come on; out wid it!"

Nickel-or-Million Connor looked sheepish. Then he took a deep breath. "It's about Dick then."

"Dick?" said Tugboat Annie with a grin. "There's a heap o' Dicks. There's Dick Finnigan, what runs the speakeasy; and Dick, the pal o' Tom and Harry, and—Dick who?"

"Dick Simonds, my nephew. The—the young—" Ty Connor struggled with his temper.

"Didn't know ye had a nevvy, Ty."

"He's a worthless scamp," said Nickel-or-Million violently, "even if he is my sister's boy. All he thinks of is a good time; spending money he doesn't earn—cocktail parties, brawls, and the like of that. And his elbow's developed a universal joint lifting drinks in night clubs. I—I— The young devil!"

"Think a lot o' that boy, don't ye, Ty?" Tugboat Annie said quietly.

"Suppose I do?"

"Oh, don't git mad! There ain't no law against it," Annie reassured him hastily.

Connor continued to rumble. "Final straw today though. He promised to take a job in my office and straighten up and behave himself, and was supposed to start this morning. By 10:30 he hadn't shown up, so I went to his flat. He'd just got home from an all-night party, with a hangover. I was firm with him. I said, 'You go and have a bath and change your clothes, you young whelp! Then you're coming with me! I'll wait!' Well, I waited for forty minutes and nothing happened. Then I went in"—Ty Connor's face turned a bright and congested magenta—"and what do you suppose?"

"Don't keep me in suspense."

"His clothes were floating around in the bathtub and he was asleep on his bed."

"Hmmph! Well, we're on'y young once."

"Once is all the Lord allows, Annie. But what am I going to do? I can't cut off his money, for he's got plenty of his own. I thought you might be able to suggest something."

Tugboat Annie thought hard for a moment, rubbing her nose vexedly with her knuckles. "Seems to me a feller as smart as you could think up some scheme.... I ain't exactly a authority on rich men's nevvys, but my method'd be to kick 'em in the pants and put 'em to work. Tell ye what, Ty; we're sailin' late tonight to pick up a schooner off Flattery and tow her in, and atween now and gettin' back, I'll think it over."

The shore whistles, blowing for the noon meal, interrupted her, and she lumbered to her feet. "Well, I'm a bowlegged rattlesnake if it ain't dinnertime already. Ty, what about j'inin' us? Pinto's cooked up a swell mess o' spareribs and sauerkraut. Smell it?"

The shadows lifted from Ty Connor's heavy face. He sniffed, then grinned. "Lead me to it, Annie!" he said.

"If there's anything in the way o' vittles what makes me stummick yelp wid delight," said Tugboat Annie, five minutes later, as she tucked her napkin under her chin and removed the cover from a steaming dish, "it's spareribs and sauerkraut. There's jest a leetle somethin' dainty about 'em what appeals to—to—"

She stopped abruptly, bent forward and inhaled the uprising steam. She reached with a fork, speared a shred of sauerkraut and conveyed it to her mouth, where she tasted, gingerly. Then her angry roar shook the emergency lamp in its gimbals: "Pinto! Pinto!"

SPARERIBS AND SAUERKRAUT

The cook stuck his startled head in the doorway. "Ya-as, ma'am?"

"Who dropped the soap in the sauerkraut?"

"Soap?"

"That's what I said! S-o-p-e——Soap! Who done it?"

"Why, ma'am, I dunno. Shif'less was foolin' round the galley awhile this mawnin', helpin' me wash the cookin' pots, so's I could git away ashore this afternoon."

"I might ha' knowed!" Annie barked wrathfully. "Every time there's trouble on this craft, that ganglin' lump o' suspended animation's at the bottom of it. Where is he?"

"He run below and hid, ma'am, when he heard you beller."

"And me wid me mouth all set fer a swell spareribs-and-sauerkraut dinner. I'll hang him over the side fer a fender, one o' these days. Take this mess away and break out some beans, or somethin'!"

She rumbled and bumbled through the rest of the meal, but by the time she had cleaned up the beans and stowed a quarter of a pie and three cups of coffee below hatches, she felt better. "Beans is fillin', even if they ain't a delicacy like spareribs and sauerkraut....Brrp! Excuse me, Ty!...What? Must ye be going? Well, so long, ye old gafoozler. And if I git any bright ideas about l'arnin' your nevvy to behave hisself, I'll let ye know."

But Tugboat Annie found no time during a busy day to devote thought to Ty Connor's problem. Routine duties on a big, efficiently run, deep-water tug are manifold, and as Annie's interest in her command was considerably more than academic, there was plenty with which to occupy herself. And all through the afternoon, rankling was the memory of that lost spareribs-and-sauerkraut dinner.

For dinner there were pork chops and applesauce, and rich brown gravy over snowy mashed potatoes, with corn and peas, hot biscuits, a creamy rice custard, and fragrant coffee; but Annie, after two generous helpings, shoved her empty plate away. "Seems like when I git me mouth set fer a treat," she grumbled to Peter, the mate, "other kinds o' vittles jest aggravates me. Me appetite jest flits away"—she made a massive gesture of snapping her fingers—"like that! Anyways, I feel restless tonight—kind o' skittish, or somethin'."

"Mebbe it's spring fever, or the hives," suggested Big Sam, the engineer. "Why don't ye go ashore, or take a good dose o' sulphur and molasses?"

"Sam's had a idea; somebody must 'a' left it to him," Annie gibed to Peter. "Still, mebbe I will step ashore, at that. We ain't sailin' till midnight. What about you and Shif'less comin' along, Sam? I'll have to take that numbskull along to make sure he don't set fire to the tug, or give it away, while we're gone. What do ye say? We'll take in a movie, and mebbe have a bite to eat some place."

"We-ell, I dunno, Annie. There's a powerful lot to do."

"I got twelve dollars and thirty-seven cents."

"Fine," said Big Sam enthusiastically. "Let's go!"

Tugboat Annie went to her cabin and made what was, for her, a careful toilet—that is to say, she discarded the battered hat of her late husband, Captain Terry, for her prize possession, a shore-going bonnet of ancient vintage, crowned by a raffish feather that teetered and dipped like a tipsy harridan in every breeze.

From her blouse she suspended a watch with a broken clasp, which Captain Terry, in an absentminded moment, had bestowed upon her. Upon the belt of her voluminous skirt she moored an ornate but somewhat shabby reticule.

Then she donned a billowy tweed coat with a moth-eaten fur collar and puff shoulders, and after smiling complacently at herself in the cracked mirror over her bunk, she made for the door. Here, for a moment, she halted, hands on hips, and turned to the smirking likeness of her late helpmeet in its plush-and-gold oval frame. "No clownin' whiles I'm gone," she adjured it with fond severity, and sallied forth to the deck.

Her satellites were waiting for her, Shiftless in the dubious garments inherited from a defunct gentleman he had fished out of the dock, and Big Sam in a rusty black suit and celluloid collar. Tugboat Annie inspected them both critically.

"Hmmph!" she said to Shiftless. "If you was a kangaroo ye'd have some place to stow that Adam's apple o' yours." And to Big Sam: "Don't ye ever scrub yerself below the collar, ye dirty ape? Look at Shif'less there, neat as a weasel, bar his ears, while you—you— Oh, well! P'raps folks'll think ye're wearin' black underwear. Come on; let's git goin'!"

They piled into Big Sam's car, an Elizabethan relic, and rattled and jolted up the hill toward the bright lights of the theater district. Signs glittered, movie palaces beaconed. They passed up The Lingerie Lover at one place, and Purple Pathos at another. Then the lurid posters of a gangster picture, One-Way Ride, held them, and Tugboat Annie, with lively recollections of her morning's reading, decided for them.

"I'm kinda curious to see how them fellers does their stuff," she said. "We'll go in."

They emerged from the theater an hour and a half later; Shiftless breathless with excitement, Big Sam still somnolent.

Shiftless commented: "They s-sure is a lot o' t-t-t—"

"Tough," helped Annie.

"—tough guys, them gangsters!"

"They ain't so much," Tugboat Annie told him scornfully. "Didja notice how that Bonelli crawled when the cop put the bee on him? Huh? They're hard till ye git 'em in a conundrum, that's all. Then they ain't so tough. They're yeller. All the pitchers shows ye that. . . . Well, what say we eat?"

"Suits me," said Big Sam, waking up.

"You're tellin' me! Say, while we're bein' so gay and all, what about goin' to a nightclub fer a bite? I never been in one, and after what Ty told me about his nevvy this mornin', I'm kinda interested."

"S-sure. Which one?" asked Shiftless.

"I dunno. Wonder if this taxi driver'd know! Pull up, Sam."

Following the taxi driver's directions, they came presently to the Racket, newest, brightest and smallest of the city's nightclubs. It was well named, for when the trio went through the door, Annie waddling in the lead, a burst of noise and merriment struck them. Although the hour was not late, things already were well underway, due mainly to the efforts of a party of young college alumni to outstunt the early show of blues singer and scantily clad chorus.

"Sa-ay, this is somethin' like high life!" Annie grunted admiringly, when they had been conducted to a table near the orchestra platform. "Like things ye read about. Ain't a big place, but it's kinda genteel and all. Look at them fellers wid the full-dress suits and cute little black ties like Buck Murphy wore at Harrigan's wake. This must be a real tony place. It'll be sorta nice to think back on when we're pushin' up the sound tonight, hey? . . . Gosh, I'm hungry!"

A waiter handed each of them an impressive menu and hovered over them. "Would madam like," he asked presently, "a bottle of—er—ginger ale? Right off the boat," he added confidentially.

"So's shellac and bilge water," Tugboat Annie told him. "Go blow yer nose, young feller, and don't bother me while I pick me vittles." She studied the menu. "Le's see now. What time's the next train leave fer Chicago?"

"Sh-h-h! That ain't a time-table," reproved Big Sam solemnly.

Annie tittered. "That's jest me joke, ye big lummox. Look at all them figgers: 1.75; 2.50; 3.25; and such like."

While they considered, the lights were dimmed, and to a blare of music, a dancing turn, with chorus, took the floor. During the number Big Sam with bovine placidity masticated a match end, but Shiftless's pop eyes bulged as the girls flashed their bare limbs among the tables.

"Skinny lot o' shads," said Tugboat Annie compassionately. When the lights went up, however, and Shiftless's fascinated gaze had followed the last of the girls into retirement, her face had cleared.

"Stop yer clappin'!" she told Shiftless; then she beckoned the waiter. "I don't need the meenu," she said with a grin. "Fetch Shif'less here a coupla chicken legs—that's what he seems to have his mind on. And Big Sam"—she regarded his frayed match end—"he'll have a plank steak. And me—why, jest dish me up a nice mess o' spareribs and sauerkraut."

"But, madam—"

"And tell 'em to make it snappy. I'm starvin'."

The waiter retreated under her formidable gaze. A few moments later he returned:

"About the spareribs and—"

"What about 'em?"

"We'll have to send out for them. It will take some time. Wouldn't something else——"

"Spareribs," Annie rumbled, "and sauerkraut. Plenty o' kraut! Now get goin', young feller, and quit starin'. We ain't no zoo."

The waiter retreated, muttering, and Tugboat Annie sat back with a grunt of satisfaction and sociably nodding feather, to watch the riot on the dance floor and the antics of the crowd. After an interval, the food for Shiftless and Big Sam appeared. Tugboat Annie watched its consumption, and her heavy face lengthened and grew dark. Time passed. She moved restlessly in her chair, her eyes on the swing door to the kitchen.

"Quit chompin'!" she admonished Big Sam. "And don't stuff yer bazoo like that. There's tomorrer!" She beckoned the waiter. "When's me grub comin' along?"

"It won't be long now, madam."

"Hurry it up, or ye'll have to carry me out o' here in a rough box!"

A half hour went by. Annie drummed on the table, her mastiff face registering a rapidly rising temper. Finally, spying her waiter as he dodged between the tables, she got to her feet.

"Hey, there, flop-ears!" she roared. "Where's my spareribs and sauerkraut?"

"Coming now, madam," he replied, and hurriedly ducked through to the kitchen. He emerged a moment later with a laden tray, and Tugboat Annie's features underwent a miraculous transformation. Smiling broadly, she rubbed her hands and tucked her napkin, with happy anticipation, into her bodice.

As the waiter passed the orchestra stand, there was a sudden

SPARERIBS AND SAUERKRAUT

crashing blow near the door. A man stumbled backward through the doorway, and while the startled room froze to stillness, fell across a chair, staggered to his feet, both hands clapped to his bleeding face, and collided with the waiter. The tray and its contents flew ceilingward, and spareribs and sauerkraut descended in a scalding shower, but the attention of the room was centered on the doorway, through which came two slender young men in dinner suits, one of whom, with a blue-steel automatic pistol, leaned negligently against the door frame, while the other, also with drawn weapon, entered the room and said harshly: "Put 'em up!"

Tugboat Annie stared, uncomprehending, for a moment; then, spurred on by her famished stomach, the disappointments of the day culminated in an explosion.

"Hell and hardtack! That was my dinner ye sp'iled, ye impident vagabones!" she trumpeted.

Her feather quivering pugnaciously she got round the table; then, with congested face and a bellow of fury, she charged. The bandits hesitated and half turned, and in a moment they were the center of a group of fighting men as the alumni entered the fray. Tugboat Annie went through the scrimmage like a torpedo, caroming struggling forms right and left. Snatching a large, empty, brass jardiniere as she passed the orchestra platform, she galloped into the wild melee of arms and legs and thudding fists, and caught a flash of a slender young man waving a gun. "Out o' me way, ye dock wallopers!" she panted. "He's my meat!" —and raising the inverted jardiniere with both hands, brought it down on his head. Blindly he fought, but it cased him to the chin like a helmet, and he could not pull it loose.

"Sam!" bellowed Tugboat Annie. "Sam! C'mere, quick! I got a idea! Grab this sculpin!"

"What ye goin' to do, Annie?" Big Sam puffed, as he pinned the captive's arms.

"Never mind! Get him outa here and into your car!"

The captive renewed his struggles, but with Annie, Sam and Shiftless giving him the bum's rush, he was shot through the door to the street, across the sidewalk and into the back seat of Sam's chariot. Tugboat Annie plumped her bulk on his chest, while Shiftless clung fearfully to his kicking legs.

"Git underway, Sam!" Tugboat Annie ordered. "Back to the Narcissus!" The car jolted into life, and Annie, blown but jubilant, her bonnet askew and the feather in a paroxysm of crazy triumph, bounced up and down on her victim's chest to squash the fight out of him. "Durn me," she chortled, "if this feller had a mite more sauerkraut on him, I could eat him fer a sparerib."

SPARERIBS AND SAUERKRAUT

Down on the wharf, the captive was hustled on board the Narcissus, his head still imprisoned in the jardiniere, whence came, at intervals, muffled growls, grunts and snorts.

"Shove him in your cabin, Sam, and lock the door," Annie said. "Then go below. It's time we was underway for Flattery. We'll tend to him further when we git out in the sound where he can't jump ashore." She raised her voice: "We'll prob'ly have to saw off his ears to git that kettle adrift, but that's all right by me. Here's one tough gunster's goin' fer a different kind of a ride!"

The shore lights gleamed as the Narcissus, northbound for the Strait of Juan de Fuca, left the harbor astern and took a whiff of spray over the nose as her bow fender smacked into a brisk sea. The night was raw and overcast, with promise of more wind, but the powerful seagoing tug liked hard weather and snouted through it like a grampus. With Secoma's lights twinkling in the distance like tiny jewels, and the wooded land on each side too far to swim to, Tugboat Annie summoned Big Sam from below, and together they went along to his cabin.

"What ye goin' to do with him?" Big Sam asked.

"Do wid him? I'm goin' to work the burr off'n him! I'll put him below at the fires wid you, and ye can haze him plenty. Then there's a few other odd jobs what nobody likes to do on this hooker, such as bilge divin' and the like. And when we get back to port I'll turn him over to the flatfeet. They'll nurse his calluses fer him. He'll be pretty scared by now, I guess, so he'll be easy to handle. But if he gits fresh, Sam, jest slap him good. Come on; unlock the door."

Big Sam fitted the key and turned. Then he grasped the knob and pulled. The door did not move. He stood back after a minute and scratched his head.

"Look out fer splinters," warned Tugboat Annie. "Why don't ye unlock the door?"

Big Sam tugged again. "It is unlocked," he grunted, "but—it—won't—open! Something's queer. What'll I do?"

"Peep through the winder, o' course; ye can use 'em on both sides! I never seen such a dumbhead!" Annie told him impatiently.

Big Sam applied his features to the small, square pane. "Heh!" he said, after a minute. "Hah!"

"Quit makin' them jackass noises," snapped Annie, dancing with uncertainty. "What's wrong in there? Ain't got away, has he?"

"No-o," said Big Sam, his fascinated gaze still directed through the window. "But he's got the door roped fast inside, and he's got the pot off his head and his shoes off, and he's lyin' in my bunk readin' a magazine and smokin' my cigarettes!"

"Wha-at? Lemme see!" Tugboat Annie peered through the window. Then a low rumble shook her and she rapped angrily on the pane. "Hey, there, you gangman!" she bawled. "Git out o' that bunk and open the door!"

The slight, recumbent figure appeared not to hear her, and it was not until she had garnished her command with seagoing variations that she drew a response. The captive put down his magazine, yawned, sat up and directed a pair of cool gray eyes at the window. He stared, blinked rapidly several times, stared again, and ran his fingers through his crisp black hair. Then he shook his head.

"D.T.'s!" he said definitely. "It must be. I saw it at the Racket, and here it is again!" He made a gesture of dismissal at the window. "Go away," he said severely, "and send me some nice pink elephants."

"Open that door, ye sassy divil!" shouted Annie. "D'ye hear?"

"It barks. I wonder if it thinks."

"Sam!" rasped Tugboat Annie. "Get a ax and poke that winder in. Then turn a high-pressure hose on him. I'll l'arn the impident scamp to sass me."

"But it'll wet all me cabin!"

"I can stand it. Come on; I'll help ye."

Big Sam went aft, and together they coupled up a hose and dragged it along the deck. With the brass nozzle Sam pushed the window in. "Go on," Annie encouraged him; "let him have it!"—and Sam turned the valve. A powerful shaft of water roared into the cabin, and odds and ends of gear went flying. Sam shut off the valve and peered inside.

"All me gear is soaked," he moaned. "But I don't see the crook."

"Were you looking for me?" said a voice behind them. They wheeled and looked into the grinning face of their captive.

"Well, cuss me!" snapped Tugboat Annie. "How'd you git out here?"

"Through the door, when you went for the hose. And now, what about putting me ashore?"

"You ain't goin' ashore till we git back to port, ye nasty feller," Tugboat Annie told him furiously. "And then I'm goin' to turn ye over to the cops. And in the meanwhile ye're goin' to see what seafarin' folks does to thugs like you, what goes around holdin' up places and sp'ilin' people's dinners. Ye got no pals to help ye now, so take off that coat and shirt, and git below to the engine room wid Big Sam here. Ye'll be wid us fer a day or two, and I'm goin' to make it lively fer ye."

The young man appeared to ponder. Then he shook his head.

"No," he said at length. "No, I think not. I don't mind a short sea voyage. But work?" Again he shook his head. "No!" he said firmly, and grinned.

"Grab him, Sam, and throw him below," Annie directed. "And don't be afraid to hurt him a leetle."

As Big Sam ponderously advanced, the captive backed away. "I wouldn't do it, if I were you," he said mildly, still smiling.

Big Sam lunged and tried to close. The captive sidestepped with practiced skill. There was a quick flurry of arms, a sharp smack, and Big Sam went down with a crash, knocked stiffer than a plank. The young man, breathing easily, wiped his knuckles on his trouser seat.

"Well, I warned him," he said.

"But—but——" Tugboat Annie stammered, staring down at the recumbent Sam. She gulped. "But you ain't supposed—I mean, you gunsters is all yeller. I——"

He looked at her for a moment in the light of the dingy bulb that struggled through the broken cabin window. Then he smiled broadly and bent to haul Big Sam to his feet. "We have our moments," he said. "Here, give me a hand with him."

They propped Big Sam against the house to recover. He waggled his head, still slightly groggy, and when he saw his late adversary, made mechanical motions of combat.

Annie stopped him. "That'll do. Ye've had enough," she told him sharply. "Didn't ye see he was only feintin' wid his left, so's he could slip over that right hook? I'm ashamed o' ye!"

"You seem to know something about it," said the captive.

"I've handled me dooks now and ag'in," Tugboat Annie admitted, not without pride.

"Battling Bertha," he murmured. "You're the cook, I suppose. Now, what about a nice fat sandwich and a cup of coffee before I turn in?"

"I ain't the cook," she growled. "I'm the master o' this tug, and you're goin' to work, not eat. Now, will ye go below wid Big Sam here, or will I call all hands and have ye throwed down?"

The young man spread his hands. "Okay, Helen, if you're going to make a point of it. I always have been interested in engines—"

"Me name ain't Helen, ye impident baboon! It's——"

"Helen!" he told her firmly over his shoulder as he moved away. "Helen of Troy—the face that sank a thousand ships."

At dawn, the Narcissus was belting into the stiff gray seas that rode through the Strait of Juan de Fuca under the lash of a whistling half gale. It was cold and gray; the tug was wet, and the forested shores and mountain peaks of the Olympic Peninsula and the opposite coast of Vancouver Island alike were obscured in driving rain. Tugboat Annie shivered as she left her cabin, and pulled her old red sweater closer about her massive frame. Outside the engine room she encountered Big Sam.

"Br-r-r-r!" she said. "A mornin' like this gives me goose bumps as big as punkins. How'd that fresh gangman behave hisself last night?" She chuckled. "I bet he's nursin' a few blisters right now."

Big Sam looked slightly uncomfortable. "Well, not eggsactly, Annie. Ye see, I put him to work all right, but every time he lifted the scoop he hit the side o' the fire door and scattered coal all over the deck plates. The pressure dropped, so I had to stoke the fires meself, for I'd told Hank he could turn in when I brought the crook below. By the way, that reminds me; we got a coupla leaky tubes."

"Trust you to do the stupid thing!" Tugboat Annie raged. "Didn't ye know he was spillin' coal a purpose? What did he do wid hisself then?"

Big Sam coughed. He said sheepishly, "Why, we had a yarn or two, and he telled me he was a amateur boxer." He fingered his jaw reminiscently. "He's a little guy, but I never seen such a feller. He's got a kind of a way about him. Anyways, he said he was cold; so I lent him a blanket and he rolled up and had a snooze. And when I come off watch he was up in the galley stuffin' hisself."

"Where was Pinto?" Annie demanded.

"He was there. This feller helped him build up the fire, and they got real friendly. Pinto give him a good feed. But I don't think he's feelin' so good now. There he is, standin' in the rain, lookin' over the bows. Guess he ain't accustomed to rough water."

Annie turned and stared. "Say!" she yelped suddenly. "That's Peter's oilskin what he's wearin'. Where'd he git it?"

"He won it off Peter rollin' the bones in the messroom, when Peter come from the wheel. I telled ye he had a way with him."

"Hmmph! I'll 'way' him—soft-soapin' the lot of ye and makin' hisself to home! I'll fix him!"

Bracing her sturdy legs against the wild pitch of the tug in the rising sea, she barged forward to where her captive stood leaning into the wind and rain, bareheaded, and with the oilskin wind-molded around his slight, sinewy body.

"Hey, there, you gunster!" Tugboat Annie hailed. "You git back out o' that! I got a job o' work for ye!"

He turned, grinning uncertainly. "My pal!" he said.

"Now looka here! I had enough o' your lip last night, and I'll take no more of it. I'm goin' to l'arn you a good lesson, and you're goin' to—to l'arn it," she ended lamely.

"Sure," he agreed cheerfully. "Some other time. It looks kind of rough out there. When are we turning round?"

"We ain't turnin' round," Annie told him grimly.

"You mean" —he looked uneasily at her and pointed ahead to where the roaring combers of the open Pacific flung their white crests against the storm-black sky— "You're going to take this tub out in that?"

"Sartinly! Why not? We got a job to do out there, and this vessel can take a awful beatin' —as ye'll prob'ly discover afore the day's over." She watched him contemptuously. "What's the matter— gettin' yeller? I thought it'd come out!"

"Maybe that's it," he admitted slowly. "Don't you find the—the motion sort of uncomfortable though?"

"So that's it, too, is it?" Annie chuckled. "Gettin' green around the gills, huh? Well, well! That's jest fine. Go on and get sick. The ocean's yours, and the sicker ye get the better I'll like it. Now go on aft there. The mate's got a job o' bilge divin' for ye, and mebbe if ye behave yerself, ye'll git some nice fat salt pork fer dinner. Go on, git movin'!"

She herded him aft and turned him over to the mate, and he obeyed meekly enough. A half hour later the mate reported to her. "Annie, he's awful sick, pore feller. He can't work. Ye'd better let him up."

"He ain't sick; he's jest scared, that's all. Needn't think he can get on my soft side. I ain't got any!" She rubbed her nose angrily with the back of her wrist. "Drat him, anyhow! Oh, well, if he's so sick, and ye're feelin' sorry fer him, let him lie in your bunk fer a spell."

"In my bunk?" barked the chastened Samaritan.

"You heerd what I said."

Clear of the cape, the Narcissus took the seas smack over the nose, and the captive was catapulted out of the mate's bunk, and crawled feebly to the deck, where he clung to the handrail near the engine-room door and looked acutely miserable. The tug's gyrations were a trial to even the hardened stomachs of her crew as she steamed doggedly out to sea.

By two o'clock she was well clear of the land, and shortly thereafter, with the wind increasing to gale force, they sighted the rolling topmasts of their prospective tow. She was a big four-masted schooner, the William Chapman, from Honolulu, in ballast; and it was plain, as the Narcissus bulled through the combers and drew nearer, that she had been through something. Her mizzen and jigger masts had been carried away, and what little canvas she had bent was close-reefed. She rose and fell in a welter of foam and her remaining sticks cut wild arcs against the stormy sky as she wallowed and pitched from crest to crest.

"Better if she hauled out to sea again, and we picked her up when the weather slacked," Peter commented moodily to Tugboat Annie; but Annie shook her head decisively.

"Don't talk so silly. How can she beat out now, agin this wind, crippled the way she is? We got to pick her up and drag her in. See everything's made ready aft there."

During the tricky and arduous job of maneuvering close enough to get a line and the heavy steel towing hawser on board the schooner, Tugboat Annie had no time to think further about her captive; but once, when the job was completed, and the lift of a great sea rose between tug and schooner, and all that could be seen of the latter were her spindling topmasts above the roaring crest, Annie spied him, face still pale, but his illness apparently forgotten, staring with fascinated eyes at the wild-sea picture. "He looks as if he was beginnin' to enj'y it, the young sculpin," Annie growled to herself. "But I'll show him yet."

In the middle of the afternoon the hawser parted, and the great steel coils, striking back with lightning speed, flicked around the side of the house and struck down a fireman and a deck hand, who were talking near the galley door.

"Here comes the grief," Tugboat Annie grunted as she ran down from the pilothouse and assisted in the removal of the men to their bunks. Both were painfully, but not seriously, injured; still, it was enough to make it impossible for them to carry on their duties, and Annie frankly was anxious as she surveyed the stretch of angry water between them and the comparative safety of the strait. By the time the Narcissus had battled around, rolling rails under, and again got a line on board the rapidly drifting schooner, wind and tide had taken them dangerously close to Tatoosh Island and the dreaded rocky shoals to the northwest.

Tugboat Annie shielded her eyes from the bulletlike spray as the tug again took up the strain of the fifteen-hundred-foot steel towing hawser, and stared resolutely shoreward. "I hope this cussed line holds, Peter," she commented to the mate. "This here'd be a swell place to pile up a hundred-thousand-dollar schooner, if it don't. Dark comin' on too! Oh, well, we'll trust to the luck o' the Brennans. I ain't never lost a ship yet, and by Barney's bull, if the schooner goes, we'll go wid it! . . . What's became o' the queer feller?"

"Talkin' to Big Sam at the door o' the engine room, last I seen of him. They's great pals . . . Say, he ain't sich a bad kid, Annie."

"You give me the gripes—you and the rest!" Annie said angrily.

"He's jest a lazy little crook, wid a yeller streak a fathom wide; and jest because he's got a grin and a smooth way wid him, ye all think he's the white-haired boy. Well, we're short-handed now, and he's goin' to work."

She waddled aft. Her captive was clinging to the big towing winch in the stern, watching the plunge and scend of the schooner at the end of the towline, as she reared like a frightened horse against the cross buffets of the seas, lifted her graceful bows, then plunged them to the capstan in snowy foam as she rushed down the slope of a wave.

Tugboat Annie prodded him with a horny thumb. "Hey, gunster," she said.

He turned. His face was pallid, but his eyes held queer sparks. "Why, hello, Graceful! Say, this life's kind of exciting after all—I mean picturesque, you know! Do you often come out here?"

"Come on," she said bluntly. "You been a passenger long enough. Playin' sick, and all. Now ye're goin' to work yer passage."

"I wasn't playing, sweetheart," he told her. "And as for work, I didn't ask to come along; so work is still out. But I'm beginning to enjoy myself."

Tugboat Annie's heavy jaw set. "Listen to me, ye no-account little crook! You think ye're pretty smart because ye got a gift o' the gab and can use yer fists a little; but ye're jest a cheap little yeller rat just the same, lookin' fer the easiest way to git by, because ye ain't got the spunk to earn the bread ye eat! Other folks makes a little money by honest work, and you takes it away from 'em wid a gun. I'm a woman, and old enough to be your grandmaw, but I give hard work for what I get, and take part o' me pay in self-respect, and so does my crew. I'm sick and tired o' yer smart-aleck ways. So either you go below and grab a shovel to take the place o' that fireman what got hurt, or I'll call the rest o' the boys and have 'em beat hell out o' ye. Now make your choice, and make it quick, for I'm short on patience right now!"

"I've made my choice," he said unsmilingly— "and work still is out."

Without a word, Annie turned, her face grim with purpose. She saw Big Sam coming hurriedly toward her. "Git a coupla the boys, Sam, and come back here," she ordered. "This gunster's goin' to take a lickin'!"

Big Sam shook his head. "Ain't got no time to fool wi' him now, Annie. We got some bad trouble below."

"Trouble?" she said sharply. "What's wrong?"

"Boiler tubes leakin' like a rusty kettle. Unless they're plugged in a hurry we're goin' to be in an awful jam."

"Hell and hardtack! Ye can't let the steam down now, Sam! Wid this wind and the set o' the tide, us and the schooner'd be ashore inside half an hour!"

Big Sam looked over the shouting seas to the loom of the land and the breakers smashing in creamy thunder against the rocks. He said phlegmatically: "Ye'll be ashore, anyway, if them tubes ain't plugged."

"Who'll do the pluggin' job?"

"That's what's botherin' me. Wi' them two men out, Shif'less is all we got left. We got to have a man on deck and one at the wheel. Shif'less is below now. He's scared stiff, but he'll have to do it. I got everything ready."

"Go ahead then. Peter's at the wheel. I'll give him his instructions, then I'll come below." She turned to the captive for a final shot. "You a good swimmer?" she rasped. "If ye ain't, ye got something to be yeller about now, by heck!"

Big Sam already was on his way below; and when Tugboat Annie followed him a few minutes later, she found the captive standing at the foot of the engine-room ladder. "What you doin' down here?" she demanded. "This is a man's job, so clear out."

"I guess I'll stick around," he said.

The port furnace was roaring full blast, trying to keep the steam pressure up to one hundred and sixty-five pounds, and it radiated terrific heat into the starboard chamber, from which the fire had been drawn and the door left open. The bed of the chamber was a mass of incandescent coals. Long tube-stopper rods, with their plugs and nuts, were laid out on the deck plates, ready; but there developed a sudden obstacle: Shiftless flatly refused the job.

"Not me, Annie," he wailed. "I got a weak heart and bad lungs, and two minutes in that heat'd kill me deader'n a doornail. I can't do it!"

Tugboat Annie raged, cajoled and threatened. Shiftless would not budge.

"Prob'ly he's right at that, Annie," Big Sam conceded. "Better git one o' the other boys down. But, Lord"—he wiped the sweat from his face—"it's goin' to be a narrer squeak!"

"Suppose you let me have a try at it, Sam," said the captive suddenly from the foot of the ladder. "If you'll show me what there is to do——"

"This job takes guts!" growled Tugboat Annie, her face tense with worry. "Guts, and lots of 'em, and that's more'n a yeller gunster like you's got! . . . Shif'less, run up and tell——"

The captive stepped around and faced her. "That'll be all from you, you fat cow!" he snapped. "You dragged me on this tub, and you've had a lot of fun calling me yellow. Perhaps it's true—I don't know, but I'm curious to find out. So quit squawking and get out of the way! . . . What do I do, Sam?"

Too astonished and indignant to reply, Tugboat Annie did not move. He pushed her roughly to one side and stepped forward. Big Sam explained:

"There's a space in back o' the boiler called the back connection. Ye can stand upright and see where the other ends o' these tubes comes through. But it's hot as the pit o' hell in there, and hotter still gettin' there. I'll pass these tube-stopper rods through the tubes that's leakin', and you plug 'em and screw 'em tight at that end. That'll stop the steam escapin' and keep it where it's needed. They ain't nothin' to it, on'y ye'll have to work mighty fast, wi' the heat and fumes and all. Now here; wrap these sacks around ye——"

Quickly he was enveloped in a thick layer of water-soaked sacking, legs, body and head. Two heavy planks were shot through the fire door onto the coals of the fire bed for him to walk over, and a water hose was made ready to play on him when he was inside. He squirmed through the aperture, and although he flinched when his hands were seared by the hot metal of the casing as he went in, he did not hesitate. Already the planks he was to walk over were beginning to char. He reached back through the door. "Give me the hose!" he gasped, and with the stream of water playing over his head and body, he advanced steadily through the inferno of the fire chamber toward the back connection. Gouts of steam and burning soot bombarded him from the leaky tubes as he went, and the gas fumes made him stagger with dizziness; but he went forward, regardless, and at last dipped under the end of the big boiler and stood upright in the back connection.

"Okay?" shouted Big Sam, already shoving the tube-stopper rods through the defective tubes.

"Okay, Sam!" the muffled response came back.

Unable to control her anxiety as to their position, Tugboat Annie went on deck. The wind was freezing after the superheated atmosphere of the engine room, and it tugged at her whipping skirts as she fought her way along the deck and up the ladder to the wheelhouse. It was nearly dark, and the flash of Tatoosh light, which guarded the iron cape, was sending its three rapid blinks at thirty-second intervals into the gathering night. The thunder of the surf sounded like the explosions of artillery as it beat over the shoals. Annie peered astern. The schooner was a wildly pitching silhouette against the faint lemon of the western sky, her high sides a fair target for the giant push of the wind, which rapidly was driving her shoreward. The tug's propeller was turning lazily now—fifteen or twenty revolutions a minute, which was just sufficient to keep the towline from fouling the blades; and Tugboat Annie's stout heart contracted, for she knew that the precious reserve of steam quickly was being depleted, and if it failed before the tube-plugging job was done and both fires again working up the pressure, nothing could save them from disaster. There was nothing she could do on deck, however, so she again made her way below.

"He's done it, Annie!" Big Sam shouted, as he saw her descend the ladder. "He's comin' out now!"

Shielding her face from the terrific heat that beat out the open door, Annie peered into the starboard fire chamber; saw her captive's legs, incased in flaming sacking, staggering along the fiercely blazing planks. She saw him stumble and fall to his knees, struggle upright with indomitable purpose, waver, then fall again with a crash and a shower of fiery sparks, and lie still, a yard from the door, while the flames licked hungrily around him.

"He's down, Sam! Do something quick!" she yelled. "Where's that other hose?"

Big Sam turned in consternation, unable to cope with this emergency; but Tugboat Annie, turning with ponderous agility, grabbed Shiftless. "Gimme a hand, Sam!" she cried; and together they hoisted him from his feet and crammed his head and shoulders through the narrow door. "Now you git hold of him, Shif'less," Annie panted, "and we'll pull. And if ye don't get him, we'll hold ye here till ye roast wid him!"

Shiftless, forced half his length into the fire chamber, locked his arms around the prostrate figure and with the desperation of sheer terror tugged and hauled; and presently, burned and scraped, they both were hauled out, and the captive dropped to the deck plates.

"Leave 'em lie!" Tugboat Annie snapped to Big Sam as he bent over them. "We got to get this job done first."

She grasped a coal scoop and stoked the port fire, while Big Sam, working like a maniac, took shovelfuls of live coals and threw them on the bed of the starboard chamber. Fuel followed, and quickly the blaze roared into life. The door was slammed shut, and presently both fires were doing their full job and the water in the steam-pressure gauge commenced slowly to rise. The job was done.

Shiftless, who was more frightened than burned, was restored to coherency and action by a couple of hearty cuffs from Tugboat Annie, and assisted Big Sam to get the unconscious captive up the ladder into Annie's bunk.

Leaving him there under the ministrations of Shiftless and Pinto, the cook, Tugboat Annie returned to the pilothouse.

Peter was spinning the wheel, his cheek white against the quid he had tucked in a corner of his mouth. He was sweating, but triumphant. "We just made it, Annie!" he grunted. "Another ten minutes or less, and we'd all have piled up. Feel that?" The deck beneath them trembled to the increased revolutions of the big propeller. "We'll snake off fine now, and be well in the strait in another hour." Peter chuckled in the vastness of his relief. "What was your tough little crook doin' all this time, Annie—saying his prayers? I'll bet he was wishin' himself safe in jail."

"In jail, is it?" snapped Annie. "It's goin' to take the hull police force o' Secoma and a shipload o' marines to arrest that kid offa this tug, crook or no crook. And I'm through wid gunster pictures!"

At five o'clock the next afternoon, after the Narcissus had placed her tow safely alongside a Secoma wharf, she returned to her own berth; and when she was made fast, Tugboat Annie went to her cabin. She stood over her bunk for a minute, looking down at the cotton-embellished figure of her captive, and her grim jaw was set.

She said huskily: "They'll not take ye, gunster, if I has to fight the hull caboodle of 'em. So don't you worry. And when ye git on yer feet again I'll give ye a good job."

The captive opened his seared and lashless eyes, and managed a grin from the corner of his blistered mouth. "Hello, Peaches," he said hoarsely. "What's that you're mumbling?"

"Ye heerd what I said, ye impident feller!" she told him. "The cops ain't goin' to git ye if I can help it—not after what ye done."

"The—Oh, yes; I see. But didn't you say something about a job too?"

"I did—if helpin' Big Sam ain't too honest a occupation for ye?"

"I'll try and bear it. Say, you're not such a bad egg at that, Annie. Were you always so good-looking?"

"Don't you be so damn sassy! Kiddin' a old woman like me! I'm goin' ashore fer a few minutes. Ye can sleep till the doctor comes."

In the company office at the end of the wharf, she reported the result of the voyage to Alec Severn, her boss.

"It was quite a gale, Annie," he said. "It had me kind of worried. Have any trouble beyond the boys that got hurt?"

"Nothin' to speak of, Alec," Annie returned. She took a newspaper from his desk and idly scanned it. Then, suddenly, she sat bolt upright, staring. "Say, Alec," she said presently, in queer, strained tones, "lemme use your tellyphone."

After a minor but interesting altercation with the operator, she got her number, and while her astonished boss listened with drooping jaw to her ensuing monologue, she talked earnestly and vehemently for two minutes. Then she hung up with a bang.

"I'll be gettin' back to the Narcissus now, Alec," she said without ceremony, and, taking the newspaper with her, sashayed rapidly down the stairs and along the wharf. Back in her cabin, her eyes hard, she approached the bunk. "Hey, gunster!" she said.

He opened his eyes. "More beautiful by the minute!" he grinned.

"Quit the funny business!" Tugboat Annie told him shortly. "Say, what's your name?"

"Queer," he said, "I've forgotten. Can it be Scarface Boloney?"

"No, it can't!" she snapped. "It's Dick Simonds—and here's yer pitcher!" And opening the newspaper, she showed him a reproduction of his photograph, under a scare head which read: Search Continues for Kidnaped Millionaire.

"Ye're Ty Connor's nevvy," Annie said dully, "and I'm mighty sorry to hear it, for although Ty's a bit stupid now and ag'in, he's honest, and he don't deserve a dirty little crook in his fambly. He thinks a hull lot o' you, though why he should I dunno, after the lousy way ye treated him. Anyway, he's comin' down here—'in nothin' flat,' whatever that means. And I—I——"

"What makes you think I'm a crook, Annie?"

"You was in that nightclub wid a gun in your hand, wasn't ye? Ye was holdin' it when I crowned ye. How do ye explain that?"

Dick Simonds smiled as broadly as his cracked lips would allow. "Remember when you went into action and upset the two bandits? Well, I socked one of them as he went down, and grabbed his gun. Then you socked me, and I took a sea trip for my health. And now look at me."

"Well, I ain't sorry," said Annie, beginning to see the light. "Mebbe it'll l'arn ye better sense than to go playin' around nightclubs all yer life. And why didn't ye tell me who ye was?"

"What and miss all the fun of a cruise with Tugboat Annie?"

"Fun, was it? Hoomph! Ye got peculiar ideas o' enj'yin' yourself. Well, I suppose ye'll not be wantin' that job now."

"You suppose wrong, Annie. A tugboat's life is the life for me from now on. . . . Say, what's that I smell?"

"Smell?" Tugboat Annie raised her mastiff nose and sniffed. "Smell? Why, that's supper, o' course. I ordered it special. Pinto's dishin' it up now."

"Annie, if it's what I think it is, I'll love you——"

"It's spareribs and sauerkraut, wid plenty o' kraut."

"—forever and ever!"

IRON JOHN

It was one of those leaping mornings when the world seems to have been sluiced in a bath of rarefied sunlight, then hung on a celestial clothesline to dry. The brilliant day, the sharp invigorating breeze, gave to the Secoma waterfront a staccato air, so that harbor shipping appeared to move with greater alacrity, the ferries shuttling across Puget Sound tootled with a shriller exhilaration, and even the shabby dockside loungers seemed to loaf at a quickened tempo. And Tugboat Annie Brennan, master of the ocean-going tug Narcissus, lumbered briskly on deck, glanced humorously about at the deep blue sky, the rippling harbor and the bobbing rubbish in the slip, and hummed with gay discordance her favorite tune:

> *Oh, happy days is here some more,*
> *O-o-oh, happy days is*———

She stopped abruptly as her eyes traveled across the slip and encountered the bright black shoebutton orbs and the roughhewn, uninspiring countenance of her detested rival, Horatio Bullwinkle, master and owner of the deep-water tug Salamander.

"Mornin', horse-face," said Annie affably. "Swell day, ain't it?"

Mr. Bullwinkle could not believe his scrubby ears. Tugboat Annie friendly?

"You ain't went crazy all of a sudden, have you?" he asked suspiciously.

"Ain't you the old tweaser?" Annie replied roguishly. "But ye can't get me mad. This ain't me fightin' day." She struggled mentally for a moment, then succumbed to need for a confidant: "I got some good news this mornin'."

"Somebody goin' to bump ye off?" inquired Mr. Bullwinkle sourly.

"No, sir! I got a letter from a old friend o' mine—Captain Iron John McGinnes, o' Portland. He's comin' up here to spend a few days wid me. He was a pal o' me diseased husband, the late Captain Terry, too. They sowed their wild onions together. Dear, dear"—Annie chuckled reminiscently—"there was a pair o' hooligans for ye. Then Iron John's wife sued him for bigamony, and——"

A hard-featured towboat captain who was passing paused interestedly.

"Annie, did I hear you say Iron John McGinnes was coming up here?"

"Yeah, this afternoon, Curly," said Annie happily.

"That's swell, Annie! There," said the hard-featured man admiringly, "is a real towboat man!"

"Humph! Towboat man, is he?" said Mr. Bullwinkle derisively.

"Best on the coast—present company not expected!" Annie told him promptly.

"Oh, yeah?"

"Oh, yeah, ye big boot!" said Annie, stung by his tone. "Iron John's tugboated all over the world—and Europe too. He's worked on tugs in Antwerp, and Sydney, and Hong Kong, and in the Irish Sea——"

"Aw, rats!"

"It's true! There was a shipmaster come in here wid his vessel once—he was a Englishman from—Cockney I think it was—and he telled me he seen Iron John on a tug in——"

"I don't believe it!"

"Ye're just sayin' that account o' sour apples," Annie rebutted scornfully. "But it's a fack. . . . Ain't it, Curly?"

"Sure is, Annie!" said the hard-featured man, and passed on.

"See, smart guy?" said Annie triumphantly. "And wid all that experience, o' course he's a pretty hard customer. They don't call him Iron John for nothin'!"

Mr. Bullwinkle laughed unpleasantly.

"Ye can laugh," said Tugboat Annie comfortably. "Only I'd advise you not to cross his bows while he's here. There's many a tough seafarin' mug fancied hisself, till Iron John showed him how much water he drawed." She chuckled again, admiringly. "Oh, he's a tartan, all right!"

"He gets in today, you say?" said Mr. Bullwinkle with an ironical smirk. "Mebbe I can do somethin' to help entertain him. How'd he like to see me beat you to the business of towing down that schooner, the George Cary, what arrives off the Cape from Honolulu, tomorrow?"

"It's day after tomorrer, smarty!" corrected Annie promptly. "We got a wireless message——" She halted abruptly as she saw his dawning grin. "That is——"

"Thanks!" said Mr. Bullwinkle maliciously. "That saves me the trouble o' findin' out. I wasn't sure. Is Iron John a smart businessman, like you?"

"Mebbe he'll have a chance to show you—although towin' a schooner is small tomatoes to a man wid the experience of Iron John!"

"I spose," said Mr. Bullwinkle sarcastically, "he's ten foot tall, and two foot between the eyes. Well, the bigger they come the harder they fall."

"And the harder they bounce back," Annie reminded him with a grin. "So mind yer p's and g's!"

Mr. Bullwinkle hoped his snort of derision sounded genuine, but he was vaguely disturbed as he turned away; and as the day wore on, and he noted the reaction of the waterfront to the impending arrival of Tugboat Annie's formidable friend, Iron John, his uneasiness grew.

During a midday session at the Greasy Spoon, a popular eating place where all the waterfront gossip was exchanged, the coming of Iron John was a popular topic; and as Mr. Bullwinkle listened to tales of his prowess—tales generally linked with instances of Iron John's fierce and effective loyalty to Tugboat Annie—he thought, with a faint regret, of certain dubious trickeries in his own past business rivalry with that redoubtable woman; and he began to ponder if he might now, without undue ostentation, make some small gesture of conciliation before the arrival of Iron John. As a rough-and-tumble fighter Mr. Bullwinkle had commendable skill, nor was he wanting in courage; but as the legendary figure of the prospective visitor grew in his mind he reasoned that there was no use in asking for trouble. Outwardly, he pretended to scorn. "Hell!" he grunted disdainfully. "Nobody could be as good as they say this guy is!" But his tone lacked conviction, and as no one listened to him anyway, he left the Greasy Spoon, where generally he raised a leading voice, and made his way thoughtfully back to the Salamander.

Beyond towing a dumb barge to an oil dock, Mr. Bullwinkle had an easy day, and he spent the afternoon alternating restlessly between the deck and the pilothouse, observing all of Annie's movements on the Narcissus across the slip. And at about four o'clock his

IRON JOHN

patience was rewarded, for Annie appeared primped and sprazzed, in her best shore-going gear, and about to set off for the station.

She wore her time-battered reticule moored to her waist, her precious watch was anchored to her massive bows with a bent safety pin in lieu of a catch and aloft, pushed in her excitement and hurry to the back of her head, was the pride of her life—an ancient bonnet whose main ornament was a decayed but still madcap feather that, overcome by the importance of the occasion, dangled and bobbed in a hysteria of condescension at more lowly chapeaux.

Tugboat Annie stepped upon the wharf, apparently looking neither to right nor left. "I see ye, Bullwinkle, sneakin' behind that wheelhouse!" she shouted complacently; then, with a shake and a settling jerk at her stays, she proceeded on her way.

Mr. Bullwinkle watched her as she rolled and wallowed along the wharf and over the tracks, disappearing finally behind a great dray; and then, his curiosity whetted insufferably, and scarcely able to control his impatience, not unmixed with trepidation, for a sight of the famous Iron John, he fumed and fretted away the interval until they should arrive.

A half hour elapsed, an hour. Time they were coming, and as the big moment approached, Mr. Bullwinkle, spurred by his uneasy imagination, drew a deep breath and made a heroic resolve. After all, he considered, he and Tugboat Annie—and Iron John, too—were all Pacific Coast tugboatmen, and fellow members of a vast and loyal guild; therefore, it behooved him to forgive Annie the few times she had outwitted him in business deals of the past. He would swallow wicked pride; he would demonstrate to her his true greatness of character by going across to the Narcissus's pier and being the first of Tugboat Annie's friends—for so he had promoted himself—to extend the hand of welcome to her gallant champion, Iron John. He'd have to meet the—the man sometimes; so, best to have it over with, and get credit for a good deed in the bargain. Annie might misunderstand. Probably, in her uncouth way, she would try to be comic; but Mr. Bullwinkle, with dignified restraint and a tolerant smile, would overlook it.

In this state of righteous resolve, and feeling very noble, he stepped ashore; but to so high a spiritual plane had he worked himself that he became careless of mundane things, and thus failed to see a carelessly left bucket, over which he tripped and fell flat on his face. He arose with stinging palms and had a bit of a struggle with his temper—a struggle rendered rather acute by the audible titters of a couple of passing longshoremen; but with great presence of mind he pretended that he had fallen on purpose, and with hot eyes and suffused cheeks continued augustly on his way.

At the shoreward end of the Narcissus's wharf he took post, with his back against the cargo shed, and waited. The sun had clouded over early in the afternoon and it smelled like rain. Time passed. Shadows lengthened and deepened, and the bright water of the harbor faded to a nacreous gray. Still no Tugboat Annie. Still no Iron John.

Mr. Bullwinkle, whose muse had been occupied with the formation of a few well-chosen words of welcome—a balanced combination of bonhomie and condescension would be about the right note—was brought back, at length, from his vacuous contemplation of the beer sign above the Hotel Neptune across the tracks, by a splash of rain on his nose; and, simultaneously, he became aware that he was the object of observation on the part of an unprepossessing individual who had materialized out of the shadows, and who stood hesitantly regarding him.

He was a bandy-legged little man, with a hard hat, a new check suit two sizes too large for him, a greasy black string tie in a cracked celluloid collar, a prim little mouth, a bulbous nose and a modest downcast eye. He seemed on the point of addressing Mr. Bullwinkle; indeed, he coughed faintly, clearing his throat to this end; but when he found that gentleman's bold eyes focused upon him in active distaste, he gulped quickly and looked away.

The stranger seemed meek and harmless enough, but Mr. Bullwinkle desired no witnesses to his meeting with Tugboat Annie and her formidable friend, Iron John. He stared, therefore, as offensively as possible, until such time as the little stranger, with an uncertain, ingratiating smile, felt compelled again to raise his eyes.

Mr. Bullwinkle scowled.

"Go away!" he said.

The little man blinked. "What?"

"Beat it! Get outa here! You ain't deef, are you?"

"N-no," the little man stammered, "b-but——"

"Go on, then—scram!"

The little man met his glare tremulously.

"B-but I'm looking for somebody. Mebbe you could——"

"Who you lookin' for?"

"Mrs. Brennan. Tugboat Annie Brennan."

Mr. Bullwinkle's business instincts came to the fore. His manner became kind, his good resolutions forgotten.

"Annie's went ashore to meet a friend, mister. But if you got a towin' job for her, why, I'm her pal, and I'll take care of it for you. That's my tug there—the Salamander."

The little man shook his head regretfully.

"No, it ain't that. She went to meet a friend, you say?"

"Yeah, up to the railroad station. Now get the hell outa here!"

"But I didn't come by train. I come up on the bus."

"You——"

"Sure!" The little man nodded amiably. "I'm the one she went to meet."

"You're a liar," said Mr. Bullwinkle. "She went to meet Iron John McGinnes, from Portland." Taking a small anticipatory liberty, he added: "He's a friend o' mine too. Now beat it!"

"But"—the little man swallowed hard—"that's my name—McGinnes."

"Not Iron John?" yelped Mr. Bullwinkle, aghast.

The little man's eyelids fluttered modestly.

"Yes, sir."

Mr. Bullwinkle's reaction, after a moment of doubt, was devastating. This—this wart, this insignificant little sprat, Tugboat Annie's friend, the famous and terrifying Iron John? A tornado of indignant resentment stormed in Mr. Bullwinkle's brain, but there came to calm it a feeling of relief; a relief which so swiftly grew that it almost swallowed his fury. No need now, in deference to the mythical Iron John, to suppress his natural talents; no further need to make friends with Tugboat Annie. He could have shouted; he could, for a brief moment, almost have liked the scrap of nonentity who stood before him eyeing him with anxious gaze. He became the full-blown Horatio Bullwinkle again, self-confident, swaggering and contemptuous. His chest swelled, his fists instinctively closed. But, for fun, he dissembled.

"Well, well, well—so you're Iron John, eh?" he said with deceptive cordiality.

"Yes, sir!" said the little man, and metaphorically wagged his tail.

At that moment, from the corner of his eye, Mr. Bullwinkle saw Tugboat Annie hurrying along in the rain under the arc light of the tracks. He grinned and spat suddenly at the little man's feet and made him jump. He did it again—and again.

Tugboat Annie had seen them by now, and with a shake of her stern increased her speed. Mr. Bullwinkle, hugely enjoying himself, gauged his time. Then he put forth one powerful hand, and with four fingers on the brim of the little man's hard hat and a thumb under his nose, he squeezed, suddenly and excruciatingly.

"Ouch!" yelled the little man, and struggled ineffectively, his eyes filled with smarting tears. "Ouch! Leggo!"

Mr. Bullwinkle let go, but only to bring the palm of his hand down upon the hat, cramming it firmly over the little man's ears. He heard with delight Tugboat Annie's belligerent roar:

"Hey, you big cloghopper, you let him alone!"

With a triumphant grin Mr. Bullwinkle stepped away; then he saw the little man's humble cane suitcase reposing on the wharf. His grin widened. He raised his foot, and with a mighty kick sent it and its wildly dispersed contents flying into the dock. Then, with a wary glance at Annie, charging down on him, he turned, and went swiftly but jauntily back toward his Salamander.

Annie changed course and made for him, but in so doing she tripped, tried to recover, stumbled again and came heavily down in a puddle. She did not immediately arise; and as she sat there, her hat with its bedraggled feather over one ear, and her foot doubled beneath her, the angry red of her face was drained to a painful white.

Wrenching his hat from his ears, the little man ran toward her, venting a series of dismayed bleats.

"What's the matter, Annie? Are ye hurt?" he stammered.

Annie looked up with a twisted grin. "H-hello, John! It's me ankle." She gasped. "I—I think it's broke."

And as he bent anxiously over her there drifted to them from the rain-veiled shadows of the Salamander's deck the derisive accents of Mr. Bullwinkle.

"Iron John!" he said.

Annie's ankle was not broken, it was badly sprained; but tugboat work must go on, and the orders of her doctor and of her employer could not defeat her determination to remain on the Narcissus.

"What?" she roared. "Let that big whiffle-snaffle think he can put me out o' commission? Nothin' doin'! I kin still keep a-goin', so you quit yer quacklin'. I'll stop on board, and Iron John here'll run the Narcissus for me. The finest towboat man on the coast, John is. . . . Ain't you, John?"

"I guess so, Annie," said Iron John modestly.

"Sure ye are!" said Annie heartily. "And we'll get along fine. We got a job early tomorrer mornin'——"

So it was that the Narcissus, in pursuance of her trade, bucketed through the darkness and the slanting rain and the short harbor chop at four o'clock next morning, to pick up a couple of gravel barges at the Rainier barge pool. While Tugboat Annie tossed in uneasy slumber in her bunk, confident that her Narcissus was in good hands, Iron John balanced his diminutive frame easily at the wheel, which he handled with caressing skill. And a quarter mile astern, also bound for the pool to drill out a scowload of lumber for transshipment to a Japanese steamer, was Mr. Bullwinkle's Salamander.

In the darkness, and the rain which descended in blinding sheets, there was some delay at the pool in picking out the Narcissus's barges; and while, with the assistance of the night watchman, it was being accomplished, the Salamander entered the pool and ran alongside the other side of the wharf.

While Mr. Bullwinkle's crew got their line on board the big lumber scow, Mr. Bullwinkle, attracted professionally by the lights of another tug in the pool, donned his oilskins and stepped on the wharf. The night watchman, his job with the Narcissus done, joined him, and together they watched her lights, shining like splintered jewels through the rain.

"Say," said Mr. Bullwinkle, "ain't that the Narcissus?"

The night watchman agreed. "Tugboat Annie's laid up, I hear," he supplemented. "Who do you spose is in command?" He paused as if on the brink of some momentous and gratifying revelation.

"Iron John McGinnes," said Mr. Bullwinkle promptly, and snickered.

"That's right!" said the night watchman, feeling cheated. "Say now, there's a towboatman, who——"

"Yeah, I know," said Mr. Bullwinkle carelessly, and his grin increased, "He's a world-beater all right, but I've took his measure. Well, I got to be goin'."

The night watchman, eager to be under shelter, went up the wharf. Mr. Bullwinkle was about to return to his tug when he noticed that, although the Narcissus was getting slowly underway with her barges in tow, the sternmost barge, although her mooring lines had been cast off, still was alongside the wharf, the slow-moving tug not yet having taken up the slack in the towing line as she moved out of the pool. And Mr. Bullwinkle, noting the possibilities thus presented to one of a playful mind, was seized by a Puckish whimsy. He moved quickly and effectively for a few moments. Then, bottling down his laughter with an effort, he stepped back on board the Salamander, rang the engine-room jingle and, with his scowload of lumber, presently was underway.

In the wheelhouse of the Narcissus, Iron John felt the resistance as the tug straightened out her charges with gentle compulsion. He felt the pull as the first barge swung into line, and he headed out between the lights of the pool entrance toward the broad, rain-lashed reaches of the sound. A few seconds later he sensed the strain of the second barge and increased the tug's speed. The big propeller accelerated its beat under the Narcissus's counter, and Iron John leaned contentedly forward, straining his eyes through the murk, and set his course on a tiny beacon winking faintly ahead through the rain. The Salamander passed him on a diverging course, and appeared, with its scow-load of lumber, to be moving with extraordinary speed, compared with the progress of the Narcissus.

"That there tug's got plenty of power," thought Iron John, not recognizing her in the thick weather. "Wonder who she is?"

He settled down to his task.

After a half hour had passed, a worried line appeared between his wrinkled little eyes. The distant beacon light should be fairly close at hand by now, to indicate a change of course; but it actually appeared no nearer than when he had started from the pool. Was it optical illusion, due to the rain?

He proceeded for a few minutes more; then his active uneasiness demanded an answer. He released the wheel, and, stepping out onto the wet and windy deck, he looked astern. And the startling and humiliating truth kicked him in the face. The entrance lights to the Rainier pool still flanked the beam of the foremost barge and, at the length of the long towline, the mooring line of the sternmost barge was still made securely fast to the wharf. Except for running the length of the towlines, which had taken her out of the pool, the Narcissus had not progressed one inch.

Iron John's brows worked agitatedly. He shouted for Shif'less, the deck hand.

"Wasn't that last barge's mooring lines cast off from the dock?" he asked.

"They sure was, cap'n!" said Shif'less, still drowsy from his surreptitious nap in the galley. "I seen the night watchman cast 'em adrift. Why," for the first time the uniqueness of the situation struck him, "somebody must 'a' made 'em fast again!"

"But who?" said Iron John, without heat, and his eyes made a series of rapid blinks.

"I dunno," said Shif'less; then recollection painfully worked. "Sa-ay, while we was in the pool, Bullwinkle came in with his Salamander. Mebbe it was him."

"Ah-h!" said Iron John softly, and his prim little mouth took on an extraordinary resemblance to a steel trap. "Mebbe he did."

Mr. Bullwinkle was not one to conceal his triumphs; and long before noon that day the Secoma waterfront had been informed, with characteristic Bullwinklean embellishments, of the discomfiture of the famous Iron John. Yet somehow, the reactions to his tale in the crowded Greasy Spoon were not quite what he had expected, for those of his hearers who did not openly disbelieve were silent. His humorous account caused no one to explode in a roar of delighted appreciation. Rather, Mr. Bullwinkle found himself regarded as serious men might look upon a brash and reckless youth who found his amusement in teasing a buzz saw.

Red Halloran, master of the Firefly, shook his head portentously. "It'll make him mad, Bullwinkle. That ain't so good for you."

"Mad?" snorted the exasperated Mr. Bullwinkle. "O' course it'll make him mad. That's what I done it for. I dunno what's the matter with all you mugs! Why, that little runt ain't even a false alarm. To hear you spout——"

"Wait a minute. Here he comes now!" someone said; and Iron John, with his bandy legs, and blinking, screwed-up eyes, and ridiculous little body, came in the door. He answered greetings with a queer, shy smile, and headed for a table. As he passed his glance met the bold, appraising stare of Mr. Bullwinkle and his eyes demurely dropped. He did not speak.

Mr. Bullwinkle laughed nastily and winked at his audience, but before he could speak Iron John halted and turned, and then, as if with painful resolution, came slowly back to him.

"You reely shouldn't ha' done that at the pool, you know," he said diffidently. "Ye reely shouldn't!"

"No?" said Mr. Bullwinkle humorously, and again winked at the bystanders. "And why not, Clarence?"

"Well——" Iron John seemed to hesitate. His tone was almost apologetic. "It was behind me back. It—it wasn't fair. I come up here for a holiday——" He paused again, embarrassed.

"Yeah?" said Mr. Bullwinkle encouragingly. "Go on, I won't hurt you."

"And now"—Iron John's chin quivered—"I got to get even with you. It—it's kind of a bother." His eyes, raised for a moment, were those of a hurt child.

"Get even with me?" asked Mr. Bullwinkle with a bellow of delight. "Why, you little rascal! I've a good mind to paddle your tail for ye! Get even, eh?" Mentally, he digested this marvel.

Iron John's gaze again sought the floor. "Yes," he said forlornly. "I don't like quarrelin' with people and makin' 'em feel bad by gettin' even with them, but this time I gotta. I promised Annie."

"He promised Annie!" Mr. Bullwinkle relayed rapturously. "Why, the little cuss!"

"Don't say I didn't warn ye," said Iron John timidly. "I'm goin' after your business."

"You are, hey?" said Mr. Bullwinkle admiringly. "Well, ain't that swell?" His manner changed abruptly. He became harsh, threatening, triumphantly domineering. "Now listen, shrimp! All these guys think you're somebody; but I think you're Mr. Nothin', see? And if you monkey around me any more, I'll chew ye up and spit ye out. It's gettin' so that every time I scratch meself you hop out. I'm gettin' tired of it! So stay away!"

Iron John shook his head.

"Ain't no use coaxin' now, I'm goin' after you. I got me mind set on it. That schooner tomorrow mornin'——"

Mr. Bullwinkle stared.

"What about it?"

"I'm towin' her in from the Cape. That'll be a start."

"So ye figger ye can take that job away from me, hey?"

"I'm goin' to," said Iron John mildly. "I promised Annie."

"Would ye like to bet on it?" asked Mr. Bullwinkle softly.

Iron John nodded. "I own two tugs down to Portland. One of 'em's as big as your Salamander, and she's more up-to-date. But mebbe"—he seemed to relent—"ye wouldn't want to bet the Salamander against her. Mebbe ye'd rather bet money."

"You mean," snapped Mr. Bullwinkle, and in spite of himself a note of respect crept into his voice, "you'd risk bettin' your tug you can beat me to that schooner job tomorrer?"

Iron John met his scowl timorously. "I ain't riskin' nothing," he said. "I'm sure to win." He added, as an afterthought: "I got a lawyer outside ready to fix up the papers."

"Wha-at?" roared Mr. Bullwinkle in consternation. "Say, how did you know I'd bet?"

"Annie told me. And I figgered if I brought the lawyer, ye'd see I was on the level, and put up or shut up. I—I hope you don't think I been too forward."

"You're crazy!" Mr. Bullwinkle's laugh was distinctly hollow. "Think I'd bet my tug on a little job like towin' a schooner?"

"I guess that's right," agreed Iron John humbly. "It wouldn't be fair for me to take your livin' away from you. Anyway, I brought a little change along, too."

Mr. Bullwinkle's expression cleared. "Oh, I don't mind riskin' a little dough, just to make it exciting," he said largely. He looked around the ring of intent faces that had gathered from the tables of the Greasy Spoon. "But no piker's bets, mind."

Iron John stood, hesitant and embarrassed. He reached into his pocket and hauled out a crumpled wad of notes. "Mebbe this ain't enough," he said anxiously. "I only brought a thousand."

There was that deep, sinking feeling at the pit of Mr. Bullwinkle's stomach but it was too late to back out now. Still—a thousand dollars! He cleared his throat uncertainly.

"Well, as it happens, I haven't got that much loose cash just at the moment, but I could raise mebbe——I mean, I've got five hundred——"

For a moment Iron John's prim little mouth looked stubborn. Then he nodded.

"Sure. That's okay. I—I hope ye can afford to lose that much."

He folded the creases from five hundred dollars in crumpled currency, and handed the money to Red Halloran, and arrangements were made that Mr. Bullwinkle was to give him a check for an equal amount.

"Well, sir," said Iron John with a little sigh, when the transaction was completed, "it sure was nice of you to give me that five hundred; and—and mebbe, if ye don't hold no spite after I've collected it, I won't get even with you no more."

"Don't be so damn cocky!" bellowed the outraged Mr. Bullwinkle. "You ain't won it yet!"

Iron John looked ashamed. "I've as good as," he said.

The sporting instinct of the Secoma waterfront had been aroused to feverish heat by the wager between Mr. Horatio Bullwinkle and Iron John, and there were many minor bettors who wished Mr. Bullwinkle to cover their money. In spite of his loudly stated confidence, however, he was wary, for he did not yet know the true professional attainments of Iron John. But after he had observed his handling of the Narcissus in various small jobs throughout the afternoon, during which Iron John twice bumped the dock, and once the Salamander, in coming alongside, and nearly collided with a ferry, his fears gave way to jubilation, and he took on all comers until his money ran out.

"Towboat man!" he snorted contemptuously to his mate. "That bozo couldn't navigate a stick across a bathtub!"

Even Tugboat Annie was alarmed.

"Hell and hardtack, John!" she yelled irritably, the second time he collided with the wharf. "What's the matter wid you? You used to come aside so gentle ye wouldn't crack a egg!"

"I'm sorry, Annie!" Iron John apologized. "But Bullwinkle was watching me—and he might have a few dollars to bet still in his jeans. Time I bump a coupla more times, he'll have bet everything down to his shirt. Funny, I don't know why I don't like him, Annie. But I don't."

When, in the late afternoon, the two tugs left for the Cape, they had a goodly escort, not only of tugs but of other small craft. When inbound sailing vessels were expected off the Cape it was the practice, in good weather, for competing tugs to lie anchored off the entrance to the strait, awaiting the arrival of the prize, and then to outbid or outsmart one another for the job. But on this occasion the presence of tugs other than the Narcissus and the Salamander was more or less a gesture, for sportsmanship among the tug fleet is strong and the interest lay in watching the champions fight it out.

The weather had cleared to a flat calm, and the fleet kept fairly well together on the way up the sound toward the Strait of Juan de Fuca. There was no object in racing, at this stage, for the George Cary would not arrive off Flattery until an hour or so before dawn. But midnight saw them well down the strait, and by two in the morning the fleet was anchored off the Cape.

The Narcissus rose and fell with the deep breathing of the Pacific, and the Salamander floated tranquilly a hundred yards away. The air was warm, and there was a moon which turned the smooth Pacific to a sheet of iridescent silk and bathed in majestic splendor the black mass of the frowning Cape.

Tugboat Annie, assisted by Iron John and a pair of makeshift crutches, had been deposited in a chair on the forward deck. Across the still water the intermittent glow of a cigar upon the Salamander's upper deck indicated that Mr. Bullwinkle also was enjoying the beauties of the night. Big Sam, the engineer, came up from the Narcissus's bowels, wiping his hands on a piece of cotton waste and, joining Annie and Iron John, leaned idly across the rail.

"How's your hoof, Annie?" he asked.

Tugboat Annie grinned.

"I can't exactly play flopscotch wid it yet, but it's comin' along. That reminds me, Sam—did I ever tell ye the antidote about the country girl and the city slinker? Well, once——"

"There's Bullwinkle, watchin' us!" said Sam hastily.

Annie looked.

"Yeah, the big ape!" She raised her voice. "Hey, fish-ears! You want to double that bet?"

"I got it doubled, ye old cow!" returned Mr. Bullwinkle ungallantly. "I bet wi' Red Halloran and Louis Torgeson and Charlie Skewis. Oh, I wasn't born yesterday!"

"You wasn't born at all—you was hatched out under a brick!" Annie told him joyously. "And ye sure pulled a bonehead, runnin' foul of Iron John here."

But Mr. Bullwinkle only laughed harshly and relapsed into silence.

"Better watch him, John," Annie said quietly. "He'll prob'ly sneak up his anchor toward mornin' and drift out a mile or two on the ebb o' the tide. That'll give him a start to the schooner."

"Don't worry, I'll watch him," said Iron John quietly, and his prim lips looked more like a trap than ever.

The moon waned and died, and after Annie had turned in, Iron John occupied her chair, his wrinkled eyes alternating between the riding lights of the anchored tugs and the dense blackness that hung like an impenetrable curtain over the open sea. After a time a slight breeze sprang up, sending tiny wavelets lapping against the Narcissus's hull. A shiver ran through Iron John's meager frame. He looked across at the Salamander's lights, listened intently, then, hearing nothing untoward, he went aft to the galley to make himself a pot of coffee. A bar of light cut through the darkness as he opened the galley door, then was shut off as he disappeared within; and, as though it were a signal, a boat swung noiselessly and by minute degrees down from the Salamander's well-greased davits and floated free, a deeper blob of shadow in the universal darkness.

With a light touch of the oars it drifted to a position three hundred feet or so astern of the Narcissus. Here it hung for a time, while its three occupants worked busily and strenuously, but without audible sound. There was a barely perceptible splash; then the boat, paying out a strong, light hawser, crept noiselessly up under the Narcissus's stern. One of the men went overside and worked, with time out now and again for all to listen. Once again, silently they dropped astern, and by degrees crept back to the Salamander, and the boat was hoisted once more to its davits. There was a smothered chuckle or two, and again stillness encompassed the dark waters.

Iron John emerged from the Narcissus's galley bearing a steaming granite mug of coffee and a thick cold-beef sandwich, which he consumed in his chair. He became aware, as he did so, that Mr. Bullwinkle had resumed his place at his tug's rail, for, through the darkness, his cigar end winked and stared at Iron John like a red, sardonic eye. For a long time he and Mr. Bullwinkle, acutely conscious of each other, dueled mentally in the dark; then, with a short laugh which carried a definite note of triumph, Mr. Bullwinkle flipped his cigar in a sharp red arc over the side and left the rail.

At intervals for the next hour Iron John climbed to the wheelhouse and peered seaward for the first glimpse of the schooner's running lights; and presently he was rewarded. Quietly he summoned his crew. The windlass commenced to clatter, and with a series of jarring clanks the dripping anchor chain began to come through the hawse pipes.

Almost immediately the rattle of the Salamander's windlass commenced and the contagion spread through the anchored fleet. Faster and faster the cables came in as the excitement increased. Faster, that is, on all of them save the Narcissus.

Iron John, in the wheelhouse, knew immediately, with that extra sense of the experienced towboat man, that something was amiss. He stuck his head out the window. Shif'less and Peter, the mate, were at the windlass below. "What's the matter?" he piped.

"Dunno, John. We can't seem to get the cable up and down. Somethin' appears to be holdin' us at the stern, like that night up at the pool. But I don't see——"

Iron John glanced toward the Salamander. He could not make out her hull, but he saw the dim flash of phosphorescence as the flukes of her anchor broke the surface, and heard the faint jingle of her engine-room signal and the slow thump of her propeller as she began to get underway.

"Annie!" called Iron John softly, and Tugboat Annie appeared in the doorway connecting her cabin with the wheelhouse. She was supported by one leg and a crutch.

"What's wrong?" she asked quickly.

"I dunno. Here, hold the wheel a minute. . . . Oh, I forgot——"

"I can hold it!" said Annie grimly. "This is some o' Bullwinkle's monkeyshines. I kin smell it!"

Iron John did not stop to answer. He grabbed an electric torch, ran aft and put the spot over the stern. And instantly he realized Bullwinkle's stratagem. He had dropped a not too heavy anchor, probably bought cheap at secondhand, astern of the Narcissus attached to a length of strong towing line, which had then been securely made fast to the Narcissus's rudder post under the counter. Thus the tug was anchored at both ends, and unable to move, except at risk of tearing the rudder adrift.

Frantically Iron John yelled: "'Vast heaving!" and the mutter of the windlass ceased. There was a circle of moving lights over the water, and he looked up as the Salamander, coming about on her course for the schooner, swept around the Narcissus's stern.

"What are ye doing?" asked Mr. Bullwinkle's raucously triumphant shout. "Picking daisies?"

Iron John did not even see her diminishing stern light. He obtained a pike pole, ordered Peter to pay out the forward anchor cable and shouted to Sam, the engineer, to give her a slight kick astern. "Not too much," he warned, "or we'll foul that line."

With the pike pole he hooked the line, and, working under desperate difficulties, managed to sever it with his razor-sharp clasp knife. The end dropped with a splash, and he again addressed Peter at the windlass. "Heave up!" he shouted.

The tug moved forward, the windlass rattling furiously as the chain came in; and presently, with the anchor awash, the Narcissus swung around and set out in pursuit of the distant fleet. As Iron John passed the engine-room door on his way back to the wheelhouse, he encountered the broad, anxious countenance of Big Sam.

"What was the trouble?" asked Sam.

Iron John blinked at him. "Trouble?" he said. "There was no trouble. It was only Bullwinkle trying to have a joke."

He resumed the wheel, still panting from his exertions. Tugboat Annie sank on the small settee and listened to his account of Bullwinkle's duplicity.

"He's a smart one, Annie," he said nervously. "I'm mighty glad I didn't underestimate him."

"Seems to me ye did," she said tartly. "He certainly put one over on us."

"That don't count," he said, with his wry little smile. "It's what's goin' to happen now that counts."

"It's no good, John!" she rasped. "He's got too much of a start!"

"Oh, I dunno. The feller what's tied to the tail of the bull travels as fast as the feller what's holdin' the horns," he reminded her quietly. "So we'll keep a-goin'."

The lights of the tug fleet were dancing yellow specks in the blackness ahead, with the Salamander well in the lead; but ten minutes is a big handicap in a close race. And, although in the long run to the schooner the Narcissus left the other vessels biting her wake, it was a toss-up, with the odds against her, that she would be able to overtake the Salamander, even though she had a quarter-of-a-knot advantage in speed. But Iron John hung grimly on.

"Drat it!" said Annie, thumping the settee tensely with her fist. "We got to win, John! The hull waterfront's bettin' on you! You can't let 'em down!"

"Who's lettin' 'em down?" he replied. "We ain't licked yet. Look at the way we're comin' up on her." He was silent for a moment, then he resumed. "I'm sorry I give you all this worry, Annie, but that schooner's still near a mile off, and we can pass the Salamander any time we like now."

"What?" Annie bounced up off her seat, and her game leg bounced her down again; but in the quick glimpse through the window she had seen that it was true. The Salamander was a bare one hundred and fifty yards ahead.

"Ye know, Annie"—Iron John's voice was slightly querulous—"I

IRON JOHN

think I'm gettin' kinda cross at Bullwinkle again. I just happened to think o' something."

"What was that?"

"Well, I hate to mention it, but this is two nights straight runnin' he held me back by the tail. I ought to do something about it. I reely should."

"No time like the present!" she assured him.

"I believe you're right," he said, and, reaching out, jingled for half speed.

"Here, what are ye doin'?" Annie roared. "This ain't no time to dawdle!"

Iron John shook his head.

"It ain't good business to have too many bidding for the job, Annie," he said diffidently. "It pulls the price down."

"But ye got to get in there and underbid Bullwinkle to get the job at all!"

"That ain't my way at all, Annie," he said. "I never did intend doin' that."

Tugboat Annie stared. "What's came over you, John?" she asked, curiosity overriding her eagerness to beat the Salamander. "You ain't afraid o' Bullwinkle, are ye?"

"No-o, I don't think so," he replied. "I'm kinda mad at him, though. Look. He'll be lyin' off alongside the schooner in a coupla minutes now, biddin' for the job. . . . Gosh, it's a black night. I bet he's feeling pretty good now, thinking he's beat us, eh, Annie?" He leaned out of the window and bawled: "Shif'less!"

Shif'less appeared.

"Go below quick," said Iron John, "and tell Sam to switch off every light in the vessel, except what he needs below, and keep the engine-room door shut. And when he hears me give one short blast of the whistle, tell him to switch 'em on again and throw the engines ahead, slow. Well, go on, move! Or do I have to fetch you a kick in the ribs?"

Shif'less disappeared. A minute later the lights of the Narcissus winked out and she surged softly ahead in a pool of complete blackness, indistinguishable from the night.

"I ain't a-goin' to stand another minute o' this nonsense——" Tugboat Annie began, in the darkness of the wheelhouse. But Iron John interrupted her.

"I'm sorry if ye're sore, Annie," he said humbly. "I only wanted to show Bullwinkle a wrinkle in towboatin'."

"Ye might as well go ahead wid it now," she returned glumly. "We're did for, anyways. I wash me face of the whole affair."

She stood up despondently in the darkness and watched the dancing lights of the Salamander as she rounded to, off the black bulk of the schooner, visible only when outlined against the stars. Iron John had called the mate and instructed him, in low tones, to bend a hauling line to the towing wire, and a shot line to the hauling line and stand by to heave it when Iron John gave the word. The mate, with a puzzled frown, obeyed.

In silent darkness the Narcissus dropped down upon the barely moving schooner. Through the open window of the tug's wheelhouse was clearly heard the growling bass of Mr. Bullwinkle, bargaining terms with the Swedish shipmaster, and it was obvious that their parley was near an end. And the Narcissus, unobserved without lights, coasted silently almost under the George Cary's bows, while upon the schooner's foc'sle head her mate and his men waited for the end of the bargaining, so that they could take the Salamander's towing wire.

Mr. Bullwinkle's voice arose, rich with triumph:

"Okay, captain?"

Iron John stiffened in the dark.

"Okay!" the shipmaster replied.

Iron John waited until the Salamander had sheered around preparatory to sending a shot line on board the schooner. Then like a flash he reached for the whistle cord and gave one sharp toot. Instantly the Narcissus's running lights came on. Iron John stuck his head out the door while his hand spun the big wheel. He shouted, sharp and clear:

"Heave 'em the line, Peter!"

Peter expertly sent his shot line whizzing up and across the schooner's foc'sle head, where the mate and his men, under the impression that this was the tug that had won the job, hauled the heavy towing wire on board and made it fast. The Narcissus picked up speed, the wire rapidly unreeling from the towing drum in the stern.

There was confused shouting, and a roaring on the Narcissus's starboard quarter, as the cheated Salamander surged up, a full two minutes too late. The outraged Bullwinkle stood outside the wheelhouse.

"What the hell kind of a game is this?" he demanded, his voice thick with fury. "You let go that schooner! You hear? That job's mine!"

Iron John cupped his hand to his ear. "What's that?" he asked mildly.

Mr. Bullwinkle repeated, with variations.

"I'm sorry," said Iron John tremulously. "I can't let go. Ye see, this is my job now." He looked aft, beyond the surge of the towing wire, to where the schooner, behind the powerful haul of the Narcissus, was slowly gathering way. He looked back then at the silhouetted figure of Mr. Bullwinkle. "I—I hope you don't mind," he said.

"You stole that job!" screamed Mr. Bullwinkle, punctuating each word with a blow of his clenched fist on the rail. "I'll sue you! I'll have my rights. I tell you!"

Tugboat Annie hobbled to the window.

"Ye'll have a apologetic fit, if ye ain't careful," she told him calmly. "I telled ye what would happen if ye started throwin' your weight around wid Iron John."

"I'll protest it to the schooner captain!" thundered Mr. Bullwinkle. "He gave me the job!"

Iron John made small, reproving sounds with his tongue.

"Ye ought to know better than that, Mr. Bullwinkle," he said with mild scorn. "And if ye was a real towboat man, you would. Ain't nobody ever told you that once a vessel accepts a tug's line, the towin' job is legally hers. I am surprised at you." He coughed diffidently. "Come down to Portland sometime. I'd be glad to give ye a few lessons."

Without awaiting Mr. Bullwinkle's foaming reply, he closed the door, then faced Tugboat Annie defiantly.

"Well?" he said tentatively.

"I'm sorry, John; I should ha' knowed. But I near had a heart attack it was that close. And as fer Bullwinkle——"

"I hope he ain't too mad at me," said Iron John. He ventured, embarrassed, but eager for her praise, "Did I do all right?"

"All right?" echoed Tugboat Annie glistening with joy. "You was grand! You was swell! You—you was even inelegant!"

MR. BULLWINKLE EARNS HIS PAY

Although the hour was only four in the afternoon, yellow oblongs of light from Secoma's shops and office windows and the chromatic fantasia of illuminated advertising signs shone over the wet pavements, fighting back the gloom of dense, low, storm clouds driven in ragged frenzy across the weeping sky by a boisterous wind. Through sheets of slashing rain, shoppers made their purchases and fled, dripping, homeward, and breathless pedestrians with water running from their hat brims bent their heads to the downpour and with one exception scuttled from awning to doorway, seeking shelter.

The exception was Tugboat Annie Brennan, master of the deep-water tug Narcissus, ashore for an afternoon of pleasure. She had thrilled to Tangled Hearts at her favorite movie theater, had sucked up a strawberry soda, bought a pair of long gray woolen drawers for Big Sam, the engineer, two plugs of tobacco for Peter, the mate, and a cake of bright-pink, sweet-smelling soap for Shiftless, the deck hand, and now was on her way home, as impervious to rain and wind as a chunk of weathered teak. She rolled happily along, munching sugared popcorn from a sodden bag, her big frame enveloped in a worn yellow oilskin, and flaunting aloft from her shore-going bonnet, a raffish veteran of a feather that, despite its bedragglement, pranced and caracoled and flounced in high disdain of less-fortunate, non-seagoing chapeaux. Annie's massive, good-humored face was streaming moisture, and her cheeks were red in the lash of the wind, but her shrewd blue eyes were alive with simple enjoyment of her excursion ashore, and she thought with lively anticipation of the hearty supper that would await her in the snug mess room of the Narcissus when she arrived home.

She left the business section and halted momentarily on top of the steep street that led down through the wholesale section and the ship chandlers' shops to the railroad tracks and the waterfront. She loved it all—the rain and mist mixed with sooty smoke from a passing freight locomotive at the foot of the hill, the taste of brine in the rough sea wind, and the vista of busy shipping alongside the wharves. She breathed deeply, and the nostalgic hooting of an inbound liner in the storm-shrouded harbor evoked in her breast a response that was inarticulate but deep. She descended the hill, feeling that this was indeed a swell world.

"Le's see, now," she murmured contentedly. "Pinto'll have some nice steaks frizzlin' on the galley range, and baked murphies wid a lump o' butter meltin' in their stummicks, and fried onions, and—— Oh, dear! Did I forget to tell him stewed corn? Yeah, that's right—corn! And a growler o' beer and hot mince pie, and coffee wid lots o' steam to it. Oh-h——" Unable longer to contain her happiness at this savory vision, she burst into song:

> *"Happy days is here some more,*
> *Oh-h-h, happy——*

"Oof!"

Waddling around a car that had slowed for a corner, she ran smack into a tall, heavy-set, oilskin-clad figure, plodding with bent head up the hill. The man staggered and nearly fell, and a savage growl burst from his throat. He looked up, revealing the depressing features of Horatio Bullwinkle, master of the tug Salamander, and Tugboat Annie's bitter business rival.

"What the hell!" he rasped.... "Oh, it's you, clumsy, is it?"

"Yes, it's me!" snapped Annie, eager for battle. "Any projections?"

"Why don't you keep your eyes open, then?"

"I'd ha' kept 'em twice as open, and both hands on me purse, if I'd knowed I was to meet you!" returned Annie. "There ought to be a law against ye!"

"Where I come from," Mr. Bullwinkle informed her sourly, "they haul things like you away in dump carts."

"And when they find things like you, where I come from," countered Annie, "they buries them! Now go about yer business, ye dirty ox, afore I fetch ye a good kick in the puss!"

They circled warily around each other, and as Mr. Bullwinkle, with a malicious grin, departed, he suddenly planted his big foot in a puddle and bespattered her. Annie turned like a somewhat torpid

BULLWINKLE EARNS HIS PAY

tornado and launched a hearty kick, which missed him by a fraction of an inch; then, both feeling much refreshed, they went their separate ways, Annie to her cozy haven on board the Narcissus, and Mr. Bullwinkle to arrange a minor towing job with the Pearson Marine Contracting Company uptown.

After transacting his business, and feeling the need for rest and refreshment, Mr. Bullwinkle bought himself an afternoon newspaper, fresh on the street, and repaired to a beer parlor, where, with a foaming stein at his elbow and his feet on a chair, he settled down to enjoy a quiet hour. He unfolded his paper and was about to turn to the shipping news when an illustration of a steamer on the front page caught his attention. He examined it, read the caption, and both feet hit the floor with a crash. Excitedly he read the short dispatch that accompanied the picture, under a heading:

CARGO STEAMER RAMMED AT SEA

A radio message received early this afternoon from the S.S. Snoqualmie of this port reports that she was in collision at noon today with the Swedish tanker Hudiksvall at a point approximately 300 miles west by north from Cape Flattery. The Snoqualmie, with part of her bow sheared away, is in a sinking condition, with the Hudiksvall standing by. There was no loss of life. According to Murdoch McArdle, millionaire shipowner of Secoma, and owner of the stricken vessel, the Snoqualmie's pumps thus far have kept her afloat and available. The Snoqualmie, 4500 tons, and commanded by Captain J.C. Millward, of Eugene, Oregon, sailed yesterday morning from Bellingham, for Kobe with a general cargo.

Hastily Mr. Bullwinkle detached the page, folded it and stuck it in his pocket, started for the door, remembered his beer, returned and gulped it, wiped his mouth with the back of a hairy paw and steamed off, full ahead, for the office of Murdoch McArdle.

Mr. McArdle, famous among Secoma seafaring men and the shipping fraternity alike for his taciturnity, his parsimoniousness and his not-always-ethical business acumen, snapped "Send him in!" when his secretary announced the arrival of the tugboat master. His little eyes in their bony caverns surveyed Mr. Bullwinkle without expression as that breathless mariner pulled off his hat and advanced from the door. Mr. McArdle's piano-wire lips opened. "Well?" he asked.

Mr. Bullwinkle pulled the newspaper from his pocket.

"It's about the Snoqualmie, sir. It looks like it might be a towin' job. I've done good work for ye in the past——"

"Bad, too!" reminded Mr. McArdle.

"I always done me best."

"Shut up!" Mr. McArdle took a cigar from his desk, clipped the end, which he placed in a small tin box, replaced the box in his waistcoat pocket and lighted his cigar with the utmost economy of flame from a cheap lighter. For a minute he lay back and closed his eyes. When he opened them, they were bright as steel. "Sit!" he said.

Mr. Bullwinkle sat, on the edge of a chair.

"Been trying to get hold of you for an hour," rasped Mr. McArdle. "Need two tugs. Get Tugboat Annie's Narcissus. Leave at once."

"Oh, now, come, sir!" protested Mr. Bullwinkle in consternation. "My Salamander's big enough to handle this. It'll be cheaper too."

"Don't count. This is on no-cure, no-pay basis, as customary. If you bring the Snoqualmie in, you get paid. If not, you don't."

"But——"

"If that don't suit, get out."

"What about Tugboat Annie? Will you tell her to lay off?"

"No. She's got a good tug. First there gets the job."

"But I——"

"Final!"

"Very well, then, sir. What's the Snoqualmie's position?"

Mr. McArdle told him, adding other terse, necessary details. When he had finished, Horatio Bullwinkle replaced his hat with a satisfied air. He said: "I'm certainly obliged to you, sir. It's——"

"Shut the door after you," said Mr. McArdle.

Mr. Bullwinkle found himself once more upon the teeming street, feeling much as though he had been physically propelled there. He thought of Tugboat Annie with a frown. Speed and secrecy were imperative, but how to keep her from knowing—if indeed she did not already know? He reflected, however, that she had left the town before the paper appeared; and simultaneously he recollected the towing job he had arranged for that afternoon, and his frown dissolved in a grin.

"Mebbe I've been kind of hard on poor Annie," he said to himself. "P'r'aps a friendly little gesture——"

His grin widened. He stopped in at a telephone booth and telephoned the Marine Contracting Company.

"Mr. Paul Pearson in? . . . Oh, hello, Mr. Pearson. Bullwinkle. . . . Yeah. Say, I forgot I had another job for tonight when I was talking with you. I'm sorry. I'm afraid I won't be able to make it. Spose I tell Annie Brennan—that's all right with you? . . . Sure! Annie's all right! . . . Well, thanks. . . . I'll tell her."

As quickly as possible, he made his way through the steady downpour to the waterfront. Deserted decks and the clatter of voices from the Narcissus's lighted mess room indicated that her crew were still at supper.

He could hear Tugboat Annie's voice, in high good humor, spinning a yarn:

"But—ha-ha!—hang onto yer ears while I tell ye this one! Ye'll scream! Well, my pa, he come from a Irish family o' great extinction, but his on'y drawback, barrin' the whisky heaves, was that he was bald as a egg. Now, he was sittin' one day——"

Mr. Bullwinkle's curiosity was aroused; he would have liked to hear the rest of the story, for he dearly loved a yarn; but time was precious. So, omitting the effete formality of knocking, he entered the mess room.

Tugboat Annie, who had paused in her anecdote to convey to her capacious mouth a forkful of hot mince pie, paused and lowered her fork. Apparently not seeing the bulky, rain-glistening form of Mr. Bullwinkle, she sniffed, looked about her and sniffed again. She bellowed suddenly:

"Pinto! Pinto!"

The cook put his head through the connecting doorway.

"Ya-as, ma'am?"

"You keepin' any dead cats around here?"

"Why, no! No indeed, Mis' Brennan! I——"

"'S funny!" said Annie. She sniffed again. "There's somethin'——"

"Now, Annie," began Mr. Bullwinkle placatingly. "Is that a nice thing to say, when I've come to——"

Annie eyed him coldly. "Never mind, Pinto!" she bawled. "I've found it!"

"Look, Annie," resumed Mr. Bullwinkle earnestly. "I come to do you a favor—honest!"

"Wid yer pockets full o' pizen ivy, I spose?"

"No, listen. I felt kinda bad talking to you the way I done this afternoon. And after I left you I got two towin' jobs, and I can only handle one, because they both got to be done at the same time. I might have gave one to Red Halloran, o' the Firefly, or one of the other boys, but——" He paused, embarrassed.

"Come on, Analiar," said Tugboat Annie grimly. "Spill it!"

"Well, Pearson, of the Marine Contracting Company, gave me a job to pick up a dredge barge over at Bremerton and tow it up to that new channel job at Everett. I'm sposed to do it right away. Then I dropped in on McArdle, and he gave me a job too—a little-better-paying one—what has to be done at once, also. I know you and McArdle ain't exactly pals, so——"

BULLWINKLE EARNS HIS PAY

"You're right! Go on."

"Well, that's all. If you want the barge-towing job, it's yours. Only, you'll have to leave right away."

Annie said: "Whatever you're up to, Bullwinkle, it's got pimples on it. Why should you——"

"Mind, Annie," Mr. Bullwinkle interrupted artfully. "I'd expect a little percentage on the job. I ain't forkin' out charity."

"Oho! Now ye're squawkin' more natural. How big a percentage?"

"Ten percent."

"Wait here a minute," said Annie.

She grabbed a sou'wester and her oilskins from a hook, and lumbered quickly up to the company offices alongside the wharf. In a few minutes she returned. Mr. Bullwinkle, who hastily was wolfing a piece of pie, looked up and swallowed, innocently blinking his little eyes.

"It seems all right, but I still don't trust ye," said Annie, absently pushing the pie plate out of Bullwinkle's range as he reached for another piece. "I tellyphoned Pearson's office, and they said I was to have the job. But how a bandy-legged ostrich like you can change yer spots in a coupla hours beats me. However——Come on, boys, and finish off your combustibles and we'll get goin'." Her eyes fell on her empty plate. "Hey, Bullwinkle," she yelped, "that was my pie what you et!"

"'Twas only a snack, Annie," said Mr. Bullwinkle, his bold little eyes a-twinkle.

"Go on, get outa here! Ye'll be helpin' yourself to a bed next!"

"Okay. But don't forget my ten percent, Annie."

"You'll get it!" said Tugboat Annie grimly. "And that ain't all ye'll get, be a coupla broken legs and a stove-in physiography, if I find you been trickin' me!"

Mr. Bullwinkle stood on the wharf, unmindful of the downpour and the wind that tugged at his flapping oilskins, and watched the Narcissus cast off. He grinned as he thought of her trip to Bremerton and the long, slow haul with the sluggish dredge to Everett. And by the time that Annie heard about the Snoqualmie, the Salamander would be clear of Flattery, and beyond any possible pursuit. The running lights of the Narcissus flashed in the rain in splinters of vivid color as she backed from the slip and turned about. Then, as her stern light dwindled from sight, Horatio Bullwinkle hurried around the head of the slip to his waiting Salamander.

A watery dawn, spreading over the tumbling gray wastes of Puget Sound, disclosed the Narcissus, with the dredge in tow, passing slowly between Whidby Island and the mainland, with Everett only a few miles away. The rain had ceased, but the sky was still overcast and the wind was blowing fresh. And far down the Strait of Juan de Fuca, the Salamander, with a fine bone in her teeth, was plowing steadily toward the open sea. At about the time she cleared Cape Flattery and took the first of the cold Pacific combers over her blunt snout, the Narcissus was delivering her dredge at Everett and, this accomplished, surged briskly home to Secoma, arriving shortly after one o'clock in the afternoon.

Tugboat Annie's employer, Alec Severn, president of the Secoma Deep-Sea Towing and Salvage Company, was on the wharf to meet her. Annie saw him from the pilothouse.

"Oh-oh! Trouble's broilin'! Look at Alec!" she said to Peter, the mate, as they entered the slip. "He's got a face as long as a cow fiddle."

"Bull fiddle, Annie."

"Don't be so finickety!" said Annie testily. . . . "Hello, Alec. Somebody put a cramp in your coffee this mornin'?"

"Hello, Annie," said Severn. He jumped on board as the tug made fast. "I've got some bad news for you."

"Don't tell me. Let me guess it!" croaked Annie with a terrible flash of intuition. "Bullwinkle!"

Severn nodded.

"I knowed it," Annie moaned. "Give that lizard a inch and he runs away wid a furlough. What's the grief?"

Severn handed her the morning paper. "Read that," he said. "Mind, it isn't your fault, Annie."

"Hold yer tongue," said Annie impatiently. She grabbed the paper and hurriedly scanned the indicated item:

LOCAL TUG WILL SALVAGE DAMAGED STEAMER
Captain Bullwinkle to Rescue

The powerful Secoma salvage tug Salamander, Horatio Bullwinkle, master, departed last night shortly after dark to go to the rescue of the S.S. Snoqualmie, seriously damaged yesterday at noon by collision. . . .

Tugboat Annie read on; then she looked up, her face as hard and formidable as Gibraltar's rock.

"So that was it! a little job from McArdle, eh? Well, give the dirty still-pigeon credit; he certainly done me up brown!" She made a visible effort at restraint. "Oh, well, what's spilt gathers no moss, and I spose I'd have did the same in his place." She reflected for a moment. "I wonder if we could catch——"

"And him with seventeen hours' start, Annie? Don't be silly."

"You're right, Alec." She simulated brisk indifference. "Deary me, there's no use makin' a mountain into a mole-hole. Now, let's see; this is Wednesday. He should pick her up sometime tomorrer evening, if she's three hundred miles off the Cape, as the paper says. Well, I tell ye this much, Alec Severn: If Bullwinkle gets her in here widout scrapin' her paint off against the trees, it'll be because they moved the shore line back to let him get by. I know that joker. He'll yell for help yet. You wait and see!"

Wednesday passed into Thursday; and Friday, then Saturday arrived, with nothing beyond a laconic message from the Snoqualmie on Thursday night to the effect that she had been picked up by the Salamander at eight p.m. that day and was returning slowly to port. Then, on Saturday night at about 9:30 o'clock, shortly after the Narcissus had returned from a towing job at Olympia and Annie was preparing for bed, there was a sharp rap at her door. It was Alec Severn.

"It's come, Annie," he said, trying to speak quietly, but the redness of his face and the sparkling eyes behind his glasses belied the casual tone.

"Can't ye be more implicit? What's came?" said Annie.

"A radio message sent from the Snoqualmie by Bullwinkle. He says——" He searched his pockets vainly. "Damn! I left it in the office. Anyway, it said: 'Come at once. Need Assistance. Urgent.'"

"What's her position?"

"It was in the message. 48.12 north, 128-20 west, if I can remember rightly. Anyway, you can check. She's about one hundred and fifty miles west by north of the Cape. I phoned McArdle, but he refused to have anything to do with it. Said you'd have to make your own arrangements with Bullwinkle."

"Humph! I ain't worried about that. Now, look; if I leave right away——"

"But what about supplies and equipment?" Severn asked.

Busy little zephyrs moved in Annie's wake as she waddled hastily, clad in her old wrapper, into the pilothouse and busied herself with a chart and dividers.

"Ain't I been ready for this minute for days? We'll leave in a half hour or less. That'll give me time to fill me tanks and bid ye a fond adoo. They'll be makin' maybe three miles an hour toward us. . . . Yeah, that's right! We ought to be up wid them about eighty miles off Flattery soon after nightfall tomorrer night. That is, if Bullwinkle ain't sunk them wid all hands and the bos'n's cat, afore we get there!"

The weather outside Flattery was overcast, and although the wind was moderate, it had changed direction, creating a small, lumpy sea that came over the Narcissus's rail in lumpy gray dollops as she left Swiftsure Lightship astern, shortly after noon the next day. When darkness fell, after a diffused and angry sunset, the tug was fifty miles offshore; and shortly thereafter, Tugboat Annie clambered to the top of the pilothouse with a pair of binoculars. At 8:30, just as the pilothouse clock gave its single liquid chime, she reappeared.

"I've saw 'em!" she told Peter, who was at the wheel.

Peter hoisted his paunch and expectorated. "How far off?" he asked.

"'Bout three miles, I should judge. Well," Annie chuckled, "they're still afloat, anyways. I better gird up me whatcha-ma-call-its and get ready for a argument wid Bullwinkle. My pa allus used to say——Oh, my! That reminds me! I never finished tellin' ye that yarn about me pa's bald prate the other night!"

"Don't bother, Annie," said Peter hastily.

"Oh, ye'll enj'y this one. Ye'll howl! Well, he was settin' out on the deck of his tug one evenin', talkin' wid Cap'n Chesley—you know him—when a Chinese steamer come into the slip alongside. It was a hot night and pa's dome was shinin' like a piston rod. And the cook in the Chinyman took a hen out o' the coop and was about to hack off its head, when the naughty fowl give a squawk and broke loose. She fluttered over the rail——"

"Hey, Annie, Bullwinkle's signalin' us. I can see his lights winkin'," Peter interrupted.

"Huh?... Oh, so he is, drat it! Just when I come to the most interestin' part!" said Annie irritably. "Well, don't forget to remind me, and I'll tell ye the rest later."

She gave three long blasts of the whistle, then went on deck. The wind had slackened considerably and the sea was fair, but the night air was cold as she stood watching the lights of the approaching vessels. The Snoqualmie, down by the head, was being towed stern first to minimize the pressure of the water against the damaged bow plates and the protecting inner bulkhead while the ship was in motion; and as they drew closer, Annie could hear the faint wheeze and suck and pound of the powerful pumps as they strove to keep down the water within the big hull. The discharged sea water was spouting in cataracts from her rusty side; and as the Narcissus drew close, she loomed, an enormous black shape against the starless sky, like a great sea animal, gasping and wounded unto death.

The Narcissus curved widely, then reduced speed and ranged parallel with the Salamander, a few yards off. Horatio Bullwinkle, in his shirt sleeves despite the damp chill of the air, was leaning against the rail. He stared at Annie with his bold, unwinking eyes for some moments without speaking.

"Well," said Annie testily, "cat run away wid yer tongue?"

Mr. Bullwinkle made an airy gesture. He said:

"H'are ya, baby?"

"I'm better off than you, be the look o' things!" said Annie, retaining a tenuous grip on her temper. "And I got plenty to say to you when we get in, ye impident louse! But business afore pleasure. What's happened?"

Mr. Bullwinkle spat over the rail and jerked his chin at the wallowing Snoqualmie.

"She's been takin' in water faster than they can pump it out, and we're only making three miles an hour. At this rate, we'll maybe lose her before we can get her in. If the water puts her fires out and the pumps quit, she'll sink like an old can. All I'm hoping for now is to get her close enough to shore to beach her."

"Got tarpaulins lashed over the hole?"

"Everything possible's been done. I been on salvage jobs before!" he told her testily. "But still the water is creepin' up."

"Prob'ly bent a few plates under the keel."

"Prob'ly. But standing there making wise guesses ain't helpin' us any."

"I jest wanted to check up on ye," said Annie calmly. "You ain't the best salvage man in the world, by a coupla million better ones. Now what's your proposition? You ain't expectin' me to help ye for nothin', in return for the favor ye done me Tuesday night, I take it?"

Mr. Bullwinkle grinned. "I still got me 10 percent coming on that, don't forget. But on this job—how's 20 percent of the salvage money?"

"You been readin' the funny papers, I see."

"That's a fair offer, Annie. You——"

"If I help ye here on a percentage basis, it'll be fifty-fifty. But I'll make no agreement until I've been aboard the steamer and had a look around."

"There's no need to do that, Annie."

"This ain't my first salvage job neither, Bullwinkle," Annie reminded him tartly, and the Narcissus swung astern.

Annie put the Narcissus's powerful searchlight beam on the Snoqualmie's bows, which had been almost completely sheared away. Ragged curls and ribbons of steel bulged under the heavy but inadequate emergency collision mat lashed over the rent, and Annie could hear the sough and wash of water as it lapped fretfully against the bulkhead within the steamer's hull.

BULLWINKLE EARNS HIS PAY

Annie shook her head doubtfully, then took the Narcissus alongside the Snoqualmie and requested permission to come aboard with Big Sam, the engineer; and ten minutes later, after some tricky maneuvering to avoid crushing the Narcissus against the steamer's rolling side, they mounted a sea ladder and stood upon the Snoqualmie's deck.

"Hello, Annie," Captain Millward said. "I'm glad you've come. The Salamander's done her best, but I'm afraid it's not good enough."

He detailed to her the full extent of the damage so far as it was known, and she agreed with him that Bullwinkle had done the utmost possible without assistance.

"I'll jest take Big Sam here—he's me engineer—and we'll have a peek in your engine room, captain, if ye don't mind."

"Certainly, Annie. You'll find Mr. Bogle, the chief, below. But don't forget, every hour is going to count, and the sooner you tail onto a line, the better." He added bitterly: "I wish to God McArdle was on the blasted crate. Then she could sink and be damned to her!"

"Why, what——"

"She's parish-rigged, the same as all his ships. Keeps us short of red lead and paint, till her plates are half rusted through and thin as cardboard. No equipment on board to take care of emergencies like this. If she'd been a fit vessel we wouldn't have sustained half the damage we did. Oh, well! What's the use of talking? He's probably got her insured for twice her value, so if she does founder he'll be that much ahead. What are a few seamen's lives to him? Hurry up and get us in, Annie."

"I'll do me best, captain," she promised; and accompanied by Big Sam, she entered the oily, superheated atmosphere of the engine-room housing and made her way below, balancing against the erratic roll and swing of the vessel as they descended the steep and slippery ladders.

They were met at the bottom by a rawboned man, dressed in a grease-stained boiler suit. He had small, shrewd, close-set eyes and the high, broad cheekbones, horselike jaw and thin, pawky lips of the Orkney Islands Scotsman.

"Who are you?" he demanded in astonishment at seeing a woman in the engine room, his voice carrying with the ease of long practice over the grind and whir and bang of hard-working machinery, fans and pumps.

"I'm Tugboat Annie Brennan, and this is——"

"Och, aye! Ah've heerd tell o' ye. Ah'm Andra Bogle, the chief engineer. Whut are ye wantin'—a sphere aroond? Ye'll find ut a prime sample o' one o' McArdle's coffins."

"How fast is the water making?"

"Ower two inches an hoor."

"And it's eighty miles to the Cape." Annie shook her head.

"Och, wi' two tugs we'll mak' six knots. We'll do ut easy!"

"If ye're blessed wid a propeller for swimmin', instead o' legs, ye might," Annie conceded. She noted that the pumps were working at high speed; yet a special sense, born of her years of experience, told her that all was not as it should be in the engine room of the Snoqualmie. Mr. Bogle, she thought, was a shade too smart.

They went into the stokehold, alive with the clang of shovels on gritty steel deck plates as half-naked firemen, gleaming with sweat in the blistering heat, toiled at the roaring fires. A lean-waisted, broad-shouldered fireman, black with grime, leaned on his shovel and wiped his neck with a dirty sweat rag.

"It's a hell of a job keeping up steam pressure with that muck, chief!" he said, jerking a thumb at the coal that spread on the plates under the bunker bulkhead.

"You're paid for whut ye're doin'!" said Mr. Bogle. "So shut yer gob!"

"The guy's right, Annie," Big Sam commented. "That's an awful poor grade o' coal they're usin'."

"Poor?" echoed Mr. Bogle scornfully. "Ut's trash. Half fu' o' slate!" He put his lips close to Tugboat Annie's ear and chuckled. "Ah don't mind usin' guid steam coal tae drive a shup ahead on her v'yage when she's makin' money, but ah'll no waste ut on a vessel whut's mebbe sinkin'!"

Annie looked startled. "But that's foolishness! The pumps——"

Mr. Bogle shook his head obstinately.

"The pumps is my business. And Andra Bogle's no the man for tae fling awa' anither man's money—not even a corby crow like yon McArdle."

"You don't like him, huh?"

"Ah'd fork ower half a day's pay to gi'e him a good dunt on the skull wi' a slice bar. But he's a canny businessman and ah'm worrkin' for him, so ah do me best. O'coorse," he added cautiously, "this is strictly atween oorsel's, mind!"

But Annie was no longer listening. She was thinking. And her preoccupation continued during her leave-taking of the economical Mr. Bogle.

On deck, once more, she sought out Captain Millward.

"Say," she said abruptly, "that engineer o' yours is losin' ye the chance o' makin' port. He's——"

"Bogle is McArdle's pet. And he won't stand for interference in the engine room!"

"But he's usin'——"

"For heaven's sake, Annie, haven't I got troubles enough, without shouldering Bogle's? Anyway, he knows his job, or McArdle wouldn't have signed him on." Millward looked overside. "And I'd suggest that you get on with yours."

"But, captain—he's——"

"I've no time to listen, now!" the shipmaster said impatiently. "We've got to start moving faster, that's all!"

Annie was about to protest further, when the chief officer came up, and engaged the captain in urgent and technical discussion about the weakening forward bulkhead. "Good-bye, Annie—I'll see you in port," Millward said over his shoulder, as they walked away.

For a minute Annie paused, irresolute; then she shook her head and clambered over the rail and down the sea ladder. When she had returned to her Narcissus and was again in conversation with Horatio Bullwinkle, her mastiff face wore a worried frown.

"Well," said Mr. Bullwinkle jovially, "if you're through with your snoopin', we'll come to terms. I'll give ye 30 percent of the salvage fee. I'm nothing," he supplemented, "if not fair."

"Ye're a kind of a growth," said Annie. "But I've changed me mind. I want a flat price, win or lose, of three thousand dollars."

"And I spose ye'd like Santy Claus twice a year," gibed Mr. Bullwinkle; but assurance was lacking from his voice. "Why, you stand to make twenty-five or thirty thousand by splitting the salvage."

"Don't try a game o' bluff wid me, flop-ears," said Annie crisply. "Wid my help ye've only got a hundred-to-one chance o' gettin' the Snoqualmie safe in, or ye'd never have offered to share wid me. Widout my help, ye've no chance at all." She wagged her head. "No, thanks! Ye can do yer gamblin' alone. I'm playin' safe for three thousand."

"To hell with you!" roared Mr. Bullwinkle. "I'll be sunk if I'll let you get away wi' that!"

"Ye'll be sunk if ye don't!" Annie assured him grimly.

"Ye won't help me, then?"

"For three thousand bucks."

"Lord!" breathed Mr. Bullwinkle, his face dark with thwarted fury. "I have never seen such a stubborn old mule!"

"A mule is a very fine animile," Annie said comfortably. "It talks wid its heels, so ye never misunderstand it. Well, auf wienersehn, or whatever it is."

She stepped into the pilothouse and jingled the engine-room bell, but before the Narcissus had gathered way, Mr. Bullwinkle surrendered.

Tugboat Annie ranged the Narcissus close aboard the Salamander in the now nearly smooth sea, and Mr. Bullwinkle, watching his chance, leaped across. And in Annie's cabin, after further rabid protest, he agreed to pay to her, upon their return to Secoma, the sum of three thousand dollars in consideration of her assistance, regardless of his ultimate success with the salvage.

"Can ye write?" said Annie innocently. "Ye supprise me. Well, here's the place for yer moniker. That's it." She picked up the paper and waved it to dry the ink. "It's prob'ly a forgery," she snickered, "but I'll have to take a chance."

When the transaction was complete, Bullwinkle returned to his tug and the Narcissus swept ahead, and with one steel towing wire from the Narcissus to the Salamander and another from that vessel to the Snoqualmie, the convoy picked up speed and proceeded at a trifle more than six knots toward the distant strait.

The night was a ceaseless vigil for the crews of both tugs. With the increased speed, it appeared for a time as though they might succeed in getting the steamer at least close enough to shore to be beached in shoal water for temporary repairs, with the possibility of eventual salvage; but the drag on the towing wires increased perceptibly as the water gained in the sluggishly rolling hull. Tugboat Annie spent the time alternating restlessly between the pilothouse and the deck. Her rivalry with Bullwinkle forgotten in the interest of a common cause and professional pride, she prayed wordlessly that he might succeed. But experience of the ways of the sea and ships denied hope. And as she stood, at daybreak, haggard and red-eyed from lack of sleep, and sensing, rather than seeing, the sinister wallow and pitch, and occasional crazy lurch of the barely visible Snoqualmie behind the long stretches of straining towing wire, her suspicion became certainty. She hailed the Salamander, and Bullwinkle came forth.

"She's not goin' to make it," Annie told him soberly. "She'll founder sure, before we reach the coast."

"Guess you're right, Annie. She's got her boats swung out, and the captain's goin' to signal if they have to abandon. But hang on as long as you can. She's good for a few hours yet, and we might make the beach." His voice, Annie noted, had a fighting edge, and in spite of herself, she warmed to him. He concluded: "I ain't goin' to quit till I'm forced to."

He disappeared within the cabin and Annie, shaking her shaggy head, resumed her endless pacing.

The sun arose in a burst of golden splendor behind the distant coastal mountains and ignited their icy peaks with points of dazzling fire, and in a swift spreading of the flooding light, day was born. A fresh breeze swept away the mist in ghostly shreds that melted quickly in the warming rays, and the clear, serene blue of the sky appeared. The Pacific was a dimpled, gently heaving floor of translucent ultramarine; a magnificent and fitting stage for the last throes of the dying ship. And the tugs carried on.

In mid-morning, with the surf breaking in snowy thunder against the gold-and-emerald coasts of Vancouver Island and the Olympic Peninsula, flanking the entrance to the Strait of Juan de Fuca, only a scant four miles away, Annie went aft to the galley for a hasty mug of coffee. And as she raised it to her lips, she heard an excited, warning shout. "She's going!" someone yelled; and she rushed on deck and looked astern.

Three long jets of steam plumed white against the deep blue of the sky from the Snoqualmie's funnel, and in a few seconds the sound reached her—three hoarse whistle blasts—the traditional farewell of the sea. Annie's throat contracted swiftly and her eyes filled.

"Durn me fer a sentimental old fool," she muttered huskily. "She's only a buckety old tramp."

Irritably she rubbed her nose with her knuckles; then the need for instant action snapped her back to her rugged, normal self. She gave rapid orders, which Bullwinkle was duplicating on the Salamander, and with the towing lines dropped clear, the two tugs curved around in swift, foaming arcs and raced back toward the foundering steamer. The Snoqualmie's boats, crowded with men, dropped from their davits, as direct as spiders at the ends of their silken threads. They pulled frantically clear, then, at a safe distance, halted and floated, mirrored on the sea with only the jeweled drip of the oars to break the still surface, waiting for the end.

Silently, majestically, the stern of the Snoqualmie rose high in the air, lifting with it a bridal veil of glittering water. The great hull turned slowly, stood almost on end; then, with appalling suddenness, she plunged, straight as a dart, to the green depths. For minutes after she had disappeared there was nothing to mark her passing save an ever-widening whirlpool whose rim spread, eddying, over the glassy water; then, with a bubbling roar, a geyser of smoke and steam broke the surface and erupted with terrific force, covering a wide area with splashing debris.

In the Secoma papers next morning, headlines, photographs and stories of the participants in the sea drama made a stir in the city, but along the waterfront there was matter-of-fact acceptance of it as one of the tragedies inseparable from the risks and labors of a seafaring life. Business is business; and as soon as the last of the reporters had departed from the Narcissus's decks, Tugboat Annie donned her shore-going finery, and with wildly capering bonnet feather sashayed off around the slip to interview Mr. Bullwinkle. Her visit was not a social one, but was for the purpose of collecting, with the least possible waste of time, certain moneys due—to wit, three thousand dollars. And in order to collect, Annie was prepared, and indeed a little more than willing, to do instant and vigorous battle.

Mr. Bullwinkle, however, was strangely subdued. To her aggressive rat-tat on his door, he gave but feeble and grudging reply; and when she entered she found him in a chair, somewhat in the position of Rodin's famous Thinker, his fingernails in his mouth to assist cerebration.

"Hmph!" said Annie. "What are ye chawin' yer fists fer—tryin' to p'izen yerself?"

"Shut up," said Mr. Bullwinkle, "and get out!"

"Right away is twice too quick for me," Annie told him tartly. "After ye've paid me what ye owe."

"What's the matter? Don't you trust me?" asked Mr. Bullwinkle, with a not very successful attempt at pathos.

"No, I don't. I want me money."

"Go away," mourned Mr. Bullwinkle. "I got a terrible headache. Nearly a week of hard work and worry and strain and damaged gear—and for what? To give you an excuse for pesterin' me."

"I'm keepin' right on pesterin' till I get that three thousand bucks."

"I've got no money. You know that. Ye can't squeeze milk out of a turnip."

"Mebbe not," said Annie grimly, "but ye can drop it in hot water and make it loosen up! Now, do I get me dough?"

"You get a kick in the ribs if ye don't get outa here!"

"Okay!" said Annie briefly. "You own the Salamander. I'm goin' up to the courthouse and slap a attachment on her."

Mr. Bullwinkle jumped to his feet.

"Listen, Annie; you can't do that! She's all I got!"

"What about McGargle? What's he goin' to pay ye?"

"Not a thing. I took on the job on a no-cure, no-pay basis and he's holdin' me to it. I telephoned him this morning. He was pretty nasty too."

"He was, huh? Well, McGargle's your bellyache; but you're mine, and I'm goin' to be paid. And if you have to sell your tub to do it, I ain't goin' to shed no tears. Goo'bye!"

Deaf to his renewed pleading, she slammed the door and started for town.

Mr. Bullwinkle agitatedly paced the floor, pausing now and again to pull back the window curtain and direct venomous glares at the Narcissus, peacefully moored on the opposite side of the slip. Bitterly he regretted that he had not, in the past, adopted toward Tugboat Annie a more conciliatory attitude. Justice compelled him reluctantly to admit that what he had invited, with many unethical tricks, he was now deservedly to collect. Regretting, however, would get him nowhere; and on a sudden impulse, although realizing the futility of it, he clapped on his hat and, with grim, determined jaw, set off ashore to interview Mr. Murdoch McArdle.

Mr. McArdle was in his office, and Mr. Bullwinkle, after considerable display of firmness, was admitted. And at the end of a hectic and perspiring half hour of pleading, Mr. Bullwinkle was exactly where he had started.

"Deal's a deal!" said Mr. McArdle coldly. "No use coming sniveling to me. No salvage, no pay. Beat it."

"But what about my time and supplies, and my crew's pay and the gear I had to use? I done my best to save your ship for you, sir. You've lost nothing. You collect a fat insurance on her, and——"

A satisfied gleam lighted the ice of Mr. McArdle's eyes but failed to melt it.

"That's my affair. You failed. Open-and-shut little job, and you muffed it." He raised his voice, seeking to bring the interview to a close. He had enjoyed it at first, but now he was bored. "You're a lazy dog! Inefficient. There's not a decent tugboat man in the port, and you're the worst of the lot. Now, get out."

"Froze-face," said a rasping voice from the door, "ye're a cockeyed liar!"

They whirled, and saw in the doorway the formidable, menacing figure of Tugboat Annie. Hat feather frantic with indignation, she advanced and shook a rough and calloused forefinger under the astonished McArdle nose.

"How dast you to lay yer dirty tongue on us towboat men, ye dirty little widget!" she bellowed. "Take them words back! Take 'em back! Bullwinkle here may be a this-and-that, but he's a fine towboat man! He done all that mortal could possibly do to keep that berry basket o' yours afloat, and he's entitled to his pay, no matter how many agreements ye had!" She shook with fury. "You lemme hear ye squawk about us tugboat people again and I'll chaw ye up and spit ye out the winder!"

For a moment, like the calm that follows the typhoon, there was silence. Then McArdle, who did not lack courage, recovered his poise.

"Get out of here, you old baggage!" he snarled. "I made my deal with him! It's finished! Now get out, both of you!"

Mr. Bullwinkle looked at Tugboat Annie uncertainly. To his astonishment, she winked. "Wait outside, horse-face," she said in a guttural and perfectly audible whisper. Mr. Bullwinkle, looking puzzled, obeyed.

"If he starts anything with you, Annie," he said from the door, "just call me."

"I'll call ye to bury him, mebbe," she said, and closed the door. She advanced again upon the shipowner. He reached for the telephone.

"I'm going to have the police throw you out, you disgraceful harridan," he said.

"Not if ye expect your insurance on the Snoqualmie, ye won't," she returned quietly. "Ha! That hits ye where it hurts, don't it?"

He hesitated; set down the phone.

"What's that got to do with it?"

"Plenty. I was on that salvage job, too, ye know."

"That's evident. The ship sank."

"Have your fun; I'm enj'yin' meself too. Listen, McGargle; do ye know what barratry is?"

Under her meaning gaze, he subsided to cold but puzzled immobility. She went on:

"I'll refresh yer memory. The book says: 'Any willful and unlawful act by the master or mariners of a vessel, whereby the owners sustain injury.' But where the owners stands to gain by such a act— Whoa! Wait a minute! I ain't accusin' you—yet. I just want to put things to ye the way they might look to the insurance underwriters."

"Well?"

"Well, I boarded the Snoqualmie wid Big Sam Doolittle, my engineer, and we went below to the engine room. The chief engineer was a Scotchman name o' Bogle. And he boasted to us that he was keepin' the pumps goin' wid coal—'trash,' he called it—that was half full o' slate, because he wouldn't waste good steam coal, what he had plenty of, on a sinkin' ship. You and him's brothers under the

BULLWINKLE EARNS HIS PAY

skinflint, McGargle, and that's what your cheese-parin' methods done for him. But the important point is this: If he had used the good coal, he could have got enough pressure in the b'ilers to double the discharge efficiency o' the pumps, and the Snoqualmie would ha' been afloat today and Bullwinkle would ha' brought her safe to port. See what I'm drivin' at?"

"Go on," said Mr. McArdle uneasily.

"Well, if the underwriters learns that your chief engineer—your servant, so you are responsible—let the ship sink, how much insurance would ye collect? Not one red cent, and ye know it! And ye'd be out nearly a million dollars' worth o' vessel and cargo!"

He was about to protest, but she stopped him:

"Oh, I know Bogle didn't mean no harm, and you hadn't nothin' to do wid it. But accordin' to the strict letter o' the law, the underwriters could refuse to pay; and they might stick ye in jail for barratry—and ye wouldn't be the first innocent employer what went to jail for the senseless act of a employee. Now think that over."

Mr. McArdle lay back in his chair with his eyes closed and his fingertips together. After a moment, he opened his eyes and indicated the absent Mr. Bullwinkle with a jerk of his head.

"He know?"

"Do ye think ye could have bluffed him out if he did?" Annie asked contemptuously. "Now then, don't ye think that after all the time and work we put in on the job, we ought to be paid?"

Mr. McArdle pursed his lips.

"M'm'm—possibly. How much do you want to keep quiet?"

"I don't want nothin' to keep quiet. All I'm after is fair pay for our labor. We'd ha' got the ship in if it hadn't been for Bogle, and the steamboat inspectors would ha' awarded us sixty thousand, at least. But we'll be content wid half o' that."

"Thirty thousand? Ridiculous!"

"Okay," said Annie patiently. "On'y Big Sam's a awful talker when he gits started. Well, I'll be seein' you."

"No-no! Wait a minute. Where does Bullwinkle come in on this?"

"He'll get his share, fifty-fifty. And look; make the check out to the Secoma Deep-Sea Towin' and Salvage Company, and mark it, 'Payment o' salvage work on the S.S. Snoqualmie.'"

Tugboat Annie and Mr. Bullwinkle walked slowly back to the waterfront together. It was a queer walk, with half remarks and constrained silences.

"How did you come to be in his office, Annie?" asked Mr. Bullwinkle at length.

"I went to check up on ye and see if ye was lyin' about not gettin' any pay. Ain't yer tongue blistered up tellin' the truth for once?"

"It was good of you to stick up for me like that, Annie."

"Stick up for you? Humph! 'Twas meself I was stickin' up fer. I'm a towboat man, too, ain't I? Imagine me stickin' up for the likes o' you!"

Silence.

"Annie, I still don't figger out how ye got that check out of him."

"Oh, 'twas easy. He's got a heart as soft as a cargo winch if ye know how to get around it."

"Gosh, that's swell! Fifteen grand apiece!"

Annie shook her head. "Ye got a poor memory. I got three thousand comin' out o' your end, don't forget."

"Wha-at?" Mr. Bullwinkle jumped as though he had been stung. "That deal's all off now! Where do you get off, to——"

"I still got your note, ye ungrateful ape!" said Tugboat Annie pugnaciously. "Ye get twelve thousand, and that's all."

Mr. Bullwinkle thought hard and rebelliously for a minute. Then he shook his head.

"Guess again, ye dirty chiseler!"

"What do ye mean?"

"What about the 10 percent on that job I put you next to last Tuesday night?" he chortled triumphantly. "Guess that'll hold you for a while!"

They walked in silence to the head of the slip wherein rested, on one side the Narcissus, on the other the Salamander.

"Well," said Annie, "I'll not detain ye. By the way, don't ye ever want to bite holes in yerself because ye haven't got a good tug like my Narcissus?"

Mr. Bullwinkle gazed judicially at the Narcissus.

"Yeah, it floats," he said. "I don't know how it does, but it does."

"Go on, beat it!" snapped Annie. "Afore ye turn me stummick."

"You're nobody's blessin'," Mr. Bullwinkle told her with fervor. He started around the head of the slip, then paused. "Sa-ay, Annie——"

"What do you want?"

"Say, what was that yarn you was telling the boys the other night about your pa's bald head—remember?"

"Do I remember?" Annie turned to him with a glad light in her eye. "Hey, wait a minute, pal. Don't go! Lissen; ye'll die laffin'! Well, a hen got loose from the coop on a Chinese steamer in the slip alongside, and flew over the deck where pa was settin', lookin' for a place to land, and afore ye could wink, she was settin' right on top o' pa's shiny, bald head!"

"She must 'a' went crazy," said Mr. Bullwinkle.

"No, not crazy, just ambitious. O' course," Annie continued gleefully, "pa pretended it was a joke; but—lissen to this; ye'll scream!—he went ashore to a hair store the very next day and bought hisself a nice new curly soufflé!"

A MATTER OF BUSINESS

Alec Severn, president of the Secoma Deep Sea Towing and Salvage Company, took a last look over his tidy office desk.

"Got my train reservations, Miss Walker?"

"Yes, sir; all in that envelope there."

"Thank you. And the——"

"Yes, your car is waiting at the head of the dock. Your bags are in it."

"That's fine.... Now look, Annie——" He leaned across the desk and addressed Tugboat Annie Brennan, master of the tug Narcissus, and senior skipper of the company fleet, who stood beside the open window, noisily munching a red Wenatchee apple. "Annie!"

Tugboat Annie took quick aim and flung the core out the window. There was a startled and indignant yelp from the dock below, as she turned back into the room with a grin.

"Right in the ear!" she said.

"Who?"

"Bullwinkle. He was passin' below. That'll l'arn him to show his dirty mug on this side o' the slip."

"Well, quit your fooling, Annie," Severn said testily, "and listen to me."

"I'm listenin'," said Annie, aggrieved. "I been listenin' all along. Now, what is it?"

"You'll be in charge as usual, while I'm gone. There's nothing very important coming up that I know of, so just coast along, and don't go snooping around after trouble."

"Snoopin' fer trouble?" echoed Annie scornfully. "I don't have to snoop for it. It flies right in me lap. And its name is generally Horse-face Bullwinkle."

"We'll not go into that, Annie," said Severn hastily. "You know my views, I think."

"Oh, sure! Well, what else?"

"There's just one thing outside of routine stuff. It's—Miss Walker, where's that letter that came yesterday from Mr. Henneberger? . . . Ah, thank you! . . . Now look, Annie——"

"Hamburger? Is that the——"

"Henneberger, Annie! For Pete's sake don't start calling him——"

"Yeah, I know—him what's startin' that steamer service from Boston to the Northwest here. I seen it in the shippin' news this mornin'."

"That's the man. Jim Henneberger. I met him in the East a couple of years ago, and when I heard he was coming out here, I wrote him. Be nice if we could get his towing business, huh?"

"Sure. But that's easy!"

"I hope so. Anyway, I'm sorry this confounded San Francisco business won't allow me to wait over until he arrives. But you can look after him, Annie. Entertain him; show him the harbor; demonstrate how well we can take care of his steamers. There's one on the way north from the Canal now, by the way—the Minute Man. She was off Cape Blanco day before——Let's see; this is Friday. Yes, that's right—day before yesterday. She's the smallest of the fleet."

"What's he like?"

"Who—Henneberger? Well, he's a chunky kind of man. Well built. Red face. Looks like a retired naval officer; in fact, he was in the service during the war. He doesn't look his years, by a long way. He's about fifty-two, but looks forty. He likes a laugh too—but don't let that fool you, Annie. He's pretty smart."

"Hmmph! He'll have to be, to shake loose from me. Could I go to the deepo and meet him?"

"No need to, unless you like. He'll look us up." Severn glanced at his watch. "Hey, I've got to get a move on. Be good, Annie, and stay out of trouble."

"Okay, Alec. Don't take no nickel nutmegs, ye old warthog!" Annie cried affectionately, as her employer disappeared through the doorway.

Alone in the office, she sat at Severn's desk and complacently surveyed her little kingdom. She seized the telephone and, after a little experimenting, sorted the receiver from the mouthpiece.

"Number, please," said the operator.

"Hello, there. How are you today?" said Annie affably.

A MATTER OF BUSINESS

"Number, please."

"What numbers ye got?" asked Annie with great good humor.

"Number, please, madam!" the operator said, with asperity.

"Ye needn't to git uppity," said Annie indignantly. "I was jest tryin' to be sociable!"

She hung the receiver upside down, tore a page off the desk-calendar pad, only to perceive, too late, that Miss Walker already had performed that service, and opened and closed a drawer or two. Unable, for the moment, to think of other executive gestures she might practice, she reluctantly arose from the desk, and in so doing found herself in violent conflict with Severn's lean-back chair. She extricated herself after a struggle, and went hastily into the outer office.

"Say," she panted, "have one o' the boys take out that swizzle chair of Alec's, will ye? It's got a spite agin me."

"Glad to, Annie. I'll have another kind put in right away."

"Thanks. I'll be on the Narcissus, where I'm safe, if ye want me," Annie chuckled, and clumped contentedly down the steps leading from the office to the wharf. She managed, somehow, in spite of her uncouth and mammoth frame, to give an impression of briskness and energy as she crossed to the Narcissus, pausing a minute to glance at the company tugs, rubbing gently against the creosoted piling. Then she looked out over the harbor.

The morning mist was like an artist's virgin canvas as it hung over the placid water; then the muffled roar of a big steamer's whistle echoed against the cargo sheds, and there appeared slowly on the screen, as a photographic print takes form in its bath of solution, the shape of a gigantic white liner. Escorted by a diminutive tug whose funnel was a splash of warm salmon pink against the mist, she moved majestically up the harbor, her flaring bows and soaring superstructure a sharper white against the thin vapor as she slipped in grace and beauty to her anchorage.

Annie sighed happily and stepped over the rail.

"Look at that, Shif'less. Looks kinda magniferous, don't she?" she said to the Narcissus's deck hand, who sat on an after towing bit, splicing an eye in a new hawser. "Who'd want to buy a farm and leave the sea, huh?"

"Annie——"

"What?"

"Annie, kin I go ashore for a while?"

"Gosh sakes!" said Annie. "I never seen such a gudgeon for wantin' to flirk yer work! What do ye want to go ashore for?"

"I gotta buy some socks, and——"

A MATTER OF BUSINESS

"Oh, my; ye're more worry to me than all me money. Did ye write that letter to them dandruff-exterminator people like I told ye to?"

"No, Annie. I forgot."

"Well, write it afore ye go, and post it ashore. Tell 'em how silly it makes ye act every time ye take a dose. Make that letter good. Put lots o' verbs in it. D'ye hear?"

"Yes, Annie."

"And don't be long. Now Alec's away to San Francisco I'm in charge of the office, and I want ye handy."

"How long's Alec away for?"

" 'Bout a week, he said. And I want to show him how good we can handle things while he's went."

In high good humor she mounted to the upper deck and glanced hopefully across the slip to the berth of the Salamander, Horatio Bullwinkle, master.

Mr. Bullwinkle, to her unspeakable gratification, was standing on her stern, his bandy legs apart, glowering.

"Hey, Annie, you puffed-up cow!" he shouted. "Was that you what corked me in the ear wi' that apple?"

"How should I know?" said Annie comfortably. "Cruisin' around like you do, wid a pair o' stuns'ls nailed to yer head, anything's liable to happen."

"You're too damn fresh!" he told her warmly. "I'd like to——"

"I can guess the rest," she grinned. "Well, I can't spend all day listenin' to you gas." She shouted, then, so Mr. Bullwinkle could get a proper earful: "Shif'less! Go along to the Daffodil and tell Perry Moore he's to pick up a barge at Svensen's Mill and take her across to Pier 50 at nine o'clock. And when the Asphodel comes in, send her after that tanker along at Jones' Cove. Hustle, now. Ho-hum-m!" She yawned ostentatiously.

"Showin' off, huh?" sneered the disgruntled Mr. Bullwinkle. "Tryin' to make out you got plenty o' work to do. Don't yer dispatcher give the orders?"

"Pooh!" said Annie. "I'm only takin' care o' the overflow. This stuff's jest small tomatoes to us. You wait a few days. Then ye'll see us gettin' some real business. I'd turn some of it over to ye, only bein' saw wid you would get us a bad name."

"You're lying," said Mr. Bullwinkle promptly. "I know how much business there is around this port."

"This is new business. It's a pal o' Alec's. We got it as good as stitched up," Annie replied complacently.

"New?" Mr. Bullwinkle pondered for a minute. Then he grinned suddenly. "Wait a minute!" he said, and ran to his cabin. When he returned, the morning paper was in his hand and his bright, hard, little eyes twinkled satisfaction. He shouted: "Sa-ay, that new business wouldn't begin with a haitch, would it?"

"The place you'll end up in does!" snapped Annie, regretting her indiscretion in the presence of her sharp-witted rival.

"Tck-tck-tck! I thought so." Mr. Bullwinkle sagaciously wagged his bullethead. "He's got a ship on the way up here, and he gets in tomorrow morning from——Le's see"—he consulted the paper—"from Boston. Well, much obliged for the tip, Annie. We'll be on deck."

Tucking the paper into the top of his pants, he swaggered gleefully away.

During a fairly busy day, Annie recollected at intervals, with vague uneasiness, Mr. Bullwinkle's threat; but by nightfall, under pressure of work, it was completely forgotten. She arose early next morning, after a refreshing night's repose, and with that sharp exaltation which always uplifted her on the brink of a new business deal, she bedecked herself in her best shoregoing gear, and with dilapidated bonnet feather nodding benignly, set out, light of heart, to meet the morning train from the East.

She was in good time, so she refreshed herself with a cup of coffee at the restaurant, then joined a small, waiting throng at the gates as the Limited thundered in. The train hissed and panted to a stop, porters descended with their little steps, and expectant red-caps dotted the platform. Amid the pleasant excitement, Tugboat Annie eagerly scanned the passengers as they emerged and began to stream down the platform. There was a goodly number of them, and she kept a sharp lookout for one who would answer to Alec Severn's description of Mr. Jim Henneberger.

At last she saw him—a square-set, powerful figure, with shrewd blue eyes in a ruddy, weather-beaten face. He was carrying his hat, revealing smooth, iron-gray hair parted amidship; and there was that indefinable something about him which marks the Navy-trained man. It was he, she felt sure, and her heart leaped; then certainty was made doubly secure when the crowd parted for a moment, and she saw that he was in amiable and almost chummy conversation with Mr. Horatio Bullwinkle.

For a horrified moment, Tugboat Annie stood and stared, unwilling to believe her eyes. Her first instinct was to do instant and violent battle, but caution checked her in time. The visitor might not like being involved in a public brawl within five minutes of his arrival. So, reluctantly bottling her temper, she barged forward through the crowd and held out a huge red hand.

A MATTER OF BUSINESS

"Hello there, Mr. Ham—Mr. Henneberger!" she boomed hospitably. "If this ain't a sight fer sore eyelids! I'm cert'nly proud to meet youse! I—I——"

But Mr. Bullwinkle stepped forward and pressed a nickel into her palm. "There, me good woman," he said kindly. "Now run along and don't bother us! . . . It's a shame," he added in a quite audible aside to his companion, "that they don't keep these tramps off of the platform."

Annie's temper slipped its moorings.

"Step out o' me road, ye furry-headed jackass!" she bellowed. "Oh, I don't mean you, Mr. Henneberger—but ain't you ashamed o' yerself to be saw wid a low ape like Bullwinkle? Just look at the ugly——Oh, well, lucky I was in time. You come wid me, now! I got the tuggest swell—the swuggest—the tellest swug—I mean the swellest tug. . . . Hell and hardtack!" She blew up. "He's got me so mad I don't know what I mean!"

Mr. Henneberger stared. He looked for guidance to Mr. Bullwinkle.

"Just a local character, sir. They call her Simple Annie," grinned Mr. Bullwinkle. "Don't pay no attention to her. She's a little cracked in her nut."

"I'll crack you in the nut, ye flop-eared reptile!" roared Annie. . . . "Don't let that big bum throw ye off your course, Mr. Henneberger. I'm Tugboat Annie Brennan, o' the Deep-Sea Towin' and Salvage Company. Alec Severn sent me to meet ye."

Mr. Henneberger looked from one to the other, with eyes that twinkled shrewd understanding.

He smiled, and his voice, when he spoke, had a deep, husky quality, very pleasing to the ear.

"I see," he said slowly. "You're Part B of the reception committee, that it?" His smile widened. "You Northwest tugboat men get right after the business, don't you? Mr. Bullwinkle taking the train last night to some point along the line where he could come in with me this morning; and now you——"

"He's goin' to have breakfast with me at the hotel," Mr. Bullwinkle interposed hurriedly, "then I'm goin' to show him the port on my Salamander. . . . Ready, sir?"

"But, Mr. Henne——"

"Sorry. I promised him, Mrs.—Brennan, is it? Give my regards to Severn and tell him I'll be along later in the day. . . . Come along then, Bullwinkle. I haven't much time here."

With granite jaw and hands on hips, Tugboat Annie watched her prospective client borne triumphantly away.

A MATTER OF BUSINESS

It was not until she saw the Salamander lying with steam up alongside her wharf that an idea came. In an angle of the warehouse beside the Salamander's berth and a small shed, the engineer and fireman of the tug were deep in an exciting game of craps with members of the crew of a nearby steamer. For a moment Annie watched them; then, struck by inspiration, she hurried on board her Narcissus.

To Big Sam she rapidly outlined her predicament, and her remedy for it. "Think it can be did?" she concluded eagerly.

"Sure. You say the engine room's clear?"

"Yes."

"Okay, Annie."

Annie went to her cabin, and from the window watched Big Sam as he ambled slowly around the head of the slip. He disappeared behind some freight cars, his soiled blue dungarees showed for a second as he stepped on board the Salamander and—after an excruciatingly cautious look around—stepped through the engine-room doorway, and three minutes later reappeared, rubbing his hands on the seat of his trousers. Shortly thereafter he returned to the Narcissus.

"I done it, Annie," he reported.

"That's swellegant!" chortled Annie, and posted herself outside the pilothouse to await developments.

Slightly more than an hour later, a taxicab stopped at the head of the slip and decanted Mr. Bullwinkle and his new pal, Mr. Henneberger. They went to the Salamander's pilothouse, the lines were cast off and, with Mr. Bullwinkle in person at the wheel, the tug was ready to go.

The engine-room bell jingled, the propeller turned, frothy whirlpools shot from under the Salamander's stern and she moved slowly away from the wharf and pointed her capable bow toward the rippling waters of the harbor. Tugboat Annie, in her own pilothouse by now, smothered a snicker and watched with intense, expectant interest as her rival cleared the slip. For a fleeting moment, as nothing happened, she looked anxious; then her sharp ears caught the sound for which she had been listening—a confused pounding in the Salamander's engine room. Her face broke into a grin and she stuck her head out the window. "Let 'er go, Shif'less," she said quietly, and the Narcissus slid smoothly away from the dock.

A few revolutions of the propeller were sufficient to clear the slip, and the Narcissus drifted down upon the Salamander, which rested now, without forward way, a hundred yards out in the harbor. Agitated figures moved upon the Salamander's deck, and the con-

A MATTER OF BUSINESS

gested face and irate comments of Mr. Bullwinkle were creating an effect. When he saw the Narcissus bearing down, his activities became heroic, but all seemingly in vain, for, after another abortive effort of the Salamander's engines which resulted only in further clanking, she floated idle, still.

Mr. Henneberger, his face expressionless, was outside the pilothouse glancing at his watch, when the Narcissus scraped alongside; and as Annie hailed him, Mr. Bullwinkle leaped defensively to his side.

" 'Lo, Mr. Henneberger, sir," said Tugboat Annie mildly. "Would ye like a ride on a tugboat?"

"Don't you do it, sir, please!" cried Mr. Bullwinkle, distraught. "We'll have the trouble fixed——"

Mr. Henneberger hesitated; glanced from one to the other of the rival skippers with a gleam of amusement.

"Guess I'll have to, Bullwinkle," he said briskly then. "My time is limited, as you know."

He jumped across to the Narcissus, and Annie promptly jingled the bell; but before she could sheer away, Mr. Bullwinkle also was upon the Narcissus's deck. The stern of the Narcissus squatted, and with a quick curve of flowing wake she was underway. As she shot clear, the grimy and perspiring face of the Salamander's engineer poked itself from the door and frantically hailed Mr. Bullwinkle.

"It's fixed, skipper!" he shouted. "We're all right now! Some dirty so-and-so slackened both nuts on the connecting-rod crank bearing! I've tightened 'em up, so——"

"And I don't have to go to China to find out who done it, either!" sputtered Mr. Bullwinkle, with a lethal glare at Tugboat Annie's innocent profile. "You follow us, d'ye hear? I'll show this——"

The rest of his words were drowned out by the quick roar of the Narcissus's whistle as Annie yanked the cord.

For an hour, followed by the impotent Salamander, the Narcissus cruised about the harbor of Secoma while Tugboat Annie, after explaining the absence of Alec Severn, entertained her guest with a vivid discourse upon the advantages of the port. Mr. Bullwinkle, sulking in the background, vented an occasional disparaging remark upon her comments, but his brain was not otherwise idle.

In the middle of the morning, Henneberger expressed a wish to inspect a bustling cargo terminal which they were passing, so the Narcissus ran alongside and made fast, and the visitor, accompanied by his host, stepped ashore. Mr. Bullwinkle instinctively was about to follow; then he thought better of it, and leaned morosely against the rail. Annie turned on the wharf and glanced back.

"Better tell the boys to lock up their vallyables if the Bullwinkle scut is goin' to stop on board!" she shouted to Peter, the mate; then, with merrily shaking shoulders, turned away.

When they were gone, Mr. Bullwinkle left the rail and walked along the deck on the opposite side. He passed the galley, redolent of cooking dinner, then paused at the engine-room door. Through the opposite doorway he could see the blue-denimed back of Big Sam, in conversation with a boss stevedore on the wharf, and, knowing Sam's propensity for extended gossip, took a chance and ducked below. Presently he emerged, walked nonchalantly around the house and climbed to the wharf, and from that eminence signaled his Salamander to come alongside. He then boarded his vessel and, his little, black, shoe-button eyes sparkling with glee, took post.

As the sight-seers returned from their inspection, Tugboat Annie's keen eyes swept the wharf, but all was peaceful; the Narcissus rubbing gently against the piling; Mr. Bullwinkle, outside the Salamander's pilothouse, gazing woodenly at the sky above the cargo sheds.

"He's beat it, huh? That's swell!" she grunted. "Now, Mr. Henneberger, step on board—look out for your pants on that spike!—and we'll have a nice dinner on our way back. . . . Pinto! Pinto!"

"Ya-as, ma'am," said the cook, his head outside the galley door.

"Dinner ready?"

"Ya-as, ma'am."

"That's great! We'll set down and tuck into them digestibles as soon as we're underway."

She went to the pilothouse and, with the lines cast off, gave the signal to the engine room.

"I spose," she murmured as she spun the wheel, "I should be sorry for that Bullwinkle stinkpot, but I ain't. If he'd been a little smarter, now——Hey! What the heck!"

Again she tugged the engine-room jingle, but nothing happened.

"What the devil's the matter wid Sam?" she snorted. "Why——"

"Here I am, Annie," growled Big Sam's irate voice behind her. She turned, and as she looked into his chagrin-empurpled face, her heart sank with quick foreboding.

"Why didn't ye start when I give ye the signal?" she barked.

"Can't do it!" he rumbled. "There's somethin' gone wrong wid the engine. It ain't gettin' no fuel."

"What do ye expect me to do—dig a oil well for ye?" Annie stormed. "Git below and fix it, quick! I never seen such a pack o' stupid monkeys what I got on this tug!" Then she remembered her guest and turned to him with a forced, astringent smile.

A MATTER OF BUSINESS

"What is this—a game?" he asked her, with a trace of asperity.

"Oh, Big Sam's a kind of a wag. Allus playin' tricks," she told him hastily. "But we'll be off in no time now."

Five minutes passed, however, and again Mr. Henneberger consulted his watch.

"I'm afraid I don't appreciate your engineer's jokes, Mrs. Brennan," he said at length. "I'd better ask Bull——" But at that moment the Salamander appeared miraculously alongside, and the benevolent voice of Horatio Bullwinkle himself floated across.

"Kin I give you a tow, Annie?" he asked solicitously; then, when Annie's indignation suitably had choked her, he turned to the visitor. "How about you, sir? I got a good tug—the best in Secoma—with a good dinner on the galley stove and steam up, ready to go!"

Like a wrathful elephant, Annie stamped the deck, watching, with feelings too dangerously explosive for utterance, the workmanlike departure of the tug Salamander. Then, as that vessel disappeared around the pierhead, she lumbered below to demand an accounting of Big Sam. He met her at the foot of the ladder, looking exceedingly foolish.

"I found it, Annie."

"Oh, did ye, Columbus? And what was it?"

"Some person had unscrewed the nut on the oil fittin' of the fuel pump—it'd only take a minute—and the pump wasn't givin' no oil to the engine. I wonder——"

"Ye wonder who done it, I spose!" Annie roared. "Ye'll be wonderin' what yer own name is, next. Go away, and——Well, go away, afore I forget I'm a leddy and fetch ye a kick in the ear!"

It was late afternoon, and the weather had turned threatening, with dark scud traveling fast in the upper sky, when Annie heard the short toot of the Salamander as she turned, splashing in the short harbor chop, and entered the slip. She watched with dull resentment as Mr. Henneberger exchanged a cordial handclasp with the beaming Bullwinkle as the tug made fast. She strained her ears.

"I'm much obliged," Mr. Henneberger was saying. "Between you and"—he glanced at the Narcissus—"your lady friend, and what I've seen of the port, it's been a very entertaining day."

"Pore Annie!" said Mr. Bullwinkle, raising his voice. "She's kind of a joke around the port." He tapped his skull. "She's got delusions that she's a towboat man. Very sad case! By the way, tomorrow being Sunday, what about letting me take ye around a bit more? There's lots we haven't had time for today, and I'd be proud——"

"Thanks," said Henneberger. "I will. But it will have to be early. I'm visiting friends in Olympia in the afternoon."

"What about eight in the morning, then?"

"Eight o'clock's fine. And thanks again." And Mr. Henneberger, holding his hat against the growing gusts of wind, stepped quickly ashore and went back to his hotel.

At sunset the wind increased, blowing the smoke of steamers in indigo veils over the white-capped harbor, and when darkness fell, it had increased to a half gale. The fleet of weather-beaten tugs alongside the wharf moved and chafed restlessly as the wind and tide tugged at them, and small craft on the sound fled for the winking harbor lights.

Shortly before dawn, Horatio Bullwinkle was aroused, by his seaman's instinct, from deep slumber, and rolled out of his bunk, pulled clothes on and went out on deck to make sure that everything was secure. The push of the wind in his face thoroughly awakened him and, when he returned to the snugness of his cabin, he entertained himself with a satisfied review of the events of the day. But beneath his complacence a small fear worked. He knew that Tugboat Annie had overheard his appointment with the shipowner for the morning. Past experience of her resourcefulness in emergency had taught him a measure of respect; and although he had no definite doubt of the morrow, it was as well to be completely prepared.

For some time he pondered heavily; then, as a result of his cogitation, he found himself once more out upon the windy deck. With the utmost caution he descended to the wharf, blessing the storm that had brought with it inky darkness and obscuring noise, and, keeping well in the shadows, moved around by the head of the slip toward the sleeping Narcissus. So intent was he, and so particular his concealment, that he failed to see a small skiff which, laden with Shiftless and Peter and a strange, heaped-up bulk in the stern, had arrived but a moment before amid the deep shadows of the piling and the black, lapping water under the Salamander's stern.

Mr. Bullwinkle had performed his simple errand and was climbing with a jubilant grin once more into his bunk, when the skiff returned to the Narcissus's low rail. Her crew slipped quietly on board and, also strangely merry, repaired to Annie's cabin, where, with an ancient wrapper over her pink-flannel nightgown, she awaited them.

"Did ye do it widout bein' saw?" she whispered hoarsely.

"Sure did, Annie!" Peter snickered. "Just wait till the old buzzard tries to pull out in the mornin'."

"That's great!" crowed Annie. "We'll show that rat-whiskered stingaroo that there's more ways o' killin' a cat than kissin' it to death!"

A MATTER OF BUSINESS

A stormy daybreak was fighting back the darkness of the night when a telephone shrilled sharply in the cargo shed that flanked the Salamander. A sleepy watchman checked its insistent voice.

"Hello," he said.... "What? ... Who?"

As the urgent voice at the other end of the wire continued, he snapped awake.

"Yes, sir! I'll tell him right away!" he yapped excitedly, and the next minute was running with heavy feet along the wharf to the Salamander. He clambered up the ladder and pounded on Mr. Bullwinkle's door.

Mr. Bullwinkle came reluctantly awake.

"Who is it?" he demanded drowsily. "What do ye want?"

"Bullwinkle! Wake up! It's me—Strauss, the night watchman on the dock. I got a message for you from Mr. Henneberger!"

Mr. Bullwinkle instantly was alert.

"What is it?"

"He's had a wireless message from his vessel, the Minute Man. She's got caught in the gale and her cargo's shifted, opposite Destruction Island. He wants you to leave immediate and stand by her."

Already Mr. Bullwinkle was into his trousers. "What's her position?" he snapped.

"You're to telephone him at his hotel and he'll let you know."

Lights were switched on as the Salamander's crew roused out, and the clumping of heavy feet about her decks aroused first the curiosity, then the interest of Pinto, the cook of the Narcissus, who had just entered the galley to build up his breakfast fire. Every good cook is intelligent, so Pinto immediately awakened Tugboat Annie.

"Oh-oh!" she grunted, when she had verified the news by a quick glance through the port. "Bullwinkle's goin' places!" In the faint light she saw her rival, fully dressed, hurrying along the wharf to the telephone in the cargo shed, and for a moment she was panicky. Then she remembered, and with a grin she relaxed.

"All right, Pinto; there's no scurry. Git back to the galley and cook breakfast. Whatever Bullwinkle's job is, I got plenty o' time to beat him to it now."

She finished dressing and, with head bent to the wind, lumbered up to the company office.

"Bullwinkle's got a line on somethin'," she told the night dispatcher. "Check up wid the Marine Exchange and the Harbor Radio, and see if you can find out what it is."

The dispatcher telephoned, and a minute later turned to Annie, his eyes round with excitement. He was still connected.

"It's Henneberger's Minute Man," he told her. "She radioed that she might need help." And he gave her the details he had been told.

"That's what Bullwinkle's after, sure enough. Ask them what her position is."

The dispatcher put the question, scribbled the figures hastily on a pad and hung up.

"There it is, Annie," he said. "Now let's see just where she is."

Together they stood at a large chart which hung upon the wall, while Annie checked off the position of the steamer.

" 'Bout fifty mile south o' Flattery and ten mile offshore. That'll be her estimated position, o' course. And it'll be blowin' blue hell right in her teeth too. Well, blow high, blow low, the Narcissus can take it! So long. See ye sometime!" and jamming on her old felt hat, a relic of her defunct husband, she returned to the Narcissus. Horatio Bullwinkle's hoarse voice hailed her as she stepped over the rail.

"Hey, Annie, where do you think you're goin'?" he asked jovially.

"I'm goin' where ye think you are, dog-face!"

"I see; found out about the Minute Man, have ye? Smart work, but it'll do ye no good. Henneberger gave me the job."

"First there is soonest mended, ye know."

"I know more than that."

"What's that?"

"You'll find out!"

With illy suppressed merriment, Tugboat Annie and her crew hung over the rail, awaiting that hilarious moment when the Salamander should cast off and get underway. And when they heard Mr. Bullwinkle shout down to his engineer to warm her up, they almost whooped their joy.

A lazy threshing began under the Salamander's stern as the big propeller turned over, and Annie hugged herself with a thrill of anticipatory delight. The threshing increased as the bell signaled from the Salamander's pilothouse; then, unaccountably, it grew labored; then it was stilled, and only the gale shouting through the funnel stays and the wash of the water against the barnacled piling disturbed the morning.

Again the Salamander's engine-room signal sounded. Furiously, Mr. Bullwinkle's voice yelled: "What the hell is the matter? Why don't we go?"

"P'raps she ain't had her oats yet," suggested Tugboat Annie, and a roar of laughter came from the Narcissus's crew.

Horatio Bullwinkle stamped down the ladder, and at the after end of the house was joined by his mate and the engineer. After hurried and profane consultation, they moved to the stern and hung pre-

A MATTER OF BUSINESS

cariously over the fantail, peering under the counter into the swirling water. Then Mr. Bullwinkle straightened and, like a wounded hippopotamus, gave voice. The awed and delighted crews of both tugs lent respectful attention as Horatio Bullwinkle launched his monologue; and it was afterward agreed along the Secoma waterfront that for ground and lofty cursing its equal had never been heard. Eventually, because he must, he paused for breath.

"What seems to be the trouble?" asked Tugboat Annie. "Is it a little flea what's nibblin' youse?"

"It's you! You so-and-so and this-and-that!" thundered the infuriated tugboat master. "You fouled that purple-starred moorin' line into my propeller! Ye snuck over last night in the dark and——" Mr. Bullwinkle's flight of profane fancy reached hitherto uncharted heights.

"Oh, my, ye dirty man!" cried Tugboat Annie, daintily stopping her ears. "On Sunday mornin' too! But I spose ye got yer reasons. Anyway, ye can drydock her, or a diver can clear it for ye in four-five hours. Sorry I can't wait. Shall I give your love to the master o' the Minute Man?"

While she was speaking, a taxicab had deposited Mr. Henneberger at the head of the slip. He walked rapidly along the wharf to where the Salamander lay.

"What's the delay, Bullwinkle? Why haven't you left?" he said sharply. "I've radioed the Minute Man that you're on your way."

With notable restraint, Mr. Bullwinkle told him, but in the middle of his explanation Tugboat Annie broke in.

"It's on'y a fair sample o' Bullwinkle sarvice, Mr. Henneberger," she said sorrowfully. "But we'll go out and stand by yer vessel. . . . We're all ready to go, ain't we, boys?" Then, without awaiting an answer, and to demonstrate how spry the Narcissus could be, she ran heavily up the ladder to the pilothouse, while Shiftless cast the mooring lines adrift.

"Looks as though she's scuppered you, Bullwinkle," Henneberger said, with grim amusement. "And I'm hanged if I've ever seen such a seagoing circus as this before!"

"Sh-h! Wait a minute!" said Horatio Bullwinkle, gripping the other's arm; and upon the tugboat master's face appeared an expression of utmost beatitude. "By the holy cat, I'd almost forgotten!"

"Forgotten what?"

"Never mind. Watch the Narcissus."

In the Narcissus pilothouse, Annie, swelling with pride, tugged at the bell pull. And, as Mr. Bullwinkle so futilely had done, she pulled and pulled again. Nothing happened. Quick annoyance dented her satisfaction. "What the——" she began, and tried again. Still the Narcissus did not move.

"Sa-am!" she bellowed suddenly, premonition clutching at her heart. . . . "Peter, run down and see what's the matter. . . . Never mind! . . . Here, take the wheel. I'll go!"

She bumbled hastily below to a burst of Gargantuan laughter from the Salamander's deck. And when she reached the engine room she found Big Sam staring forlornly at the big diesel engine.

"Why'n't ye get under way, stupid?" she said frantically. "I give enough jingles to last ye over Christmas!"

He gazed dejectedly at her out of red-rimmed eyes. "Can't do it," he mumbled. "Some lousy swab's went and stole the lever off the air-startin' valve—it was only fastened with a cotter pin through a bolt—and the engine won't run."

For a moment Annie was floored, but she came up fighting.

"What can ye do about it then?" she snapped. "Ye got to find some way. Think, quick! I promised Alec——"

"We-ell," said Big Sam, after maddening deliberation, "I got a piece of flat steel down here. I could mebbe make a temporary lever that might do, but it'll take a coupla hours."

It was nearly two o'clock of the following morning before the Narcissus, with Tugboat Annie grim-lipped at the wheel, turned off outside Cape Flattery and took a blinding green sea smack over the nose as she started her battle southward in search of the partly disabled steamer; and astern of her, about five hours in time, and perhaps fifty miles in distance, the Salamander was slogging along under forced draft through the Strait of Juan de Fuca, also headed seaward. For the Narcissus it was a gamble and nothing more, since the Minute Man would be expecting the Salamander, and there had been nothing in the set, noncommittal face of Mr. Henneberger as the Narcissus left port to indicate that he had changed his plans. Possibly, if the steamer was in urgent need of assistance—and this had not been mentioned—her master might use the Narcissus; otherwise, she almost certainly would hold off until the arrival of the other tug.

"Still, I'm trustin' to a good vessel and the luck o' the Brennans," she told Peter as she braced her feet against the swing of a sea and fought the wheel. "This fog that's blowed up, along wid the wind and dark, ain't helpin' things. I hope we kin find her."

They found her shortly after daybreak, much farther north than they had expected—a rust-streaked steamer of about two thousand tons, with a cloud of wind-snatched smoke from her tall, rime-coated orange funnel smudged across the murk. The seas were spouting against her listed port side and exploding in bursts of savage spray, as she rolled and pitched and crawled painfully toward Cape Flattery and the entrance to the Strait.

Annie pulled the whistle cord, and an answering plume of steam broke from the steamer's funnel. The Narcissus ran as close as was safe, and Annie, with a megaphone in her hand, braced herself between the pilothouse and the rail and bawled up at the Minute Man's captain as he leaned over a wing of the bridge.

"Stand by to take our line!" Annie bellowed.

"What tug is that?"

"Narcissus, o' Secoma."

"Did the owner send you?"

"No-o, but——"

"Can't use you."

"Listen, captain? Ye're in a bad way——"

The shipmaster shook his head.

"We're all right. I'll wait," he said.

Dipping and plunging crazily, and controlled by Annie's superb seamanship, the Narcissus clung to her post to weather of the listed side of the Minute Man, in such a manner that her sturdy hull acted as a breakwater and destroyed the force of the seas that were battering her with insatiable and unending fury; and while she kept position, Tugboat Annie pestered the steamer's master with every argument she could invent, born of her years of seafaring, in vain endeavor to have him accept her help. But the captain was adamant.

"I know my way about!" he shouted angrily, at length. "We don't want your line, so you needn't wait! The other tug'll be in sight anytime now—and you needn't think you'll get anything by shielding our exposed side either! We—don't—need—you!"

Doggedly, however, Tugboat Annie hung on, fighting against time and the imminent arrival of Horatio Bullwinkle.

"She's far too close inshore now," Annie said worriedly to Peter, as they watched the steamer laboring through the heavy seas, half obscured in fog and the smoking crests. "Look, ye can't see the coast at all now, behind that mist. I'm goin' to have another try at him."

The bow of the Narcissus plunged, and there loomed ahead the lift of a gigantic sea that blotted out the sky and, with translucent green light shot through its deep-curved belly, commenced to curl over with thunderous, hissing crest. Annie watched it warily, as a boxer watches his opponent; then she shifted the wheel slightly. The sea roared down and under, and the tug flung hundred-foot fans of milky foam over its broken back, then staggered and broke through.

"Whoosh!" said Annie with a strained grin, as she glanced sideways at Peter's pallid, sweating face. "We don't want to meet wid the grandfather o' that one!"

She wrestled with the wheel, hooking her leg over a spoke and utilizing her weight to keep it down, while the Narcissus bashed and battered her way once more as close as possible under the Minute Man's bridge.

"Better take our line, captain; I'm tellin' you!" she bellowed. "The weather's thickenin' and——"

"Will you get the hell away from here, you lunatic!" yelled the exasperated shipmaster. "Do you want to get stove in against our side? I know what I'm doing, so let me alone!"

Annie shrugged. It looked, at last, like a losing battle; and for a half hour she was silent. Then freshly anxious, she stared again in the direction of the coast. Through the welter appeared a faint, dark haze.

"He'll run her ashore, sure as shoutin'!" Annie rasped. "I've got to tell him! Look, the fool's beatin' right into Mukkaw Bay!"

Once more, battered by shotlike spray, she stood outside the house and hailed the steamer.

"I don't care if ye take our line or not," she screamed, above the roar of the wind, "but change your course! Ye're standin' straight for the south side o' Flattery, and afore ye know it ye'll be piled up ashore!"

The shipmaster turned and looked into the shouting maelstrom shoreward. Then he nodded quickly and ran into the wheelhouse. Slowly the steamer's bows swung out, pointed seaward. Annie wiped her brow and gave a sigh of relief.

"Well, Peter, we've did our best now. Bullwinkle can have her, and welcome. It's been a good day's work."

"What are ye so happy about? We didn't get the job."

"Well, ye've heard o' the hen what sat on a duck's egg and hatched somethin' just as good, only fatter, ain't ye?"

Peter shifted his quid. "Ye're prob'ly goin' out of your mind," he said equably. "Sounds like the first sign to me."

Annie made no further attempt to communicate with the steamer, and by noon, the increasing gale having blown the fog clear, they passed Flattery and entered the Strait. And as the wind-scoured sea road stretched before them they discerned a black dot riding on a white bow wave, and black smoke pouring from her funnel, and recognized the approach of the hard-driven Salamander.

Tugboat Annie gave her a wide berth, and watched as the other tug ran alongside the Minute Man and put a line aboard, then forged ahead with the steamer in tow. Then she sighed, not unhappily.

A MATTER OF BUSINESS

"I'm feelin' tired, Peter," she said. "Let's go home."

It was late the following afternoon before the Salamander and her tow limped into port; and shortly thereafter, having delivered her charge at a wharf, the Salamander breezed triumphantly home. Mr. Bullwinkle's bright little eyes eagerly searched the Narcissus as he came expertly to his berth and made fast, and as he came out of his pilothouse he shoved his hat on the back of his head.

"Scared ye off, did I, Annie?" he chortled. "Well, let that be a lesson to you!"

"Yeah, mebbe ye did scare me off, Bullwinkle. That face o' yours would scare a locomotive off the track," she admitted soberly. "Ye must be feelin' pretty good, ye look so unpleasant."

He let the insult pass. "It just goes to show," he said pedantically, "that cheaters never prospers. And ye see what happens when a woman tries to play a man's games. What? No snappy comeback?"

"I'll have mine later," she replied, standing with hands on her big hips, on her face an enigmatic smile. "If ye're feelin' so swell, make the most of it. It might not last long."

Mr. Bullwinkle jerked a thumb at Henneberger, who was approaching along the wharf.

"It'll last as long as he says it will!"

"That," said Annie cryptically, "is jest what I was figgerin' on."

She climbed stiffly to the wharf, for the beating she had taken in the heavy seas had bruised her bones, and waddled ponderously around the dock. She boarded the Salamander and, ignoring the grins of the crew, went to the quarters of Horatio Bullwinkle.

"Well, sir," Mr. Bullwinkle was saying within, as Annie paused outside, "I spose, as you say, that seven hundred and fifty is a fair price. It ain't a fortune, of course——"

"It's fair enough for what you had to do," said Henneberger crisply. "I really should have let Annie take charge, I suppose. If you're not satisfied——"

"Oh, sure, I'm satisfied," Mr. Bullwinkle assured him hastily. "Especially now, since I spose ye'll give me all your towin' business when your vessels make this port."

"And that," said Tugboat Annie calmly, as she pushed open the door, "shows how crazy ye are."

"Hey, get outa here!" shouted Mr. Bullwinkle. "Who invited you?"

"I didn't need no invite. And if ye don't like it, ye can spiff off yerself! I just sashayed around to see that ye didn't sell Mr. Henneberger no gold brickbats." She turned to the shipping man. "Has he?"

Henneberger's eyes twinkled. "Not so far."

"That's swell. Because I got one o' me own to sell. . . . So ye're fixin' to get his towin' business, eh, Bullwinkle?"

"It's mine!" said Mr. Bullwinkle promptly. "Ain't that so, sir?"

"Possibly," Henneberger said. "Unless Annie—Mrs. Brennan——"

"Tugboat Annie's me name. I ain't ashamed of it!"

"——unless Tugboat Annie can give me some better reason than she has, up to now, for deciding otherwise. The captain of the Minute Man told me she made quite a pest of herself outside the Cape."

"I dunno about that," said Annie placidly. "All I want is to put in me claim for salvage."

"Salvage?" echoed Henneberger with a frown. "Now, look here——"

"Bein' silly again, eh, Annie?" Mr. Bullwinkle put in, with a wink at the shipowner. "The Minute Man come in under her own steam, and I picked her up and helped her down, after"—he emphasized—"after he refused your help."

Annie shook her head.

"He didn't refuse it. He took it. That's why I'm claimin' salvage."

Henneberger stared at her.

"What are you getting at?" he asked quietly.

"It's very simple, sir, and like cases has been won on less grounds in every salvage court in the country. Marine law says that when a vessel is in danger, from possible or undisclosed perils, and unsolicitated advice is accepted what saves her from them perils, then the adviser may place legitimate claim fer salvage."

"Well——"

"Well, I saved the Minute Man from runnin' ashore on Cape Flattery yesterday mornin'. She was standin' straight inshore in the fog and murk, and the master didn't know it till I telled him. He didn't ask for me advice, 'tis true, but he took it immediate, when I gave it, as I've me crew to prove. And it saved his ship."

"Nonsense!"

"Ask yer shipmaster, sir. He'll tell ye. And I been seafarin' too long to come around wid a claim I can't back up. Even Bullwinkle's got brains enough to tell ye that. You, sir, wouldn't have no ship now," she told Henneberger soberly, "if I hadn't been standin' by like I done. She'd be pounded to bits and all her crew drownded at the foot o' Flattery. Call that nonsense if ye like."

"But——"

"It's as I say. I'm entitled to salvage; and if me case ain't good fer a five-thousand-dollar award in any maritime court, I'm a four-legged hummin' bird! Mind you, I don't say that I'm goin' to be bullheaded about it." Her eyes sought the deck head above. "If I was gettin' reg'lar towin' jobs on a contract, say, from a man what owned the ship—like yourself, say, Mr. Henneberger, and you a friend of Alec Severn, and all—I wouldn't dream o' nickin' ye fer five thousand bucks. 'Twouldn't be good business. I'd throw in that salvage job as part o' the contract and call it sarvice. Now——"

"Hey!" yelled Mr. Bullwinkle, who could see how a straw blew in the wind as well as the next. "You're trickin' him! You can't get away wi' that, you lyin', cheatin', old cow! . . . Can she, sir?"

Mr. Henneberger pursed his mouth, and a glint of humor wrinkled the fine network about his shrewd blue eyes.

"She's got a pretty good argument," he said slowly. "And she seems to have a head on her."

"So's a glass o' beer, but that don't mean nothin'," growled Mr. Bullwinkle.

"Suppose," continued the shipowner, addressing Annie over Mr. Bullwinkle's further and anguished protests, "I did give your company my towing business——"

"In writin'!" said Annie bluntly.

"——in writing. What would you do for me?"

"Do?" roared Annie with a grin. "I'd send Bullwinkle here a nice pointed straw hat wid holes what he could stick his ears through; then I'd take you and Peter and Big Sam and Shif'less—I got twelve dollars saved!—and we'd go ashore tonight and raise whoopee!"

"IF THE CAP FITS"

Darkness had fallen over the harbor of Secoma, and the rumble of trucks, the clatter of ships' winches, the pious ejaculations of stevedores were stilled, and the only sounds were the merry voices, deep laughter and the music of a fiddle and a harmonica issuing from one of a line of moored tugs tied up at the Deep-Sea Towing and Salvage Company dock. Tugboat Annie Brennan, master of the deep-water tug Narcissus, was giving a party.

Burly men of the tugboat fleet moved down the wharf and boarded the tug; a door opened and hearty voices shouted: "Happy birthday, Annie!"

"Happy birthday yerself, ye old gafoozlers!" Annie roared, her massive face gleaming with pleasure and exertion as she made her guests at home. "My, what ye got there? A present for me? Sa-ay, ain't that swell of ye!"

Beer flowed, and other liquid cheer; vast stacks of sandwiches, plates of pickles, cheese and doughnuts melted like snow, to be perpetually replenished; and the fiddle and harmonica staged a musical feud, but nobody minded that; the boys were having high jinks, and everyone was happy.

There came another bang at the messroom door. Annie, at the table with a massive granite cup in her hand, her mouth full of corned-beef sandwich, looked up. "Come in!" she bellowed merrily. "If it won't open, kick it down! What the heck do we care, now?"

The door opened, and a powerfully built, bandy-legged man with a bristle of hair on his bullethead, bright black shoe-button eyes, a package held behind his back and a broad grin on his face, stepped

"IF THE CAP FITS"

over the coaming. And as he entered a hush, affecting all but the most bibulous guests, fell upon the room.

"Oh!" said Annie, her cup suspended. "It's the horse's tail! Well—what do you want?"

"I want," floridly replied Mr. Horatio Bullwinkle, master of the tug Salamander, and Annie's bitterest rival, "to wish a happy birthday to me old pal, Tugboat Annie. Happy birthday, Annie!"

"Happy birthday," grunted Annie. "Who invited you?"

"Aw, be neighborly, Annie!" cried Mr. Bullwinkle, his little eyes sparkling with malicious amusement. "Can't ye let bygones be bygones? Look"—he produced the package—"I brought ye a present."

"Ye did?" In spite of herself, Annie was intrigued. "Well, that was nice of ye, I guess. All right, folks"—she waved to her guests—"don't let this big baboon stop yer fun." She relented a trifle. "What's in the parcel?"

"No-no, Annie!" Mr. Bullwinkle was massively coy. "It's a surprise. Ye're not to open it till I'm gone. I went to a lot o' trouble to buy you that, Annie. There ain't an appropriater gift in the whole o' Secoma!"

"Thanks!" said Annie, touched. "I guess mebbe I been misjudgin' you a mite, Bullwinkle. Have some beer. Don't mind the cup. It's only had pea soup in it."

"Some birthday party, Annie," commented her guest admiringly, making the comestibles vanish. "How old are you? Tck-tck!" He chided himself. "I'm sorry! I forgot ye can't count that high."

Annie eyed him, dourly speculative. "That sounds like a crack to me! I got a good mind——"

"You got me wrong, Annie!" protested Mr. Bullwinkle virtuously. "I don't care if you are that old. You're a good egg. By the way"—his voice became casual—"are you goin' up to the shipyard tomorrow with your boss, when Keane awards that drydock-towin' job?"

"Oho!" cried Annie in a voice that made her guests stop and stare. "So that's what ye come here for—to pump me, was it? Well, grab yer hat, ye snake in the bush! You're goin' home!"

"But, Annie, listen!" Mr. Bullwinkle protested loudly, shocked at this swift penetration of his strategy. "I was just——"

"Out ye go, ye deceitful wagabone! Beat it, afore I kick yer ears adrift!"

She clapped his hat on his head, someone obligingly opened the door, and Mr. Bullwinkle, still clutching his beer and two sandwiches, was thrust into the night. But instead of looking dejected, his

"IF THE CAP FITS"

uncouth countenance was extended in a smile. "Don't forget to look at your present, Annie!" he roared through the closed door, and hastily departed.

"Golly, that's right! I forgot!" said Annie, within. And, puffing but complacent, and with no compunction for the donor, she opened the package, while her festive guests stared, with happy anticipation, over her big shoulders. She covered her eyes with one hand, while with the other she fumbled in the parcel. "Eenie-meenie-miney-mo——" Annie cried archly, drew forth the present, and uncovered her eyes. Mr. Bullwinkle's gift was a large, rough straw hat of the sombrero type, and at the juncture of crown and brim were two large, red-taped ear holes.

"Haw-haw-haw-haw!" suddenly brayed a tactless guest. "That's a good one, that is!" And Tugboat Annie, forgetful of her obligations as hostess, enthusiastically boxed his ears.

Next morning, as Annie was on her way to the wharf office of her employer, Alec Severn, she was hailed by the irritating voice of Mr. Bullwinkle, who lounged with his elbows on his tug's rail, his bright little eyes fixed derisively upon her. "Have a happy birthday, Annie?" he inquired solicitously.

"Ye needn't try to git me mad, Bullwinkle!" bellowed Annie, stung. "But I got a mind to go over there anyway and lend ye a good smack on the pout!"

Encouraged by the cheers of a group of elated tugboatmen on the wharf, Annie rolled up her sleeves, squashed her old felt hat belligerently upon her skull, and was about to carry out her threat, when the rotund little figure of Alec Severn, her employer, appeared on the landing above. "Annie!" he barked. "Stop that brawling and come up here. I won't tolerate your quarreling with that fellow any longer." He led the way to his office and plopped into his chair.

"He started it," Annie grumbled. "One o' these days——"

"Twenty minutes ago I sent for you, and——"

"I was comin'," said Annie, "But there's somethin' about that stingamaroo——"

"You leave Bullwinkle alone. I particularly didn't want you to get him sore today. He joined up with Red Halloran, of the Firefly, and Clay Kniss, of the Sea Scout, to bid against us on that drydock-towing job that Tom Keane is awarding this morning. But if he's in an ugly mood he'll down his price just to spite us. I want to talk to you about this job. As you know, Keane is head of the Keane Engineering Company, of Skagway. He's had this floating drydock built here, and it is to be towed to Alaska in three sections."

"Think we'll get the job, Alec?"

"IF THE CAP FITS"

"We stand the best chance, because we own a number of tugs and our operating expenses are lower. But Keane is peculiar. He has requested, for instance, that the tugboat captains who might tow the first section also be on hand at the shipbuilding offices today."

"That's why ye wanted me there, too, huh?"

"Yes. It's the biggest towing job of the year, Annie, for whoever gets it will tow the first section north tomorrow and provide tugs to tow the other two sections at intervals of a week. That means, if we land it, that three of our heavy-duty tugs will be employed for from three weeks to a month. But remember what I told you about Bullwinkle, and keep clear of him, both here and at the shipyard. If there's any kind of trouble or scene before Keane, it might lose us the contract."

"Sure, Alec!" Annie promised fervently. "I'll be as peaceable as a cockroach. I wish there was some way o' stoppin' Bullwinkle from bein' there, though. I don't suppose it would do," she suggested, hopefully, "if I snuck up on him and knocked him subconscious——"

"Someday," Severn rapped, "your ideas will land you in the hoosegow. I've got to go uptown now, but I'll meet you in the shipyard offices at eleven o'clock."

"Okay, Alec," said Annie, highly elated. "I'll be seein' ye. And don't take no nickel nutmegs."

She rolled breezily out the door, which slammed behind her, and down to her tug. Mr. Bullwinkle, she observed from the corner of her eye, had not moved. " 'Lo, Annie," he said, mockingly placating. "What time ye going to the shipyard?"

Heroically Annie fought down the impulse to hurl a reply, and climbed the ladder to her cabin.

"Mind if we go up together?" pursued Mr. Bullwinkle, his impudent little orbs upon her retreating back. "Well, I'll be waitin' for you across the tracks."

Despite her vow to Severn, Annie knew that any further traffic with the aggravating Mr. Bullwinkle could have but one result; therefore his threat to accompany her to the shipyard occasioned her considerable perturbation. She changed; and when, at length, with her reticule pinned to her waist and the slightly daffy hat feather of her favorite chapeau jigging haughtily aloft, she was ready to depart, she saw through the curtained porthole that Mr. Bullwinkle, shining with soap and malice, was waiting on his side of the dock, ready to bear her gallant company.

Anxiously Annie consulted the watch pinned on the bosom of her blouse. Preoccupied with thought, it had taken her longer to dress than she had anticipated.

"IF THE CAP FITS"

"Golly! It's ten of eleven!" she muttered desperately to herself at last. "I gotta make the best of it and go!"

Affecting not to see Mr. Bullwinkle as she left her tug, Annie bustled ashore and along the wharf. But Mr. Bullwinkle was something of a wag. Since she had so delayed her departure, it would be necessary now, he knew, for Annie to engage one of the three decrepit taxicabs from the stand at the head of the dock, and he planned, for a little light fun, to delay his joining of her until the last possible moment, then step into her conveyance. So he allowed her a fair start, then set out in leisurely pursuit. Annie broke into a ponderous canter. Mr. Bullwinkle increased his pace. Annie, inwardly raging, pounded across the tracks toward the taxi stand.

The driver of the nearest leaped from his seat and opened the door, but Annie, with a last lethal glance over her shoulder, had an idea.

"Hey, wait a minute!" she panted, and bustled to the other two cabs in turn, and crammed a dollar bill into each man's hand. "Here!" she gasped. "Go have yerself a dollar's wuth o' taxi ride!"

"B-but, lady! Where——"

"I don't care where ye go! But move away from here quick, and don't take no other fare till the dollar's gone!"

She hastened back to the first. "Start the bus!" she said as she fell inside; and the three conveyances started off just as Mr. Bullwinkle, curdled with indignation, reached the spot.

"Hey, there! Wait a minute, Annie!" he bellowed frantically. "Hey! Taxi! Taxi!"

"Giddap!" said Tugboat Annie.

The meeting in the offices of the shipbuilding company was well underway, and the competing bids already had been opened and read, when Annie, still breathless, ambled in. She was scrutinized by Mr. Keane, a compact, square-shouldered man with a pleasant, weather-tanned face, graying hair and shrewd eyes.

"Who is this—this lady?" he asked, surprised.

"Mrs. Annie Brennan, my senior captain, in command of the Narcissus," Severn replied.

"You mean, a woman skipper, to tow my drydock section north?" demanded Keane incredulously.

Severn replied: "There's not a more capable, experienced tugboatman on the coast, Mr. Keane. Even my business competitors and their captains will tell you that. Isn't that so?" He appealed to the group of mahogany-faced men who lined the walls of the office.

"She's terrible!" said a carrot-whiskered giant of a tugboat captain, who sensed a chance to put Severn out of the running.

"IF THE CAP FITS"

"Sa-ay, Red Halloran!" growled Annie. "If I had you outside——"

Keane demanded silence. "Well, I don't know——" he said dubiously. "You had the low bid, Severn. But frankly, I wouldn't care to trust a tow worth a quarter of a million to a woman captain." He addressed the others. "Are any of you gentlemen prepared to meet Mr. Severn's figure?"

Halloran spoke again. "Well, sir, me and Clay Kniss and Bullwinkle, of the Salamander, put in our bid together. If only Bullwinkle was here now——"

"Where is he?" Keane asked. "He was told to be present."

"I dunno, sir. But if we had a little more time——"

"That's not fair," Severn protested hotly, his round face turkey red. "Mine was the low bid, and——"

"Listen!" Tugboat Annie shoved her bulk forward. "You let one of our other skippers take the Narcissus, Alec. I ain't goin' to stand in the way o' the job."

"That's an idea," said Keane; but Severn, after a glance at her troubled face, and a brief pause, shook his head.

"No!" he said. "If I get the job, then I appoint the one I think fittest to carry it through."

"I'll have to think about it," Keane said slowly. "I appreciate your stand, Severn, but this is business, and——"

A sudden commotion outside arrested him. There was a clerk's remonstrating voice; the sound of someone being thrust violently against a partition; heavy running feet. Then Mr. Horatio Bullwinkle, wild-eyed and furious, burst into the room. "Where's Tugboat Annie?" he demanded.

"Here I am, ye ugly trollop! What about it?" roared Annie.

"What's all this about, Captain Bullwinkle?" Keane snapped.

"It's her, sir! Tugboat Annie! She tried to stop me comin' up here this morning"— and he spluttered forth an account of her taxicab trick. "And with the taxis gone, I had to wait twenty minutes for a streetcar."

Keane turned to Annie. "Is it true that you took that means to prevent the arrival of a competitor?"

"It is!" Annie grunted, scorning excuse.

Keane took in her truculent, mastiff face, her heavy-set, formidable figure, and the feather nodding raffish defiance from her hat. "That settles the towing job, then!" he said abruptly.

"Thank ye, sir!" Red Halloran said.

Keane shook his head. "You misunderstand. Mrs. Brennan gets the job. She has the kind of quick thinking in an emergency that I require. Good day, gentlemen."

"IF THE CAP FITS"

Daylight the following morning struggled through a fine, mistlike drizzle of rain, and the plaintive hoot of the Black Ball ferries as they shuttled across added a melancholy note to the unpromising day. But mere bad weather could not dampen the spirits of Tugboat Annie and the crew of the Narcissus as that capable vessel left her wharf. Soon thereafter, with the lumbering, unwieldy bulk of the floating drydock section in tow, the Narcissus was pushing her blunt snout through the heavy, rain-laden mists, Alaska bound.

"Ain't it swell?" Annie commented to Peter, the mate, in the warm snugness of the wheelhouse, as she peered out the window at the raw, shrouded grayness of the strait ahead. "And the Pansy and the Rose is goin' to tow the other two sections up in a week's time!"

Through the long day the Narcissus plowed steadily north. The sea was smooth, but the weaving curtain of mist thickened, as evening advanced, to dense fog. Periodically the shattering roar of the tug's whistle blasted into the gathering darkness, warning other seafarers of her approach; and her speed was reduced to conform to the regulations governing the progress of vessels in fog. But since fog is a commonplace hazard in a Northwestcoast tugboatman's life Annie kept a good lookout, and sharp hearing for answering fog signals, and did not worry.

After dark, the increased lift of the crestless swells told Annie that they had cleared sheltered water and were crossing abreast the inside entrance of Juan de Fuca Strait.

"I'll be glad when we get across here, Annie," Peter said as he came from below to relieve her at the wheel. "Some o' them big liners in a hurry to make port don't slacken down much for fog, or——"

His words were drowned in the whistle's deep-throated roar as Annie pulled vigorously on the lanyard. When the sound had died away, she said: "I been listenin' for the last ten minutes to a vessel blatterin' about ahead of us there, somewheres. Listen!"

They waited; heard only the lap and hiss of the bow wave, the creak of the tug, the smooth panting of her diesels.

"It's okay, I guess," Annie said. She added, with a grim chuckle: "We'd look kinda silly if anything happened now, after our swell send-off and all. I——"

The brazen clamor of a vessel's siren roared earsplittingly about them, blotting out the frantic warning scream of Shiftless on the forward deck below. From out of the fog ahead loomed a cargo steamer, bearing down on them, her navigating lights vague colored blurs. Automatically Annie threw her weight on the wheel and put it hard over, but for an agonizing moment the tug, hampered by the bulk of the floating dry-dock section, failed to respond. The flaring bows of the steamer soared over them. The roar of her bow wave was like thunder in their ears, and a tiny figure on the towering fo'-castle-head waved excited arms and added a shrill, futile pipe to the wildly bellowing sirens of both ships. Then, leaden slow, it seemed, the Narcissus's bow swung away and the stranger, with only yards between, ran parallel and slid into the fog.

"Thank the Lord——" began Annie deeply, when from astern came a crashing jar, and the scrape of shearing steel, and the Narcissus was shaken from truck to keel.

"She's hit the drydock!" gasped Peter. "Annie! She's hit——"

Her heart tight with anxiety, Annie lumbered hastily outside, her nostrils assailed by the wet, salt fog. But her voice was steady as she gave calm, curt directions; and after twenty minutes had passed, she reentered the wheelhouse and met Peter's apprehensive gaze.

"The drydock's been holed bad, Peter. It's takin' in water pretty fast," she said quietly, her tone denying the anxious sweat that stood out on her ruddy face.

"Can we patch her and pump her out?"

"Unh-unh! We gotta beach her. And I only hope we can make the shore afore she sinks on us!"

While the tug picked up way she studied the chart.

"Whip Island is nearest," she announced presently, "and just inside Willamute Head is Crescent Beach—that's firm sand, and fairly well protected. We'll put her ashore there."

Peter changed course and the tow proceeded. Progress across the tidal current was heartbreakingly slow, and adding to their difficulty were the fog and darkness, making their destination hard to find. But Annie's years of experience in waters that she knew like the inside of her pocket guided her. Night had gone, however, and the fog was beginning to blow clear before a fresh morning breeze when the dark smudge of Willamute Head appeared and the Narcissus approached the sandy indentation of Crescent Bay.

The tide had changed and was with them as the tug, having taken in her towing wire, pushed the sluggish, water-heavy drydock section toward the beach. It struck, the lighter end slid hissing over the foreshore and, with the tide at high-water slack, it settled down like a stranded leviathan onto the sand.

"Now what?" asked Peter as the Narcissus backed away.

"Now," replied Annie grimly, "we'll slink over to Port Townsend wid our tail atween our leg and phone the j'yful news to Alec Severn. By the way, did anybody happen to see the name o' the steamer what hit her? Shif'less, you was on deck at the time——"

"IF THE CAP FITS"

Shiftless wagged his head. "She was on us and away too quick."

"Why the devil wasn't her fog whistle blowin'?" Annie growled.

"It was," Shiftless told her. "She sounded off same moment we did, just a minute or two before she struck. Guess our whistle stopped you hearin' her."

Annie shrugged. "Both of us obeyin' the rules, and nobody to blame."

"I guess," said Peter slowly, hitching up his paunch, "Keane'll cancel our contract to tow them other two drydock sections now, hey?"

Examination of the stranded drydock later revealed that the damage was too extensive to repair without additional salvage equipment, so the Narcissus crossed the strait to Port Townsend. The fresh breeze had swept the last of the fog away and the day was bright with sunshine and blue, wind-rippled water. Annie's face, however, was dour, her eyes troubled.

"I wouldn't feel so bad if I hadn't let Alec down wid Keane, like this," she said as she jammed her old felt hat on her blowsy head and prepared to go ashore. "I dunno how I'm goin' to tell him. Sam, you come wid me whiles I tellyphone."

"Aw, Annie, I wouldn't know what to say either," Big Sam demurred.

"Ye're comin'," replied Annie adamantly, "whether ye like it or not."

Together they moved reluctantly along the wharf toward a telephone booth. Big Sam looked sideways at Tugboat Annie. "What are ye talking to yourself for, Annie?" he asked curiously.

"Hold yer tongue! I'm rehearsin' what I'm to say."

"Better make it good," he cheered her.

In the telephone booth, Annie gasped and clapped her hands to her stomach. "Oo-oof!" she said.

"Whassamatter?" ejaculated Sam, startled.

"I—I ain't feelin' so good. It—it's a attack o' pneumatic fever, or somethin'."

"Golly!" Big Sam cried. "Kin I do anything for ye?"

"No. It'll be all right if I stay out in the air. You go in and phone Alec, Sam."

"Oh, no!" yelped Sam. "Oh, no, ye don't, Annie! Ye can't fool me. Anyways," he added virtuously, "I was below in the engine room when it happened."

"All right, ye big coward!" Annie grumbled crossly. "But you stick around. Now don't go 'way!"

"IF THE CAP FITS"

She requested her number, and presently was in communication with Severn.

"Hello, Alec, ye old stoge-poach!" cried Annie, with the good-humored heartiness of one hoping to cushion bad tidings. "How are ye today? Say, I got a little news fer ye.... Huh? What's that?... How did the paper find out?... Oh, I see. H'm'm!... Eh?... Who's the laughin' stick o' Secoma?... We are, huh?... Is Keane sore?... Why, Alec Severn; you, usin' such langridge!... Well, I am sorry it happened, Alec, honest!... If ye'd let me explain.... Okay, then!" Her voice hardened.... "What's that?... Bullwinkle? No, I ain't seed nothin' of him.... Yeah, yeah! Go ahead. I'll listen."

She listened while Severn told her what he wanted her to do. They discussed the condition of the drydock section, and methods of repair; and when finally Annie hung up, her stubborn jaw was set.

"Come on, brush the cobwebs offa ye," she said to Big Sam. "We got work to do."

"Was Keane sore?" Sam asked as they started back to the tug.

"Sore as a boil on a broken leg. Alec says he's canceled our contract to tow them other two drydock sections north." Annie snorted. "Said he should have knowed better than to trust a woman wid the job in the first place!"

"That's too bad, Annie. How'd the papers find out about it so quick?"

"That steamer—she was the Knight of Malta— reported it when she went into Bellingham."

"What was that about Bullwinkle?"

"Oh, yeah, I almost forgot. Alec says that soon as the word got around that we'd been in collision, Bullwinkle cast off his Salamander and headed north. I wonder what that furry-headed tarantella is up to? By the way, Alec and Keane is comin' up to Crescent Bay in the Pansy right away. So we better be gettin' back."

It was evening when the Narcissus again rounded Willamute Head and opened up Crescent Beach, whereupon reposed the dark bulk of the drydock. But where Annie had expected to see only the deserted beach, the stranded drydock and the black sentinel pines reflected in the still water, she saw in addition the yellow glow of an anchored tug's riding light; and it was still sufficiently light to recognize her as Mr. Bullwinkle's exceedingly capable Salamander.

"And hey! Look!" squawked Shiftless. "There's lights and people on the drydock too!"

"Shut up!" rasped Annie. "Put us alongside the Salamander!"

Scimitars of reflected sunset color rippled across the mirrored bay as the Narcissus curved alongside the other tug. Annie left the wheelhouse for the deck.

"Where's that——" She swallowed. "Where's Bullwinkle?" she demanded of one of the Salamander's grinning crew.

"He's on his drydock," the man answered promptly.

"What do ye mean—his drydock?"

"That's what he's calling it. Why don't you go over and ask him?"

"Mebbe ye think I won't?" Annie muttered dangerously. "Take her inshore, Shif'less."

The Narcissus floated off the stranded drydock, set high on the sand by the receding tide; and Annie was about to hail Bullwinkle when that gentleman detached his bandy-legged person from two companions at the end of the structure and peered at the Narcissus.

"Could it be somethin' I et," he inquired drolly, "or is that me old pal Tugboat Annie come to offer congratulations on me salvage job?"

"Get offa that drydock, ye boot!" cried Annie. "Ye got no business there!"

"Why, Annie," returned Mr. Bullwinkle, in sorrowful reproof, "this is my drydock! I find an abandoned vessel—a wreck—piled up ashore, and accordin' to the law of salvage, she's mine."

"Oh, Lord!" thought Annie, with a further swift sinking of the heart. She said: "Don't be silly. That's my tow."

"Was yours," corrected Mr. Bullwinkle jovially. "It's mine now, and it looks pretty good."

"Mebbe ye'll find out that all that glitters ain't a gold brick."

"I know—and everything that swims ain't a fish, neither." He chuckled. "It was kind of ye to leave her here for me so neat. Always the pal, eh, Annie?"

But Tugboat Annie, for the moment, was not listening. Something that he had said had plucked a vague, almost forgotten chord in her memory; and in her predicament instinctively she groped for it—something to do with fish that didn't swim? No, that wasn't it. But almost.

Bullwinkle's voice recalled her: "You ain't asked how I found you, Annie."

"I'll bite," she rapped. "How did ye?"

"Well," said Mr. Bullwinkle, enormously enjoying himself, "when the master o' that steamer mentioned where he'd struck you, I knew that the handiest place, if ye had to beach the drydock, was here. So I took a chance on your goin' for help, and here I am."

But Annie, preoccupied again with that irritating little bur of recollection that Bullwinkle's words had stirred up in her mind, was not even listening; and Peter, who had come up and spoken to her, grasped her arm. "Annie, what's the matter wi' you?" he said. "I tell you the Pansy is coming in the bay."

The Narcissus came about in a swirl of foam and headed to intercept the other tug. Severn and Keane were on the Pansy's forward deck; and when the Narcissus was within hailing distance, Severn summoned Annie on board. She obeyed, affecting a cheerfulness she was far from feeling.

The meeting was unpleasant. Keane and her employer sat at the Pansy's messroom table. For a moment after Annie entered, neither man spoke.

Annie coughed. "Ye—ye must have et starch for supper," she essayed at length with hollow good humor. "Ye act so stiff."

"Skip the comedy, Annie!" her employer told her curtly. "What's the situation? Can she be patched up here and towed off?"

"Well," admitted Annie reluctantly, "she's holed pretty bad, and she's beached hard. I had to do it, or she'd ha' sunk. The sand's buildin' up around her, and I guess, after she's patched temporary and pumped out, a dredge will have to cut a channel for her back to deep water."

"But that's a two-week job!" protested Keane angrily.

"Who's that other tug in close there?" Severn asked Annie abruptly. "What's she doing?"

"Why——" Annie cleared her throat. "It—it's the funniest thing, Alec. Ye'll die laffin' when ye hear this."

"We need a laugh!" Severn replied grimly. "Go on."

Annie told him; and when she had finished, there was silence.

"How good is his claim?" Keane asked quietly, at length.

Severn replied, "I'd say it's a damn sight too good to be laughed off. With Bullwinkle holding the aces, especially."

There was another silence. Keane, a repressed volcano by now, broke it:

"First, against my better judgment, I employ a woman to do a man's job. Second, she gets my drydock smashed in, beached and abandoned. Next, it's claimed for salvage by a seagoing bandit, and it seems I don't even own it anymore!" He looked at them angrily. "Anything else?"

"Maybe it's not as bad as it seems," Severn countered. "Anyway, we'll go across and have it out with Bullwinkle. Annie, you go back to your tug. We'll join you later. Annie! Do you hear me?"

"IF THE CAP FITS"

Annie started. "I'm sorry, Alec. I was thinkin'. What did ye say?"

"I'll tell you later, with additions," Severn snapped. "Come on, Keane."

Mr. Bullwinkle was delighted to see his visitors. He told them so, fulsomely. He even invited them to inspect his property. And when, a half hour later, with tempers ragged and in a highly abusive mood, they boarded the Narcissus, they were not inclined to temporize. But Annie, when she met them at the rail, seemed to have lost her preoccupation. She was her rough but capable self again, her manner indicating excitement, rigidly repressed.

"What happened?" she asked, almost gaily. "Did ye sweat the tar outa him?"

"We got nowhere!" Severn told her savagely. "And he had the gall to offer to hire our two tugs to help him salvage!"

"He did, huh? I hope ye accepted. Ye might as well make all ye can out of it, Alec."

Keane said icily: "I admire your ethics, Mrs. Brennan. Snatch what you can out of the mess for the benefit of the Deep-Sea Towing and Salvage Company! But what about me?"

"What was you plannin' to do, then?"

"Do? I'm returning to Secoma at once, to get an injunction restraining Bullwinkle from touching that drydock!"

"I wouldn't." Annie sagely shook her head. "In this case that'd just be cuttin' off yer face to spite yer nose. Listen. To get that drydock section back to Secoma, it's goin' to take tugs, and men, and a dredge, and mebbe drivin' piling to shore up the channel that'll have to be dug, to get her afloat again after she's patched. All that's goin' to cost a lot o' money!"

"We know that!" answered Severn impatiently. "Get to your point!"

"Me point," said Annie proudly, "is simple. Let Bullwinkle do it."

Keane looked at Severn. He said wearily: "Can't we discuss this without Mrs. Brennan? I am beginning to find her humor rather trying."

For a moment, Severn did not speak. Then he nodded. "Mr. Keane is right, Annie," he said heavily. "I'm afraid I've got to let you go."

"Ye mean," cried Annie, "fire me? Fire me off me old Narcissus?"

"That's what I mean. I'm sorry, Annie. But you've become more of a liability to us than an asset. Perhaps later on, if things change, I can take you back again. But you've had a long, useful life afloat, and——"

"Okay, Alec," said Annie huskily. "Ye needn't go on. Only, when

"IF THE CAP FITS"

I start a job I like to finish it, and this job ain't finished. But o' course if I ain't workin' for ye any more, Alec, ye won't want to hear me plan. Will ye?"

"Darn you, Annie! You got more cussed ways of getting around me!" cried Severn, exasperated, yet relieved. "Go on, then. What is this scheme of yours?"

"If you two cooing doves will excuse me," said Keane, a shade sardonically, "I'll be getting back to Secoma."

"No, sir!" exploded Tugboat Annie unexpectedly. "We'll not excuse ye till I tell ye somethin' I been achin' to say ever since ye aired yer silly views the other mornin' on women what has to go to sea fer a living!"

"Now Annie——" Severn interposed; but Annie fiercely wagged her shaggy head.

"Don't you butt in, Alec Severn! He's goin' to hear this, since them views o' his cost me me job!"

She turned back to Keane.

"Ye'll find at the steamboat inspector's inquiry, that neither us nor the steamer was to blame fer the collision. It was a risk seafarin' people has to take in heavy fog, and we was unlucky. And if a god in pants like yerself had been in command o' the Narcissus, ye'd ha' called it a act o' providence or peril o' the sea, and made the best of it. But because a woman was skipper, ye call it poor seamanship and bad judgment, and ye cancel Alec's contract and git me the sack! But don't you forget, me fine-feathered friend"— and Annie waggled a large, work-calloused finger under Keane's astonished nose—"that it was a woman what l'arned you to eat, and talk, and walk, and blow yer nose, and put yer little britches on! And—and," she concluded lamely, deflated now, "I guess that's all. I'll be goin' now."

Keane looked at her for a long moment. Then: "I'm sorry, Mrs. Brennan," he said quietly. "I see that I've been a little hasty in my estimation of you."

"A little hasty!" snorted Annie. "Hmmph!"

"If you'd care to finish what you were saying, about a possible way out of this——"

Annie hesitated. "If what I say shows ye how ye'll have yer drydock back in Secoma widout cost to yerself or Severn, will ye give Alec here the job o' towin' them other tow sections north?"

"I will."

"Okay, ye rat-whiskered old son of a gun!" cried Annie, happy once more. "Listen, then. Bullwinkle pulled a crack this evenin' about everythin' that swims not bein' a fish. It didn't make sense, but he had to sass me back wid somethin' and that happened to be it.

"IF THE CAP FITS"

But it set me rememberin' a similar remark what I'd read in a book years ago—and it had somethin' to do wid a floatin' drydock too. Guess that's what made it click in me head. See?"

"Not yet. But go on."

"Well, while you two was over jawin' wid Bullwinkle, I had me thinkin' cap on pretty tight; and finally I remembered. A floatin' drydock had caught fire in a Eastern port and a tug had pumped water and put it out, and then claimed salvage. And the judge in the case had said, when he give his decision, 'Everything that floats is not a vessel.' That's the remark that Bullwinkle's crack set me rememberin'. And that's the reason why I advised ye to let Bullwinkle go ahead and do this job—at his own expense."

Keane and Severn exchanged glances. "Well?" said Severn.

"Now," Annie continued heartily, "we'll hire our tugs to him, and clap a lien on the Salamander to make sure we git our pay when the job's done, for he's goin' to be plenty sore at us then. Then we let him go ahead wid his patchin' and pumpin' and dredgin', and the like, and return the drydock to Secoma for overhaul—all at his own expense, since he'll expect to repay hisself out o' that nice fat salvage. Dearie me!" Annie wiped her eyes. "I could die laffin' at him over there, workin' away, bless his heart, and me here, cuttin' the ground right out from under him. Him and his salvage! That's the joke, d'ye see?"

"What joke?"

"Why, there won't be no salvage! Here; I'll git the book what gave that other case, and read it to ye!"

She waddled away, and returned presently with a dog-eared, salt-stained volume on admiralty law.

"Here 'tis. The tug claimed salvage for puttin' out that fire. But the judge, when he give his decision, said: 'Everything that floats is not a vessel. A drydock, though floating, is not used for the purpose of navigation and therefore is not a vessel. And a structure that is not a vessel is not, and cannot be made, a subject of salvage!' Now do ye get me point?"

"You mean," cried Severn jubilantly, "that if Bullwinkle goes ahead with it, he'll have all his trouble and expense for nothing!"

"Ye couldn't put it clearer. And Keane gets his drydock back and it don't cost him a cent. Later, if ye liked, ye could get the insurance company to allow Bullwinkle his bare expenses, since the job's got to be did anyway and, give the devil his due, he'll do it well. But let him finish the job and make his salvage claim, then spring this on him. It'll scare him stiff as a plank, and l'arn him a good lesson!" Annie chuckled. "I got somethin' personal to spring on him meself, the day

"IF THE CAP FITS"

he returns the drydock to Secoma and tries to collect. Want to see it?"

She went to her cabin and returned with a carelessly wrapped parcel.

"What's that, Annie?" asked Severn.

Annie undid the paper and drew forth Bullwinkle's birthday gift to her—the big straw donkey hat.

"I'll have to enlarge the ear holes a mite, o' course," she grinned, "but I got a card that's all made out to send wid it."

Proudly she displayed it. The card read: "If the cap fits, wear it!"

TUGBOAT ANNIE SAILS AGAIN

Alec Severn, president of the Deep-Sea Towing and Salvage Company of Secoma, raised his round and beaming face to meet the inspired gaze of Tugboat Annie Brennan, master of the deep-water tug Narcissus and senior skipper of the fleet. Her big, capable body was planted solidly on the floor, her broad, weatherbeaten face with its twinkling blue eyes expanded into a huge grin as she returned her employer's gaze, and it was plain that she was supercharged with renewed energy and fairly sparking to go places and do things.

"No use telling you how delighted I am to have you at work for us again, Annie," Severn told her smiling. "You've had a long stretch on the beach——"

Annie's mastiff face grew serious. "You're tellin' me?" she said soberly.

"——but the way business is picking up, we'll be in the clear again before long. The Narcissus is back in commission."

"Yes, sir, my old Narcissus!" Her eyes misted with overpowering emotion. "Alec, I dunno how to thank ye. I—— I——" She blew her nose happily, dabbed her eyes. "Dear me, I must 'a' ketched a cold someplace." To hide her feelings, she glanced out the office window down onto the dock. "Look at the wuthless old wagabone!" she said huskily. "Rubbin' her pelt agin the pilin's as though she knowed we was talkin' about her!"

"Perhaps she does," said Severn, smiling again.

"Think I ought to run down again and see that everythin's sprick an' span?" she suggested eagerly; but Severn checked her.

"Just a minute." Severn's face settled back for a moment into the deep lines that a series of reverses had etched. "I've been through a pretty tough time, too, Annie, or I'd never have let you go. And——"

"I know ye have, Alec!" said Annie with quick sympathy.

"We still have four tugs laid up, and only the Narcissus and Daffodil ready to work. To put the others back means a hard grind—a hard, bitter fight for all the business we can get, no matter how small. And everything's going to depend on how loyally you support me."

"I'll find ye the business, don't worry!" Annie told him confidently. "I'll git it if I have to kick the stuffin'——"

"That's what I'm afraid of," Severn interrupted. "You got us in too many jams in the past by those methods. Quarreling with Bullwinkle——"

"That bilge creeper!" snapped Annie, instantly aroused.

"You see?" Severn barked. "All I do is mention him and——"

"Mention who?" asked Annie artlessly, taking quick warning. "Oh-h, ye mean Bullwinkle? Why"—she rasped out a merry laugh—"I allus liked the—the man. We're practically chums. Besides, he's went back to Portland——"

"He's back here again," Severn informed her.

"Wha-at?" Annie's eyes goggled.

"Rushed back as soon as business began to pick up. Right now he's on his Salamander, working in the South Waterway, tending a hydraulic dredge. He may be looking for trouble when you meet. But you've got to mind your own business, no matter what he says to you."

"I'll cultivate a skin like a epidermis!" Annie promised eagerly. "I won't even cuss him back. And just as a symptom o' me friendship——"

"I'm warning you," Severn told her, unimpressed by her ready promises. "One slip, and you'll find yourself on the beach again, and the Narcissus with a new master! And now here's your first job." He handed her a slip of paper. "Siwash Oil Barge Fourteen, in Rainier Pool. Shift her across to the oil company's dock. Phone me from there, case there's anything else." He stood up and held out his hand. "And good luck, Annie. No use me telling you how happy I am we're together again."

"Me, too, ye lobster-faced old gafoozler!" said Annie deeply. "Jest you leave everythin' to me! Well, spilt milk don't gather no moss! G'-by, Alec!"

She turned, her big body fairly jigging with delight. "Oh-h, happy days is here some more!" she hummed with discordant self-appreciation, blew out of the door like a merry hurricane, and the office shook as she thundered down the outside stairs.

Halfway across the wharf to the Narcissus her commands exploded like signal guns: "Shif'less, ye lazy lout! Peel yer backside off that deckhouse and stand by to let go! . . . Sa-am!" The placid face of Big Sam, the engineer, pushed itself with unwonted alacrity from the engine-room door. "Sam! Get below and start yer coffee pot grindin'!" Annie bustled ponderously on board. "Pete, take the wheel and git under way. Rainier Pool! Oh-h, happy days is here some more!"

While the engine-room signal jingled and the tug trembled under the thrust of the big propeller as it got under way, Annie dug into a half-unpacked suitcase and took therefrom the loadstone of her life—a large tinted chromo of her late husband, Captain Terry, in its oval plush-and-gold frame.

She sniffed it suspiciously. "Hmmph! Drunk again! . . ." she scolded automatically, and stuck it on its old hook on the bulkhead above her bunk. "Now mind what Alec told us about fightin' wid Bullwinkle, ye old divil!" she adjured, wagging a huge forefinger. Then: "Oh, Terry!" Meeting the blandishing eyes that seemed to gaze so responsively back at her, she gulped. "Ain't it great to be home again?"

The day was gray and raw, with a spit of rain, but this was duck soup to the disreputable old tug as it sloshed through the short harbor chop, headed for the South Waterway, beyond which lay the inner harbor and the Rainier Barge Pool. The tug's bow swung into the South Waterway, and Annie settled against the rail for a comfortable chat.

"Did ye ever hear tell about the time Terry and me was took up be sassiety, Peter?" she asked affably.

"I heard about the times he was took up be the police," Peter said, with a grin.

Annie snorted. "There was nothin' unusual about that. This was different. It was at the Seamen's and Firemen's Ball in Seattle one time . . ."

Her voice trailed abruptly off; and Peter, glancing at her, followed her suddenly tense gaze to where, in the waterway ahead, a hydraulic dredge was busily sucking mud and water through a large pipeline strung squarely across the channel, the pipe's connections supported by a series of small floating tanks, and linked by massive hose connections. It was neither pipeline nor dredge, however, that had so rigidly nailed Annie's attention. It was the supporting or tending tug, a powerfully built, efficient-looking ruffian; for upon its stern were the sinister letters SALAMANDER, SAN FRANCISCO, and its master was Annie's arch enemy, that massively built, bandy-legged,

134

bristle-headed and superabundantly efficient tugboat master, Horatio Bullwinkle.

Annie's crinkled eyes raked the long, speedy-looking black hull, white superstructure and canary-yellow funnel, while the muscles knotted ominously in her bulldog jaw. Then, in time, she remembered, and on her broad face there appeared a frozen smile.

"Well, well!" she grunted. "If it ain't me old pal Bullwinkle!"

Her hand went to the whistle cord and she hooted the required signal, indicating her desire that the Salamander tow the dredge to one side to allow her room to pass. In response, a bulky figure appeared on deck and looked toward them; and distance may have concealed the start of surprise with which he recognized the oncoming Narcissus. If so, he speedily recovered, for he spat lazily over the side and indolently reentered the Salamander's pilothouse.

Annie's face looked a bit mottled as she compressed her lips and again yanked the whistle cord. The Salamander did not budge.

"Heh-heh!" She shook her head in simulated mirth. "That's Bullwinkle for ye! Allus the wag!"

By now the Narcissus was close to the pipeline, and Annie's repeated and increasingly impatient hootings having no effect, she spoke to Peter, who put the wheel hard over. The tug swung in a wide smooth arc abeam of the Salamander, which lay close in to the bank, and stopped a dozen yards away. Annie's fist clamped the whistle cord and held it down till the earsplitting racket worked on her adversary's nerves sufficiently to impel him once more to the deck.

He stepped to the rail, hands in pockets, two hundred and twenty pounds of bone and muscle, surmounted by a thick, corded, weather-beaten neck and a round bullethead covered with ginger bristles. His small black shoe-button eyes, close set and shrewdly humorous, surveyed Annie unblinkingly from beneath heavily thatched brows.

Annie waved her fist with what was meant to be, not too successfully, bonhomie. "Hi there, ye—" She swallowed, then tried again. "Hi, there, Bullwinkle! It's me! Yer old sidekick, Tugboat Annie!"

Mr. Bullwinkle affected deafness; cupped his big hand, with an exaggerated gesture, to his ear and comically inclined his head. "How's that?" he said innocently.

"You heard me!" replied Annie, struggling valiantly with her choler. "Swing that dredge over, will ye? I wanta git past!"

After another full minute of calm scrutiny, Mr. Bullwinkle turned a puzzled face to the mate of the Salamander, who lounged, grinning, against the pilothouse doorpost. "Funny," said Mr. Bullwinkle, perplexed. "Must be a circus in town. You heard anything about a circus, Jake?"

Jake shook his head. "Uh-uhn!" he said.

"There must be," persisted Mr. Bullwinkle, and jerked his thumb toward the Narcissus. "There's the Ark—and there's part o' the zoo."

He turned and squeezed past Jake into the pilothouse, where the mate presently followed.

On board the Narcissus, Annie performed a suppressed but interesting species of sun dance, accompanied by homicidal mutterings. "I can't help it, Peter!" she choked. "I gotta do somethin' to that you-know-what or bust!" Again she grabbed the whistle cord, jetting plumes of indignantly screaming steam. But the only result was another appearance of the maddening Mr. Bullwinkle, who gazed vaguely at the sky.

"My! Ain't the birdies singin' pretty tonight?" he queried appreciatively, and again disappeared.

Tugboat Annie stopped her dance. "All right, he axed for it!" she rapped, her mouth a grim white line. "Here, gimme the wheel!"

Jingling for full speed ahead, she made a wide half circle, then, with every ounce of energy that the powerful diesels could impart, she aimed the weather-faded bow fender of the Narcissus full at the center coupling of the pipeline. The rig's quick surging bow wave grew to a roaring white wall, there was a heavy bump, the shriek of rent metal as the hose couplings parted, a wild, spouting cataract of mud and water from the severed pipe ends that missed the tug by inches, and the Narcissus was through.

"Take the wheel," she told Peter, and went back on deck.

With angry shouting, Bullwinkle and Jake raced out on deck and wrathfully surveyed the damage. Gone, now, was the cool aplomb of the Salamander's master. His contract called for maintenance of the pipeline, and to repair what Annie had done meant two hours of hard and dirty work.

"All right, Annie! You wait!" he yelled, shaking his fist at the retreating Narcissus. "I'll fix you for this!"

"Tell it to the birdies!" Annie yelled back. "I'm comin' back this way in a few hours, and if ye don't move pronto when I toot, I'll bust it again!" And with a quick, derisive lift of her beam she waddled triumphantly back to her pilothouse.

As darkness fell, rain pelted the chugging Narcissus while she snaked the oil barge from the pool and bucketed it across the inner harbor, but within the Narcissus it was warm and cozy, and Annie, with a comfortable cargo of beans, sauerkraut and frankfurters, golden fried potatoes, fresh bread, another section or two of flaky raisin pie and three cups of fragrant coffee stowed within her hold, was happy. She'd had her first bout with Bullwinkle and given him more than he'd bargained for, and having convinced herself that she honestly was not to blame for what had occurred, and hoping that Severn—if he heard of it—would regard it in the same forgiving light, she was content. She delivered the oil barge to its destination, picked up two dead barges and conveyed them to the pool, then telephoned the office from the shanty on the pool dock.

Severn was mildly elated. "Got another job for you, Annie," he said breezily. "You know the Justine—that big wooden car barge of the Transcontinental and West Coast Railroad? Well, she's gone aground on Foss Island with twenty loaded boxcars on board."

Annie was derisive. "How could she? There's deep water almost all around the island, and there ain't been much wind."

"She hit a deadhead and it rammed a big hole in her. She began to sink, so the tug's master—Red Halloran, of the Firefly, it was—pushed her ashore quick. He needs help to get her off when repairs are made, and the insurance underwriters phoned me. Now get up there soon's you can, Annie. There's no immediate danger, but the wind's blowing up a bit, and if she isn't snaked off soon, it's liable to push her right on the beach, to stay."

"Okay, Alec, I'll yank her off!" promised Annie briskly, and hustled back to the Narcissus.

The pipeline was once more in position, and a string of red lights crossed the fairway, shining like splintered jewels through the rain, as the Narcissus, bucking the rising wind on her return trip, swung once more into the South Waterway. Annie's eyes puckered a little with worry as she hauled down on the whistle cord and the raucous hoot gave warning to the Salamander to move the dredge. Bullwinkle's silhouette appeared briefly against the light within as he opened his pilothouse door. But having seen that it was only the Narcissus, he went inside again, closing the door with an audible slam.

Annie said things behind her teeth, and repeated the signal. No response. She ran the Narcissus alongside the high bank and, with considerable difficulty and much expenditure of wind and temper, climbed to the top and made her way past the dredge to where the Salamander lay, separated from the channel bank by two or three floating logs, so that she could not climb down.

Oilskins glistening and rain streaming from her red, angry face, she cupped her mouth and yelled, "He-ey, Bullwinkle!"

After what seemed an interminable time, the pilothouse door on the shoreward side opened and Mr. Bullwinkle thrust out his bullethead.

"Hey, you rat-eared coffin robber!" bawled Annie, desperately. "Get that pipeline out o' my way or I'll——"

"Was that someone cryin' on us?" asked Jake with mild curiosity.

Mr. Bullwinkle shook his head. "Only a jackass brayin', somewhere over on the bank. Voice sounds familiar at that. Ho-o-hum!" He yawned elaborately and looked at the dripping sky. "Sure is a wet night."

The door closed.

Tugboat Annie, tears of fury mingling with the raindrops that coursed down her cheeks, stamped back to the Narcissus, slid down the bank and on board, and again took the wheel as the tug's nose straightened out for the boom. She gave Big Sam the jingle, and the tug's powerful engines responded in an irresistible rush—irresistible, that is, until she had smacked the pipeline head-on at a hose connection as before, snapped it and gone through. Then something went wrong. With a shivering tremor that rattled the entire tug, her impetuous way was checked, then stopped. And simultaneously hundreds of gallons of stinking water and liquid mud splashed pilothouse and deckhouse with filth and began to pour into the Narcissus from the severed pipeline.

Thrown nearly from her feet by the sudden shock, Annie recovered and raced out on deck, to be spattered instantly from head to foot with evil-smelling slime, splashing over from the viscous flood that was rapidly filling the Narcissus's newly overhauled innards.

"Oh, the louse! The dirty man! It's Bullwinkle! He's stretched a hawser along the pipeline!" she yelled.

She grabbed an ax from the fire-hose bracket and ran below and forward, struggling through the river of mud that sluiced nearly knee-high across the deck. Then leaning far over the bow she hacked at the thick wet hemp hawser that held them back. It parted, and once again the Narcissus leaped forward, the broken pipe spewing a farewell cataract as she surged through.

And as the Narcissus, her propeller shaft turning in thick slime, painfully resumed her voyage, she was followed into the gloom and the rain by the raucous jeering laughter of Mr. Bullwinkle and his friend Jake.

Useless now, to think of going to the rescue of the car barge. With three feet of mud and water in the engine room, the galley and saloon swamped, and the tug looking, from water line to the top of the pilothouse, like some disreputable garbage that had been dredged from the festering ooze of the ocean floor, it was all the Narcissus could do to limp home.

Alec Severn was at the dock when the Narcissus skulked alongside and made fast, and his eyes grew wide with amazement, then narrowed, as he took in her doleful plight. Determined to get it over with quickly, Annie clumped down the ladder and climbed to the dock to meet him.

"Gosh, Alec," she said, forcing a chuckle. "We had the dangdest time."

"So I see," said her employer grimly, glaring from her clay-plastered face to the equally unlovely Narcissus. "What happened?"

"Well, when we got into the South Waterway, Bullwinkle——"

"Bullwinkle?" His chin set. "You've been fighting with Bullwinkle again?"

"Yeah. But——"

"I see." He looked at her squarely. "You know what this means, of course."

"But, Alec——" Annie began miserably.

Obdurately, he shook his head. "I told you before you left. One slip and——Well, you're out. At the end of the month."

It cost five hundred dollars and three days of back-breaking labor and a lot of lost business before the Narcissus was again her shining, efficient self; and Annie's spirits, as she moped dejectedly about, superintending the job, were not improved by echoes of the titanic laughter which rocked Secoma's waterfront at her expense. Horatio Bullwinkle's account of the affair lost nothing in his vivid and skillful telling; and the situation further was aggravated for Annie by her rival's triumphant proximity, for, the dredge-tending job completed, the Salamander had returned to her old berth on the opposite side of the Narcissus's slip.

"Nothin' like a beauty bath and a mud pack to make an old battle-ax look purty," Mr. Bullwinkle chortled on the morning when, her refurbishing completed, the Narcissus again was ready to work; but beyond heaving at him, with praiseworthy accuracy, an open can of red paint, she was too wrought up over her own misfortunes to reply.

"Guess I'm gettin' too old and cantankerous to even fight no more," she confided morosely to the chromoed likeness of her departed spouse, when she had sought the refuge of her cabin. "Mebbe if you hadn't guzzled yerself into the ground, ye big bum, ye'd be here now, God forbid, to help me out o' these conundrums!"

She yanked off her hat, pushed her blowsy hair irritably from her face and was about to fling herself on her bunk, when the dispatcher called from the top of the office steps:

"Annie! Come up here! Alec wants you!"

The call was relayed by Shiftless from the deck below, and

reluctantly Annie obeyed. Since the night of the debacle there had been a coolness between Severn and herself which no simulated camaraderie of Annie's could dispel.

Severn was seated behind his desk when she entered, and he waved her to a chair.

"It's about that car barge," he said with cold abruptness. "Her sinking's snarled up the whole railroad freight service to Port Angeles and Port Townsend, and the company's going crazy. The insurance people are calling for bids to salvage her and we're entering a bid for the job."

"What's her position?" Annie asked.

"That's what you're going up to find out. I hear she's slipped and settled on rocky bottom. That means she's pretty badly strained. And you know what outside pressure does to the caulking in the v-shaped grooves of those wooden scows. The tides are running in and out of her like a sieve."

Annie thought hard. "I'd say, speakin' left-handed, it'll need derricks to lift them cars off, and what wid floatin' the barge and takin' the boxcars to the railroad connectin' apron and all, it's a ten-day job at least. Prob'ly more." Then recollection smote her, and she colored up. "I—I—Alec——" she stammered awkwardly. "Me-me month'll be up afore then. D'ye spose, if I done good work on this job, ye could lemme—lemme——"

"No, Annie." Severn avoided her eyes, plucked at his blotter. He went on, not unkindly: "You had your chance, and you let me down. With the hole you put me in, I've got to go to San Francisco tonight to raise some money, so we can finance this job if we get it. No, at the end of the month you're through."

"Okay, Alec." Annie swallowed the lump that had arisen so often these last few days in her throat. "I don't know's I blame ye."

She got up, walked to the window and looked down at the Narcissus, noting mentally that the Salamander had left the slip and was surging north across the now bright waters of the bay. When she had got hold of herself a bit, she turned back into the room, rubbed her hands and gave a rather pallid imitation of her usual cheerfulness.

"When do I leave?" she asked.

"The bids have to be in by nine tomorrow morning, so you'd better go right away."

It was mid-afternoon when the Narcissus, rounding a point fragrant with thickly ranked firs, came upon the scene of the stranding. The sunken Justine, her upper half showing, lay about a hundred feet offshore, beaten by the slow lazy roll of the seam which surged against her defeated sides in a smother of creamy foam and sluiced in and out of her opened seams with the ebb and flood of the tide. The weather had turned fair, however, and Annie knew that soon the water would be smooth as glass.

First it would be necessary to remove the cars with derricks. This would allow the wooden barge to float, and she could be towed to an even bottom, which would pull her plans or framework back into place. With the leaking seams recalked, she could be pumped out and taken to the dry-dock.

It was a straight, matter-of-fact job, but a lengthy and laborious one, and this opinion was concurred in by the masters of half a dozen rival tugs which fussed around sizing up the situation for the same purpose as herself. And prominent and vociferous among them was Captain Horatio Bullwinkle.

"Ye know," he confided to Henpeck Brown of the Pelican, his voice booming with unnecessary loudness over the water, "Severn ought to be ashamed to bid on this job. If Annie'd been tendin' to her knittin' 'stead o' playin' pranks in the South Waterway the other night, the Justine wouldn't need salvagin'! What's more," he ended triumphantly, "I'm goin' to tell that to the underwriters."

He cast a malicious eye Annie-ward to see how she was taking it, but that chastened mariner, fighting down with noble self-control the impulse to send her Narcissus crashing through the Salamander's sleek and arrogant side, pretended not to hear him, and set her course back to Secoma, with Bullwinkle, in his Salamander, following a derisive hundred yards astern.

Back in Secoma, instead of proceeding directly to the company's office, Annie visited numerous friends among the divers, calkers, chandlers and ship's carpenters of the port. She placed the salvage problem squarely before each in turn, and from the information about prices thus obtained, and adding the rental of floating derricks, which from long experience she already knew, she was able to form an accurate estimate of what the rival tugboat companies' respective bids would be. Thus armed, and with the addition of a scrap of gossip picked up on the T. & W. C. Railroad apron at dockside, she returned to the company wharf.

Mr. Bullwinkle was sitting outside his pilothouse, chair tilted back, his little black shoe-button eyes fixed upon her with malicious enjoyment as she trudged across the tracks.

"If ye're figgerin' on biddin' on that salvage business, Mrs. Cow," he remarked with a grin, when she drew abeam, "ye can forget it. I've as good as got it right now. It's in the bag."

"Keep talkin', prattle puss!" rejoined Annie. "Mebbe it'll make ye forget ye ain't got no brains."

"I don't need none when I'm dealin' with you," he retorted; but Annie, disdaining further repartee—since she could not think of any—climbed ponderously up the office steps and entered.

Annie's employer greeted the sum of her investigations with an approving grunt and a slight relaxation of his aloofness, and something of their old-time intimacy crept over them as they figured their bid.

"The job'll cost between thirteen thousand and fourteen thousand, five hundred," Severn remarked, sitting back and surveying the figures. "There's none of the rest will bid below twenty thousand, because"—he added a touch of irony—"none of them need money as badly as we do. Suppose we bid the bare maximum cost, plus thirty percent. Say eighteen thousand, five hundred."

Annie shook her head. "You gotta make surer than that," she said. "Do it for cost. Fourteen thousand, five hundred."

"But that doesn't give us any profit!" Severn protested. He sat back and stared at her. "Are you crazy?"

"Sure, crazy like an ox! Listen, Alec." She leaned forward and excitement crept into her lowered voice: "The railroad freight agent down at the apron's a friend o' mine, and he telled me the road's sore as hell at Halloran's company fer pilin' up the Justine, so they're cancelin' their towin' contract."

"What of it?"

"Don't be so dumb! Whoever does this salvage job quickest and cheapest is likely to pick up that towin' contract as well. Mebbe we don't make no profit from the salvage, but that towin' contract means twenty-five thousand a year. Ain't that worth a gamble?"

"By golly, you're right!" Severn rose excitedly from his desk, slammed his hand down on it. "Annie, we've just got to get this salvage job!"

"Don't worry, Alec. Wid a price like that we can't miss. Even Bullwinkle, the—the"—she met his eye and swallowed—"the dear sweet feller, wouldn't dare match that!"

"I hope you're right." Severn crumpled the penciled notes he had made and threw them in the basket. He sat down again. "You'll have to represent me tomorrow morning up in the underwriters' offices, when the bids are opened. I'll leave you power of attorney, as usual. And when you get up there, mind your manners. J.J. Pendleton is going to be there——"

"What?" Annie was impressed. "Not the big railroad pontoon?"

Severn nodded. "He's vice-president of the T.&W.C. Railroad. This stranding's disorganized their whole Puget Sound system and he'll be pretty touchy. So talk civil to him."

"I'll take him up on me lap and pat him, if ye say the word," said Annie. "When'll ye be back?"

"I don't know, Annie. But if we get the job, Jerry Bacon'll handle it with the Narcissus, and you can take over the Daffodil until—" He stopped abruptly.

"I know—until the last o' the month. Don't spare me feelin's, Alec." Annie got up. "Well, I'll not let ye down this time."

Unhappily, Severn watched her broad back as she waddled slowly to the door and went out. Then he shrugged with irritable self-impatience. "Damn me for a sentimental fool!" he muttered aloud, then banged his desk. "No, sir! I'm not going to weaken this time!" he swore, and summoned his secretary while he dictated the car-salvage bid.

Shortly after dark, with Severn on the southbound train and Annie, in her cabin on the Narcissus, contemplating, with what cheer she could muster, a singularly bleak and frightening future, Mr. Bullwinkle's pal Jake drifted over to the Narcissus's wharf, where, engaging in conversation with the night watchman, he invited that perpetually arid individual across the tracks for a drink.

Severn's dispatcher was in the Daffodil's galley, having a mug-up and a chat with the cook; so Mr. Bullwinkle also moved, by a cautious and involved route, around the dock and behind Severn's private office. A ladder, previously spotted, gave him access to a window, which he gently forced.

Ten minutes later he was back in his cabin, where, behind drawn curtains, he spilled from his shirt onto the table the booty he had removed from Severn's wastepaper basket.

"Now," he grunted with deep satisfaction as he spread the papers flat and sat down for expert perusal of their penciled figures and notations, "we'll see what we'll see!"

Shortly thereafter, looking somewhat puzzled, but complacent, he drew pen and pencil toward him and began rapidly to write.

Annie, who had been kept awake most of the night by the rats of worry that gnawed unceasingly at her mind, was early on deck, and watching a telegraph messenger boy who kicked his way down the dock. He stopped and glanced up at her, and she looked with interest upon his impudently engaging face.

"Ye know, sonny," she told him amiably, "if ye had a few more freckles a pusson'd take ye for a palmetto."

"Never mind the wisecracks, missus," he replied with a grin. "You Tugboat Annie Brennan?"

"That's me, ye sassy little sculpin!" she grinned back. "What of it?"

"For you!" he said, and handed up a telegram.

She tore upon the envelope and scanned the message within. Then: "Oh, my! Oh, my, I don't believe it! I—I— Shif'less! Go fetch me me horn-brimmed specks!" she cried. "No, never mind! C'mere! I kin read it! Listen! It's a tellygram what Alec sent from Klamath Falls this mornin'!"

Shaking with jubilant excitement, she grasped her deckhand's arm till he winced, and read aloud:

DEAR ANNIE RECONSIDERED DECISION STOP IF WE GET JUSTINE SALVAGE YOU KEEP YOUR JOB STOP IF NOT YOU'RE THROUGH STOP REGARDS ALEC

She hopped up and down in an ecstasy of relief. "Ain't that great?" she chortled. "I'm stoppin' on the Narcissus!"

"If we get the job, Annie," Shiftless reminded her, rubbing his arm.

"'Course we'll get it, ye silly goat! How dare ye— Where's me hat? Get me coat! I'm goin' ashore right now and make sure!"

In a dither of excitement she rushed into her cabin, threw on her shoregoing finery, crowned herself with her ancient hat, its feather jiggling in a delirium of triumph, and bustled ashore, performing, as she crossed the tracks, a ponderous measure of the mazurka. "Oh-h, happy days is here some more!" she chanted, and tramped gaily up the hill.

Representatives of the competing tugboat companies, including Bullwinkle, looking singularly pleased, were already assembled in the big board room of the Underwriters' Association, when she arrived, panting but confident, and took her place. The chairman looked at her.

"What name, please?" he asked.

"Tugboat Annie Brennan, o' the Deep-Sea Towin' and Salvage Company—and take that smirk off yer ugly puss, Bullwinkle, afore I slap it off!" she replied in one breath.

The gentlemen present exchanged startled looks. Then the chairman indicated a quiet, gray-haired man at one end of the long table.

"This is Mr. Pendleton, vice-president of the Transcontinental and West Coast Railroad—er—Captain Brennan," he introduced, and Tugboat Annie's feather dipped a gay acknowledgment.

"How-de-do, sir. . . . I'm all ready, gents," she said happily, and settled back in her seat.

The chairman, with the sheaf of bids before him, leisurely slit the first envelope and extracted the contents.

"Rainier Tug and Barge, twenty-one thousand, four hundred and twenty dollars and ten days," he announced, and laid it aside. "Northwest Towboats, Incorporated——"

He droned on, all the bids approximating between $20,000 and $23,000, with an almost unanimous time stipulation of ten days. Then he opened the Deep-Sea Towing and Salvage Company bid, and Annie squirmed with pleased anticipation in her chair.

This is more like it," the chairman commented. "Fourteen thousand, five hundred dollars and ten days." He looked across at Annie's glowing, triumphant face. "You mean this, Mrs.—er—Captain Brennan?"

"It's in black and white, ain't it?" Annie asked, grinning, and got to her feet. "Now, if ye'll just make out the contract, so we can get started——"

"Just a moment!" They turned at the cool, demanding tone of Horatio Bullwinkle. "You ain't opened my bid yet!"

"Your bid?" Annie snorted scornfully, but a sudden chill of unease crept through her brain. "These gents'll be lucky to get outa here wid the gold fillin's still in their pouts!"

"Keep your big mouth outa this!" chided Mr. Bullwinkle. He turned to the chairman. "Are you goin' to open my bid?"

The chairman picked up the envelope—the last on the table—opened it and glanced at the contents. Then he turned to the room.

"Tug Salamander, Incorporated, Horatio Bullwinkle, owner and master, bids fourteen thousand, four hundred—one hundred dollars less than the best previous offer. Time, ten days."

For a moment Tugboat Annie could not move. She was speechless, stunned. Gone, her fine dreams, her renewed hope; and as the black shadow of a jobless future once more enveloped her, the blood drained slowly from her mastiff face, drawing with it the last of her happiness and leaving only a grim white mask of fury. Slowly she turned, and meeting Bullwinkle's triumphant and insolent grin, she lumbered menacingly toward him, doubling back her sleeves.

"Put up yer dooks, Bullwinkle!" she roared. "You found out what our bid was and double-crossed us, you swivel-eyed scupper rat! Put up yer dooks and step out here! I'm goin' to give ye the lickin' o' yer life!"

She made a sudden lethal rush at him, its success hindered by the hard interposed bodies of the tugboat skippers present, most of whom were her friends.

"Here, quit it, Annie!" Henpeck Brown panted, struggling with her wildly flailing arm.

"Quit nothin'! I'm goin' to tear his head off and use it fer a anchor!"

"Not now, Annie! Not in here!" pleaded the husky master of the Rosy B. "Wait till ye get back to the waterfront! Then ye can drownd him if ye like!"

"Drownd him?" yelled Annie, struggling furiously. "Hell and hardtack! Ye couldn't drownd him! That big wooden head o' his'd swell bigger'n it is now and keep him afloat! No, sir! I'll——"

Suddenly, miraculously, she ceased fighting. Her arms dropped to her sides, and slowly the dawning light of an idea suffused her fury-blanched face. "Wa-ait a minute!" She looked dazedly around at them. "By jabers, I believe I've got an idear!"

Uncertainly they released her and drew back, watching, while she stood alone in the middle of the room, almost audibly thinking. Then she snapped her fingers and turned to Pendleton.

"You're vice-president of the road?" she asked.

"I am," he said stiffly. "And I must say this whole affair is most——"

"Sure, sure!" Annie interrupted impatiently. "Sure it is! But 'twas all me fun! Listen. How bad do ye want the Justine refloated?"

"Don't stand there asking damn silly questions!" Pendleton snapped. "Her sinking's tied up our whole Sound system and the delay's costing us thousands a day! It's time, not money, that counts with us."

"That makes it just dandy, then," beamed Annie. "If you'll give me this contract, I'll guarantee to get that car barge afloat, pump her out, make temporary repairs and deliver the boxcars to the railroad apron in twenty-four hours!"

There was a roar of incredulous protest from every tugboat man present.

"Don't you pay no attention to her; she's loony! She always was!" shouted Bullwinkle excitedly.

"Wait a minute," said Pendleton, who, meanwhile, had been attentively studying Annie's flushed, bulldog and undeniably capable face. "Perhaps she has an idea."

The chairman snorted. "The thing's ridiculous, sir! It's absolutely impossible, and I think it's only fair to award the job to Captain Bullwinkle. He's not a crackpot theorist, nor——"

"No, he's only the biggest crook unstrung!" put in Annie vehemently, and again addressed herself to Pendleton.

"Look here, mister. I'll even go ye one better. I'll complete the job in less than twenty-four hours!"

"Now I know she's nuts!" howled Henpeck Brown, but Annie turned on him in a fury.

"How long've ye knowed me—fifteen years?" she demanded fiercely. Henpeck nodded. "And did ye ever once, in all that time, know me to say I'd do a thing I didn't do?"

"No, Annie," he confessed. "I never did."

"That's that, then!" she rumbled, and turned again to Pendleton. "I'm in charge o' the company whiles me boss, Alec Severn, is in Frisco, and I'll stake our biggest tug, the Narcissus—and she's worth a hundred thousand dollars in the water today—against this job! If I'm successful, ye pay me fourteen thousand, five hundred, same as me original bid, plus one thousand for every hour under the twenty-four that I complete it in, plus yer towin' contract! And if I ain't off the job at the end o' twenty-four hours, all ye lose is that time, and ye can keep the tug. Now, am I talkin' turkey?"

"You certainly are," said Pendleton. "I'll accept that offer, if the underwriters have no further objection—and I wish you luck!"

Tugboat Annie breathed deeply, and her face was grim as she looked around the room. "Get yer lawyers in," she said. "I'm itchin' to go! ... And as for you"—she turned to Bullwinkle—"this is one time I'll show you somethin', my fine fettle!"

Late that evening, when Alec Severn arrived at his San Francisco hotel, he found waiting for him a panicky wire from his secretary, outlining the details of Annie's mad bargain.

Immediately, on the thin rim of apoplexy, he bombarded Annie with frantic wires, addressed to his office, the text of them varying from "You're fired!" to "I'll have you shut up in an asylum!"

These feverish communications resulting in no reply, he telephoned, to be told by his trembling-voiced secretary that Annie was not there.

"Where the hell is she, then?" he demanded furiously.

The secretary was not sure, she told him shakily. All she knew was that Annie had departed for points north at noon that day, with the Narcissus, the Daffodil and two scowloads of sawdust.

Groaning, he hung up the receiver, only to lift it a minute later and charter a plane.

Fog grounded them at Portland, so by the time he got home and hired a boat, daylight was well advanced.

Too worried even to taste the steaming coffee prepared for him, Severn slumped in a chair outside the pilothouse, oblivious of the raw, chill morning air, and alternating desperate reflections on a bankrupt business and a ruined life with more comforting visions of the punishment that he intended to mete out to his demented employee.

Time passed. The little vessel puttered along, and Severn, in a fit of violent shivering, started back to awareness that fatigue had conquered him and he had fallen asleep.

It was broad day. The fog was thinning, the sun trying to thrust its pearl-pink rays through the blanketing mist, and Severn stood up and yawned, shuddered convulsively and began dully to think of nourishment. He turned, his hand on the handle of the pilothouse door, then stopped dead, listening. Yes, there it was again—that vague, far sound, carrying through the dripping fog; the sound that had awakened him from his uneasy slumber and that he had attributed to the imaginings of an overtaxed and nightmarish brain. The sound of singing—Tugboat Annie singing, raucously and off key as always, her favorite song:

"Happy days is here some more! Oh-h, happy days is here some more!"

Severn turned, his white-knuckled hand gripping the rail as he peered ahead, anger rumbling volcanolike within him, trying to pierce the swirling opaqueness before him.

A vagrant wind arose, blowing the fog aside, thinning it. And slowly, as a pattern comes upon clouded glass when light strikes through, the shape of the Narcissus took form, showing ever plainer through the dissolving mist ahead. And alongside her, made fast with stout hawsers, was a giant rectangular shape, slapping playfully over the waves as it responded to the powerful forward thrust of the tug; a shape with the large painted letters T.&W.C.R.R. on its housing—the shape, unbelievable and miraculous, of the car barge Justine, with twenty loaded boxcars borne lightly in her water-free hull.

Even as he watched, he heard again the rolling lift of Tugboat Annie's song, and that doughty skipper herself appeared, hair blowing in the morning wind, cheeks whipped red and shining in the cold morning air, as she walked energetically around in front of the pilothouse, chest out, full of life and vigor and energy, and happy as a forest full of larks.

Almost immediately she saw the oncoming vessel, and her glad hail came booming over the water.

"Hi, there, Alec! Why, ye old alligator, what brings you here?" she chortled. . . . "Hey, Peter, wait a minute!" Bells jingled in the Narcissus's depths, and she glided almost to a halt, the smaller vessel swept in a graceful curve alongside and Severn jumped to the tug's deck.

He swayed with mingled fatigue and relief, and she stepped forward with quick concern, an anxious hand on his arm. "Are ye all right, Alec?" she asked.

"Barring a touch of apoplexy, heart failure, exhaustion and general cussedness," he assured her testily, "there's not a thing wrong. What I want to know is how the devil did you work this miracle?"

"Oh, there's more ways than one o' skinnin' a dead cat," she told him airily. "I had a bit of a rumpus wid Bullwinkle—the monkey's orphan!—and somethin' I telled him about that big wooden head o' his swellin' if it was dunked give me an idear."

"Will you talk sense?" Severn demanded impatiently.

"I am, ain't I? It reminded me that wet wood allus swells," she replied indignantly. "So I took the Narcissus and the Daffodil and two scowloads o' sawdust and went up to the wreck. It was smooth water, so I moored the sawdust scows alongside the Justine, and the rest was easy as a bump on a log."

"Maybe it's me that's stupid," Severn grunted. "Go on."

"Well, I put the Narcissus's hose inside the barge and begun pumpin' out, while the Daffodil's hose washed them tons o' sawdust outa the scows around the car barge. The suction pulled the sawdust into her seams and swelled 'em tight, and when I'd pumped enough water out, she riz outa the water like a balloon, boxcars and all. And here we are!"

"Yes," said Severn deeply, "here you are."

"We'll have the cars on the apron at six this mornin'—six hours under contract, at a extra thousand a hour, and the towin' contract is ours to boot," she crowed jubilantly. "Ain't that somethin'? Oh, wouldn't I love to see Bullwinkle's ugly mug when he hears tell o' this!" In the exuberance of her feelings she broke into a happy bellow, "Oh-h, happy days is here some more; oh, happy days is here some more! ... Say, Alec——"

"What, Annie?"

"Could I ax a favor of ye?"

"What is it?"

"Well, the other night when I was ashore I seen somethin' in a joolry store what kinda took me fancy. And if ye could mebbe let me have a teeny advance on me pay — It ain't expensive, but——"

"I'll buy it for you, Annie," Severn told her. "What was it?"

"Wait till ye see it!" Annie exclaimed, her shining eyes upraised in blissful anticipation. "It's a beautiful grindstone brooch!"

TUGBOAT ANNIE SAWS OFF A LEG

The morning breeze, fresh with the tang of pines and the sea, blew down the strait, dissipated the thin mist that veiled the innumerable green gems of islands, whispered hello to the deep-water tug Narcissus, Tugboat Annie Brennan master, as it chugged prosaically across the rimpled blue floor, filched an added fragrance of breakfast coffee and broiling bacon from her galley, and meandered on. And Tugboat Annie herself, after setting the tug's nose for French Frigate Point, turned the wheel over to Shiftless, the deck hand. "Now mind the course, whiles I'm below eatin' me combustibles," she warned, "and don't go writin' yer name in the wake, or I'll bump yer thick head together!"

Her appetite sharpened by the smell of cooking as she stepped out on deck, she filled her big chest, rubbed her hands, forgot the problem that had been haunting her since the previous day and clumped down the ladder to the messroom.

"Oh, was that you eatin'?" she said with a grin, to Big Sam, the engineer, who had already started his breakfast. "Be the sound o' the chompin', I thought it was a horse!"

Tugboat Annie sat down in high good humor, and Pinto, the cook, brought her a plate that was heaped with fried eggs, crisp bacon and cottage-fried potatoes, together with hot rolls, honey, strawberry jam, a butter-drooling stack of golden toast and a large cup of coffee. Fifteen minutes later, halfway through her second plateful, she looked across at Sam, her mastiff face creased with puzzled vexation.

"What's the matter wid you this mornin', Sam?" she asked. "Ye ain't spoke a single verb since I sat down."

He looked bovinely across at her. "I been thinkin'," he said with a note of somber pride.

"Oh, well, in that case——" Her voice was solicitous. "Ye mustn't give that noggin' o' yours more'n one chore at a time. What was ye thinkin' of?"

"Oh, of all them repairs to be made down below, and no money to do 'em with, since Alec's so set on puttin' the Pansy and the Hyacinth back in commission fust. And where he's goin' to find the money for that——"

"That's why we're up here seein' Ole Olesen, ain't it?" she asked with some acerbity. "To dig that twenty-two-hundred-dollar towin' bill he owes us out of him."

"Dig is right! Gettin' money outta Ole's like openin' a drum o' fuel oil with a toothpick."

Annie pretended a confidence she did not feel. "He's gotta pay, Sam. He's owed us nearly a year now."

"And if he says 'no,' then what? Alec won't take him to court, 'cause he won't git no more of his towin' business. Ye can ask him, Annie, but he'll just look at ye wi' them fish eyes o' his——"

Annie pushed her fourth egg irritably with her fork. "Hell and hardtack!" she roared. "Ye've sp'iled me breakfast wid yer gloomin'!" She lapped up the egg, polished off another roll or two and heaved herself regretfully from the table. "Mebbe if I tapped Ole's noodle wid a spanner," she ventured, "and got him to sign a check whiles he was subconscious——"

"That hard head o' his 'ud break the spanner," said Sam.

When Annie regained the deck, her mind again busy with the problem of Ole, the tug was entering Deep Sound—a long arm of the sea that thrust itself, rimmed by a forest of dark giant pines and wrapped in primeval stillness, far into the heart of the great peninsula. The water was an unblemished sheet of indigo glass, disturbed only by the Narcissus's gently hissing bow wave, the silence broken only by her softly panting diesels, as she swung around the point. A flock of cormorants passed in lovely, effortless flight across the bows, and in the distance the mighty snow-capped pinnacles of the Olympic Range glittered frostily in the pure air. It was a morning for exhilaration, optimism, a quickening of the blood, but Annie experienced none of these as she tramped the deck, while the Narcissus bored deeper into the silence of the sound.

At about ten o'clock a jet of steam against the dark pines of the far shore indicated human activity, and the tug's nose swung over. Presently she was sweeping in a rippling curve alongside the wharf of a small logging village at the mouth of a swift-flowing river. All around were rafts and log booms; millions of board feet of scarred forest veterans that had been cut and floated down in the spring drive; and even as the Narcissus came alongside, another magnificent spate of logs swept into view around the river's curve and into the protected rafting pockets where pond monkeys in their sharp-calked boots poled them into booms.

Annie's expert eye automatically was measuring the cut as the Narcissus was made fast, and her heavy face lightened a little. She went into her cabin, crammed her old felt hat determinedly onto her untidy head, shook her fist with mock warning at the blarneying chromo of Captain Terry, her departed husband, in its oval plush-and-gold frame, and stepped ashore.

She barged into the offices of the Deep Sound Logging Company.

"Hi, Johnny, ye ol' brush cat!" she boomed at the chief clerk. "Where's that skimflint boss o' yours?"

"What do you want him for, Annie?"

"Ye'd never guess," she told him sardonically. "We only been billin' ye once a month for the last nine months."

"Oh, that! Well, he's up at Camp Two, or in the woods beyond, with the crews. And listen, Annie"—he leaned confidentially over the counter—"keep your hair on. He's been kind of sour this last week or two."

"I ain't been feelin' too sugary meself," Annie told him, "so we'll get along just elegant. Camp Two, did ye say?"

He nodded. "I'll send you up on a speeder. You might have to walk a piece though."

Annie did. After the gas car had deposited her at railhead, she trudged through nearly three miles of heavy mud that clung to her skirt and balled constantly under her flat-heeled shoes; but somehow she did not mind it, for in the dim cathedral arches of the forest the dew still jeweled the leaves, and the fresh earthy smell of the mold underfoot, the resinous scent of pines, and the schools of salmon swimming lazily in amber pools beneath snowy cascades of the tributary streams soothed and heartened her.

Presently she heard the puffing of donkey engines, the shrill signals of the whistle punks, the clatter of tractors, and the long-drawn warning cry of "Timber-r-r!" as a forest Goliath crashed and filled the air with dust and widow-makers. Then, abruptly, as she rounded a curve in the boggy trail, the colorful activity of the loggers was spread before her.

The crews were logging across a narrow valley, and the steel cables of the high-line skidder brought the forest giants crashing through the smaller growth to the setting, there to be bucked into logs and sent down the rollways into the river. But it was all old stuff to Annie, and her eyes swept around for Olesen. She found him presently, superintending the topping of a lofty head spar; and even before she addressed him, she was reminded, by the driving force of him, and the way the men jumped to obey, that he was a formidable figure with whom to deal.

Annie came up behind him, and indefinably was aware, even though he did not turn, that he knew she was there. She coughed genteelly. No result. She coughed again, significantly; but still his gaze remained upturned to the lofty treetop. Annie, after a third abortive whoop, lost patience.

"Hey, Ole! What do I have to do—tear me bellers adrift afore ye'll notice me?" she snapped.

He turned, tall, paunchy, broad-shouldered, with a shock of yellow hair, and his eyes, set in a broad, high-cheekboned face, were chips of blue ice. "*Ach*, it's you?" he said indifferently, and turned again to watch his men. This, Annie felt, with a sudden sinking of the heart, was going to be more difficult even than she had anticipated.

"Sure it's me," she said, with an attempt at playfulness. "Who did ye think it was—the Queen o' Turkey?"

He turned again; surveyed her phlegmatically. "How did you get up here?" he demanded.

"Why, be the speeder——" she began, but he interrupted.

"Ay ban charge you fifty cents," Olesen said, and extended his hand toward Tugboat Annie.

Annie stared. "B-but——"

"Fifty cents," he repeated inexorably. "Ve ain't carrying no deadheads on our road."

"Well, I'll be——"

"*Ja*, but it's fifty cents yust the same!"

Boiling inwardly she dug down and handed him fifty cents, which he pocketed without comment, and once more turned away. Red-faced, she waddled aggressively around and confronted him.

"Looka here, ye aggravatin' feller," she rumbled. "I didn't come all the way up here to look at yer back, so let's get down to brass knuckles!"

"What is it ye want?" he said.

"Twenty-two hundred bucks, what ye've owed us fer nine months fer——"

"Can't pay it," he said calmly.

"Can't pay it?" she echoed incredulously. "Why, I ain't never heard such hokey-pokey! Ye've cut over twenty million feet this spring."

"And ain't sold a foot of it!" he returned coolly. "And the way things look yust now, I ain't a-goin' to. How'm I goin' to pay bills and make a little profit if the mills ain't buyin'?"

"What's been holdin' up yer sales? Surely ye can sell logs like them."

His eyes lit with cold fires. "Sure, a leedle here, a leedle there, but dat ain't the vay I do business. For the last five years I've sold all I could cut to Bob Anderson, of the Port Orcas Lumber Mill. Know him?"

"Yeah, a little. He's a pretty close trader."

"He's a shark—a robber," said Ole flatly. "Yust because I did him a little on price last year, now he does me a dirty trick. Lettin' me t'ink he vas goin' to buy my full cut, so I turned down a coople good other offers. And now he writes me the lumber market's fell off and his ponds is full of enough logs for four months ahead and he can't buy mine. And my note fallin' due at the bank next veek."

"Yeah," agreed Annie diplomatically. "That is kinda tough."

"He's bluffin' because he don't vant to pay my price. Plenty o' logs! His mill cuts two hundert t'ousand feet a day, so how the hell could he have plenty logs dis time o' year?"

"He's prob'ly picked 'em up on the quiet, here an' there. How much ye askin' fer yours?"

"Twenty-two dollars a t'ousand feet."

Annie's mouth pursed. "That's pretty high."

"For the best logs on the sound?"

"Yeah, they're that all right. But ye could shave that price a dollar or two and still make a nice profit."

"After I pay off the bank, where's the profit?"

"That reminds me," said Annie brightly. "About that bill ye owe us——"

"If ye keep vorryin' me about dat, I'll take my towin' business someveres else. There's a feller named Bullvinkle, vit' a fine tug——"

"Now, now! Don't git yer tail in a uproar!" soothed Annie hastily. "Mebbe there's some other way——"

"The only vay you'll get your money outta me," he told her dispassionately, "is if I sell my logs to Anderson."

"At your price, huh?"

"At my price!"

Annie, thus left high and dry, sat on a stump and thought furiously, but to no purpose. Ole was good for the money eventually, but "eventually" did not settle current bills. Still, if she could get him to acknowledge the debt in the form of a note, perhaps Severn could get some ready cash on it by selling it at a discount. It was worth a try, so she waddled back to him. "Lookit, Ole," she said. "If ye'd give me a note fer what ye owe, mebbe I could help ye sell yer logs. I could——"

"You needn't bother. I'm coming out in four-five days to see for myself."

"But won't ye just put the debt in writin'?"

He took out a tin of snoose; stuffed a pinch in each nostril, snuffed it up, and dusted his hands. "My vord's enough. You can take it or lump it!" he said flatly and turned away.

Only by tremendous effort was Annie able to control the unruly epithets that crowded her tongue. Swallowing hard, her bulldog face purple with rage, and muttering wildly to herself, she commenced the long backward trail toward railhead. She had gone but a few yards, however, when Olesen's voice recalled her. With a quick flash of hope, she tramped back to him. His cold little eyes surveyed her.

"You goin' back now?" he asked. She nodded.

"It's a long valk," he said. "Fourteen miles."

"What?" Surprise overcame even the dashing of her optimism. "Why, it's only a coupla miles to railhead. Then I'll take the speeder——"

He held out his hand. "That'll be another fifty cents," he said.

Annie's indignation was at white heat, and it was not till the Narcissus was well out into Puget Sound and headed south for Secoma that she recovered her composure sufficiently to retail her encounter with Olesen in coherent form.

"Well, what do ye think then, Annie?" asked Peter, the mate, shifting his cud. "Has Anderson really got plenty of logs? If he has, Ole's in a spot, all right."

"Pshaw!" Annie exploded irritably. "Mill men is all liars when they're dealin' wid a logger in the spring and don't want him to know how bad they need logs! And Anderson's even foxier than most. He might have had a pond full o' logs when he wrote to Ole and then again mebbe he ain't. Anyways," she concluded, "we'll see what Alec has to say."

What Alec Severn, her employer, had to say was very much to the point, when Annie faced him that evening across his desk.

"You keep your nose out of it, Annie," he warned her, when she had explained the situation and expressed her desire to check up on Anderson's stock of logs. "If Olesen's coming down in a few days, he'll find out for himself. Then, if Anderson buys his logs, we'll get paid."

"Yeah, when he's good and ready! And we can't wait that long, Alec! There's two or three good towin' jobs comin' along, and we're gonna need them other tugs in commission, as well as repairs on the Narcissus."

"You don't have to remind me!" he said morosely.

"And all I want is one teeny little peek into Anderson's log pockets. It's only a short run over to Port Orcas, Alec."

"Those mill men resent any snooping around their ponds! Some of that towing business we hope to get is Anderson's, remember, and we can't afford to get him sore at us. Forget it, Annie. I'll find money some other way."

But forgetting, for Annie, was impossible as long as there was an unanswered question in her mind. She worried about it all that night, and the following morning she again faced Severn across his desk. But this time she was tight-lipped and grimly determined.

"I'm goin' across to have a look at Anderson's mill today," she announced bluntly.

Severn sat bolt upright. "I told you yesterday——"

"I'm goin'," said Annie stubbornly.

"Not in one of my tugs, you're not!"

"Okay then. Gimme the day off and I'll go be ferry."

"You're not going at all, I tell you!" Severn stormed. "Your job's to run the Narcissus and obey my orders, and leave the business end to me!" He glared at her, his usually good-humored face choleric with worry and resentment.

"Listen to me, ye red-faced little sprat!" said Annie, growing angry in turn. "Mebbe you are runnin' the business, but I'm runnin' the Narcissus, as ye just telled me, and she can't go around no longer the way she is, widout them repairs. So I'm goin' over there if I hafta walk, swim or fly; and if I make a mess of it, ye can do yer bellyachin' after I git back."

The building shook as her heavy feet pounded down the outside stairs, and a minute later Severn watched, with angry eyes, as the Narcissus cast off and pulled out of the slip.

The curving conformation of the harbor of Port Orcas, Anderson's private milling hamlet across the sound, was such that as Annie approached in her Narcissus, it was impossible for her to see any of the mill's log pockets or ponds; and since a log boom was drawn across the mouth of the waterway to prevent the logs within from being sucked out by the tides, it was not feasible for her boldly to run up and have a look.

So, trusting to providence and the luck of the Brennans, she made the tug fast to the town wharf and walked across to the mill.

TUGBOAT ANNIE SAWS OFF A LEG

The big plant was working full blast, the great saws screaming, steam whistling and puffing, and huge transporter cranes running about the yards, when Annie entered the main office and, staking everything on a frank interview with Anderson, requested to see him.

"Have you an appointment?" asked the switchboard girl.

"No, young leddy, I ain't. But it's about a towin' job."

"Just a moment, please."

The reply was prompt. Mr. Anderson was much too busy to see anyone. Annie shrugged dispiritedly. It was impossible for her to enter the yard gates without a pass, and beyond nosing about outside the high board fence around the plant, there seemed nothing she could do. Then desperation struck from the flint of her obstinacy the spark of an idea. She again approached the information desk and whispered genteelly.

The girl nodded, smiled. "Certainly," she said. "Along that hall. The third door to the left."

Annie thanked her meekly and proceeded along the hall, past the third door, the fourth and the fifth, till she came to a stair leading upward. This she followed, and in due time reached the stockroom. Then, guided only by instinct, she crossed the room, calmly disregarding the interested stares of the employees, and at length waddled over the covered bridge that led into the mill itself. Without hesitation, weaving between the glittering saws and shuttling carriages, she crossed to the water side for a look into the ponds which she knew would lie below.

She reached a high-silled window, craned and peered over. Then, "Oh-oh!" she said deeply to herself, and looked again. The expansive ponds and pockets spread below generously reflected the golden glitter of the waning sun—too generously; for that expanse of placid water, which should, according to Anderson's letter to Olesen, have been covered with millions of board feet of logs, housed little beyond one big raft, or boom, and the reflection of the sky.

"How much did Ole say they cut here?" Annie calculated rapidly to herself. "Two hundred thousand feet a day?" Again her expert eye measured the logs below, and inwardly she whistled. "Why, he's hardly got enough here for a week, let alone the four months he was braggin' to Ole about!" This meant, she thought jubilantly, that Anderson would have to buy Olesen's logs and Severn would get paid after all. She was stretching her massive body for one final verifying peek when a harsh voice behind her froze her rigid. "Hey!" it rasped, loud above the noise of the biting saws. "What the hell are you doing there?"

Stricken, Annie turned to look into the thin, grim face and blazing eyes of Anderson, owner of the mill.

"Why—why, hello, Bob," she stammered lamely. "I—I thought mebbe some day I'd need me a wooden leg, so I was jest lookin' yer lumber over. An' then I—then you—Well, well!" She shook her blowsy head in astonishment. "If this ain't a coincidink!"

He said no further word; simply gripped her arm in iron fingers and dragged her away and across the mill to his office. He faced her there, tense and angry. "Now then," he snapped. "Come clean! What's the idea?"

"Well, I'll tell ye," she said haltingly. "I was up seein' Ole Olesen yesterday, and——"

"Oh, so that's it!"

"Yeah. He owes us twenty-two hundred dollars fer towin'."

"Just a minute. That reminds me." He buzzed for his secretary. "If we get any towing bids from the Deep-Sea Towing and Salvage Company in the future, throw 'em out!" he ordered, and turned back to Annie. "Go on," he said grimly.

Annie gulped, driving her heart still further down toward her boots.

"So he—he told me he'd had a letter from you, that ye had logs enough for all summer, and if ye didn't buy his, he couldn't pay us. So——"

"So he sent you here to spy on us, and now you'll go back to report and get paid off. Is that right?"

"No, it ain't right, ye scrawny catapult! All I wanted to know was what chances we had o' gettin' our bill paid, that's all!" Her anger at his insinuation rose. "And I gotta mind to fetch ye a good kick in the pants!"

"You mean," he asked incredulously, "you're not going to——"

"——to tell Ole you ain't hardly got a log to bless yerself wid, and is just tryin' to outbluff him and git his logs cheap? No, I am not! . . . Least," she amended shrewdly, seeing his thin lips relax, "I wasn't till you begun to git tough. After all," she concluded loftily, "if we ain't goin' to git no more business from you, why should I start gettin' big-hearted?"

"Sit down a minute," he said abruptly; and he sank into his own chair, folded his hands and looked at her.

"I suppose there's no use trying to disguise from you that——"

"No, there ain't," she said bluntly. "There ain't enough logs in them pockets to more'n last the week out."

"And you'll give me your word you're not working for Olesen?"

"Sa-ay!" She began to rise from her chair, but he waved her back.

"All right, all right! I may as well tell you, then. Olesen's a hard, shifty customer, and I'm in a jam. I've got orders for lumber for months in advance, and I need Olesen's logs. But he wants too much for them. That's why I bluffed him about having all I needed for the summer. But he don't bluff easily. He hung out longer than I figured he would."

"And now ye can't buy logs anywheres else, so ye're out on a leg and he's goin' to saw it off."

"Not quite. He doesn't know yet."

"But he will. He's comin' down here in a few days."

Anderson was startled, and showed it.

"Ye can't keep it from him," Annie went on placidly. "He'll ask to go through the mill to see how yer present stuff's cuttin'. It's the custom; and if ye refuse, he'll know then, for sure, ye was bluffin'."

Anderson groaned audibly. "Then how the devil am I going to get out of it without paying through the nose? When he finds out the fix I'm in, he'll jack his price higher still!"

"Why ask me?" said Annie indifferently. "I got nothin' to do with it. Anyways, I hope ye do have to buy 'em, 'cause that's the only way he'll pay us. Come to think of it, I don't see why I shouldn't tell him the spot ye're in now. You ain't been so nice to me. Now have you?"

"Listen, Annie——"

"Oh, it's 'Annie' now, is it?" she retorted, beginning to enjoy herself. "Not so long ago——"

He pressed the buzzer. "Miss Burns," he said, when his secretary responded, "cancel that order about the Deep-Sea Towing and Salvage Company bids. Make sure they come to my desk marked for my special attention."

The girl withdrew, dazed, and Annie grinned. "That's better," she grunted. "Now we're pals. Though I still dunno how I can help ye."

"All I ask is that you don't say anything to Olesen," he assured her. "I'll have to figure some way out. Will you promise?"

"Yeah, I'll promise. Allus the softhearted booby, that's me!" She crossed to the door. "An' if I have any brain waves I'll let ye know—at a fair price, o' course. Well"—she opened the door—"don't take no nickel nutmegs."

On the way back across the sound, Annie pondered the problem anew, and not even the blistering dressing down she received from Severn for her insubordination could dent the shell of her mental concentration.

"I've a mind to fire you!" he barked. "I——"

"Hold your tongue, Alec!" she reproved impatiently. "How do ye expect me to think?" She shook herself angrily. "There now! I had an idear almost in me head and that big bazoo o' yours blowed it right out!"

Still angry, but knowing from long experience that nothing could move her in this mood, and that the most surprising consequences might come of it, he subsided, and Annie lumbered thoughtfully back to the Narcissus, tripping over objects on the wharf as she went. She gobbled her supper in deep cogitation, absentmindedly eating, in her abstraction, Shiftless's wedge of pie and almost forgetting to consume her own.

After supper she drifted like a ruminative hippopotamus to the upper deck and sat outside the pilothouse in a tilted chair, where she contemplated, almost unseeing, the winking harbor beacons, the blazing reflections of passing ferries over the black water, and the more intimate, restless heaving and shifting of orange crates, boxes, paper, grapefruit rinds and sticks under the wharf light, as the changing tide filled the slip with debris, drew it out and pushed it back again.

Passing her hand over her aching brow, she dismissed for a few seconds the puzzle that beset her, to watch, with idle interest, a swirling mass of close-packed driftwood as the tide pushed it compactly into a corner of the slip.

She looked away, and when her gaze returned, the mass had moved, drifting with the secret currents toward the channel, and leaving clear the patch of shining water that but a minute or two before had been covered. Then, as her eyes caught the flotsam's slow but inexorable return, the solution that had been tap-tapping at her brain crystallized in a thought that drew together all the tangled threads of speculation, and stunned her with its simplicity and common sense.

Her chair legs hit the deck with a thump, and she hoicked in excited, bumbling progress across the wharf toward the company office. She rushed in, upsetting the night dispatcher, who was reading with his feet on the desk.

"The tellyphone, quick!" she panted. "Git me Bob Anderson over at Port Orcas! Hustle, will ye, Tom? Oh, my! I never seen such a stoge-poach!" She beat his back in a tattoo of impatience. "Hurry up!"

Anderson, who was about to go home to a belated dinner, after hours of fruitless wrestling with his problem, felt a quick uplift of hope when he heard her thrill-charged voice.

"What is it, Annie?" he asked, his own voice sharp with anticipation. "Have you got something?"

"What'd ye think I called ye fer—to tell ye a bedlam story?" she replied with merry excitement. "Where are ye?"

"In my office, you fool!" he snapped. "Where do you think you were calling me?"

"Thass so! I forgot! Now look, pal. Don't stir hide nor pelt till I get there!"

"But, Annie——"

The telephone clicked.

An hour later she barged into Anderson's office, her vast frame quivering like a horse of war whose nostrils are full of the jubilant scent of battle.

"I got it!" she exulted. "He's out on the leg now, an' I'm gonna saw it off!"

"Who is?" he demanded, shaking her. "Calm down and tell me about it!"

"Who is? Why, Ole, o' course—the fish-eyed haddock! But listen; ye got to tell him he's got to pay up what he owes us first, or ye don't buy his logs!"

He sat back, suddenly disappointed and utterly spent. "What are you talking about?" he demanded. "Did you come across here and keep me from my dinner just to talk about your confounded towing bill?"

"O' course!" she said. "But that's only part of it. The rest comes next!"

He summoned patience. "Let's get this straight," he said wearily. "Do I understand you have a scheme to make Ole sell me his logs?"

"Certainly! That's what——"

"At whose price?"

"Why, yours, o' course! That's what I'm tryin' to tell ye. He's in the bag, wid the ends tied up!"

"Would it be too much if I asked you to tell me how you propose to do it?"

"It would," she said promptly. "I got the idear all right, but I ain't givin' it to ye fer nothin'. I seen enough o' the way you and Ole chisel each other for me to make sure I ain't goin' to be squoze between ye like a nutcracker. Not"—she grinned complacently—"that I ain't a pretty hard nut. Where's a pen and paper?"

He shoved writing materials toward her. She sat at his desk, and her capable business brain subdued her bubbling spirits as, coldly and clearly, she detailed her terms. "There ye are," she said, when she had done, and passed the paper over to him.

He read with mounting color, and when he had finished, he

looked up; repeated the astounding details in a thick, choked voice:

"First, I'm to collect that towing bill of twenty-two hundred dollars he owes your company. Right?"

"Right!" Annie agreed heartily. "Otherwise, ye don't buy!"

"Second, you want a ten percent commission on any resale I may make of surplus Olesen logs. Right?"

"Sure. Lumber's bound to rise when summer construction begins. That clause should bring me in about six thousand bucks. Go on; read the next! I can hardly wait!"

"Third, I'm to award the contract for towing Olesen's logs down to this mill to your company. Right?"

"It'll be a two-month job," said Annie blissfully, "and it'll take three of our tugs. A nice stroke o' business, if I do say it meself!"

"Fourth, I'm to advance all expenses incurred by you in putting over this scheme. 'Said expenses' "—he consulted the paper—" 'not to exceed fifteen hundred dollars; costs over that sum to be borne by the Deep-Sea Towing and Salvage Company,' or, if less, the difference to be kept by you. Right?"

"Ye read fine," Annie said admiringly. "Well, what do ye say?"

"I say you're crazy!" he shouted, with sudden passion, rising to his feet. "Do you think I'm going to turn my company into a damn collection agency for you and submit to a highbinder's contract like that on the strength of some insane scheme you haven't even told me about? I ought to boot you right out of here!"

"Go ahead," she told him calmly. "But don't forget; at the same time ye'll be bootin' out the only chance ye've got o' lickin' Olesen. And if ye'll trouble to read that paper again, ye'll see there's a qualifyin' clause that reads ye're only bound by this contract 'providin', within the limits of Olesen's visit to you, he sells ye his full spring cut o' logs at a price that you shall name.' They ain't much of a gamble in that, that I can see! And as for the advance, ye can allus sue us and collect."

He calmed down. Yes, that had escaped him, and it did put a better complexion on things.

"How are you going to work it?" he asked heavily.

She handed him the pen and indicated a space at the bottom of the paper. "On the spotted line fust, pal," she said jocosely.

Reluctantly, slowly, and after further careful scanning of the document, he affixed his signature and handed it across. She folded it and tucked it in her shirt front. "Now the check for expenses," she reminded him.

He made it out and gave it to her. She put it away and sat back, beaming. "Whoosh! I feel better!" she told him. "Now we can really get down to business. Fust thing ye do is wire Olesen to come down here day after tomorrer and look over yer ponds."

"That's a swell start," he said disgustedly. "One look and he'll know he's got me!"

"Mebbe," said Annie. "But I'm gonna be here when he does stick his ugly puss outta them winders! It'll even up a little for what I had to take off'n him yesterday!"

"I hope you're right! What else?"

"Nothin'." Annie got up. "Just get Olesen down here. Ye can leave the rest to me! . . . Oh, I near forgot. Kin I use yer telly-phone?"

"Help yourself," Anderson told her.

He lighted a cigar and leaned back, listening idly, while she called her first number. Then, as he heard question and answer, his eyes bulged and became fixed, his cigar cold and forgotten; and for an hour he sat, fascinated, while Tugboat Annie, wheedling, coaxing, bribing, even mildly threatening, but mainly gaining her way through rowdy but good-humored repartee, made call after call. And gradually, listening, his stiffness and unease dissolved, his eyes crinkled, as, bit by bit, her plan progressed. Then when she had done and, standing, looked at him, her tired face expanding into a wide exultant grin, he gave way to gales of helpless, cackling laughter.

Mr. Olesen, attired in the stiff blue serge of his city best, responded with cold alacrity to Anderson's invitation to come to Port Orcas. He could not quite understand his rival's initiative in asking him down, but put it down to the other's acknowledgement that Ole had called his bluff. The icy light of triumph in his eyes was heightened when he left the ferry landing and walked toward the Port Orcas Mill, for its accustomed activity was subdued, almost stilled. This could mean but one thing. His informants had been right, and production was curtailed for lack of logs. The game was entirely in his own hands.

His first intimation that all might not be what it seemed occurred when, after being ushered into Anderson's office, his chilly gaze fell upon the broad, good-humored countenance of Tugboat Annie.

"Hi, froze-face!" she greeted him affably; but he ignored her and turned to Anderson, who was seated at his desk. "Ay ban in hurry to get to Secoma for some supplies," he stated without preamble. "So if you vant my logs, say so."

"Logs?" said Anderson ingenuously. "Who said I wanted your logs?"

A faint angry flush dyed Ole's high cheekbones. "I got no time for yoking," he said coldly.

"I'm not joking." Anderson shook his head, puzzled. "I told you in my letter that I didn't need——"

"Is dat so?" interrupted Ole calmly. "Then why are ye nearly closed down?"

"That's the lumber business for you," replied Anderson with sad disgust. "You get all stocked up with logs, then the bottom drops out of the construction market and you're stuck, with no place to sell 'em. I was hoping maybe you could advise me what to do."

Something unpleasant clutched Olesen's inside, and his small eyes bit into his adversary's face; but he saw there only a sorrowful graph of adverse business conditions. He swung from Anderson to Annie, but her mahogany countenance was blandly innocent. The logger's knuckles whitened. He smelled a trick, but could not fathom it.

"You're lyin'!" he rasped. "You ain't got logs enough for——"

Anderson sighed at such stupidity. "Have a look, then," he said, and gestured indifferently at the window.

In what seemed a single stride, the logger was at the window, staring down, and Annie and the mill man joined him as his shocked and incredulous eyes swept over the mill pockets and ponds, every nook of them bursting with huge pine logs. Logs everywhere, packed so tightly together and ranging so far that they seemed countless, endless; more logs than Olesen had ever before seen at one mill.

"Well?" said Anderson quietly at his elbow.

Feeling slightly ill, Olesen turned back into the room and stared wordlessly at each in turn. His mouth opened to speak, but no words came.

"Would ye like a sup o' water?" Annie asked solicitously, but Olesen's hard eyes snapped at her a look so savage that even she momentarily was quelled.

He started for the door, and for one quick, apprehensive moment Annie and her partner feared that they had lost him. But business is business and Mr. Olesen still had twenty-four million feet of logs on his hands and a thumping loan due at the bank. He turned, one hand on the knob, and Anderson, knowing they had won, lighted a cigar with a flame that trembled a bit.

"Okay," said Ole dully. "What'll you give me for my cut?"

"I just told you," said Anderson. "I'm not buying."

"Tventy-vun fifty a t'ousand feet?" suggested Ole desperately.

"Don't be silly," said Anderson.

"Tventy-vun?"

"I better be gettin' along, pal," said Annie briskly to Anderson, "seein' ye won't be doin' no business today."

Ole glared at her. "Tventy?" he said.

"M-m-m. We-ell——" Anderson appeared reluctantly to deliberate.

"Make it nineteen——"

"——fifty!" cut in Olesen.

"Nineteen, and not a cent more!" said Anderson with finality. "Mind, I don't really need your logs, so you can——"

"——take it or lump it!" supplied Annie with some relish, remembering where she had last heard the phrase.

Again he favored her with his malevolent stare, then turned to Anderson.

"It's a deal," he said sourly. "But you've got to take the lot."

"That's okay," Anderson replied indifferently, and rang for his secretary. She brought in the contract already prepared, and her employer handed it to the logger.

Ole read it, and as he perused the first clause, the pink crept once more into his cheekbones.

"What's this about payin' dat fat cow tventy-two hunnert dollars?" he rasped.

"It's what ye owe me, ye horse's tail!" snapped Annie. "And if ye don't pay it, ye don't sell yer logs. . . .That right, pal?"

"That's right," Anderson confirmed. He turned to Olesen. "Annie's company is handling my towing now, and they'll need a little capital to get those logs of yours down here."

For a full minute the other deliberated, but the temptation to get out from under was too great, and reluctantly he stretched out his hand for a pen.

When the contract was signed and witnessed and notarized, Anderson deposited it in his wall safe and turned to Tugboat Annie.

"Well, I guess that's it, pal," he grinned. "You can tell 'em to go home now."

Annie stepped to the window and, pleasurably aware of Olesen's baleful eyes upon her, stood full in view from the ponds below and waved both her big arms. Immediately they heard the sound of chugging diesels. Anderson joined her.

With quick suspicion Olesen also crossed the room and looked out, just in time to see the Narcissus, the Pansy and the Daffodil, of the Deep-Sea Towing and Salvage fleet, swing into the ponds, pick up the tow lines of the three huge log rafts and begin slowly to chug away.

"Hey, what's this?" Ole yelled, his smoldering suspicions bursting into angry flame. "Where are they takin' dem logs?"

"Why"—Annie turned to him, her beaming physiognomy the picture of artless candor—"they're takin' 'em back where they belong."

"You mean"—Olesen turned on Anderson, his bony face drained white with fury—"you don't own 'em?"

"Course not," Annie cut in, her voice rich with innocent surprise. "He never said he did. Them ponds out there looked kinda bare widout logs, and we wanted ye to feel at home, so we rented or borrered 'em two nights ago from every mill in Secoma—and now, o'course, we gotta tow 'em back."

Oblivious of the logger's tongue-tied rage, she turned to Anderson. "Well, pal," she said, "I gotta be sashayin' along. . . .Oh, an' by the way"—she again addressed Olesen, with the utmost good humor—"if ye want to ride wid me back to Secoma, I'll be glad to oblige. It'll cost ye fifty cents."

TUGBOAT ANNIE WINS HER MEDAL

Evening descended like a silken, star-spangled blue veil over the coast of Southern California as the big ocean-going tug Narcissus, flagship of the Deep-Sea Towing and Salvage Company, of Secoma, Washington, under propulsion of her powerful diesels and with a large, new and heavily laden steel oil barge in tow, chuffed steadily out through the gap in the San Pedro breakwater and swung her weathered-hemp bow fender on the long course for Puget Sound and home.

The Narcissus was still in her variegated war paint of greens and browns and blues, for, though the war was over, the need for prosaic, workaday sea commerce such as she so unromantically represented had not slackened with the coming of peace and reconversion, and there had not been time to lay her up long enough to metamorphose her back to the red deckhouse, black hull and yellow funnel which had become famous in all the Northwest ports before the war.

Astern, the early lights of San Pedro, Wilmington and Long Beach blinked over the calm, shining tide, and the broad harbor was crammed with the gray fighting shapes of anchored battleships, cruisers, destroyers, giant carriers and transports, home once more from the slugging agony of beating into submission one of the most fanatically warlike nations upon earth.

Up in her cabin, which formed the after end of the pilothouse, Tugboat Annie Brennan, master of the Narcissus and for many years senior captain of the Deep-Sea Towing and Salvage fleet, sat at her table, checking over the paperwork in connection with the voyage, that she had been too busy otherwise to attend to in port. And as she worked, wetting the stub of a much-chewed pencil, her broad nostrils appreciatively sniffed and her mastiff face lifted in lively anticipation to savory odors from the galley below, where Pinto, the cook, was preparing a succulent supper of richly nourishing vegetable soup, crisply grilled lamb chops, mashed potatoes with lashings of gravy, fresh garden peas, mint sauce, hot biscuits and syrup-dripping deep-dish apple pie.

"Oh, my; oh, me!" exclaimed Annie to herself, and pushed her blowsy hair back under the aged and battered felt hat she wore at sea. "What I ain't goin' to do to all them elegant combustibles!" And so, relishing her happy dream of nutriment to come, and humming contentedly to herself her favorite song, "Happy days is here some more," she bent her shaggy head again to her work.

With Point Firmin light blinking its message of homecoming cheer far off on the starboard quarter, and night gathering in, Annie was still hard at it, when suddenly the nerve-shattering roar of the Narcissus's siren jerked her head up again. "What's that fool Shif'less up to now?" she demanded, mentally cuffing the gangling deck hand at the wheel. "Is the skinny wagabone soundin' off to keep his lazy carcass awake? Or——"

Again the siren hooted, but Annie now realized that this was no casual rules-of-the-road warning or letting off of exuberant spirits which sometimes, among tugboat folk, was a reflection of too much spirits within. No, there was about this enthusiastic shattering of her concentration a note of triumph, of greeting, of congratulation for a job well done.

Leaving the table, Annie waddled hastily to the window, and when she saw and understood, the heart beneath her capacious though none too tidy gray flannel shirt swelled with appreciative approval, for there, not two hundred yards off, and answering the tug's brazen-voiced greeting with jets of steam and sound from her giant whistle valve, was passing a great Army transport, crammed to the rails with cheering masses of Khaki-clad troops—a converted liner returning to the shores of home the battle-worn veterans of Guadalcanal, Saipan, Tarawa, Iwo Jima and all hot points north, south and west.

And viewing this shipload of triumphant youth, and reflecting suddenly upon the thousands like them who had been left in their lonely Pacific island graves and for whom the lights of home would shine no more, Tugboat Annie's weather-lozenged throat constricted, her sympathetic eyes misted suddenly, and she found herself reaching for a handkerchief and matching the joyous sirens of the two vessels with sonorous trumpetings of her own.

She watched until the surge of white foam beneath the transport's bow and the long, sleek, high-tiered length of her had slid past; then she returned to the table, sniffling. "Must 'a' ketched a cold someplace," she told herself mendaciously, but as she sat down again her eyes encountered the hand-tinted likeness of her long-defunct helpmeet, Captain Terry, as he ogled down at her with impudent boldness and a smirk on his mustachioed mouth from his plush-and-gold oval frame.

"Go on, stare at me, ye drunken old divil!" she murmured in fond abuse. "Well ye know what I'm thinkin'! Yes, the time you come home to me after the last war. You was young then, ye naughty ratscallion, and so was I. And when they let ye out o' the brig and I sobered ye up, we had a bingo!" Her big head waggled and a grin crept over her face as she remembered the details of that rambunctious and faintly disgraceful but glorious celebration.

To what further extent her sentimental musings might have carried her was forever lost, however, in the sudden clamorous ringing of the supper bell; and Annie, ever alert to postpone the nebulous for the practical, jumped up, shoved her papers tidily in order, and descended, with further happy sniffings, to the deck below.

The lighted cabin, with its air of good cheer, and the healthy, weather-beaten faces of her shipmates around the well-laden table, drove from her mind the last faint traces of her recent nostalgia, and as she sat down and tucked her napkin into her neck, she was garrulous and beaming and in great fettle.

"Ain't it great?" she chortled. "All them boys comin' home after fightin' the Nutzies and the Japs? Peter"—she addressed the solemnly munching mate of the Narcissus—"you was out in Japan. Is it true the Japanese women ain't got no toes—only a big toe and a foot?"

"Naw!" said Peter. "It's the socks they wear. Like our mittens."

"That explains it, then," said Annie complacently. "No wonder they got queer ideas, wearin' mittens on their feet!" She tittered massively. "What else do they do—put their nightgowns on their heads and sleep in their hats?"

Peter having expounded to them the wonders of Japan and his own considerable and hair-raising experiences transporting fighting troops onto the invasion beaches of the South Pacific, the conversation turned upon the war generally, but presently Big Sam, the phlegmatic and slow-thinking engineer of the Narcissus, noticed that Annie, from having sparked the discussion, seemed now sunk in a glum reverie, with but little to say. He turned to her.

"What's wrong, Annie?" he asked solicitously, a load of mashed potatoes and gravy suspended expertly on his knife. "Got the dyspepsia? Time was when you could stow away double that cargo o' vittles an'——"

"Yeah! 'Time was!' That's it!" she answered morosely. "Why good-fer-nothin' hooligans like you was born men, and me a woman, I'll never know!"

"It's nature, Annie, you can't go agin it," Peter comforted her, but she was not to be appeased.

" 'Member when the war broke out?" she demanded. "And I axed the Navy to take me—me, that knows ships and the sea like the inside o' me hat? 'Ye're a woman,' they says! Then, later, when they started takin' women, what happened? 'Ye're too old,' they says! Too old fer the Wacs an' the Waves an' the Spuds——"

"The Spars, Annie," corrected Pinto, the cook, entering with another heaped-up platter from the galley.

"Whatever they was, God bless 'em!" said Annie. "And keep yer big pout outa this, Pinto! Jest because you was cook on a curvette—"

"Corvette, Annie."

"Hell and hardtack!" roared Annie, thoroughly aroused now. "I was so far outa the war I don't even know the lingo!"

"I dunno's I'd call what you done 'out of it,' Annie," said Peter slowly. "Ye took the Narcissus around to Boston, then across to London, even before we was in it, an' that was right in the middle of the Battle of the Atlantic. Was that fun?"

"We-ll," admitted Annie reluctantly, "it wasn't no Mexican sleighride. But——"

"An' what about towin' that torpedoed English cruiser from Murmansk to Yarmouth?" supplemented Big Sam warmly. "Ye said yourself that when one bomb landed, it blew the Narcissus so far outa water a seagull flew under her keel!"

"Not forgetting," put in Clem, the tug's radio operator, "that time later on when the Japs chased you out of Attu only one jump ahead of a salvo, and if it hadn't ha' been for the fog——"

"Sure!" said Annie disparagingly. "Sure, I was bummed and torpedoed and shot at! So what? I drew good merchant-service pay and a bonus for every hour I put in, didn't I? But that ain't fightin' is it? Why, in all that time I never as much as fired a peep shooter! But any one o' you fellers, every one o' them kids comin' home, has got a right to call hisself a American! And all I can call meself is a wore-out old sculpin they wouldn't trust to skipper a Navy scow! It"—her big fists clenched and her usually good-humored face was congested with rage—"it makes me blood bristle jest to think of it!"

"But even Bullwinkle had trouble gettin' into the service——" began Hank, the other deck hand, a husky young ex-gunner's mate, but at mention of her detested business rival of prewar days, Annie interrupted with a hamlike fist on the table that made the dishes tremble.

"That's what I mean!" she thundered. "The big bilge creeper! He fit the Coast Guard once, years ago when he was a rumrunner! But in 1941, which he talked 'em into believin' all them cases o' booze clumb aboard his schooner by theirselves when he was takin' a sea v'yage fer his health, they even took him. An' made him a lieutenant, no less!"

"He's a commander now, Annie," Peter volunteered. "I met him ashore at Wilmington. That was his ship—the big Coast Guard cutter that was here off Long Beach. An' by the way, he said to give you his regards."

"Hmmph! Is that the way he put it?" demanded Annie skeptically.

"We-ell, just about."

"Go on," said Annie grimly. "What did he say?"

"He said," went on Peter reluctantly, "to tell ye to keep the home fires burnin', an'—now don't get mad, Annie!—an' if you had to stoke 'em wi' some of that excess tallow o' yours, it was all right by him."

"Impident widget!" growled Annie. "When's he gettin' out?"

"Next month. And he's headin' straight back for Secoma."

"But I heard his Salamander was sunk at Wake!" said Annie, startled.

"She was, but the Government's givin' him a better one. He's callin' her the Salamander too."

Clem chuckled. "The waterfront sure will pop when he gets back!" he prophesied. "All the towing business we get with him around, we'll have to take with a shotgun in the dark of the moon!"

He grinned; then, suddenly catching Annie's lethal eye, he was abruptly solemn. Annie got up.

"If ye know any more bad news," she told them sourly, "ye can make yer own nightmares wid it! . . . No," she added to Pinto, who was coming in with the dessert, "I lost me appetite fer pie! That is"—she reached out and helped herself to a generous slab and a hunk of sharp yellow cheese—"Well, mebbe one teeny piece." And demolishing a half of it with one exasperated bite, she climbed heavily topside to relieve Shiftless at the wheel.

Night closed in, and while the Narcissus with her tow surged peaceably on her way, with her running lights sparkling emerald and ruby and topaz over the smoothly heaving bosom of the sea, another vessel about forty miles away, the 14,000-ton combination cargo-

and-passenger vessel City of Bangor, crammed to capacity with jubilantly celebrating veterans of the Pacific fighting, was clipping off her steady sixteen knots, inward bound from Saipan. Cigarettes glowed in a myriad sparks as they crowded the decks and rails, chatting, singing, playing mouth organs, indulging in happy horseplay or just gazing ahead, eager for the first lights of home.

Then, abruptly, the quiet sea night was shattered by a stupendous explosion, and the fore part of the City of Bangor spouted upward in violent disintegration, to splash its debris over a wide area of the star-reflecting waters. Yells arose, and agonized screams, and disaster gongs clanged throughout the stricken vessel, while in the partially destroyed radio room frantic messages for help went out through the calm Pacific night: "Struck drifting mine . . . sinking forward . . . watch for rafts and boats," followed by the ship's position and urgent appeals to hurry.

In swift response, rescuing Navy and Coast Guard vessels sped from the harbors of San Pedro, Santa Barbara and San Diego, with other home-bound transports and fighting ships closing in. And while the City of Bangor slowly settled, there appeared above the surface a half mile away a long, slender piece of metal tubing from which a cowllike eye traversed a quadrant of the sea ahead and came to rest upon the crippled ship, which now shot gouts of flame from exploding ammunition lockers toward the stars. For minutes the periscope remained motionless; then, slowly, it disappeared beneath the smooth black water and only a faint and ever-widening circle of ripples showed where it had been.

In Annie's cabin, she and Peter were playing cards, with Big Sam earnestly and inexpertly kibitzing behind her. The radio was on, and beyond the subdued melody of shore music, the hiss of water along the Narcissus's rugged hull and Annie's labored mutterings as she tried to decide between discarding a five of spades or a seven of hearts, the room was quiet, the night at peace.

"No, Annie!" Big Sam protested earnestly as she started to draw the seven from her hand. "Don't spoil yer run of hearts!"

"Be the purple-starred Bull o' Bashan!" Annie roared. "He's ginned me twice wid you to help him, and us playin' fer a quarter of a cent a point!" She turned around, glaring. "Now will ye quit belchin' down me sarcophagus and go park that big fat starn o' yours over on the settee! An' turn the radio up. I want to hear the news."

Docilely, Big Sam complied; sat meekly on the settee, while directing yearning glances at the two sports, and twiddled the radio knobs. The volume swelled, and presently the staccato voice of a newscaster filled the cabin. It was Peter's deal, and while Annie's

TUGBOAT ANNIE WINS HER MEDAL

thick, clumsy fingers were arranging her cards, she sat back to listen.

"And here is the latest report," said the newscaster, "upon the sinking of the Army transport City of Bangor which, laden with homecoming veterans, struck a floating mine and went down about sixty miles off Point Firmin, at nine o'clock tonight."

Shocked to rigid attention, Annie and her shipmates stared at one another. "Why," said Annie, "that was jest an hour ago, whiles we was chuggin' along as peaceful as a flea on a pup! Listen!"

The radio reporter's voice was continuing: "First reports of heavy loss of life were modified, when it was learned that most on board were saved by the proximity of other inbound transports. But the anxiety of the Navy and Coast Guard lest there be other drifting messengers of death is increased by the fact that vessels crammed in every available space with our returning fighting men are coming into West Coast ports at the rate of thirty to fifty ships every twenty-four hours. To prevent a duplication——"

Suddenly the broadcaster broke off, and when he resumed, his tone was agitated, tense. "Attention, folks!" he rapped. "We've just had a flash"—his voice rose, almost hysterical with excitement—"that there have been two more sinkings, with probably heavy loss of life, within a mile of the first—a United States heavy cruiser of the Indianapolis class and the huge former passenger liner Australasia, inbound from Yokohama with more than three thousand troops on board. Both vessels went down while rescuing survivors of the City of Bangor, and it is authoritatively stated, based upon a message from the Australasia's master before she disappeared, that all three disasters were caused, not by floating mines, but by torpedoes launched from a giant Japanese submarine——"

"He's crazy!" Peter gasped. "The war's over!"

"Sh-h-h-h!" warned Annie tensely.

"——the commander of which, true to the grim and suicidal code of *Bushido*, is still carrying on his private war of extermination against the enemies of the Son of Heaven! A state of war emergency is again immediately being imposed on the California coast line south of Eureka, with total blackout orders being issued to ships at sea."

"Turn it off, Sam!" Annie snapped, lumbering to her feet....
"Peter, tell Clem to get the Coast Guard on his radio phone and ax fer instructions!"

But before Peter could get to the door, Clem stumbled in, face white, eyes staring. "Annie! Annie!" he stammered. "There's—I just heard a Navy shore station. There's ships bein' sunk and—and——"

"I know it!" said Annie forcibly. "Don't git yer tail in a uproar!

Keep calm!" She removed her hand of cards from the bosom of her shirt, into which, unaccountably, she had stuffed them. "What did they say?"

"Lights out, proceed in blackout, same as wartime!" said Clem. "Maintain total radio silence, both phone and otherwise! That's important, Annie! And the whole coast's been put in a state of war alert."

"Okay! Slap into it, you fellers!" said Annie promptly. "Sam, git down to the engine room and make sure everythin's runnin' smooth.... Peter, take over the wheel from Shif'less——Or no! I'll do that meself! There'll be no smokin' on deck an' no matches struck! Git movin'!"

She snapped out the cabin lights and, like a human hurricane, essayed to leave the cabin. But the gloom was punctuated by a sharp crack, followed by an explosive and agonized "Oof!"; then her suddenly belligerent voice howling, "Put up yer dooks like a man, consarn ye! Swat a leddy in the dark, would ye?" followed by the scuffle of hasty shadow-boxing.

"What is it, Annie? Who hit ye?" bellowed Big Sam, charging blindly to her rescue.

There was a small pause, a silence. Then: "Nobody," replied Annie with sheepish meekness. "I—I jest run into the door jamb."

With the lank dark blob of Shiftless up in the bows keeping lookout, and the other deck hand, Hank, performing a like duty on top of the wheelhouse, and Annie, with Big Sam for company, in the blacked-out wheelhouse, the Narcissus panted steadily up the coast. And as the night grew darker and the stars dwindled, the huge steel oil barge at the end of the towing wire astern, deep in the water with her enormous head, could no longer even faintly be seen.

Hours passed, but nothing was sighted except a lean-hulled destroyer which knifed suddenly out of the gloom, loomed briefly near to have a look at them, then went around on her heel like a dancer and slid, ghostlike, into the blackness to seaward. And gradually the tension of watching lessened, and Annie, one knee hooked over a wheel spoke, keeping the tug on its course, allowed her thoughts to wander.

"I'm gittin' mad, thinkin' o' that murderous yeller divil lurkin' out there somewheres, Sam!" she said, with an angry wave of her paw toward the invisible horizon. "What good does it do him, drowndin' our boys like that? This country's licked and the war's over! And when his fuel and ammunition's gone, he won't even be able to get home again!"

"I dunno, Annie." Big Sam wagged his stolid head. "But I've

heard the Japs sneaked in before the war an' hid big stores of ammunition and stuff among the Mexican sand dunes along the lower coast o' Baja California. And if he could get some fuel oil——"

"Yeah, but where?" asked Annie triumphantly. "When his tanks is empty, he's a gone goon!"

Sam broke the brief ensuing silence. "Be kind of a Christmas treat for him," he said slowly, "if he could pick up somethin' like our barge astern, Annie. He's got eight thousand barrels o' the last fuel oil on earth in her and——"

"Eight thousand bar'ls. Le's see," Annie figured mentally. "Forty-two gallon to the bar'l . . . three hundred and thirty-six thousand gallons. . . . Hey! don't go sayin' things like that, ye old coffin creeper! It gives me pimples big as doorknobs jest to think of it! Why, if he got ahold a that barge he could keep this coast in conniptions fer a year!"

"Well, he ain't got it," Big Sam replied comfortably, "an' he ain't likely to. Her freeboard's so low ye can hardly see her in daytime, much less at night. And it'll be light in another six hours and he won't dare show his nose. Hey, Annie! Ain't you listenin'?"

"Yeah. Go on talkin'. I want to think."

There was silence for perhaps ten minutes. Then Tugboat Annie's iron fist grabbed Big Sam's arm so tightly that he yelped. "Sam!" she said, and her voice was a hoarse, excited croak. "You heerd me soundin' off down below tonight, didn't ye?"

"Pretty hard to tell," he returned phlegmatically, "when you're soundin' off an' when you ain't."

"I mean about havin' done nothin' fer me country asides drawin' good pay in wartime, ye dolthead! An' this is kinda wartime all over again, ain't it?"

"I suppose——" he began dubiously.

"Okay! An' here's all our boys comin' home an' that bloody-minded feller settin' out there waitin' to blow up more ships, an' wonderin' how he can keep on blowin' 'em up! Am I right?"

"He's in a submarine, Annie. It ain't settin' on the surface."

"At night it is!" Annie's voice tensed a little more. "They allus runs on the surface, nights. An' I jest been thinkin' o' somethin' my Terry—God rest his rum-pickled hide—used to say. That ye don't ketch vinegar wid flies."

"Who wants to catch vinegar?" asked Sam practically.

"Don't take me so illiteral!" cried Annie, exasperated. "It's jest a old adverb, but it means somethin'!" She wagged her untidy head portentously. "It shore does! Sam, that Jap sub come a long way, didn't it?"

"From Japan. Any fool knows that."

"An' he prob'ly ain't got any too much fuel oil left."

"Look, Annie," said Big Sam uneasily, "when you get to talkin' like this, it generally means trouble ahead. Whyn't you just go turn in an' have a nice quiet little nap?"

"An' if," went on Annie impatiently, "he even smelled a chance to git some oil, he'd sprain his brain tryin', even if it meant takin' big chances. Do ye foller me?"

"No."

"Swell! Now I know me idear's good."

"Oh-oh!" groaned Big Sam. "She's got an idea! Oh-oh!"

"Look!" Annie suddenly was galvanized into action. "Go tell Hank to come and take over the wheel. You an' me's goin' places!"

"What places?" asked Big Sam, his uneasiness growing by the second.

"The engine room fust!" said Annie, with a large and satisfied grin. "An' we gotta work fast!"

Ten minutes later the Narcissus and her tow still were panting steadily on their course northward, but now from the tug's side poured a steady stream of fuel oil that spread in an ever-widening film as it disappeared into the darkness astern. Then the oil pump ceased, and Annie and Big Sam emerged from the engine room to the darkness of the deck, and Annie stumped hastily aft to look out over the counter at the black, oil-filmed water. And when the slick that she had created was lost in the night astern of them, she turned again to Big Sam.

"Get it?" she asked.

"No," said Big Sam again.

She shook her big shoulders irritably. "Ye're as dumb as I am!" Then, pointing astern, "That's me gift to the Jap sub."

"How far do ye think he's goin' to get on that?" demanded Sam scornfully. "Even if he could pick it up, which he can't."

"He'll git further perpendick'ler than forwards, I hope," replied Annie enigmatically. "Come on back to the wheelhouse. We'll keep agoin' fer another hour, so's to git well clear. Then we'll do what's next!"

The end of the hour, however, found her in her own cabin with the curtains tightly closed, figuring out her position from the coast. She jotted it down on a scrap of paper, glanced at the chronometer on the bulkhead, then, snapping out the light and with the scrap of paper in her hand, went rapidly along to the radio cabin.

Clem was at his set, listening intently to nothing. He looked up as she barged in, and shook his head. "H'llo, Annie," he greeted.

TUGBOAT ANNIE WINS HER MEDAL

"There ain't been a thing. I been listening. And——"

"Never mind," she told him briskly, and pointed to the radio telephone. "Git the Coast Guard wavelength at Wilmington an' call 'em!"

"Are you nuts?" He stared his amazement. "I told you the orders, Annie! Total radio silence, both standard and phone!"

Annie placed her fists on her broad hips and glowered suddenly, intimidatingly, down at him. "Who's skipper o' this home fer aged bilge rats?" she demanded.

"Why"—he stared uncertainly up at her—"why, you are. But——"

"And who gits shoved in the clinker if what I do ain't right?"

"You. But——"

She grinned broadly. "Okay, then! Do what I tell ye!"

Reluctantly, with trembling hands and quavering voice and a heart weak with misgiving over incurring the combined wrath of the Navy and the Coast Guard, he obeyed.

The Coast Guard operator at the base ashore jumped as though he had been poked with a red-hot wire, listened intently and incredulously to a loud and terrified female voice that had so unexpectedly blasted into his ears from somewhere out on the dark Pacific; then, panicky, he summoned his superior, a lieutenant, from his desk in the next room.

"There's some crazy woman breaking radio silence, sir!" he gasped. "Says she's on a tug off Santa Barbara and she's scared of that Jap submarine and wants to talk to Commander Bullwinkle!"

"Have you been drinking?" the officer demanded suspiciously. He grabbed the phone. "Hello. . . . What? . . . Who? . . . Look, I don't care who or what you are, madam! You're endangering yourself and every ship along the coast, breaking radio silence like this! . . . What? . . . No! You can't talk to Bullwinkle! You can't talk to anybody! . . . What's that? . . . But, woman, you mustn't do that! If that Jap commander found a barge full of——What? You'll do it unless you talk to Bullwinkle? Wait a minute."

He turned to the operator. "Get hold of Commander Bullwinkle! You'll find him at the briefing in the Operations Room! Tell him there's some maniac that calls herself Tugboat Annie raising hell on a tug off Santa Barbara, and she won't shut up for anybody but him! Ask him to come at once!"

Annie, sitting at the radio phone in Clem's small, cluttered cabin, waited, while Clem's white, scared face stared at her. "Happy days is here some more," she trolled discordantly, her big foot keeping time, "Oh-h-h, happy days is——Hello!" Suddenly she became alert, but her voice, as she spoke into the radio phone again, was trembling, charged with a fear that bordered on hysteria. "Oh, h-hello, Bullwinkle. Is—is this you? . . . W-well, how are you, ye——I—I mean, ye old ga-foozler! This is Tugboat Annie talkin'. I——"

At that well-remembered voice, quavering though it was, Horatio Bullwinkle, sitting at the shore end of the phone, felt the red bristles on his bullethead tingle now with the old hostility.

"Where are you, you old cow?" he demanded, and his little black shoebutton eyes snapped with fury. "On the Narcissus? Well, what the——What's that? Speak louder!"

"I'm scared, Horatio," he heard her say, but those familiar accents from the past were freighted now with a dithering, craven terror that Bullwinkle, in years of hectic competition and mutually enjoyable bouts of personal abuse, had never heard from her before. "I been tryin' to tell them lame-brains ye got there——"

"Don't you realize, ye worm-eaten old wreck," interrupted Bullwinkle violently, "that there's a Jap——"

"S-sure! That's what I'm tryin' to tell ye, ye aggravatin'——I mean Bullwinkle, ol' pal, ol' pal! That's what I'm ascairt of. That's why I dropped that oil barge I was towin'. She's over three hundred thousand gallon o' fuel oil in her——"

"And ye dropped it?" It was Bullwinkle's turn to grow hysterical. "Why you furry-headed——"

"But—but she was so heavy I could hardly tow her. An' suppose that Jap ketched me wid it in the mornin'? He'd blow us outa the water wid all hands an' the galley cat!" Her voice rose, terrified, "I—I gotta git outa here! I gotta!"

"A full oil barge!" groaned Bullwinkle.

"Ye can find it fast enough, come daybreak," returned Annie, more brightly now. "I pumped over a big oil slick, so's it could be easy spotted. An' it's on'y twenty mile west an' four mile north o' the Santa Barbara——"

"Will you shut up, you fool?" Bullwinkle howled. "Do you want him to pick it up?"

"He'll have a time seein' it, it's so low in the water. L-look, Bullwinkle; we was always pals, wasn't we? Send me out somebody to help me, will ya? He's apt to show up any minute an'——"

"Help you? Brother! You can make your own way! And if you never——"

"But I can't!" wailed Annie. "I got a cracked cylinder head an' I can on'y make two knots even widout the barge!" Her voice rose again on a note of high panic, "Ye gotta send out a destroyer or a cutter or somethin'! If he ketches me here at daybreak——"

"That'll be too bad!" snapped Bullwinkle. "Help you in!" Sudden realization of his own position assailed him, and again his angry hackles rose. "Furthermore, my fine—fine——"

"Fettle?" quavered Annie helpfully.

"——do you realize that by talkin' to you like this, I'm riskin' my commission?"

"Ye are? Well, ain't that great!" returned Annie promptly, forsaking her role for the moment in deliberate, calculated effort to goad her old enemy. Then, giving it plenty of time to sink in, she continued. "I—I didn't mean that, Bullwinkle," she amended hastily. "I remember there was times in the old days we had to work together to scupper the opposition an' bring home the bacon. Now be a good feller"—her voice started shaking again—"an' send me out a destroyer or a cutter or somethin' to fetch me in, will ye?"

Instantly the cool, hard, quick-thinking brain beneath Bullwinkle's unprepossessing and bristly skull began to click. He had been fooled—and badly, at first—by Tugboat Annie's panic. But her apparent delight at his prospective misfortune was like a slap in the face or the icy hand of logic on his brow. And it had set him thinking, fast. People in a paroxysm of fear such as Annie appeared to be in usually don't snap out of it to carry on personal feuds, no matter how bitter or long-standing. And her further remarks about former cooperation, which had been rare enough, gave him the missing key. So now he, in turn, dissembled, knowing she would understand.

"Listen, you old yellow-belly!" he stormed. "If you think we've got nothing to do but send out escort ships to bring a lousy little mud scow like the Narcissus into port, you're crazy! We need every vessel we've got to run down that sub! A purse seiner," he added falsely, "has already reported sighting her off San Clemente. So get off this phone and stay off! And keep your lights out!"

Tugboat Annie did as she was told, but her face, as she got heavily up from the table in Clem's cabin, was creased with worry. "I sure hope Bullwinkle ain't growed a hole in his head since he's been in the service," she muttered. " 'Cause if he has an' that Jap don't find no barge, he's gonna come looking fer us, sure as water off a duck."

"Then what, Annie?" asked Clem, still scared stiff.

"You guess!" replied Annie shortly. "But out there is scores of inbound ships, loaded to the gunnels wid American boys what's thinkin' o' nothin' but sittin' in the kitchen at home, watchin' ma bakin' them apple pies! And tomorrer night there'll be more! And the night after! An' out in the dark there is a little yeller guy wid bugs in his brain, figgerin' how he can git ahold o' that bargeload of oil! An' if he gits it—we're still towin' it, remember!—there ain't nothin' goin' to stop him! Unless——"

Leaving the remainder of the thought unsaid, she stumped wearily out, and as she rejoined Peter and Big Sam in the wheelhouse, her face was grim.

But there were no holes in Horatio Bullwinkle's head, other than those that nature had provided, and shortly after the termination of his encounter with Annie, he was consulting with his superior, Captain Bolton, across the Operations Room table.

"How do you know she really wasn't just plain scared?" asked Bolton, after Bullwinkle rapidly had outlined the situation.

"No, sir!" was Bullwinkle's emphatic reply. "Annie's an old she devil, but she's got more guts to spare than a slaughterhouse, and she wouldn't show her starn to a dozen Japs. And she's no fool either. We-ell"—he qualified hastily—"most times. But she's got somethin' up her sleeve, and I've a fair notion what it is. For if that Jap sub skipper was listenin' in—and I'd bet my ship against the Narcissus's gypsy-head he was!—look what he learned: that a barge full of fuel oil is floating around unescorted—she gave him the position exactly."

"And us!" Bolton reminded him, beginning to understand.

"And us!" Bullwinkle's tobacco-stained teeth showed in a grin. "That's what she intended, sir! And we're supposed to be concentratin' our search for him around San Clemente Island, a hundred-odd mile south o' here."

"And with a large oil slick to help him find the prize, he'll take a chance as soon as it's light," Bolton finished for him.

They looked at each other for a few tense, significant seconds. Then Bolton reached for the telephone. "Get me the San Diego Naval Air Station," he said.

Dawn broke, with the sea as still as a floor. A slight morning mist limited surface visibility and hung close over the undulating swells which rolled unbroken beneath the iridescent sheen of Tugboat Annie's oil slick. And presently there emerged from the grayness the long, sleek shape of a gigantic Japanese submarine, cruising along the surface with hardly a sound beyond the faint ripple beneath the bow. The conning tower was open, the deck guns manned, and behind the protection of the small bridge, the sub's commander, a stocky, round-faced man with a shaven pate beneath his small-visored cap, was searching the surrounding area with sharp, sea-wrinkled eyes. Then suddenly he tensed, looked up and listened, and immediately shouted staccato commands. A gong clanged below and the guns' crews started along the narrow deck on the run.

From the air above them, the sea was a wrinkled blue floor only slightly diluted by the surface mist; and as the squadron of Navy dive bombers roared across the pure, clear arch of the sky, keen young eyes looked downward. The squadron leader saw their objective first—a long, wide, nacreous film of oil rising and falling to the slow breathing of the sea, and even as he wiggled his wings in signal, the others spotted it too, and something else—the long, cigar-shaped hull of the submarine.

In beautiful, space-consuming curves the dive bombers peeled off; dwindled to faint, screaming specks far below. Then, abruptly, the smooth carpet of the Pacific was stippled with the spouting geysers of exploding bombs. And suddenly, from the center, slowly and majestically, rose a higher column black with smoke and the debris of twisted steel and shattered human flesh. It fell back in a thousand minor diminishing splashes; and now, joining the filmy veneer that already lay over the water, there was a heavier slick brown and thick and slow moving bubbling up from the depths, and writhing in shifting, ropy coils the epitaph of the last active underwater fighting ship of the Imperial Navy of Japan.

Eighteen miles to the north, Tugboat Annie stood outside the wheelhouse of the Narcissus, with Big Sam, anxious-eyed and uncertain, at her elbow.

"I dunno, Annie," he said, troubled. "I got a feelin' ye're in for trouble. They could confiscate the tug for what you done last night."

"If they do," said Annie deeply, "I'll go ashore an' swaller the anchor fer good. But"—she pointed astern—"we'll soon know."

The hull-down dot they had been watching enlarged rapidly to a large, sleek and heavily armed Coast Guard vessel which overhauled them at a smooth thirty-two knots. And when it was abeam and within close hailing distance, there stepped out of the charthouse the bulky and smartly uniformed figure of Commander Horatio Bullwinkle, followed a moment later by Captain Bolton.

For a few seconds Bullwinkle looked down at the panting, disreputably sea-stained Narcissus and the wallowing barge at the end of the long towing wire.

But his face was expressionless, and presently he cupped his hands and hailed, "Ahoy, the Narcissus!"

Annie turned to Big Sam. "Strange," she said interestedly, but in a voice that had carried to windward in many a gale. "We're at sea, ain't we? I could ha' swore I heerd a donkey bray jest now."

"Ahoy, the Narcissus!" hailed Bullwinkle again, a bit more florid of face now, as he became conscious of the titters of his crew.

TUGBOAT ANNIE WINS HER MEDAL

Tugboat Annie looked up; gave a start of simulated astonishment. "Well, I'll be Tom Tiddler's widder if it ain't that swivel-eared old wagabone, Bullwinkle!" she cried with elephantine archness.

"You can skip the compliments, Annie," said the recipient of her humor, restraining, out of deference to his superior officer, the more salty retort that sprang to his lips. "Lay to! We're coming aboard!"

"I told ye, Annie! I told ye!" Big Sam groaned. "This is it!"

"Shet yer gawp!" she told him tersely. "If they're gonna beach me, I'll go down wid me funnel flyin'!"

Nevertheless, it was with uneasiness, thinly masked with bravado, that she awaited their coming.

Presently, Bullwinkle and Captain Bolton stood on the Narcissus's littered and narrow deck and walked to the stern, where Annie was waiting, with Big Sam standing stoutly and loyally behind her, and Peter, the mate, in the background.

"That's her! That's Annie!" stated Commander Bullwinkle, and pointed at her. "The one wi' the shortest whiskers."

"And the same to you wid knobs on it, ye horse's tail!" retorted Annie hotly, and turned to Bolton. "What kin I do fer ye?"

He eyed her with some interest, and Annie, in return, noted, with increasing respect, the rows of campaign ribbons on his chest and the quietly seamanlike cut of his jib.

"You—are—er—Captain Brennan?"

"That's me! He ain't lyin', fer a change!"

"I am Captain Bolton, of the United States Coast Guard. Something happened last night for which I've come to——"

"Sure! I know!" said Annie unhappily. "Will I come quiet or do ye have to drag me?"

Bolton's eyes twinkled. "I'm afraid you don't understand. I've come to congratulate you."

"Congratulate me?" Dumfounded, Annie stared at him. "I don't git it!"

"That Japanese submarine you led us to," said Bolton, smiling broadly now, "was destroyed from the air at daybreak this morning."

"Glory be!" gasped Annie. "Then it worked!" He nodded. "And—and you ain't gonna confisculate the Narcissus or nothin'?"

"Far from it," he assured her. "In fact," he went on, "I think when the news gets out, you'll find yourself rather popular. . . . Eh, commander?"

"The shock o' that'll kill her!" said the gallant commander, with a grin. . . . "Muster your crew, Annie. Captain Bolton wants to talk to 'em."

"They ain't did nothin'!" defended Annie quickly. "They on'y done what I——"

"It's not that, captain. There's nothing to worry about," Bolton reassured her, and wonderingly she obeyed. So presently they were joined by Pinto, the cook; Clem; Ernie, the assistant engineer; and the two deck hands, Shiftless and Hank. They formed a semicircle, with Annie in the center, shifting about uneasily. And once again Captain Bolton addressed her.

"I don't know of any service regulation," he said quietly, "which permits the award of the Navy Cross to a civilian, and especially a woman. But if ever a good American earned one, you did last night." He paused, dug in his pocket for a small box and extracted therefrom the coveted Navy decoration. Then he went on.

"This was given for a deed of valor performed during the Battle of the Coral Sea. The citation read: 'For courage performed above and beyond the call of duty.' And as one old seafarer to another"—he smiled—"I know of no one more qualified to wear it than Tugboat Annie Brennan."

Carefully he pinned it on her massive bosom amid a profound silence, broken only by Shiftless's asthmatic snuffles and the hoarse breathing of Commander Bullwinkle, and shook her by the hand.

Tugboat Annie looked down at the bit of metal and its colorful ribbon reposing on her chest, and when she gazed at him again, her eyes were misted.

"Thanks . . . thanks!" She gulped. "But I—I don't want to denude you o' yer medal."

"You're not," he said quietly. "The medal did not belong to me. It was awarded to Commander Bullwinkle."

Annie's incredulous eyes went, first to the acutely embarrassed and red-faced Bullwinkle, then slowly back to Bolton. "Ye— ye mean that? It's really his? Ye ain't tryin' to pull the bull over me eyes?"

"It was his," repeated Bolton. "He wanted you to have it."

Annie's eyes again went to the face of her ancient adversary, while slow color flooded her neck and cheeks. "Gosh, ye—ye old— —Gosh!" she choked. "I—I'm sorry I called ye a horse's tail, Bullwinkle! You ain't that at all! Ye're on'y a horse's neck." "But——" she added prudently and with great presence of mind, thinking of the future with its prospective cut-throat business rivalries in home waters, "ye may git to be a horse's tail someday!"

THE FRAMING OF TUGBOAT ANNIE

In the joyous lift of an autumn morning, Tugboat Annie Brennan, senior skipper of the Deep-Sea Towing and Salvage Company, of Secoma, emerged happily from the messroom of her raffish but sturdy tug Narcissus, and stood for a few moments on the narrow side deck, drawing in deep and audible gulps of the salt air, laced with snows from the Olympic Range and spiced by the resinous tang of primeval evergreen forests, that blew across the island-studded reaches of Puget Sound.

"Ooof!" she grunted comfortably, and patted her capacious stomach, armed against the pleasant chill of the crisp breezes that prickled her skin. "Them flannel cakes o' Pinto's sure is fillin'!"

"How many did ye stow away?" asked Peter, the mate, who had followed her out.

"On'y ten," said Annie regretfully. "After the steak I kinda seemed to lose me appetite. I bet," she went on with a sigh of repletion, "I won't be able to eat another bite in a month o' Mondays. . . . Sa-ay"—she turned her enthusiasm in the direction of the galley—"Pinto!"

Pinto's face showed cautiously, in response to her bellow, at the edge of the galley door. "I ain't done nothin', Annie," he said defensively, ready to dodge.

"Well, don't do it again," she adjured with vast good humor. "An' look. Fer supper tonight let's have veal chops—you know how ye do 'em! In little blankets o' bread crumbs, all brown and crispy around the edges, wid cream gravy, an' corn on the cob what's drippin' wid butter, and plenty o' gnashed potatoes!"

"I thought ye said ye couldn't eat——" began Peter derisively.

THE FRAMING OF TUGBOAT ANNIE

But she cut in, her weather-crinkled eyes twinkling: "An', Pinto, mebbe ye could take Peter's head, here—he never has no use fer it—an' make us a nice punkin pie!"

Chuckling massively at her joke, she heaved herself up onto the wharf and crossed toward the company offices, humming, with off-key vigor, her favorite tune, "Happy Days Is Here Some More."

"Well, what's new what ain't been stole?" she demanded boisterously as she entered the office, but Fred, the dispatcher, looking up from the telephone, frowned and made admonitory hushing motions. "Yes?" Fred resumed into the telephone, while Annie tiptoed with elephantine caution across to the window, "Okay, Alec. She's here now. . . . Yeah, I'll tell her."

He hung up and turned to Annie. "The boss wants you to meet him in Room Eight Oh One of the Maritime Building in half an hour," he informed her, and added, grinning, "And he said to warn you to keep your big bazoo shut and let him do the talking."

"Well, I like that!" Annie yelped indignantly. "There's times past, if I'd kept me mouth shut, then this company'd ha' gone bankrupt! Wait till I see that little fat—fat——" Suddenly, curiosity overcoming her irritation, she finished on a calmer note, "What's it all about, Fred?"

"He's going up to see Captain Craig, of the Red Triangle Line."

"Hey!" Annie was excited now. "Ye mean that new cargo-steamer outfit what's makin' Secoma their western terminus?"

"That's right. Craig's been appointed their representative here. It could mean a lot of pilotage and towin' business for us, Annie, and Alec's hot after it."

"But what's he want me up there fer?" asked Annie. "Course," she added modestly, "I could be a big help to him, but——"

"Craig's a peculiar fellow, I've heard tell," Fred answered. "He came up the hard way himself, and even though Alec's the head of our firm, Craig said he wanted to size up the—the men that actually do the work."

For a moment, Annie's keen blue eyes were troubled. "What ye reely mean, Fred," she said bluntly, "is that Craig's l'arned that the skipper o' Alec's biggest tug's a woman and he don't like it. Ain't that right?"

"Well, maybe," Fred admitted reluctantly.

"So I gotta sell meself to him!" returned Annie grimly. "Still, I mind in times past, other fellers had the same idears, an', brother, how I showed 'em!"

"Now take it easy," warned Fred nervously. "Just go up there and act natural——"

"Ye mean," Annie interrupted mendaciously, "ye don't want I should show up wid a set o' false whiskers an' a soufflé on me head, an' wearin' a pair o' men's pants?"

"Don't get funny!" replied Fred, more uneasy than ever, for Annie was ever unpredictable.

"Okay, ye old coffin creeper! I was on'y havin' a smidgeon o' fun!" she grinned and waved a massive paw. "I'll be seein' ye," and she lumbered out the door.

A half hour later, decked in her shore-going finery, with an ancient reticule moored to her waist, an ornate though rather tarnished fleur-de-lis watch made fast to her expansive bosom, and on her blowsy and hastily tucked-up hair a hat surmounted by a venerable but gaily mowing and bobbing feather, she was standing with her boss, Alec Severn, before the desk of Captain Craig. The latter, a weather-beaten man of about fifty with shrewd but kindly eyes, eyed her with perhaps pardonable astonishment, then turned to Severn.

"So this," he said, with hardly perceptible emphasis upon the pronoun, "is your senior captain?"

"No, sir!" replied Annie promptly, simulating, in her eagerness to cater to his whims, a man's deep bass. "As a third-mate friend o' mine, name o' Mr. Gallup, used to say, Salvation Army has 'captains,' but commercial seafarers on'y has 'masters'!"

"Hmm-m-ph!" replied Captain Craig noncommittally, although unexpectedly the corners of his eyes wrinkled.

"An' if ye think it queer that a woman should be skipper of a tugboat," Annie went on warmly, and disregarding a warning kick on the ankle from Severn, "there's been a few women in hist'ry, like Cleopatria an' the Queen o' Sherbet, what——"

"Yes-yes! Of course!" said Captain Craig, while Severn's round little face flamed. "And though it is a bit unusual, I've never noticed that the flavor of a good lamb chop was spoiled by the little paper doodad they tie around the bone."

"Sa-ay!" Suddenly grinning, Annie stuck out her massive fist. "I like you! Ye got common sense . . . which"—she glanced at Severn meaningly—"is more'n most men is blessed wid! An' if it's work ye want did, me an' me old Narcissus'll do a better job fer ye than anybody else'd do fer half the price!"

"Double the price, you mean, Annie!" Severn corrected anxiously.

But Annie's grin only widened. "He knows what I mean!" she said, quite at home now. . . . "Alec's kinda shy," she confided to Craig, to her employer's increased embarrassment. "Did he tell ye I was the best pilot on Puget Sound and that we got the best fleet o' tugs what ever hit blue water?"

"N-no, not exactly."

"Well, we have! An' all ye got to do to prove it is give us yer business!"

"Listen, Annie!" Severn reproved her sharply. "Let Captain Craig make up his own mind!"

But Craig, who had been watching them both with veiled but sympathetic amusement, interrupted. "It's made up," he said. "At least enough to give you a try. We have a steamer now, the Corinthian of London, loaded with a very valuable cargo of English woolens, running through the Juan de Fuca Strait and bound here. Her master, Captain Bogle, is new to these waters, I understand; so, if you want to pick her up off the quarantine station at Port Townsend and pilot her down here——"

"It's as good as did!" said Annie promptly.

"And I'm very much obliged, captain," said Severn.

"Not at all." Craig shook hands with them. "And I hope this is only the first of a long association."

"We'll do our part, sir. Shall I send you the usual verifying letter?" Severn replied.

"Yes. But that won't reach me till the morning, and I don't want to wait till then to have the Corinthian picked up. The cargo owners are particularly anxious to have her start discharging here tomorrow, so——"

"Annie will leave as soon as she gets back to the harbor."

"Fine! Meanwhile I'll radio Captain Bogle to expect——" He paused; looked at Annie, smiling. "What was the name of this outstanding tug of yours, Mrs. Brennan?"

"The Narcissus," Annie told him happily. "An' it's 'Tugboat Annie' to you!"

On the run up the Sound the weather was fair, the sun brilliant over the sparkling waters and Annie was in great spirits, her naturally vivid interest in life intensely heightened by the company's good fortune, so that everything about them was the occasion of lively comment; and when, shortly after leaving the harbor, an experimental helicopter flew over them, trying out a new mail-transportation scheme between Sound ports, her naive and astonished gratification was boundless.

"Look!" she cried, grabbing the arm of Big Sam, the engineer, with whom she had been engaged in animated gossip outside the engine-room door. "What's that? It looks like a outsize in bunglebees!"

"Aw, it's jest a helicopter, Annie," said Sam, with male contempt for feminine ignorance of the mechanical things of life. "It flies up an' down and sideways."

"An' backward, too, to keep the dust out of its eyes?" cried Annie, hugely enjoying her joke. "Oh, my, oh, me! A flyin' elevator! Whatever next?" and she stumped happily up the ladder to the pilothouse, where she repeated her jest to Peter, who was at the wheel.

But Peter was unresponsive. "Yeah," he grunted. "But it might do more good if it was to sprinkle a little water on them forest fires over on the peninsula. It's goin' to be slow steamin' ahead, Annie!"

Peter was right; for in front of them the natural light haze which lay over the placid water was augmented and thickened to the density of heavy fog by the smoke of seasonal forest fires which, crackling through thousands of acres of virgin timber, billowed eastward in a dark brown, almost completely opaque blanket through which seafarers groped their way with mournful hootings. And presently the Narcissus was in the thick of it, but Annie was perturbed not at all, for she knew the local positions, tides and currents as familiarly as the calluses on her palms.

"I wonder," she said to Peter, whose jaws were moving over his cud with bovine contentment, "what that big clack-trap Bullwinkle will yap when he finds out we got the Red Triangle account."

"Bullwinkle?"

"Yeah!" said Annie impatiently. "As if ye never heerd of him! I'm referrin'," she went on with the automatic choler which recollection of her ancient business rival always aroused in her, "to that bandy-legged snake-in-the-bush what skippers the Salamander!"

"I know who ye mean!" returned Peter resentfully. "I ain't as dumb as I look! But how's he to know? He towed a sucker dredge up to Nanaimo couple o' days ago, and he'll just be gettin' back by now."

"Great!" Annie rubbed her horny palms with anticipatory jubilation. "All I want is fer him to be settin' on the dock when the Corinthian and us comes trollopin' by!"

Time passed, with the Narcissus pushing her way at reduced speed and with periodic bleatings of her fog signal through the murk, which now was so dense that it obliterated the shore line. But as if by instinct, Annie constantly was aware of their position, and presently she spoke.

"Swing inshore a leetle, Peter," she said; and, with only the hiss of the bow wave and the periodic hooting of distant ships in their ears, she listened. "Give her a bit more starboard helm," she directed quietly. "There's the three blasts o' the Marrowstone P'int fog signal now."

A half hour later they were chugging over the smooth surface of Port Townsend's harbor, and soon, off the quarantine-detention anchorage, there loomed out of the smoke-thickened noonday the bulk of the S.S. Corinthian, a fine new ten-thousand-ton cargo steamer, with her name and register on her counter and a bright red triangle painted on her brave white funnel.

There was a churn of water as the Narcissus came to a halt off the lowered accommodation ladder; and shortly thereafter Tugboat Annie, with the Narcissus standing by alongside, was on the steamer's bridge, addressing the vessel's master, a paunchy, nondescript-looking man with jowls beneath a red walrus mustache, and bags under eyes that were rheumy with a lifetime of staring over heaving oceans, and a nose that was tinted, Annie shrewdly suspected, by something more potent than life in the open air.

"I'm Tugboat Annie Brennan, o' Secoma, come to pilot ye in, captain," she told him complacently. "Would ye be good enough to have the accommodation ladder hauled up?"

"You—you're the pilot?" He stared at her with unbelieving eyes.

"Sure, I'm the pilot. What did ye think I was—the bucolic plague?" Annie returned good-humoredly. "Don't worry. I'll git ye into port widout yankin' out no tail fedders. Have ye cleared quarantine? But I see ye have—the flag's down. Well, let's git underway."

"Just a moment, madam," Captain Bogle said nervously. "This—this is my first time in these waters and I"—the uncertainty deepened in his voice—"I don't know that I care to trust my ship to a woman pilot. I—I——"

He turned and looked behind him, and for the first time Annie noticed another man standing there; a swarthy, thickset individual with sharp dark eyes, and dressed not in merchant-service uniform, but in a heavy brown tweed suit. Abruptly leaving her, Captain Bogle crossed to the man, and they engaged in low-toned colloquy. Apparently it was satisfactory, for the shipmaster returned to Annie, followed by the other man.

"This is Mr. Bendigo, one of the cargo owners, who crossed with us from Bristol," he said, and Annie acknowledged the introduction with a nod.

"You're sure it's safe to proceed in this fog, or smoke, or whatever it is?" Bendigo asked her, and there was a faint foreign intonation in his otherwise faultless English. "It's important that we begin unloading in the morning. If we're held up and the market drops, it could mean a serious loss for us."

"I'll git ye in on time, sir," Annie reassured him cheerfully. "It's easy as fallin' over a bump on a log."

Soon the Corinthian's anchor cable was clanking and dripping out of the depths, with hunks of black mud splashing back as a hose washed chain and anchor clean. Then, with the Narcissus puffing close abeam, the steamer moved slowly out toward the harbor mouth.

With Marrowstone Point half a mile to starboard, and after Captain Bogle had relayed to the helmsman Annie's directions for the course, the shipmaster joined her on the wing of the bridge.

"I'm sorry if I seem a little anxious," he said nervously. "But if anything was to happen——"

"What kin happen?" asked Annie calmly. "I been sailin' around here fer forty years, man an' girl, and ye're as safe as if we was navigatin' a boat in a bathtub."

"But I've heard these are dangerous waters in thick weather. Full of shoals and tricky currents——"

"I'm the pusson what put 'em there!" she told him roguishly. "Anyways, it'd take a congenial idiot to put a vessel ashore on a calm day like this."

"But the visibility's so bad you can't see fifty feet off the bow!" he persisted testily, his jitters appearing suddenly to intensify. "You'll tell me next that there are no tricky spots at all!"

"Oh, there are, here an' there ... if ye want to call 'em that," replied Annie carelessly, and grinned. "In fack," she continued, "we're on'y two hundred feet from land right now."

"Wha-at?"

Her grin widened. "Straight down," she explained, and chuckled.

But Captain Bogle was not to be reassured. "You may think that's funny, madam, but it's not what I mean!" he answered morosely. "What's the closest we come to shore?"

"Bush P'int. There's a long low sand spit runs out, wid a light on the end, an'——"

"Sand, you say?" he interrupted sharply.

"That's right. But——"

"How close off do we pass it?"

"'Bout a quarter of a mile. The current sets across it pretty strong at times. Then there's Double Bluff, about four mile further on, but that's high cliffs, wid shoals runnin' out——"

"How far off do we pass that?" Captain Bogle again interrupted, and Annie was aware that Mr. Bendigo had joined them now and was listening with apparently casual interest.

"'Bout a mile. So ye needn't to worry."

"Not worry?" He turned to Bendigo, said heatedly, "Here's a new ship and a valuable cargo that I have to turn over to a strange pilot—and a woman at that!—in dangerous and obscured waters, and she tells me there's no need to worry!"

But Bendigo, placing a calming hand on the shipmaster's arm, turned to Tugboat Annie.

"His concern is natural, Mrs. Brennan," he said quietly, "and he means no reflection on your ability. Actually"—and he smiled—"I should be the one to worry. After all, it's my cargo, captain."

"Aye, but I'm responsible for ship and cargo both!" Bogle said brusquely. Then, to Annie, "Where is—is this point we run within a quarter of a mile of?"

Before answering, Annie stared at him curiously, noting his anxious eyes, his trembling hands, and she guessed that here was a man insecure in his job. *Prob'ly was on the beach fer years afore the war shortage got him a berth again, an' he's so scared o' the future that he don't dare make no mistake*, she told herself mentally, and instantly she was sympathetic.

"Bush P'int," she resumed. "We'll be up wid it in a half an hour or so. I'm runnin' pretty far in to take advantage o' the current. It's so low in the water we'll prob'ly not even see it an' we'll be past afore ye can blink. Unless"—she essayed an encouraging joke—"it's come adrift an' swims out to bump us."

"Don't talk like that!" he snapped back at her. "It's nothing to be funny about! I've got my ticket to think of, and——"

"Okay, okay! Don't git so turbulated!" Annie roared, annoyed at last. "Heaven's sakes, ye even got me shakin' like a aspirin now, wid yer 'Where's this?' an' 'How far's that?' an' 'Are ye sure we're safe?'! I been pilotin' up an' down the sound since Noah was a cabin boy! I telled ye that afore! So shut up and lemme alone!"

For a few moments Captain Bogle was silent; then, unexpectedly humble, but still persevering, he said, "You will let me know when we're coming up with the point, though?"

"Yeah." Annie glanced again at his troubled face and relented. "I'll let ye know."

He turned away from her, and after pacing restlessly for a while, stood motionless by the engine-room telegraph annunciator, while the Corinthian, sounding her fog signal at proper intervals and being answered by the mournful bleats of other invisible seafarers, proceeded at a cautious reduced speed. Soon they could hear from out of the murk ahead, at thirty-second intervals, the long, dismal, abruptly terminated moo of an air fog signal.

Annie turned to where Captain Bogle was standing, his fingers drumming on the annunciator, the indicator of which was pointing to Slow Ahead, while his eyes strained shoreward through the smoke and mist.

"There's Bush P'int foghorn now," she said quietly.

"How close in are we?" he asked instantly.

"Pretty close," she told him. "We git a extra half knot that way. It's all okay, though," she added indulgently, when she saw his stare of alarm. "There's no danger. Look, there's a easterly breeze an' it's clearin' a bit. Ye'll see it in a minute."

His intent eyes followed her pointing finger, and presently, through a temporary thinning of the dark brown blanket ahead, there became visible a low, timbered point of land, terminating in a long sand spit at the end of which was a white pyramidal building which housed an occulting white light.

Captain Bogle straightened abruptly. "Listen, ma'am," he rapped, his voice a strange, tense ejaculation, "you're in too close!"

"Don't git in a flitter," she told him calmly. "I know what I'm doin'."

"You don't, you old fool!" he roared suddenly, and at his alarmed cry, Bendigo came rapidly toward them from around a corner of the wheelhouse. "Swing off! You're putting us ashore!"

Quickly he swung the annunciator handle over to Full Ahead, then, in a panic, ran into the wheelhouse, where he wrested the wheel from the quartermaster and swung it hard over. The vessel's deck plates thrummed from the suddenly accelerated beat of the propeller, and the bows started to swing shoreward.

Stunned, Annie gaped for a moment; then she, too, ran to the annunciator and slammed the handle down to Full Astern.

"Git that wheel back!" she yelled over her shoulder. "Ye've swung it the wrong way!"

Too late. Even as the engines came to an abrupt halt in response to her corrective signal, then began to pound astern, the steamer struck. Not hard, but sufficiently to slide her forefoot and a quarter of her length over the low, yielding spit of sand. And there, with a series of small tremors, she came to rest.

The shipmaster stalked from the wheelhouse and crossed to Annie, his face a mask of quiet menace. "Well, you did it, you old cow!" he said, his voice spitting venom. "You set her ashore as I knew you would!"

"I set her ashore?" Incredulously she stared at him.

THE FRAMING OF TUGBOAT ANNIE

"Of course you did!" he threw at her. "Didn't I beg you ever since we left Port Townsend to keep her far enough out? Didn't I ask——" He broke off suddenly; turned to Bendigo, who, with still, set face, was regarding them. "Here, you heard me make her name every danger point we were coming up with, so's I could check on her! And what did she do? She treated the whole thing as a joke! A joke, God save us!"

"An' if you'd kept yer clumsy meat hooks offa that annunciator," Annie roared back at him, now roused to fighting pitch, "we'd ha' been okay!" In turn, she, too, appealed to Bendigo. "You seen him put the handle over to Full Ahead, didn't ye?"

Slowly, looking puzzled, Bendigo shook his head. "No," he replied. "The only person I saw touch it was you."

Annie glared from one to the other like a goaded and baffled rhinoceros. Then, on flat feet, with congested face and big fists clenched, she shuffled lethally toward the shipmaster. "Don't you try to shove this off onto me, ye whisky-raddled twitch," she grated, "or I'll wrap ye around yer own binnacle!"

"You'll pay for the damage just the same—you or your company!" he told her, backing away. "And by the time the cargo's transshipped and the vessel refloated, it'll cost you plenty!"

"Ye can guess again!" she yelled back. "A pilot on a steamer underway is a servant o' the shipowners, an' as such is not liable——"

Annie left the sentence unfinished, for, even as she spoke, recollection clamped an icy grip upon her brain, and she knew that probably neither she nor Severn could make a case. What she had told Captain Bogle was true only when pilotage was carried out under a clause printed on the letterheads of towing companies, and over the agreement to pilot or tow. Too clearly, now, she remembered the vital clause, which read: "Officers, crew and tug shall be the servants of the owners of the vessel piloted or towed, and, as such, neither they nor the owners of the tug shall be liable for damage of any nature however, caused even by their negligence." But when service was rendered upon an oral agreement only, such protection did not exist; and although Severn and Craig had discussed the sending of a formal letter of contract, it would not take effect until delivery—on the morrow at the earliest—and meanwhile the stranding had taken place. And if Captain Bogle, fearful of the effect of the accident upon his own career, could make his accusation of negligence against her stick——

Buffeted and stunned by the implications of her position, she could think of nothing further to say, and it was into a mind numbed with despair that his next words penetrated. He was not, however, addressing her, but the second officer, who was on watch and who had crossed from the opposite wing of the bridge.

"Hail that tug off there," he was saying, "and tell it to come alongside and take this woman off!"

"Hey!" Instantly Annie was alert again. "I'm stoppin' right here till I see what damage has been did! It can't be much, because we grounded in sand, an'——"

"Will you be good enough to keep your mouth shut? You've done harm enough already!" the shipmaster told her harshly, while Bendigo nodded approval. But Annie was not so easily squelched.

"Oh, no!" she replied forcefully. "Ye telled me I was liable fer this. Okey-dope! Then I got the right to suggest remedies what'll keep that liability down. I got me tug out there"—she pointed to the Narcissus, which was hovering close abeam, her crew agoggle at the rail—"an' at flood tide we'll pull ye off."

"Why don't you"—and Captain Bogle's face suddenly was purple—"mind your own business?"

"That's exactly what I'm doin'! Furthermore"—she pointed at Bendigo and the second officer—"I'm callin' them to witness that I offered to help. So, if a blow comes up, and we could ha' pulled ye off in time to save ye, you'll find yerself in a conundrum too!"

For a moment the shipmaster glared at her, nonplused; then, after a brief exchange of glances with Bendigo, he capitulated.

"Right," he said grudgingly. "You can have a try at it. But we'll not take your line; you'll take ours!" Noting her look of astonishment, he added bleakly, "If the strain's too much you're not going to gyp us by claiming payment for a damaged hawser."

"But we'll use a steel towin' wire!"

"You heard what I said! Take it or leave it!"

Time passed, and the autumn dusk came early as they waited for the flood tide to ease the task; so it was nearly dark and the freshening wind had blown the last of the smoke and haze seaward when the Narcissus, in the capable charge of Peter, the mate, and at the end of the Corinthian's long hempen hawser, strained and panted at her job of snaking the stranded vessel off the sand bar. Annie was leaning over the wing of the Corinthian's bridge, anxiously watching operations, when suddenly, just as she was sure there was a movement responsive to the Narcissus's powerful hauling, there was a loud, explosive pop, and the tug, abruptly freed of the freighter's weight, gave a ridiculous forward surge. The towline had parted.

"Ye should ha' took our steel wire aboard, like I telled ye," she informed Captain Bogle, when reporting the mishap. "I'll hail the Narcissus an'——"

"You'll hail the Narcissus, all right," returned the shipmaster, strangely composed. "But not for the purpose you think."

"Suppose," suggested Annie, nonplused, "ye give to me in words o' one syllabus."

"Gladly! Having done all the damage one stupid, bungling female can do, you're getting the hell off this ship! In other words, I'm exercising my prerogative and getting shut of you!"

"Ye can exercise yer—whatever it is—till it's muscle-bound!" Annie retorted hotly. "But if I was to put a wire on board she'd come off easy, now it's high tide!"

"Get off or be thrown off! Take your choice!" he returned easily, and turning, he hailed a square-hewn, towheaded Finn who was passing by. "Bos'n," he said, "if this—this woman isn't off the ship in five minutes——"

"Okay, ye horse's rudder!" said Annie. "I'll go! But ye ain't seen the hind end o' me yet!"

Ten minutes later Annie sighed with relief as she felt beneath her broad soles the familiar planks of the Narcissus's deck, and that homely but capable craft scythed away from the Corinthian's side and straightened out on a course for home.

"Woosh!" she said to Peter, in the wheelhouse, as the placid expanse of water opened up before them. "I'm sure in a awful jam wid Alec an' Captain Craig, but I'm glad to be rid o' the queer feller back there. He had me nervous as a twit! Well—here, lemme take the wheel!—on'y thing I can do now is go home an' face the band. But what I can't git through me chromium," she continued as her big fists grasped the spokes, "is why he wouldn't let us make another try at haulin' her off. One more heave, if that hawser hadn't parted——"

"What do you mean, 'parted,' Annie?" replied Peter. "That hawser didn't just part. It was cut!"

"Wha-at?" Incredulously, Annie stared at him in the dim light of the binnacle's lamp.

Peter nodded solemnly. "Sure. Shif'less noticed it when he hauled it aboard."

"But—but"—Annie's thoughts were cast all adrift—"that don't make no sense! Wait a minute." She cogitated briefly but intensively, then again wagged her shaggy head. "No! It still don't make no sense!"

"What don't, Annie?"

"Well," Annie spoke slowly, cautiously testing every step of her thoughts, "on the way from Port Townsend, Captain Boogle, or Google, or whatever his moniker is, kept axin' me, where's the bad spots, an' please be careful; an' I felt sorry fer him, he was so nervous, case anythin' happened to his ship. But, countin' the fack that it was him what signaled full ahead an' put the wheel over the wrong way, that might ha' been jest tryin' to pull the bull over me eyes whiles he was fishin' me fer a good spot to cast her away."

"But"—Big Sam's mind revolved slowly but surely—"that would be barratry, Annie."

"Sure. An' if it was off a dangerous coast in bad weather, and he was in cahoots wid his owners fer a share o' the insurance, I could understand it! But ye don't sail a vessel ten thousand miles to run her ashore in sheltered waters, on a sand spit in a dead calm, and on'y forty-five miles from your port o' destination! I mean, what good would it do him? She can't be damaged bad, so the insurance'll be nothin'. So he risks his ticket and what does he git out of it? I dunno." She was not only dubious but worried, "I jest can't figger it! . . . Sa-ay!" She broke off suddenly and pointed ahead.

A full moon now was flooding down, making the island-studded Sound a fairyland of black and silver; and silhouetted in the moon's path and coming toward them was a large seagoing tug with a number of huge cargo lighters in tow, her running lights coruscating like jewels over the smooth rolling water.

"Ye're right, Annie," said Peter deeply. "It's Bullwinkle and his Salamander!"

"Hell an' hardtack!" Annie growled. "Here's me, thinkin' mebbe I'd crow over him a leetle, an'——" She swung the wheel over a little. "Mebbe if I was to skiddle to one side a mite, p'raps he won't see us!"

Such optimism, however, did injustice to the keen black shoebutton eyes and humorously malicious intuition of Horatio Bullwinkle, for as the two vessels drew closer, the Salamander's pilothouse door opened and Mr. Bullwinkle stepped out on deck. For a moment he peered at the oncoming Narcissus, then he turned and addressed his paunchy, stolid mate, who was at the wheel, in accents artfully loud, artlessly astonished.

"Why, Jake," he cried, "ain't this Tugboat Annie I see sailin' towards us? No!" Firmly he shook his bullet-head; repeated stoutly, "No, it can't be! She's piled up ashore on Whidby Island!"

"Oh, oh!" groaned Annie to Peter. "Here! Take the wheel!"

She also stepped out on deck. "Who said I was piled up, ye iggerant baboon?" she demanded irately.

But Mr. Bullwinkle appeared not to hear her. Instead, he cupped one large hand behind a somewhat cauliflower ear and assumed, eyes upraised, an archly listening attitude. "Hark!" he said ingenuously to Jake. "Ain't that a mockin' bird I hear?"

"If I'm a mockin' bird——" began Annie heatedly.

"Why, it is you!" interrupted Mr. Bullwinkle, registering intense delight.

"If I'm a mockin' bird," Annie repeated doggedly, ignoring this, and finishing in a regrettable bellow, "you're a mugwump!"

"A mugwump?" returned Mr. Bullwinkle gaily. "I don't get it."

"It's a bird," Annie informed him gladly, "what sits on a fence wid its mug on one side an' its wump on the other. On'y wid you, it's hard to tell which end is which! And now," she continued, more equably, "how'd you hear that I'd piled up?"

"The hull Secoma waterfront's talkin' about it! How ye run a steamer ashore on Bush Point in broad daylight and a flat calm. Tck-tck-tck! I could hardly believe it till they sent me along wi' these barges to transship her cargo."

"Wait a minute!" said Annie hastily and turned back to Peter. "Come about an' run abeam of him!" she directed, and when Peter had complied and the two tugs were running parallel, she again addressed Bullwinkle, "Now then! Who sent them barges?"

There was no flippancy in her tone now, and her rival, sensing her seriousness, also abandoned persiflage. "Why, Captain Craig, o' the Red Triangle Line," he told her. "The cargo owners phoned him. Said they had to start deliverin' tomorrow mornin', and——"

"I see!" Annie's big face was grim. "What time did you git yer instructions?"

"About sundown. Why?"

"But that's crazy! You're at least three hours out o' port, an' time ye got to the moorin's and picked up them barges——"

"That's right. I got me orders from Craig at five o' clock."

"An' flood tide wasn't till near six! Why, Bogle must 'a' radioed down an' axed fer them barges whiles we was still tryin' to snake her off, or mebbe before!"

"What's that, Annie?"

"Never mind!" She thought for a moment, then resumed. "Listen, Bullwinkle," she told him heavily, "I like you same as a herrin' likes a shark, but I'll give ye a tip. Watch yer step up there! There's some kind o' shenanigans goin' on, so don't let 'em mix ye up in it."

"Why should I? It's a straight business deal. And if I help the steamer meet her discharge date, Craig's promised me all his future business. That's why," and Mr. Bullwinkle, unable to contain his triumph, chortled, "Alec Severn's fit to be tied and you're likely to be lookin' fer a new job when ye get back. So long, Annie!"

It was late when Annie got in, but lights still were burning in Severn's private office when the Narcissus was made fast and her commander waddled hastily across the wharf and up the outside

THE FRAMING OF TUGBOAT ANNIE

stairs. Severn, his face set and stern, met her as she opened the door, while the night dispatcher watched with white face and frightened eyes.

Without speaking, Severn led her into his office and closed the door behind her. "Well, Annie——" he began, and since, for the moment, she could think of nothing to say, his anger, repressed through long anxious hours, blazed forth. "Why the purple-starred hell I ever trusted you——" he burst out suddenly, but this was all that Annie needed.

"Shut up!" she told him forcefully. "And git on that phone an' tell Craig to come down here!"

"Craig? Are you insane?" he returned, his round, pink, usually benevolent little face congested with anger. "Why, he wouldn't touch us with a forty-foot broomstick, much less come down here!"

"Do what I ax ye or I'll tellyphone him meself!" she shot at him, and, looking at her grim, mastiff face and deep-burning, purposeful eyes, reluctantly he did as he was asked.

In a matter of a half hour or so, Captain Craig was confronting them, his eyes raking Annie with contemptuous anger. But when he attempted to speak, "Save yer breath fer the right answers!" she snapped. "When did ye hear last from the Corinthian's master?"

"About an hour ago! From a shore telephone!" he snapped, his deep anger breaking loose at last. "And——"

"I knew it!" said Annie in triumph. "He's abandoned ship! Is that right?"

"That's right, thanks to you! And let me tell you——"

"Hold it!" Annie commanded. "I'm gonna tell you! An' if I'm wrong——"

"You're not telling me anything! I listened to you once too often before!" Craig snapped.

"Ye won't listen to me?"

"No!"

"Okay!" Abruptly she turned to Severn. "Gimme a blind check!" she demanded.

"A blind——"

"Blind ... blank ... whatever it is."

When, puzzled, he had obliged, she sat herself at his desk, grabbed a pen and laboriously commenced to fill in the check, talking as she wrote. "Out o' forty years o' work," she told them, "I've saved jest over ten thousand slappers. And here"—she completed the writing and signed her name, then handed the check to Craig—"is ten thousand of it."

"But—but——" He stared at it; met her hard, determined eyes. "This is made out to the Red Triangle Line!"

"That's right. Ye got me life's savin's right in yer paw. That's me fee to ye fer listenin' to me. If I'm wrong in what I tell ye, ye can keep it as my contribulation toward the damages what Alec will owe yer company. But if I'm right, and what I tell ye saves ye money, I want that check back and twenty-five percent o' what it saves ye, payable to Alec here, an' a promise o' yer future business."

Craig turned and looked at Severn, his face registering the utmost incredulity. "Is this woman crazy?" he asked.

"Yeah, crazy like a ox!" She stared at him demandingly. "Is it a deal?"

Uneasy, yet now somehow impressed by her earnestness, Craig turned from her to Severn; and the latter, his eyes on Annie's resolute face and deep-sparkling eyes, and with recollection of how, in the past, she had emerged from tight corners, suddenly made up his mind. "I'll string along with Annie," he said quietly.

"Thanks, Alec," said Annie, not looking at him, but her voice suddenly, gratefully, was husky. Then to Craig she said impatiently, "Come on, make up yer mind! Is it a deal?"

"Yes," he said quietly at length. "It's a deal."

"Swellegant!" and her grimness melted in a wide and happy grin. "Now then. When I left, the Corinthian was aground! Bogle put her there, not me! And when I tried to tow her off, he cut the hawser. I got the severed end to prove it!" And, ignoring their stares of blank astonishment, she continued, "Now, she's not only still aground, she's abandoned!"

"How did you know that?" Craig said.

"It's still my turn at axin'," she reminded him tartly. "Did ye ever look into Captain Bogle's past?"

"I never had occasion to. We found him during the war, and——"

"Like I suspected! Well, look it up sometime. I fancy ye'll find it both spotted an' interestin'! Who's the owners o' the cargo?"

"Bendigo and Gadstone."

"Recently incorporated fer the purpose o' handlin' this cargo?"

"I wouldn't know that. I——"

"Okay, I'm tellin' ye. Ye can check that later too. Anyways, Bendigo's wid the Corinthian now, lookin' after his interests. And ye'll find that Captain Bogle has an interest in that cargo too."

Craig stared at her. "Just what are you trying to say, Mrs. Brennan?" he asked.

"On'y this, sir," she answered quietly: "That Captain Bogle, in cahoots wid the cargo owners, deliberately put his vessel ashore on Bush P'int."

"But that's insane! Why should he? If he was found out, he'd lose his master's ticket and get ten years in jail, and what would he gain?"

"Enough to make it wuth his while, p'raps. But we'll come back to that sooner an' later. Meanwhiles, you an' Alec here is goin' up there in the Narcissus. Peter'll take ye. An' here's what to do when ye git there: Ye'll find her abandoned, but wid Bogle an' the crew on shore, ready to go back. Or mebbe they are back now, an' busy transferrin' the cargo into them barges ye sent Bullwinkle up wid. If so, make Bogle h'ist it back aboard. Then, wid the mornin' flood, have the Salamander an' the Narcissus put wires on her an' they'll haul her off, cargo an' all, as easy as pullin' a duck's tooth."

"Why don't you come with us, Annie?" asked Severn. "You seem to know all the answers."

"I do," said Annie complacently. "After I talked wid Bullwinkle on his way up there, I stuck me snoot in a book or two dealin' wid freight payments an' maritime law, an' I found what I was lookin' fer. But I want ye to go up an' prove me right so far. Meantimes, I'll set here. And I ain't agoin' to bulge till ye git back!"

Annie watched from the office window while the lights of the Narcissus disappeared around the end of the wharf; then, going down to the storeroom, she cut herself a couple of huge cheese sandwiches, opened a quart of beer, then returned to Severn's office and settled herself to wait.

The night had fled and the steely light of dawn was spreading over the still tranquil reaches of the Sound when Annie, chilled from her long vigil, awakened from a nap and waddled to the window. It was not the cold which had awakened her, however, but the familiar thump of the Narcissus's propeller. Even now she was coming alongside her berth; and moving slowly across the still harbor, escorted by the Salamander, and with Horatio Bullwinkle as pilot on her bridge, was the S.S. Corinthian, under her own power, and slipping smoothly toward a long cargo wharf nearby. Dully, Annie watched; then, rubbing her tired eyes, but with a satisfied nod, she returned to her chair.

Almost instantly she was asleep again, and when, awakened by Severn's hand on her shoulder, she looked up, he was smiling down at her. Slowly she got up, looked at Craig, who had followed Severn through the doorway, and held out her hand.

"I'll have me check back now," she said with a sleepy grin. "Where's Captain Bogle? In jail?"

"Not yet, but he will be," Craig told her, suddenly grim again as he handed her the check. "On a charge of barratry and attempted embezzlement. And Bendigo will be with him."

"Oh, so ye know now what I was holdin' out on ye?" asked Annie, disappointed that her triumph had been anticipated. "Well, come on, ye doubtin' tomcats, give!"

"I'm sorry I anticipated you, Annie," Craig told her with a smile. "But I haven't been to sea all my life either without learning some of the answers. And with the clues you gave us before we left, if they were true, there could be only one solution. But go ahead. I'll let you tell it anyway. How did you figure it?"

"Well," said Annie happily, grateful for the chance, "I figgered Bogle wasn't in cahoots wid your owners, for he had nothin' to gain, as you said. Then who was he in cahoots wid? And Bullwinkle, tellin' me the nasty feller had ordered lighters to transship the cargo even afore a tug had a chance to try an' drag him off, put me on the right smell."

"Scent, Annie," Severn corrected mildly.

"Same thing in this case, ain't it?" Annie grinned. "Anyways, if Bogle couldn't profit from the owners o' the vessel, that left on'y the owners o' the cargo. So, after leavin' Bullwinkle, I went to me cabin and started dredgin' out the law regardin' the payments o' waterborne freight. And here's what I found. Wait a minute; Alec's got a copy of it here. I'll read it to ye!"

She took from a bookshelf a slender volume on Shipmasters' Business, thumbed clumsily through it and at length found what she sought. Then, following the words with a massive forefinger, she read aloud:

"Since freight is computed on a finished voyage only, and where ship and cargo have been abandoned by a shipowner or a shipmaster legally acting for an owner, but the cargo afterward is carried forward from the point of disaster by salvors or a third party, the shipowner has no lien for freight, nor is he, in fact, entitled to claim even pro-rata compensation for that part of the voyage actually performed, even if he carry it halfway around the world to within half a mile of its destination."

Annie put the book aside and faced them. "In other words, captain," she said soberly, "not only was they out to cheat ye out o' your freight payment—from which Bogle was to get his squeeze, o' course—but you, representin' the shipowners, would ha' had to bear the cost o' that transshipment for even the measly little forty-five miles from Bush P'int to Secoma! Ain't that right?"

"That's right!" replied Craig. "All told, it would have meant a loss to us of perhaps a hundred thousand dollars. But," he added deeply, "thanks to you——"

"A mere female woman?" reminded Annie with a humorously malicious grin.

"Maybe we'd better not go into that," amended Craig hastily. "Anyway, Annie, supposing my company were to make you a present, personally, of a thousand dollars, what would you do with it?"

"A thousand dollars?" cried Annie, wide-eyed with delight. "Oh, my; oh, me! Well, le's see, now I'd put most of it in the bank, but—yeah, that's it!—I'd keep enough out so's I could go uptown to the compartment store an' buy meself a couple o' pair o' pylons!"

TUGBOAT ANNIE'S SECRET

All day the gray low-ceilinged sky had threatened the Puget Sound port of Secoma with the year's first snow, and now, with evening closing in, it had come, muffling the harbor's barnyard chorus of cautiously moving shipping and brushing with ethereal beauty such mundane things as boxcars and freight sheds, docks and barges and anchored vessels. And even so prosaic an object as the big deep-water tug Narcissus looked like something off a Christmas card as she surged in and, with running lights shining like jewels through the swirling crystals in the gathering darkness, made all secure alongside her home wharf.

Moments thereafter, Tugboat Annie Brennan, her master, clumped up the outside steps of the Deep-Sea Towing and Salvage Company offices; and when she flung open the door and entered the warmth within, her blue, weather-wrinkled eyes were dancing.

"Hi, Fred!" she boomed at the dispatcher as she slammed the door. "What's new what ain't been stole?"

"Can't you ever come in here," grumbled Fred, "without tearing the place apart?" He consulted his dispatch sheet. "There's a big steamer, the Starlight Victory, having turbine trouble up at Anacortes and she's got to be towed down here for repairs."

"Right away?" Annie yelped. "Why, I jest come in from Campbell River——"

"Keep your wig on, Annie!" Fred smiled. "She's still discharging cargo up there and won't be ready for a coupla days yet."

"Swellegant! I'll have a night in me bunk fer a change! Sa-ay, I noticed that Bullwinkle's Salamander ain't at her berth across the slip. I don't suppose she's been sunk or nothin' comical like that, huh?"

"I wouldn't know," Fred told her. "All I know is, she's been away for two, three days now. And that's not bad. It'll keep you and Bullwinkle from clawin' each other for a while."

"That horse's tail!" Annie growled automatically. "Well, guess I'll sashay up to the Greasy Spoon an' lay in some grub. Be seein' ya, boy," and with an elephantine wave of her paw, she waddled spiritedly out.

The windows of the Greasy Spoon, that popular waterfront cafe across the tracks, were hospitable orange beacons in the snowy night, its interior rich with the odors of plain but savory cooking, as Tugboat Annie barged in, exchanged salty persiflage with various acquaintances, hung up her things and, with appreciative sniffings, settled her ample frame in a cozy booth.

"Fetch me a double ration o' them nice fried trollops o' yours, Olive!" she roared good-humoredly. "An' a coupla baked spuds wid lashin's o' butter!"

Then, as she sat affably back, tucking her napkin under her chin, she became aware of someone beside her; and glancing down, she immediately recognized the bandy but powerful legs.

"Oh-oh!" she said loudly and with vast distaste. "The wind is off the dump again!"

"Sure it ain't blowin' back in yer face, Annie?" asked a dulcetly solicitous voice, and she looked up into the grinning countenance of Captain Horatio Bullwinkle.

"I knowed it, I knowed it!" groaned Annie. "Jest as I'm set to enj'y a good meal somethin' comes along an' upsets me stummick!"

"And what a stomach, Annie!" murmured Mr. Bullwinkle. "Purty soon it's gonna need four legs to tote it around."

"You'll need four guys to carry ye outta here," stormed Annie, half rising, "if ye start gittin' me dandruff up!"

"Now, now, dear," replied Mr. Bullwinkle. "I was merely admirin' your architecture."

"Well, spoof off! I'm in no mood fer idle bandage!" growled Annie. "Hey, wait a minute! How come you're ashore here an' yer Salamander ain't at her dock? Gov'ment claimed her fer taxes at last?"

"Oh, havin' a little face lifting, Annie," he replied airily.

"What'd she do—fall apart?"

"No, she did not!" replied her rival. "Fact is, it'd be worth quite a bit to you to know where she is and what's bein' done to her, because it's something that's gonna cost you some business."

"That's a laugh!" Annie said.

"Is it?" Mr. Bullwinkle became both expansive and mysterious. "Why, say, when they get through I won't even have to go aboard. She'll just go ahead an' run herself."

"In which case," sniffed Annie, "she might earn ye a honest livin' fer a change! An' as if I cared where she is or what they're——Well, go on, dang it!" she exploded, unable longer to control her curiosity. "Where is she?"

Red Halloran, master of the tug Firefly, and one of a now intensely listening group, leaned from a neighboring booth. "I heerd," he told Mr. Bullwinkle, "ye ran her over to——"

"Let Annie worry!" interrupted the Salamander's master hastily. "When she's thinkin', her brain stops and she keeps out o' trouble better."

"Poof!" said Annie. "Ye're prob'ly havin' a hull built onto her so's she'll look like a vessel, at least. That it?"

"Guess away," replied Mr. Bullwinkle, with maddening superiority. "I'll give ye one hint, though. The days o' barking-dog navigation are over, Annie. There's no guesswork in tugboatin' no more. And to survive, ye gotta be modern! Like me!"

"Yeah?" scoffed Annie. "Well, the old ways, what we l'arned be experience'll still draw enough water fer me! Ask Dog-face Jackson over there 'bout the time I berthed a ten-thousand-ton steamer years ago when the follower nut what holds the piston plate come adrift, an' I had to stop me engine! Hey, Dog-face?"

"Sure was somethin', Annie," replied Dog-face. "I was in the——"

"So what happened?" went on Annie to Mr. Bullwinkle.

"Ye run on your own compressed hot air?" he grinned.

"No, sir!" said Annie. "It was the wrong time o' tide an' a gale blowin', but I made use of 'em both, along wid the steamer's own engines, an' berthed her so neat that the shipmaster gimme a case o' sherry . . . what had turned a mite sour, I found out later. But he never did know me tug's engines was outta commission fer a hour an' a half! So tie that wid any o' yer modern fiddle-fangles!"

By morning the wind had slacked off, but the snow still fell, limiting visibility over the water, so that shipping moved at a crawl. Such weather, however, was no handicap to Tugboat Annie, who had navigated from Flattery to Olympia in rain, snow or darkness for more than forty years. And by evening the Narcissus was well to the north again, towing two large oil barges which she was to deliver at Port Townsend before running across, after a night's layover, to pick up the Starlight Victory at Anacortes. Dutifully, at the proper legal intervals, her fog siren blasted into the snowy darkness ahead, while

TUGBOAT ANNIE'S SECRET

Annie stood at the wheel in the blacked-out pilothouse and allowed her thoughts to speculate upon the whereabouts of the mysterious Salamander.

"Bullwinkle wasn't lyin'," she confided irascibly to Peter, her large, phlegmatic and tobacco-chewing mate. "She's layin' up somewhere, because this mornin' just afore we sailed, I seen him an' that fat-bellied mate o' his comin' outta Rafferty's beer parlor. An' if the Salamander was off on a job, one or the other'd sure be aboard."

"She's at the Bremerton Navy Yard," Peter told her calmly. "The night watchman at the freight sheds says she's been there several days."

"Well, of all the aggravatin' apes!" Annie yelled wrathfully. "Here's you, fair bustin' wid inflammation, while I bin sweatin' me brains out tryin' to——What's she doin' there?"

"I dunno. But Bullwinkle and Jake was joinin' her wi' the rest o' her crew today, the watchman said."

"H'm'mph!" Unaccountably, now that Annie knew where the Salamander was, though not for what purpose, she was relieved. "Prob'ly just been buyin' some o' that Navy war-surplus gear." She laughed disparagingly. "O' course, it'd never occur to Bullwinkle that new gear's no good 'less ye git the business to use it wid! . . . Yeah, Clem?" she interrupted herself, as the tug's radio operator stood in the doorway.

"Coast Guard radio at the Siwash Point station says there's a steam tug ashore in Ghost Inlet."

Annie gasped. "Ghost Inlet?"

"It's along the coast, south o' the cape," Peter supplemented.

"I know that!" snapped Annie. "I used to haul log booms outta there years ago, an' it's so fogbound 'count o' them glaciers back of it most o' the year, ye almost gotta walk along the bottom to find the entrance! What's the tug's name, Clem? Did they say?"

"Yeah. Louis F. Danforth, out of Portland."

"Oh, brother!" exclaimed Annie.

"You know her?" asked Clem seriously.

"Know her?" Annie's voice suddenly was deep with emotion. "Why, me an' Louis Danforth used to prank together as kids on the Willamette River years ago! I remember when that tug was built, even—copper-fastened and made o' live oak from the coast o' Maine! Course, they don't own it no more, but she cost aplenty even in them days. An' she may be old an' slow now—she's a coal burner—but she's still got more power for her displacement than any tug on the West Coast! What about the crew, Clem?"

"She's abandoned. They got ashore and walked overland the ten miles to the station."

"H'm'm. Mebbe she was holed bad, pilin' up; else she run outta fuel beatin' around in the fog."

"How she ever wiggled her way through that gap into Ghost Inlet——" began Peter, but Annie interrupted.

"Old-timers' luck!" she said convincingly. "Any o' these twentieth-century smart monkeys'd ha' piled her up on the rocks outside! How's the glass, Peter?"

Peter looked at the barometer. "Holding," he said. "But the breeze is swinging, and that means a sou'easter ain't more'n just beyond scratchin' distance. Why?"

"Here, take the wheel whiles I figger this out," said Annie. "Le's see, now. We drop these oil barges at Port Townsend in about a hour from now, an' we don't hafta pick up the Starlight Victory at Anacortes till day after tomorrer. That means——" Suddenly she whirled on Clem. "Listen. Try an' find out from the Coast Guard what shape she's in!"

"What's the idea, Annie?" asked Peter curiously.

"Idear?" Annie's big face was alight with inspiration. "If the Danforth kin even float, she's wuth fifty thousand in salvage alone! An' if we kin tow her home an' reconvert her to diesels, the company's got a new tug what'll knock Bullwinkle's eye out! Him an' his newfinagled thumadiddles!"

But no further information was forthcoming from the Coast Guard. They had relayed the item as part of their nightly short-wave broadcast for the information of seafarers and there was nothing to add. Annie had brought off long chances before, however, and her incurably optimistic nature would not allow her to pass this one up. Therefore, having delivered her oil barges at Port Townsend, dawn found the Narcissus plowing south outside the cape, the shores of the Olympic Peninsula to port lost in snow and swirling mist.

With the smell of hot cakes and coffee drifting up to them from the galley below, Annie and Peter stood in the raw morning, peering anxiously ahead.

"I sure hope it clears up a little," muttered Annie, brushing the snow from her lashes. "Even in midsummer there's fog around the mouth o' Ghost Inlet an' we'd wait outside fer days, sometimes, when they was loggin' in there, sooner'n take a chance on them surf-washed rocks. But winter's different. Mebbe we'll git a break."

By ten o'clock the Narcissus, although prudently well offshore, was abeam of the inlet. The snow temporarily had ceased to fall, and they could see the densely forested peaks of the mountains soaring majestically above a heavy fog bank that clung close to the land. But as the tug closed with the shore she was surrounded by the thick, clammy white veil, which restricted observation to less than 200 yards, and, as it once more began to snow, even this closed in.

"Better hold it, Annie," said Peter cautiously. "If we ever pile up here, Lord help us; 'specially wi' that sou'easter on the way. An' when that gets crackin', whether we're here or not, all that's gonna be left o' that tug inside there is toothpicks!"

"When they was handin' out crape, however did they come to overlook you?" rasped Annie. "We're stoppin' here till around sunset anyway, an' be that time it'll prob'ly clear enough for us to run inside an' have a peek."

When the day was almost gone, and the eastern sky was perceptibly darker, what Annie had foretold came true; for suddenly the snow was blown away, and Shiftless, the Narcissus's gangling deck hand, hailed from his lookout post in the bows. "Look, Annie!" he yelled. "I can almost see the surf breakin' over them shoreward rocks!"

"Sure enough!" cried Annie happily. "We'll wait outside here fer mebbe another half hour, an' if it's cleared enough——"

Abruptly, she stopped and listened, then turned to Big Sam, the engineer, who had come up from below for his early supper. "You hear anythin' queer, Sam?" she asked, puzzled.

Big Sam also froze. "I don't hear nothin' queer," he said matter-of-factly. "All I hear is another diesel tug out here with us somewheres. Pretty big one, too, by the sound o' that exhaust."

Together they stood, alert and listening, and presently the short, staccato pant of the other vessel was unmistakably clear. Instantly Annie clattered up the ladder to the pilothouse and yanked the whistle cord, and the deep-throated blast of the siren broke the stillness.

For a few moments there was silence; then, sharp and clear, came the other vessel's reply. "Toot to-toot-toot! Toot-toot!" jeered the stranger's air whistle, derision in every note, and Annie, who had been followed up by Big Sam, stared at him, aghast.

"Bullwinkle!" she grated. "How in the merry hell——"

"Listen!" said Big Sam sharply. They heard the surging roar of a big bow wave, and from out of the thinning fog to seaward materialized the rakish silhouette of the Salamander.

Then the foghorn voice of Mr. Bullwinkle roared across to them. "'Hoy there, Annie!" he cried jovially. "Fancy meetin' you here!" and his bulky figure showed dimly against the white of his wheelhouse.

"What ye doin' here yerself?" Annie bellowed back, wild with rage.

"Oh, just run down to have a look around!" responded Mr. Bullwinkle. "We got kind of a late start, but when that Coast Guard message went out last night, I smelled a dollar, same as you! Had a look at the Danforth yet?"

"Ye know damn well I ain't, ye wind-geared jackass!"

"Now, Annie, is that neighborly? Is that kind?" replied Mr. Bullwinkle in pained reproof. "After I come all the way here just to make sure ye was all right."

He retreated inside his wheelhouse, and almost immediately, in response to bells jingling in the Salamander's engine room, the bone in her teeth grew to a roaring cascade and she headed at high speed shoreward.

Instinctively, Annie yelled in warning. "Hey, ye blisterin' idjet! There's rocks ahead there! Don't go in till it clears!"

But already the Salamander was lost in the fog, and Annie and Big Sam braced themselves for the inevitable crash. Instead, there was silence.

It was nearly an hour later before the fog had cleared sufficiently to allow the Narcissus to enter the narrow rockbound channel into the calm waters of Ghost Inlet. It was well named, for burned-out and logged-over skeletons of a dead forest stood like black, forbidding specters along the shore. But Annie and her crew had no attention to waste on sentiment; for, as the Narcissus surged across the mirrorlike water, they saw that the Salamander had reached the prize first.

The Louis F. Danforth, huge and powerful-looking still, lay like a stranded whale on a short, rock-studded crescent of sand. Nearby was the bustling Salamander, the water marbling under her counter, and lines aboard the derelict tightening as Mr. Bullwinkle took up the slack. Annie watched glumly, but with professional appreciation.

"I gotta hand it to him, the bandylegged snake in the bush," she muttered to Peter, who was still at the wheel. "But I still can't figger how he was able to run in here through all that fog. An' he never even scratched——Hey, wait a minute!" and her gaze suddenly was focused upon the Salamander's sturdy mast, "I wonder if——?"

She gave Peter a quick, sharp order, and presently the Narcissus was floating alongside the straining, panting Salamander.

"Hi, Bullwinkle!" Annie hailed, and the Salamander's master crossed to his rail.

"What? You still around?" he exclaimed in artless astonishment.

Annie pointed. "That—that kinda grid thing on yer mast—ain't that——"

"Sure!" he said, gazing upward. "It's a bird cage. It holds the early bird what catches the worm. But some folks calls it——"

"Radar! O' course!" said Annie in self-disgust. "I should ha' remembered! I seen it often enough durin' the war! So that's what the Salamander was doin' in Bremerton—havin' it installed!"

"Complete wi' a trained operator," replied Mr. Bullwinkle complacently. "No more bein' fogbound or held up by rain or dark nights for me, grandma!" Then, turning away, he resumed supervision of the salvage job.

Dourly, Annie watched while, foot by foot, the Danforth was hauled clear. Then with a last ear-piercing screech of heavy timbers over rock and pebbles, she was afloat, bobbing violently. Ranging swiftly alongside, the Salamander put two of her crew on board; then, with a towing wire made fast to the Danforth's bow, the two vessels moved smoothly toward the seaward gap. And as they passed the Narcissus, Mr. Bullwinkle launched a farewell gibe. "Hey, Annie," he called solicitously, "can I give ye a tow?"

Disdaining to answer, Annie turned to Peter and dejectedly gave orders to start back.

"At least we got the Starlight Victory to pick up on our way in," she said, but this was bleak comfort, and despondently she wagged her shaggy head. "Well, there goes fifty thousand slappers, an' the Secoma waterfront's sure gonna hold me up to ridicule an' colloquy when they hear tell o' this!"

Peter, whose attention was on the departing vessels, did not immediately answer. But when he did, his tone was strangely unsteady. "Never say die, pal!" he croaked.

"Who's dyin'?" demanded Annie. "'Cept fer a chance to lend that big twit a good kick in——"

"I don't mean that, Annie! I mean——Well, look! Somethin's went wrong!"

"Wrong?" Quickly her gaze followed his outstretched arm to the Salamander and her tow, now just clearing the thundering breakers of the gap, and she saw what he meant; for the two men on board the Danforth were running with wild gesticulations up into her bows.

"Somethin's cockeyed all right," Annie grunted, puzzled. "Them guys is scared! An look, Bullwinkle's comin' about!"

In the next few minutes Annie once again had occasion to admire the prompt efficiency of her rival; for in a matter of seconds the Salamander had spun on her heel and now, guiding her tow with consummate skill back through the narrow entrance, she was moving at high speed toward the beach. Then, when it seemed that the Salamander herself would pile up, the big tug sheered away and the Danforth, carried by her momentum, but guided by Bullwinkle's superlative judgment, was grounded once more, but this time on a clear stretch of shelving sand where, presently, she hung motionless, her bow held fast and her stern in deep water.

"Oh, dear!" cried Annie briskly. "I gotta git to the bottom o' this! . . . Shif'less! Shif'less, git the dinghy over the side!"

By the time Annie had climbed on board the stranded Danforth, Mr. Bullwinkle, his face a mask of fury, already was there with Jake, his paunchy mate, and his engineer, a capable-appearing younger man named Lloyd.

"Gracious me," said Annie archly to Mr. Bullwinkle, "if you ain't the busybody! Fust ye take her away, then ye fetch her back! Busy, busy, busy, runnin' hither an' dither like a ——"

"Shut up!" rasped Mr. Bullwinkle. "And who asked you on board here anyways?"

"I come," said Annie meekly, "to see what I could l'arn. But seems ye didn't need no modern gadgets to run her ashore again. What's went wrong?"

"She's got a leak in her bilge almost as big as that hole in your head! Must 'a sprained some plankin' pretty bad when she first piled up," he explained; for Mr. Bullwinkle was well aware of Annie's professional skill, as well as of the fact that where a technical problem is concerned, tugboatmen are almost childlike in their eagerness to help solve it.

But Annie proved not particularly helpful. She said vaguely, "Can't ye patch her up some way?"

"Sure! I got a dry dock right in me pocket!" he snapped. "Anyway, with that sou'easter due to come blastin' in the entrance a few hours from now, whatever we do's got to be done quick. Got any more bright ideas?"

"Scabs of 'em," said Annie cheerfully. "What's wrong wi' usin' her main pump? All ye need do is git steam up——"

"With what, dim-brain?" he demanded. "The reason she went ashore in the first place was because she run out o' coal after runnin' around in the fog and last night's snow!"

"Well, ye got yer engineer here," Annie said placidly. "What does he suggest?"

Lloyd looked uncomfortable. "I'm afraid a steam plant's a little out of my line, ma'am," he said hesitantly.

"Yeah, son, about two generations out," replied Annie soberly. "Diesels an' electric turbines is your dish, not these old compound two-cylinder steam jobs ... But you, Bullwinkle, you oughtta know——"

"What do ye think I hire engineers for?" demanded that gentleman sullenly. "My job's topside! Always has been!"

"Above the neck excluded," said Annie complacently. "Hand pumps wouldn't control the inflow, huh?"

"My men tried that. But the water come in so fast it scared the pants offa them. Said she was sinkin'. She was too."

"Well, le's take a look below," Annie suggested. "Mebbe it'll give me the shimmerin' of a idear."

But this was fruitless also; for while the powerful, old-fashioned engine seemed in working order, with the main pump directly connected with the driving shaft, there could be, as Mr. Bullwinkle sarcastically pointed out, no steam without coal, and without steam to turn the main engine, the pump was equally useless.

"Sure is a shame," said Annie. "A fine big tug the like o' this, still good fer twenty or more years, bein' left to rot or be broke up by bad weather!" Slowly and regretfully she looked around, then commented: "H'm'mph! Her engineer had a head on him, anyways! Look, he's fastened a rubber plunger to a broomstick an' fastened the top o' the broomstick to the pump eccentric. An' see. There's the pail, full o' his dirty duds an' soapy water, so when the eccentric jounced up an' down, it done his washin' fer him, like a reggaler washin' machine!"

"Remind me," said Mr. Bullwinkle ironically, "to stick you in the bucket when it's workin' again. Well," he added, as she continued to stare at the contraption, "let's go!"

"Huh?" said Annie absently. "Oh ... yeah, yeah! But I was jest thinkin' that—that——"

"Thinkin' what?" asked Mr. Bullwinkle.

"Nothin'," said Annie indifferently. "It prob'ly wouldn't ha' worked anyway." And before he could question further, she led the way topside again. On deck she absented herself for a brief spell while she made a rapid examination of the tug's outer planking. Then, casually, she questioned the Salamander's engineer. "How fast did them men o' yours say the water was comin' in?" she asked. "How do ye know she wouldn't stay afloat till ye got her into Port Angeles, at least?"

"The water was nearly over the engine-room plates by the time we got her back in here," Lloyd told her. "She'd last for maybe twenty miles. Then she'd go down like a stone."

"Yeah? Well, that's sure too bad." She turned back to Mr. Bullwinkle. "And where do ye go from here, duperman?"

"Home, you dope! Where else?" he replied savagely.

"Jest a minute," she said quietly, and eyed him as if wondering how far she could trust him. "What about this vessel?" she pursued at length. "You don't want it no more?"

"Let the gulls have it!" he snapped. "We've wasted enough time... Come on, you two!" and he gestured the others to follow.

"In that case, then," said Annie mildly, "ye'd have no objection if I took her?"

Mr. Bullwinkle, one bandy leg suspended over the rail, stared at her. "Take her where—to Davy Jones's Locker?"

"If you don't want her I'll take her," said Annie. "An' after I've had Big Sam, me engineer, over here, an' we've sized her up together, mebbe I'll have a job fer ye, Bullwinkle."

"A job for me?" Slowly he lifted his leg from the rail and came back to her. "What kind of a job?"

"A towin' job, o' course. Towin' the Danforth home." And, ignoring the astonishment in his eyes, she added softly, "Ye'd ruther make a leetle than go home empty-headed, wouldn't ye?"

"Listen," growled Mr. Bullwinkle, every pore now crawling with suspicion. "What is this? What dirty deal you got up yer sleeve?"

"It mightn't even work," said Annie, dissembling fast.

"If it'd work for you, it would for me. What is it?"

"No use sayin' till I try it," replied Annie. "An' in any case, since ye don't know what it is, you can't do it!... Oh, all right," she capitulated, before his stony stare. "I'll tell ye! I'm jest willin' to gamble I kin keep her afloat till she gits in, that's all! That mebbe she ain't leakin' as bad as you think!"

"Oh, is that all?" Mr. Bullwinkle was at once relieved, and contemptuous again. "Come on, boys!"

"Ye mean," cried Annie with mendacious incredulity, "ye'd pass up a chance to make a easy sixteen hundred bucks?"

That stopped him again. "Like how?" he demanded.

"Like I jest told ye—be tryin' to tow the Danforth in. Look, I mean it! All ye gotta do is sign a teeny-weentsy bit o' paper sayin' ye relish all claims on this here tug, an' I'll pay ye the reggaler fee of eight hundred dollars a day fer the two days it'll take ye to git her safe into Secoma."

"Now I know it's phony!" howled Mr. Bullwinkle. "Because what about your Narcissus? Can't she tow her for as long as she'll stay afloat?"

"Unh-uh!" Annie shook her head. "She's got a job to pick up on the sound, an' it's time she was startin', afore it begins snowin' again or that sou'easter blows in. Well, what do ye say?"

"Hold on a minute!" said Mr. Bullwinkle, and with remarkable agility he tore below again in a hasty resurvey to make sure there was not some favorable condition about the derelict tug that Annie might have seen, but that he had chanced to overlook. When he reappeared, however, it was only to shake his puzzled head. "Now I'm sure you're nuts," he said deeply. "But it's your money."

"It's me boss's money," she told him with a grin. "Well, ye'll do it?"

"On one condition. When she sinks, I cast off. But you pay me the sixteen hundred regardless. Okay?"

"Carried anonymously!" Annie promptly agreed.

Less than an hour later, the Louis F. Danforth, with Tugboat Annie and Big Sam on board, was once more heading out of Ghost Inlet in tow of the sturdy Salamander, while, far ahead and hull down by now, the Narcissus, in charge of Peter, and with Big Sam's assistant in the engine room, was en route to keep her date with the Starlight Victory at Anacortes. And for long after the Salamander and her tow had cleared the gap, and with fog and snow again clamped down over the North Pacific, Mr. Bullwinkle stood on the fantail as the miles foamed astern and, regardless of the cold and the wet, stared at the snow-blurred oil lamp set on the Danforth's mast and wondered, unhappily, what was keeping her afloat. For he was forced at length to admit that she was no lower in the water than when the tow had begun. And even the slip of paper in his pocketbook, guaranteeing him payment regardless of what happened, was now of small comfort compared with what, he was forced to conclude, he had lost.

And when finally he sought refuge in the wheelhouse, he confided his depressing thoughts to Jake, who was at the wheel.

"I just don't get it!" he rasped. "She was takin' in water like a sieve when we towed her out, and now she floats as light and perky as a drunken duck. And did ye notice her bilge discharge as we pulled through the gap? It was pourin' water out of her like the main pump had never been stopped!"

Dawn saw them well within the Strait of Juan de Fuca, minutes before the dreaded sou'easter broke in smoking fury against Flattery's iron cliffs, but since the force of the gale reduced their speed, it was not until late the following day that the Salamander delivered her charge alongside the shipyard dock at Secoma. But no sooner was she made fast than Mr. Bullwinkle was on board the Danforth and indignantly demanding to know the answer.

"Ye'll laff," Annie chuckled, scratching her broad back against the lee of the deckhouse while she watched the shipyard crew prepare to dry-dock her prize. "It was almost as simple as you are."

"Ye gonna tell me," shouted Mr. Bullwinkle hotly, "or do I have to kick it outta you?"

"Keep yer bearin's cool," Annie admonished mildly. "After all, what's the loss o' fifty thousand slimoleons, when ye're agonna l'arn somethin'? Anyways, it was that homemade washin' machine attached to the pump eccentric what fust gave me the idear o' bunkoin' you; for I thought then, practically everythin' what's invented kin be made to do a double job—unless, o' course, folks is plumb iggerent, like you an' that bubble-socks engineer o' yours."

"Keep to the point!" retorted Mr. Bullwinkle.

"'Tis the p'int," Annie insisted. "An' it's too bad fer you that ye didn't know—or care—more about them old-time compound marine steam engines. For it was plain as the nose on yer pikestaff that if the engine could turn over, the main pump, what was attached direct to the drivin' shaft, would hafta work too."

"How could the engine turn over with no steam up, and no coal to get it up with?" he countered irritably.

"That's the crud o' the whole thing!" Annie cried. "We didn't need no coal! We got the engine turnin' over widout steam, an' I'm supprised ye didn't think of it yerself!"

"We'll skip that," said Mr. Bullwinkle hastily. "How was it done?"

"Well, sir," obliged Annie, affably, "since, like I telled ye, the pump—one o' the old plunger type—was actuated be direct connection wid the drivin' shaft, we jest switched the condenser intake from the sea to the bilge to take care o' the incomin' water." She paused and inquired archly, "Are ye beginnin' to git it?"

"Go on," said Mr. Bullwinkle grimly.

"Then when ye started towin' us, since we'd already removed the cylinder tops to eliminate compression, jest the movement o' the Danforth through the water turned the propeller, an' that turned over the engine, which revolved the drivin' shaft. An' that operated the main pump wid its four-inch discharge pipe, an' it kept us as dry as a bonehead all the way home! . . . Why, Horatio, what's the matter? Ye ain't leavin' already?"

But Mr. Bullwinkle had given a low moan and was already over the rail and hurrying along the pier to the more soothing environment of his Salamander.

Annie turned and slowly walked along the narrow main deck of the again forlorn and deserted-looking Louis F. Danforth, and a lump came into her throat, for to her vessels were persons, with lives and feelings of their own.

"Take it easy, old-timer," she muttered, and slapped the ancient paint work with a reassuring hand. "'Twon't be long now afore ye'll be underway again, wid yer galley cookin' good meals fer a full crew, an' you all dolled up wid diesel engines, ship-shore tellyphone, electric towin' winches an'— an'——" She hesitated, then went recklessly on, "Yeah, I wouldn't be supprised if we even fitted ye out wid—wid radar! Oh, your days o' useful work ain't done!" She shook her blowzy head with solemn relish. "No, sir! Yours, nor mine! Fer it'll be many a long day afore us two relicts is candidates fer the Indignant Old Ladies' Home!"

TUGBOAT ANNIE BURNS A BRIDGE

Gradually thickening weather, with spits of rain, was blowing in from the Pacific, shrouding in pine- and spruce-impregnated mist the vast, high forests that rose precipitously to snow line from the little cannery and sawmill town of Port Olympic. But the dull, depressing morning was no more gloomy than the thoughts of Tugboat Annie Brennan, massive and ordinarily cheerful skipper of the big Puget Sound salvage tug Narcissus, when, having delivered a bargeload of diesel fuel to the oil-company wharf, she crossed the harbor to the cannery dock at the foot of the town's main street.

"Hi, Annie!" shouted the cannery superintendent cordially as the tug glided to a stop alongside and quickly was made fast. "Glad to see you again! How you been?"

"Ter'ble!" groaned Annie as she stepped outside the wheelhouse to the rail; and her large, mastiff face registered the utmost misery. "Dunno what's clumb into me lately, Tim. Can't sleep so good, ain't got no appetite——"

"Ye had eight pancakes for breakfast," remarked Peter, the Narcissus's huge-stomached, phlegmatic mate, as he started up the ladder from the deck below. "And a platterful o' sausages an' eggs."

"Call that a appetite?" returned Annie with indignant scorn. "Did I have more'n one helpin'? An' did I as much as even snuff the breakfast steaks? No, Tim, I just ain't me usual self these days. I feel—well, I ain't got no life; no int'rest in nothin'——"

"Why not?" Peter interrupted again from the top of the ladder. "You ain't even had Bullwinkle in your hair lately. Not since he went off on that towin' job to Los Angeles."

"Poof! That lump o' horse meat!" snapped Annie; but even mention of her favorite enemy and business rival failed to arouse her usual explosive ire. "An' I'll thank ye," she roared irascibly after Peter as he disappeared into the wheelhouse, "to mind yer own damn business!" Then, after a sepulchral cough or two she turned again to Tim. "Musta ketched the bucolic plague or somethin'," she confided morosely. "Mebbe I should see a doctor, huh?"

"What about young Doc Adams, over on Quillayute Street there?" Tim suggested. "He's the doctor for most of the canneries and mills around. He's pretty good too."

"Sa-ay! Sure! I know him! Used to play around the docks back in Secoma when he was a kid. His old man runs a ship chandler's on'y a block from our home wharf. Thanks, Tim! Thass what I'll do!" She raised her voice. "Peter? Git Shif'less an' Big Sam! Ye're goin' ashore wid me! An' put yer shore duds on. Goin' like ye are, the doc'll think I mistook him fer a vet!" Quickly she turned to enter her cabin; then: "Oof!" she exclaimed, remembering that she was ill. "I hope I kin make it that fur!"

Annie was in her cabin, dressing, when there came a sharp rap at the door. "Don't come in!" she said quickly. "Who is it?"

"It's me—Tim!" the latter's voice replied. He sounded urgent. "Can you come out a minute, Annie? Maybe got a job for you."

Hastily throwing around her an old dressing gown which once had belonged to that likable rascal, her long-defunct husband, Captain Terry, Annie opened the door a crack and peered out. With Tim, on the deck outside, was a squat, burly, worried-looking man in logging clothes, whose broad, dark-tinted face and small, slant black eyes indicated his Siwash ancestry.

"This is George Swimming Seal, Annie," introduced Tim. "George—Tugboat Annie Brennan."

"Hi-ya, George," said Annie affably, and opened the door. "Come on in. Looks like a cyclone inside, but then, it allus does, so don't apologize. Set down!" She looked at Tim. "What gives?"

"Well, George here," Tim explained, "got into port in his gas boat, right after I talked to you. He belongs to a gang of hand loggers up the Koahkuddit River, over on the coast."

"Yeah, I know the place," said Annie. "Ain't that where the land curves around each side the river mouth like a pair o' ice tongs an' makes a little harbor?"

"That's right. Inside where an old logging-railroad bridge crosses the channel to open water," verified Tim. "So George and the boys have just floated their season's log cut down and started making up their boom in the harbor you mentioned. They signed a contract with that sawmill over the way there"—Tim pointed out the window—"when prices were still up, to deliver their log boom into the millpond by——What's the latest date, George?"

"Day after tomorra."

"Easy," said Annie. "It's on'y about a day's tow."

"Yeah—if the weather stayed settled," said Tim. "But take a look out and see what's building."

Annie crossed to the window. "Sou'easter," she said, after a brief glance at the roiling clouds and rain-laden sky. "Glass is fallin' too, I noticed as we come in. It's a sure sign. So?"

"So unless they get their big boom over here right away," said Tim, "it might be stormbound at the river mouth for days."

"Mebbe weeks," supplemented George. "It's happened. Them sou'easters blows right in and keeps on blowin'. And if the boom don't get here the mill cancels our contract and we gotta take much lower price. Lose mebbe three, four thousand dollars. So they sent me to hire tug."

"And I recommended you," said Tim, and grinned. "Since you're the only big tug in port."

"Why didn't they phone?" Annie asked. "I could ha' been on me way by now."

"Landslide carried their phone line away a week ago. It's not fixed yet," Tim explained.

"How many sections in your boom, George?" asked Annie.

"Twenty-five."

"Hm'm'm. 'Bout a million board feet, huh? How come ye left gittin' it over here till so late?"

"A lot of logs got jammed in, upstream, by same slide what wrecked the phone line," George told her. "Took a few days to blast it clear and float 'em down. They was making up the boom when I left. You come over and get it, mebbe?"

"Why not?" said Annie. "I got a good tug here, an' lots o' time. I'll give ye a fair towin' price too. On'y thing, I gotta go see a doctor fust. I ain't feelin' so hot. 'T won't take long. Okay?"

"Yeah, guess so," George replied dubiously, looking at Tim, who nodded. "All right, I'll wait. Don't be longer'n you have to."

A half hour later, primly arrayed in her shoregoing best, with her feathered hat bobbing deliriously on top of her blowsy head, her old-fashioned reticule moored to her ample waist, and buttressed by the solid, reassuring presence of her three shipmates, each acutely self-conscious and ill at ease in his Sunday suit, Annie entered the doctor's waiting room, groaning and bleating a little in anticipation of the ordeal to come.

"Git me in there quick, young leddy," she told the crisply uniformed nurse feebly, "'less I prespire afore yer very eyes!"

"She means 'expire,'" explained Big Sam. "But that'd take me and you and a hammer," he added skeptically.

"Don't pay no attention to the calloused ape," moaned Annie. "Where's that——Oh—hi, doc!" she cried with a little more animation as the doctor entered. "Oh, my, oh, me, how you've growed! I ain't saw you, hardly, since ye was in twaddlin' clothes!"

"Annie!" He shook hands in delighted greeting, humorous eyes twinkling behind their glasses. "I don't believe it! What brings a hardy old seahorse like you in here? Don't tell me you're ailing!"

"Me battlin' average was pooty good up till now," she informed him dolefully, "but I guess I'm all washed up. Them"—she pointed to her companions—"is some o' me boys what helped me up here." Forebodingly she tapped her capacious bosom. "Better git yer telescope out quick, an' take a peek! Now don't go 'way," she adjured her escort anxiously, as the doctor ushered her into his consulting room; "ye may hafta carry me back!"

Inside, divested of coat and blouse, and having unloaded her symptoms, Annie stood, apprehensive, while the young doctor examined her; but gradually curiosity overcame her fright and she began to take a lively interest in the proceedings.

"Tee-hee. What ya see in there, doc?" she tittered as he applied his stethoscope to her massive chest.

"Nothing much amiss, Annie," he smiled, and folded the instrument away. "You'll be roaring around for quite a while yet."

"I will, huh?" said Annie, deflated and a little disappointed. "Well, what if I don't feel no better?"

"You going to be in port for a while?"

"There's a little log-boom towin' job I gotta do today, but I'll be back tomorra, fer a coupla days."

"Fine!" he said cheerfully. "If you don't feel better by then come and see me again. Meanwhile"—he patted her reassuringly—"don't worry!"

Still not quite convinced, Annie dressed and rejoined her friends, and they emerged upon the street and headed down the steep hill street toward the wharf.

"Wh-what d-did he s-s-say, Annie?" Shiftless asked eagerly.

Relishing the drama of it, Annie wagged her head. "Couldn't find nothin' wrong wid me," she said solemnly. "That makes it all the more mysterious. Prob'ly some terrible disease nobody never had afore." Importantly she indicated her stomach. "Must be skulkin' in here someplace."

TUGBOAT ANNIE BURNS A BRIDGE

"That what's makin' ye limp, Annie?" asked Big Sam innocently. "Somethin' wrong wi' your leg too?"

"She wasn't limpin' a minute ago," said Peter practically.

"Cuss you fellers!" Annie bellowed in sudden wrath. "Can't a pusson feel bad all over if they want to?"

Snorting with indignation, she increased her waddle; but suddenly Shiftless checked her. "S-say!" he cried excitedly. "Ain't that B-b-bull-winkle's Salamander movin' out?"

"What you talkin' about?" Annie demanded, instantly alert and tense. "Bullwinkle's down south in Calif——" She stopped abruptly, staring. "It is! Ye're right, Shif'less!" she cried, bristling. "How the divil did he git up here—an' where's he goin' so fast? Looka that bow wave! Oh-oh! Come on! He don't duck in an' outta here in such a hurry 'less he's up to somethin' dirty! I wonder if George——"

Leaving the sentence unfinished in her wake, she bumbled rapidly down the hill; but as they approached the cannery wharf her uneasiness somewhat was allayed when George's squat, powerful and unmistakable figure emerged from the cannery office, followed by Tim. But the latter, seeing them, made urgent gestures to hasten, and again Annie's heart sank.

"I knowed it!" she grunted as they galloped out onto the wharf. "Give it to me quick!" she rasped as they slid to a halt before the other two. "What's happened, Tim?"

"Bullwinkle! You saw him hightailing out of here?" Tim asked.

"I saw him!" said Annie grimly. "What's bit him, though? It can't be that log boom, because George is still here; but——"

"It's the log boom all right, Annie. He's going after it!" Tim replied angrily. "Tell her, George!"

"How'n the blue-starred hell could it be the log boom?" Annie roared, her face aflame with fury, all her ills forgotten. "George give that job to me! An' what was Bullwinkle doin' in here anyways? He was s'posed to be in——"

"He stopped in to check with Secoma on his way back. And shut up, will you, while we tell you how it happened? Go on, George."

"It's your own fault," George told Annie sullenly. "I wait for you beside your tug. Then this feller comes along in big boat and ties up right astern o' yours. So——"

"I'd gone back in my office by then," Tim interrupted. "I didn't know anything about all this. Not till after he'd gone!" he ended.

"So," continued George, "this big redheaded feller asks me was I waitin' for you, and I says yes, and tells him why, and when he asks where you'd gone I told him. Well, then he says he'll do the job for you, right away, to save time, and split the profit with you."

"What did ye tell him?"

"I told him no, I'd wait for you. Well, he talked and talked. Said he was an old pal o' yours. Like a brother, he tells me, except his father only had one head, while your father——"

"Criminy!" yelled Annie impatiently. "Git on wid it, will ye?"

"Wait!" said George. "Right then one o' your men hollers out not to believe him. That he's a blankity-blank liar and you hate his guts! So I tell him to beat it. And that's what he done. He yells 'The hell with you!' and jumps on his tug, and away they go!"

"Listen!" cried Annie wildly, "ain't there some way we kin let them other loggers over at Koahkuddit know——"

"Phone line's down, Annie—remember?" Tim put in.

"An' they'll think," said George morosely, "he's the tug I sent."

"But sakes alive!" Annie said desperately. "Wid a sou'easter blowin' up, an' them havin' to git that boom away, the dirty thief won't on'y steal the gold outta their teeth, he'll snatch their jawbones too! An' he's such a fast worker that——"

"Mebbe," said George gloomily. "Mebbe not. McCann's the Bull o' the Woods across there. He's a tight Scotchman and he ain't gonna give in any more'n he has to."

"Think McCann's smart enough to pin him down to a no-cure no-pay basis?"

"You mean, if he don't deliver the logs to the mill here in time he don't get paid? Yeah! And then some!"

"What do ye mean—'n' then some?" Annie cried incredulously. "That woods boss o' yours'll be lucky to talk him into the no-cure no-pay deal! That buckaleer's the sharpest, unscruplest operator on the coast!"

George's reply was simple. "You don't know McCann," he said. "Oh, and here's something else; just before he left he wrote a note and dropped it on the dock. Said to give it to you." George handed it over; an untidy, crumpled scrawl. "It says——"

"How do you know what it says?" demanded Annie sharply.

"I can read," said George. "It says, 'Lay down. You're dead.'"

"Why that impident widget!" Instantly Annie was raging again. "So I'm dead, am I? Oh! That——Tim, how much start ye figger he's got?"

"We-ell, say thirty-five to forty minutes."

"An' he's got near a knot more speed, wid the overhaul the Narcissus needs! Well—no matter! George, we'll lug yer gas boat on board an' take ye back wid us! Peter! Sam! Git back on——"

"Hey, wait a minute!" George protested. "I got a whole list o' camp stores to order."

TUGBOAT ANNIE BURNS A BRIDGE

"Whyn't ye say so?" snapped Annie, now a dynamo of action. "Git back aboard, you other fellers! I'll not take this widout a fight! No sir!"

Under increasingly lowering skies and heavy rain squalls the Narcissus surged out of the harbor and down the coast in furious pursuit of Mr. Bullwinkle's Salamander, while Annie, who miraculously had recovered both her appetite and her energy, wolfed a couple of enormous cold beef sandwiches, and gabbed between bites with Peter, who was at the wheel.

"How's the glass?" she asked presently.

"Still droppin', Annie."

With quick competence Annie again glanced out the window and scanned sea and sky. "Give ye about twelve hours afore that sou'easter busts loose," she prophesied. "An' when it does she'll be a real hellabaloo!" Her face tightened. "So no matter who tows that log boom up to Port Olympic ain't gonna have too much time to git it clear o' Koahkuddit!" Impatiently her fist pounded on the bulkhead. "If on'y we kin make it to the river mouth afore that—that big tumble-bum closes a deal!"

As if in back-handed answer to her prayer the door opened and the worried, oil-streaked countenance of Big Sam appeared.

"Bilge pump's clogged, Annie," he announced flatly. "We got to shut down for a while."

"Hell an' hardtack!" Annie rasped. "Fer how long?"

"Mebbe an hour," he said. "Mebbe two. I'll make it quick as we can."

It was slightly more than two hours, however, with the Narcissus rolling in the heavy swell; and the afternoon was well along before the breakdown was repaired, and the vessel turned in toward the low twin spits of land which, except for the narrow channel bridged by an old deserted logging-railroad span, almost entirely enclosed the restricted estuary of the Koahkuddit River. And soon they were entering the channel entrance.

"One thing, we don't hafta stop an' go ashore to open that cussed bridge like in the old days," Annie growled, pointing to the steel framework of the heavily counterweighted drawbridge. Rust-flaked and forlorn and with the span up, it bordered the channel, with the tracks of the old logging railroad, half buried in sand and brushwood, curving away toward the mainland at either side.

"Don't often see one like that nowadays, Annie. How did it work?" Peter asked.

"Well, in them times," Annie explained, "they used to spill the logs offa the flats, an' make up their booms right in the open salt chuck there. Saved that drag acrost the inlet. An' if the bridge was down, a vessel had to tie up an' send a coupla hands ashore to work that big fandangle wheel crank. See it? Then the span went up an' the boat went through an' picked up her men on the inside after they'd let her down again."

"But why——"

"Saved the wages of a bridge tender, that's why." She glanced casually at the span. "Give her a squirt of oil an' she'd prob'ly still work. Well"—they were passing close by the gaunt, neglected structure now—"let's keep a-churnin'!"

Shoreward from the channel only the hills were visible, their thickly forested slopes now half concealed in curtains of swirling clouds; but as the Narcissus surged out onto the inlet, or lagoon, the mouth of the Koahkuddit River appeared with, on one shore, a small Indian village, and on the other a spindling jetty alongside which agile, calk-booted loggers were making up the sections of the log boom while, even at the distance of the mile that separated them, Annie and Peter instantly recognized, tied up to the jetty, the long, powerful and capable-looking shape of Mr. Bullwinkle's Salamander.

"Look at all them fellers out on the wharf too," commented Annie uneasily. "I'll bet Bullwinkle's in the middle of 'em, talkin' so fast he's trippin' over his tongue! I jest hope we git there in time to put a spoke in his eye, that's all!"

This, apparently, was mere wishful thinking, however; for as the Narcissus swept up and lay to, within close hailing distance of the wharf, Mr. Bullwinkle's bandy legs separated him from the group of loggers with whom he had been talking, and propelled him to the edge of the dock.

"Well-well-well!" he announced with loud cordiality. "If it ain't me ol' pal Mrs. Rigor Mortis herself! Thought you was bein' subdivided, up at the doc's, Annie. I hope," he added, deeply solicitous, "it was nothin' trifling!"

"Shut yer big claptrap!" she told him roughly. "Where's McCann?"

"He can't do you no good, Fatso," replied Mr. Bullwinkle affably, and waved a paper he held in his hand. "It's in the bag. All I got to wait for, now, is the boom to get finished."

"I'd like to use yer head fer a boomstick," Annie retorted furiously, and turned to the group of loggers on the wharf. But before she could speak a tall, wide-shouldered man of about sixty, with a snow-white bush of hairs over each keenly gleaming blue eye, pushed his way forward.

"You McCann?" asked Annie.

TUGBOAT ANNIE BURNS A BRIDGE

"Aye! An' who are you—another bloody vulture the like o' yon"—he jerked his formidable chin at Mr. Bullwinkle—"wha's come ower here to help pick oor bones?"

"Who—me?" returned Annie. "Why, I'm the jerk he stole the towin' job offa! How bad did he stick ye?"

"Twenty-five hundred dollars."

"Wha-at?"

"On a no-cure no-pay basis, o' coorse. 'T is less than we'd lose if he didna' tak' them."

"The dirty ratscal! He'd steal the pennies off a blind man's eyes!"

"I've ne doot. On'y, he was in such a nairvous hurry aboot getting the agreement signed that I thocht 'Oho! He's as anxious to tow the boom as I am tae get it on its way. I wunner why?' So I tested him oot. An' it wurrked—eh, Bullwinkle?"

The normally ruddy color of Mr. Bullwinkle's face suddenly deepened. And, enjoying his embarrassment, with a pawky twinkle in his cold blue eyes, McCann continued.

"Aye, he got the job on condition that if he did fail tae deliver the boom on time, not on'y would he not get paid but he'd pay us one half o' what we'd lose from the mill."

"Ye mean," cried Annie delightedly, "he fell fer that?"

"It was that or naethin'," replied McCann calmly. "If he hadna' agreed I'd ha' kept the logs here for anither year. We've lived on short commons before. O' coorse he's still got the best o' the bargain; and if on'y I'd known you were coming——"

"Listen, McCann!" said Annie. "Tell him go jump! I'll tow yer boom at me reg'lar rate——"

"Pay no attention!" Mr. Bullwinkle broke in agitatedly, addressing McCann. "The old gas bag's been dead fer years. She just walks around through force o' habit!"

"Eight hundred dollars a day, McCann!" continued Annie, ignoring Mr. Bullwinkle's fervent outburst. "An' I'll have it in Port Olympic afore daybreak tomorra!"

"You can't, and neither can he!" Mr. Bullwinkle yelled, wildly shaking the paper in his hand. "Here's his signed agreement, even if you was to offer to tow the boom for nothin'!"

"An agreement forced under duress——" Annie began.

"Ye're quite richt, ma'am," McCann said quietly. "But I passed ma worrd."

"See?" cried Mr. Bullwinkle triumphantly. "He's a gent! Now go home an' get buried right this time, will ye, dear?"

Helpless and raging, Annie glared at him, then made a final forceful appeal to McCann. But the Scotsman, while appreciating her offer, declined to change his mind—an attitude she violently disagreed with, but could not fail to respect. And, realizing at last the uselessness of further discussion, she stamped back into the wheelhouse.

"Okay, le's git outta here!" she told Peter, boiling. "There's times I even wish my Terry was still alive, the drunken sot—God rest him! He'd ha' went ashore an' blowed up like a adam bomb right in Bullwinkle's ugly puss!"

In sheer desperation, as the Narcissus came about, and lest she be tempted, regardless of its futility, to storm ashore and lethally engage her enemy in fisticuffs, Annie forced her stormy thoughts to concentrate upon the personality of her graceless but colorful late helpmeet; and on their way back to the seaward channel she entertained Peter and herself with a lively account of Captain Terry's more truculent and usually alcohol-sparked antics.

"Bro-ther," she exulted, "when he'd git hot under the collar he'd swell till ye'd swear he was twice his size—an' the on'y way ye could handle him then was to swat him over the nuggin an' drop him in the drink. Yep," she chuckled, as always beginning to enjoy these faintly scandalous but hilarious memories, "that usually shrunked him down to size again!"

While she was speaking, the Narcissus had entered the seaward channel, with the starkly forlorn and upraised steel framework of the bridge looming ahead; but for the second, still amusedly thinking of her drastic cooling off of the incandescent Captain Terry, she gave the span only a casual glance; then, suddenly, her gaze focused, and after a moment or two of frowning concentration, there leaped into her weather-wrinkled eyes the flame of a sudden inspiration, and quickly she ran out on deck and stared astern toward the river mouth. But, the intervening curve of the channel blocking her view, she bumbled excitedly inside the wheelhouse again, where Peter, startled by her sudden change of mood, stared at her in vague alarm.

"How long, ye figger, afore that boom's in shape to be towed?" she demanded abruptly.

"What's the matter—you ain't feelin' so good again, Annie?" he asked worriedly.

"Heck wid that!" Annie replied, her voice alive, crackling. "How long?"

"Oh, four—mebbe five hours. But——"

"Hallelulya!" she cried. "Look—soon's we pass the bridge ahead there, pull into the bank at the side it's raised on!"

"What fer?" Peter protested. "If we're gonna make port before——"

TUGBOAT ANNIE BURNS A BRIDGE

"Do what I tell ye!" commanded Annie impatiently. "I got the nutriment of a idear!"

And, shortly thereafter, the Narcissus was made fast alongside the narrow foreshore, just beyond the bridge abutment, on the same side as the large, hand-wheel gear.

"Now what?" growled Peter dubiously.

"Now," said Annie briskly, "call all hands. I got somethin' to say."

With the crew of the Narcissus assembled, including even Pinto, the cook, Annie briefly but forcefully explained her plan and, sweeping aside both objection and approval, she put them instantly to work. The huskier members she sent up the bank in charge of Big Sam, carrying a can of lubricating oil, crowbars, and other tools, to get the corroded gears of the lowering apparatus working in order to lower the span—a considerable project, for the span had been upright and untended for years. The other men she put ashore from the dinghy, on the opposite bank, with instructions to collect driftwood and old railroad ties and bank their harvest against the inside of the stone bridge abutment, immediately below where the span, if lowered, would join the tracks of the old logging railroad.

Willingly they set to work under Annie's increasingly dynamic supervision; but at first the bridge span, rusted by long neglect and disuse, obdurately declined to budge. Then, at Big Sam's suggestion, a rope was attached to the top of the structure, and the men on the opposite bank hauled lustily, concurrently with the working of the big gear handles by the sweating ground crew. And after a minute or two, with protesting screeches and groans of corroded metal, the heavy span began slowly to descend.

"Hooray!" yelled Annie jubilantly as the edge of the span settled into place with a scrape and a bang, and the ends of the track met. "We done it!"

"Sure," replied Big Sam, wiping his brow with the back of a grimy fist, "but if we got it down, why can't Bullwinkle get it up again?"

"He kin try," admitted Annie. She added cryptically: "An' if he don't, there's somethin' else he sure will raise, an' wid me too."

"What's that?"

Annie grinned. "A morsel o' holy hell!" she said. "Come on now, boys—over to the other bank, all of us!"

Energetically she waddled across the bridge and down the bank to the huge fuel pile set against the abutment under the now lowered end of the bridge; and as the others interestedly watched she rolled an old newspaper into a torch, lighted it, and applied the flame to the foot of the pile. At once the brushwood kindling caught and the

TUGBOAT ANNIE BURNS A BRIDGE

flames crackled upward, directed by the stone of the abutment to the joining of track and span.

"Git the fire hose out, case we need it, Sam," Annie ordered next. "We don't want the steel to melt."

"What ye tryin' to do, Annie," said Shiftless, who, being not overly bright, had not fully understood her earlier explanation, "burn the bridge down?"

"Ain't aimin' to," Annie grinned. "I'm jest aimin' to burn Bullwinkle a mite, when he shows up wid that log boom in tow, two-three hours from now. Keep feedin' that fire, boys. There's nothin' to do now but wait." She looked around, grinning widely. "Meantimes, who's fer a nice, friendly, cutthroat game o' rum ginny?"

A little more than two hours later, with darkness beginning to fall and the seaward horizon blanked out with heavy clouds, the sky filled with flying scud, and the surface of the water lashed by increasingly violent rain squalls—all presages of the dreaded sou'easter—the blunt, powerful snout of the Salamander appeared at the end of the channel; and with running lights already switched on and shining like bright jewels against the dark loom of the land, and towing the cumbersome log boom at the end of a long line, she headed slowly around.

Shiftless, planted on the bridge as lookout, shouted quick warning, and Annie and the other card players ran from the messroom and jumped ashore.

"Turn the hose on, Sam! Git that fire out, quick!" Annie shouted as she ran; and within seconds a powerful stream reduced the blaze to a heap of steaming ashes. Satisfied, Annie then trudged up the bank, and took station on the center of the bridge.

Slowly the Salamander approached; then when Jake, her paunchy mate, observed that the bridge was down, bells jingled in her engine room and brine roared beneath her counter as way was checked; and presently, the tide being at full flood, tug and boom rode motionless on the smooth, rain-pitted water. Then the burly figure of Mr. Bullwinkle appeared and he leaned over the upper rail, staring into the gathering darkness.

"Who the hell let that bridge down?" he roared angrily.

"'T was on'y little me," admitted Annie in a voice meek, but loud. "Wanna make somethin' of it?"

"You?" he yelled incredulously. "What are you still doin' around here?"

"Jist stopped fer a game o' rum ginny," Annie told him affably. "Wanna play? Ye'll have plenty o' time."

TUGBOAT ANNIE BURNS A BRIDGE

For a moment Mr. Bullwinkle was silent; and when he again spoke, his voice was heavy with suspicion and, perhaps, a faint unease. "What you tryin' to build, ye old hag?" he demanded. "I'm sendin' a coupla hands to raise that bridge, so git the Narcissus outta the channel!"

"What fer?" asked Annie mischievously. "You ain't goin' no place."

"The hell I ain't!" he roared. "I'm gettin' this boom to the mill before the sou'easter breaks!"

"What'll ye bet?" asked Annie.

Abruptly Mr. Bullwinkle retired to his wheelhouse to confer briefly with Jake. When he reappeared on deck he ordered the boom cast off—a safe procedure in that state of the tide—and when this was done, with a powerful beat of foam the Salamander swept rapidly forward and along the control-wheel side of the bank.

A few seconds later, accompanied by two of his men, he climbed to the bridge, where, without wasting further words on Annie, he confidently grasped the control handle and turned. Or tried to turn; because, even when reinforced by the two husky members of his crew, strain and sweat as they would, nothing happened.

Nonchalantly Annie waddled along to watch. "Whyn't ye git under the span an' push?" she suggested helpfully. "Ye'll shift her jest as quick."

"And why don't you mind your own damn business?" inquired Mr. Bullwinkle savagely, between panting efforts to turn the gears.

"Well now, don't git mad, Horatio—dear," replied Annie, reproachfully. "I'm on'y tryin' to save ye yer sweat, because I fixed this bridge jest afore ye arrived, so hell an' hot water won't move it 'less I say so, fer at least eight hours."

"What do you mean—you fixed it?" Mr. Bullwinkle said irately. "It was up when we come through today."

"An' now it's down! To stay! Go ahead," she said indifferently, "rassle wid it. It won't bulge a inch."

Quickly Mr. Bullwinkle turned to one of his men. "Get some more hands up here," he ordered. "Tell 'em to bring peaveys and crowbars!"

"Ye sure are a happy octupust," commented Annie with a grin. "But, like I said, ye kin allus try!"

Mr. Bullwinkle's optimism rapidly diminished, however; for after another hour of extreme exertion by the major portion of his crew, during which they attacked the obdurately immovable structure with all the tools and ingenuity they could summon, their progress was exactly nil.

"Damn thing's froze so tight between the tracks and the end of the span," rasped Jake, limp with fatigue, "it'll take dynamite to shift it. I'm tellin' you, Bullwinkle, it's hopeless!"

"What I said a hour ago," remarked Annie complacently, for she had remained a deeply interested observer. "'Twas me what froze it. An' since I'm the on'y one what knows how to unfreeze it, ye may as well give up."

"Give up?" bellowed Mr. Bullwinkle, his roughhewn, perspiring face purple with rage. "When I got a million feet o' logs that's got to be towed into port?"

"An' if ye don't git to tow 'em in—an' ye won't!—what happens? Oh, wid that hell-roarin' sou'easter due here in a few hours, an' you stuck wid a no-cure no-pay deal, o' course ye won't git no money fer all yer sweat an' hard work—to say nothin' o' havin' to pay McCann fer nonperformance. But"—she snapped her big fingers airily—"what's a few lousy thousand bucks to a hot-pot operator like you?"

"Someday, Annie," grated Mr. Bullwinkle slowly, "I'm gonna take you in my two hands an'——"

"Poof!" said Annie. "O' course, now, if you was willin' to talk turkey——"

There was a pause.

"What kind o' turkey?" Mr. Bullwinkle asked at length; and although his tone was rough Annie instantly detected the desperate anxiety beneath.

"The kind what gives me the breast an' drumsticks," Annie said bluntly, "an' leaves you to nibble the part what kites over the fence last. It ain't tasty, but it's better'n starvin'."

"Go on," he rasped through anger-stiff lips. "What's the deal?"

"Well, fust thing," she informed him cheerfully, "is to gimme your copy o' the towin' agreement ye gouged outta McCann back there."

"I'll be damned——"

"Ye sure will. Looka that sky!" There was another tense pause; then: "Oh, I'll pertect ye wid McCann so ye won't hafta pay him fer nonfulfillment," she went on. "In fack, I'll take over that little obligation meself."

"In writing?" he asked quickly.

"Okay, in writin'!" she snapped. "I never seen such a Peekin' Thomas—doubtin' every word I say! But we ain't got all night."

"All right, cuss you!" he snarled, and handed over his copy of the McCann agreement, which she promptly crumpled and threw away.

"And now that's took care of," Annie said affably, "an' ye're in the clear again, ye kin easy afford the thousand bucks ye're gonna hafta pay me fer gittin' ye off the hook."

"Hell wi' you!" His voice was an anguished roar. "What's there left in it for me?"

"Do I hafta," asked Annie patiently, "describe the geog'aphy o' that turkey all over again? Come on, make up yer beetle mind!"

There were more profane objections; but since the alternative was even worse, he eventually led the way to his cabin on the Salamander, with Annie taking Peter and Big Sam along to witness.

"Okay, there it is!" Mr. Bullwinkle growled, handing over his check and taking in return Annie's agreement to assume his towing obligation. "Now how do I get them damn logs off my hands?"

"Easy," said Annie with a grin. "Ye float 'em under the bridge an' I'll pick up the boom on the other side."

"Fine! Great!" exploded Mr. Bullwinkle. "That leaves you free to tow the boom to Port Olympic an' collect later from McCann! It also leaves the Salamander here, on this side o' the bridge. So how the devil do I get out, before that sou'easter hits? You claimed you knew how to open the span!"

"Oh, yeah—I a'most forgot that!" replied Annie with deceptive mildness. "But I'm afraid that inflammation's gonna cost ye another five hundred slappers. Okay-okay," she added indifferently, correctly and expertly interpreting the suddenly deepened tinge of his already apoplectic face, "ye kin stop here an' rot, fer all o' me. Come on, boys." And she prepared to leave.

So once more Mr. Bullwinkle was forced to yield; and muttering several remarks the originality of which aroused Annie's scandalized admiration, he scrawled out another check.

"There it is, you old coffin-creeper!" he choked as he handed it over. "So what's the answer? How do I get out of here?"

"An' have ye renig on the hull deal if I tell ye now?" responded Annie merrily. "Unh-unh!" She stuffed the checks into the safe haven of her capacious bosom and moved toward the door. "I'll send the answer back wid George We'll be passin' his gas boat on the way."

Some time later, while the Narcissus was beating north with the log boom in tow and the first outriders of the sou'easter were beginning to sweep in out of the night, Peter, who was at the wheel, pointed out a dancing light ahead which presently materialized as that of George's gas boat, as he beat his way homeward through the windy darkness. And at Annie's tooted signal he surged about and for a brief period accompanied the Narcissus close abeam, while, briefly but pungently, Annie described the beneficent change in fortune of the Koahkuddit River loggers.

"As ye know, George," she explained gleefully, "heat expands steel, and that fire we built froze that span so tight nothin' would move it 'less ye took the bridge apart. An', like my Terry when he got het up—God rest the naughty scamp!—the on'y thing what'd shrink it back to size in a hurry is the application o' plenty o' cold water."

"Yeah—but how's Bullwinkle going to——" George began; but Annie checked him with a grin.

"It's simple as he is," she chortled. "Jest tell him to play a fire hose on it fer two-three hours, an' he kin raise it an' sashay through widout no trouble at all! Well"—she waved jovially—"be peekin' at ye, George! Oh, an' say! Tell McCann the boom'll be at the mill in plenty o' time, an' all I'll charge him is me reg'lar daily rate like I promised. So long!"

George's tiny boat light danced away into a blinding rain squall astern; and for a time, as Annie took the wheel from Peter and balanced expertly to the vessel's increasing pitch and roll, there was silence in the darkened wheelhouse. Then Peter spoke.

"Don't forget, when we get back in port, Annie," he said dryly, "to go up an' visit Doctor Adams."

"Why?" Annie asked with quick concern. "Is he sick?"

"No," Peter reminded her. "You are."

"Me?" cried Annie in outraged denial. "Ye're crazy! I'm fit as a faddle! In fack," she ended complacently, "I never felt better in me life!"

TUGBOAT ANNIE LOSES A TOW

A sudden acceleration of rain-laden wind roared over foam-streaked Puget Sound, battering against the docks, cargo sheds and shipping of the port of Secoma, and almost wrenching the doorknob from Tugboat Annie Brennan's massive fist as that veteran seafarer and master of the big tug Narcissus stepped from her cabin on the way to the messroom for breakfast. And as she buckled her oilskins more securely and moved toward the ladder, a distant, muffled detonation punched its voice through the storm's tumult.

Annie's mastiff face swung sharply toward the sound. Then, recollecting, she shook her head and clumped heavily down the ladder; and when she entered the warm and cozy messroom not even the appetizing galley odors sufficed to smooth the corrugations from her brow.

"What's wrong, Annie?" grinned Hank, the husky young second deck hand. "You look like you'd relish a hunk of wildcat for breakfast."

"Naw, I ain't sore nor nothin'," said Annie glumly as she sat down and helped herself to a heap of hot cakes. "I'm just worried about pore ol' Noah Svenson, out acrost the bay there."

"Noah?" said Big Sam, the engineer, in mild surprise. "What's poor with him? That little cafe o' his is a nice business."

"And he's got plenty dough salted away too!" exclaimed Hank. "Why, Dogface Jackson, who's been doing a calking job on that old hulk Noah's got his cafe on, says that down in his cabin Noah's got an iron safe the size of a hack! The old boy never sets foot on shore, never spends a cent. So he's probably got that safe stuffed with money till it's fuller'n a Christmas turkey!"

"What ye mean, never goes ashore?" asked Peter, the mate. "How about them two weeks, every year about this time, he closes up shop and disappears? S'pose he's got a family someplace?"

"No," Annie answered quietly. "He ain't. Leastways—pass me a steak, Sam—not that I ever heerd of, an' I've knowed him since afore most o' you was in waddlin' clothes. He's reel nice too."

"Is it t-true that he was r-rich once, Annie?" stuttered Shiftless, the other deck hand.

"Sure is. Years ago he was one o' the richest maritime lawyers in the hull Northwest here. Then, when his wife died, it jest kicked the heart outta him. Affected his business judgment or somethin' too. Anyways, he lost everythin' he had."

"If he was so all-fired rich, how come he learned to cook so good?" asked Hank.

"Cookin' was his hobbyhorse," Annie replied. "When he come down on his uppers, cookin' was all he could turn to. So he bought that beat-up old dismasted schooner an' built that little caffy on her poop, called it 'Noah's Ark'—an' there he is, livin' alone wid that cat an' dog o' his, as happy as a sandhog!"

"Since he's so happy," remarked Peter stolidly, "why's he worryin'?"

"He ain't worryin'," Annie told him testily. "I am. Didn't ye hear that explosion acrost there a while back?"

"Sure. But that was just the city engineers blastin' Kings Bluff away to make room for them new docks."

"Yeah, an' gittin' closer to Noah's place all the time—an' he's right where the bluff's closest to the water."

"So?"

"Well, figger it." Annie was deeply troubled. "All that dynamitin's li'ble to fetch the rest o' the bluff ripsnorin' right on top o' that caffy o' his."

"Yeah, that's so," Clem, the radio operator, conceded. "But didn't they warn him to move?"

"They did. But where kin he go?"

"Sa-ay!" Hank snapped his fingers. "Know that big new sea-wall construction job they're building out across the sound?"

"West side o' Weyant Island, ye mean?" Annie asked.

"That's it!" Hank was excited. "Well, Tony Ruiz, who's bossing the job, he's an old friend o' mine; and only a couple days ago he said his workers were griping because the nearest eating place was at Jokisch Landing, almost three miles away. I'll bet he——Hey! Where you going, Annie?" For Annie had leaped up and was struggling elatedly into her oilskins.

"God bless ye, Hank!" she cried happily. "I'm gonna sashay over an' tell Noah! Right now!"

"Fine," said Hank with alacrity, also rising. "I'll drive you over, then I'll take a ferry across and fix it with Tony."

On the lengthy ride around the waterfront, Annie vented her now high spirits in raucous song, but as they ran below the beetling cliff known as Kings Bluff, a mass of time-disintegrated rock behind the old fish harbor, her discordant tones abruptly ceased. For moored beside the wharf was the big, powerful-looking blue-water tug Salamander. And her proud owner and master was Annie's most bitterly cherished business rival, Captain Horatio Bullwinkle.

"What the heck," Annie muttered savagely, "d' ye s'pose that monkey's orphan is doin' over here, asides from outstinkin' the fertilizer plant?"

"Probably on a towing job," Hank told her soothingly. "Anyway, why worry? He's not bothering you."

"He better not," said Annie darkly. "Who-o-oa! Stop the bus, Hank. Here's Noah's wharf now. You comin' in?"

"No, guess not," Hank told her. "I'll roll along and fix it with Tony. So long, Annie. Be seeing you."

Waving her thanks, Annie splashed out to the rickety wharf, alongside which was moored the battered hulk of a cut-down schooner, formerly a three-masted lumber carrier. On her poop, reached from dockside by an adjustable gangplank that rose and fell with the tides, was a small, attractively painted counter lunchroom, originally the vessel's charthouse, above which rose a neat sign: *NOAH'S ARK—NOAH SVENSON, PROP.* Noah himself, his sparse white hair brushed carefully back over a clean pink scalp, was a small-framed, slender man of about seventy, with gentle blue eyes that lighted with pleasure as Annie flung open the door.

"Hello there, Annie!" he cried. "What brings you over here in this weather?"

"Hi, Noah, ye old nanny goat!" Annie roared with vast good humor, slamming the door. "Long time, no peek! I——"

She halted abruptly, staring with intense dislike at the bulky, oilskinned figure of Mr. Horatio Bullwinkle, who sat at the well-scrubbed counter enjoying a sardine sandwich and a bottle of beer.

Mr. Bullwinkle stared back, with maliciously twinkling little black shoe-button eyes. He said, "Well, as I live and breathe——"

"Do ye hafta?" Annie asked brusquely and turned to Noah. "Funny what crawls outta the bilges on rainy days," she commented, and sat her broad beam on a stool. "A cup o' joe, pal, an' a coupla eggs, well strangled. Then I got news fer ye!"—and briefly she told him of Hank's felicitous brain wave. "So there it is," she concluded triumphantly. "An' I'll fetch me Narcissus over an' tow ye to Weyant Island fer free."

Before Noah could reply, however, Mr. Bullwinkle gave vent to a coarse laugh. "Dig in yer heels, chum!" he advised Noah derisively. "Any time Cow Face here does somethin' for free, Old Nick'll take up fancy skatin'!"

"Listen," Annie grated, big fists curled, "this is private business atween me an' Noah! So git on yer gorilla legs and preamble the hell outta here! Go on—puff!"

"You mean 'blow,' sweetheart?" Mr. Bullwinkle corrected archly, and winked at Noah. "Got a temper like an old seal, ain't she?" he grinned. Then, delicately extracting a sardine from his sandwich, he held it out by the tail to Annie. "Bark!" he said waggishly.

Annie rose suddenly, with a quickly snatched ketchup bottle in her hand, but Mr. Bullwinkle, hastily buckling his oilskins, retreated rapidly outside.

"Now, Annie"—Noah's faded blue eyes twinkled—"calm down. Nothing's worth getting upset over." He broke two eggs into a shining pan. "Now about that kind offer of yours."

"I'll come over for ye when ye close this evenin'," she said eagerly.

"Thanks, Annie," said Noah gently, stirring the eggs in the pan. "Fact is, though, I'm not quite ready to leave just yet. You see, each year I take a couple of weeks off. And I'd thought of leaving this weekend."

"But today's on'y Thursday," Annie protested. "An'—an' listen, Noah. Even though they have quit blastin' fer today, that whole Kings Bluff's li'ble to tumble right down on yer nubbin!"

"Maybe," he said quietly. "I doubt it, though. And day after tomorrow I'll be gone." He dumped her eggs on a plate and served the toast and coffee. "Don't think I'm ungrateful. And I'll be glad to have you help me out when I get back."

"Well, look. If things does git to lookin' bad, will ye use yer phone? I'll be over here in a cloud o' rust!"

"O.K.," he smiled. "I promise. But——" He stopped and looked, vaguely puzzled, toward the rear of the cafe.

"Yeah," said Annie. "I feel it too. Mebbe yer back door's open."

Noah disappeared behind the partition, then returned. "It was open, all right," he began, then stared, for Annie was scuttling rapidly from the window to the door.

She flung it open and bellowed irately into the wind and rain. "I see ye, Bullwinkle, ye dirty school pigeon!" she was yelling. "Snitchin' in the back way so's ye could l'arn what we was sayin'! ... Look at him, Noah!"

He hurried to the door in time to see Mr. Bullwinkle hastening with a ludicrous pretense of innocence up the gangplank and thence ashore.

"Might ha' knowed he'd come nimblin' back to spy on us!" Annie rumbled angrily, as she closed the door.

She waded into her scrambled eggs while, outside, the boisterous rain rattled off the oilskins of the perfidious Mr. Bullwinkle, who presently, in pursuit of his suddenly inspired scheming, became engaged in conversation, at a shanty door, with a city watchman detailed to detour traffic around the debris and to report, by telephone, the constantly shifting menace of the bluff. A bill changed hands, and ten minutes later the now-jovial Mr. Bullwinkle was back on his Salamander as she returned to her home mooring across the slip from the Narcissus.

When Annie—having returned by bus—was splashing around the wharf puddles abeam of the Salamander, Mr. Bullwinkle, who had been watching for her, stepped briskly out on deck.

"How are ye figurin' on taking him, Annie?" he said with a grin. "Not wi' yer wits, surely!"

"Takin' who, Ape Face?" she demanded.

"Nutcake Noah, of course! The whole waterfront knows he's got a bundle o' boodle stashed on board that old wreck. So I don't blame ya for tryin' to get yours. But how ya gonna do it? If ya'd trust me," he added piously, "maybe I could help ya."

"An' if the Lord would on'y give you brains," Annie retorted, "ye'd mebbe git promoted to a freak!" And with a contemptuous flick of her stern, she entered the company office and told the dispatcher that she was to be alerted instantly on receipt of any telephoned message from Noah.

Thoughtfully Mr. Bullwinkle watched her return to the Narcissus; then, hugging to himself a secret excitement, he summoned Jake, his paunchy, tobacco-chewing mate.

"I dunno when that cliff might start slidin'," said the Salamander's master. "It might be tonight, or maybe tomorra, or not at all. But when it does, Jake, we gotta move—and move fast!"

The call to action came much sooner than he really expected, however; for at suppertime that evening, when night had begun to deepen the rainstorm's darkness, the Salamander's ship-shore phone rang sharply, and Mr. Bullwinkle picked it up.

A moment later he hung up and hastily found Jake. "The watchman called," he said jubilantly. "The bluff's beginnin' to crack. They've had three bad rock falls in the last half hour."

"But—but ain't that dangerous for the old coot?" Jake was nervous.

"Naw! It's too far back from the water," Mr. Bullwinkle assured him speciously. "O' course, when it does let go, it'll eventually slide out to Noah's mooring. But by that time Annie'll have him in tow, an'——Say!" A sudden thought hit him. "We'll slip over there now. Someplace close, but where we won't be spotted. Then, when the time comes we'll be all set."

Annie, at supper on the Narcissus, did not notice their departure, and later she was too busy; for at about nine o'clock a frantic call from Noah sent her surging across at top speed.

Above the roar of wind and hiss of rain they could hear ominous crackings and the thunderous roar of tons of dislodged rock and earth. So, alongside the rickety jetty, with the Narcissus's broad fantail beneath the old hulk's bows, Annie issued rapid-fire orders to get a towing hawser aboard her. Then she jumped ashore and across the gangplank into the still-lighted cafe; nor did she observe, in her hurry, that she was watched by Mr. Bullwinkle from shadowed concealment on the hulk's deck; nor could she know that when Shiftless left the Ark's forecastlehead, after securing the Narcissus's hawser to her bitts, the master of the Salamander, with furtive quickness, took his place.

With utmost precaution against being seen or heard, Mr. Bullwinkle's powerful hands gathered in what hawser slack they could and belayed it, bestowing on it then, before letting it out again, some hurried but expert attention. Then, like a shadow, he was gone, over the side and ashore to his concealed Salamander in the gloom of an abandoned fish shed.

Meanwhile, inside the cafe, Annie had tried in vain to persuade Noah to accept passage on the Narcissus.

"I've got my own quarters below, Annie," he told her, gently smiling. "I'll be all right. Besides, I couldn't leave Toby and Tab."

"Toby an'——" For a moment Annie was nonplused. "Oh, ye mean yer cat an' dog! Where are they?"

"Down below. I never bring them into the cafe, of course."

"Well, fetch 'em along. Nobody'll bite 'em!"

Noah shook his head. "This is their home too," he said.

Further discussion was cut off by another tremendous rock fall that shook hulk and jetty, and Annie snapped into action.

"O.K.," she said quickly. "Git out on deck, Noah, an' when ye hear me toot the Narcissus's whistle, cast off yer dock lines!"

TUGBOAT ANNIE LOSES A TOW

Slogging through a moderate sea, with the Ark wallowing astern almost invisible in the rainy darkness at the end of a long towline, the Narcissus, with Annie at the wheel and Peter, the mate, to keep her company, moved from behind the lee of the northern headland and out into the rougher water of the open sound. As she did so, a sudden black squall bore down upon them and green water shot over the wheelhouse and poured down the windows. Impatiently Annie waited until it cleared, and the distant gleam of Seal Point Light swam hazily back into view.

"I hope Noah's all right, back there alone on that old hulk," she confided worriedly to Peter. "Here, take the wheel, whiles I go aft an' see if the Ark's makin' out O.K."

Balancing expertly, she staggered aft to the corner of the house and strove to pierce the murk astern. Then, suddenly, she froze in quick alarm.

"Oh, no!" she gasped and, turning, bumbled frantically back to the wheelhouse.

"Stop her, Peter!" she yelled. "Quick! Afore we git the propeller fouled in the towline!"

"The propeller fouled?" Peter said.

"We've lost our tow!" she cried desperately and reached past him to jingle the engine room. Then she dashed out again, to the top of the ladder, hanging grimly on as the Narcissus, her way stopped, rolled wildly in the trough.

"Hank! Shif'less!" she roared; and when they came tumbling out on deck she ordered them to lay aft and reel in the parted hawser. "Lemme know when it's secured!" she directed, then ran for the radio room.

Presently a frantic plea was cracking forth to the Coast Guard and to all nearby shipping to keep a lookout for the missing tow. But by that time Annie was on top of the wheelhouse, operating the tug's powerful searchlight, traversing, in wide sweeps, the tumbling waters around them. But of the derelict Ark there was no sign.

Presently, with the dripping hawser secured, Hank struggled up to Annie. "It's kinda queer!" he yelled into her ear. "That hawser end looked like it had been cut halfway through, then snapped wi' the strain!"

"Never mind it now!" she told him urgently. "Have Peter git underway again, whiles we turn back an' look! An' if ye know any prayers, Hank, start bleatin'! Noah might need 'em!"

With the propeller beating once more under her counter, the Narcissus swung back over her course, the searchlight still sweeping the rain-thickened darkness. But a half hour passed without result.

Then Clem's vibrant voice rode up to her from the deck below. "Annie! Annie!" he shouted. "It's O.K.! The Ark's been found! She's been picked up!"

Tightly Annie gripped the searchlight standard, shaking with the violent nausea of relief. "Tell me quick! What happened?"

"A—a tug picked her up." Clem swallowed and struggled on—"It was the Salamander! Bullwinkle just called us on the ship-shore phone."

"Bullwinkle?" Annie almost burst. "How in the blue-starred hell did he git out here so fast? Where are they? What'd they say?"

"He said they found her adrift and——"

"What about Noah?"

"He's O.K. That is," Clem amended hastily, "Bullwinkle said he broke his arm while they were taking him off the Ark. Otherwise he's fine."

"Thank God!" breathed Annie deeply. "An' the hulk?"

"The Salamander's towing her back to Secoma."

"O.K., Clem. Fine. You done swell, son!" Annie switched off the searchlight. "Better git below an' take them wet clothes off."

"Just a minute, Annie," Clem said uneasily. "There—there was another message Bullwinkle said to be sure and give you. You aren't going to like it much, but—but——"

"Well, come on!" cried Annie impatiently. "What was it?"

"Well, he said to warn you not to start any funny business about reclaiming the Ark, because after he took Noah off she was abandoned and in danger. So he—he——"

"Go ahead!" said Annie grimly. "Let's have it!"

"So he's taking possession of the Ark and all her contents," Clem finished, "as total salvage!"

"I knowed it!" Annie roared savagely at the unruly elements. "I knowed there'd have to be some cussed, skulduggin' reason why that dirty robber would hafta be Johnny-on-the-Blot!" Wildly she flung up her arms. "But wait till we git into port, brother! Jest wait!"

The Salamander was lying tranquilly at her berth, with the Ark moored close astern, when the Narcissus surged into her home slip an hour later, and Annie lost no time in storming around. Jake tried to stop her as she stepped aboard, but she disposed of him with one solid punch, then stamped up the ladder, to be confronted at the top by Mr. Bullwinkle, whose rain-wet face was uneasy but truculent.

"What you doin' here?" he blustered. "I told Clem——"

"He telled me!" Hotly she cut him short. "But how come you was so handy when she went adrift? An' what's this nonsense about salvage?"

TUGBOAT ANNIE LOSES A TOW

"It's no nonsense!" he told her angrily. "An abandoned vessel is claimable. You know that. She became abandoned the second Noah left her! And can I help it," he yelped virtuously, "if I happened to be cruisin' around out there, looking for a—a log spill?"

"Save it!" she rasped. "Where's Noah?"

"In me cabin. His arm's broke. He was outside the Ark's rail, ready to jump, when he remembered them pets o' his and started back for 'em. Then she rolled, an' he fell on my deck."

"His pets?" Even Noah's misfortune temporarily was forgotten, for with her enemy's words a glimmer of hope appeared. "Ye mean ye left his dog an' cat on board?"

"What am I runnin', a zoo?" he demanded. "Anyways, they're O.K. Ye needn't worry."

"Me, worry?" Her voice was quiet, for with everything he said, the glimmer was brightening. "It's you what's in a conundrum right now, not me!"

"How do ya mean, dear?" Since Annie no longer was perking violence Mr. Bullwinkle was amused.

"About that so-called salvage claim, Hamhead," she said genially. "Abandonment of a vessel means the removal of 'every livin' thing.' But Noah's cat an' dog is livin' things—an' you was fool enough to leave 'em on board!"

"Ye're crazy!" he yelled. "I never heard o' such a law!"

"Why should ye?" she retorted. "All you know about law is what's on a police blotter. But come wid me. I'll prove it."

"Prove it? How? Where?" Mr. Bullwinkle was badly shaken.

"By Noah, o' course! Right there in yer cabin! One time he was the finest maritime lawyer in the state. Come on, let's git this over wid." And since she energetically pushed him aside and headed for his cabin, he had no choice but to follow.

When they entered, Annie wasted no sympathy on Noah, who, with his left arm in an improvised splint, was sitting in an easy chair, eating soup. "I'm sorry ye got hurt," she told him brusquely, "but at the moment I got a tooth to pick wid Nasty-face Bullwinkle here." And rapidly she outlined her theory on the salvage claim. "So tell him what a fathead he is, then let's git outta here an' turn this cage back to the monkeys!"

For a few moments Noah was silent, his wistful, troubled eyes going from Annie's triumphant face to Mr. Bullwinkle's red and sweating one. Then, slowly, he shook his head.

"I can't tell him that, Annie," he said quietly. "And since he probably saved my life tonight, I wouldn't want to. Actually, he has a salvage claim against me. A quite legitimate one."

"B-but yer dog an' cat," sputtered Annie, aghast. "The law says——"

"No, Annie," Noah interrupted her gently, "it doesn't. You're thinking of the case of the liner Colombia?" She nodded dumbly. "She was abandoned, and there, too, animal pets were left on board, and her owners fought salvors, who claimed her, on that basis. But the court of admiralty held that the phrase 'any living thing' applied only to humans, and the Colombia's owners lost their case."

"And you mean to say," blurted Mr. Bullwinkle, staring at Noah in blank incredulity, "you'll admit, without a legal fight and after what I done to——" He corrected himself quickly, "I mean—knowin' it might cost ya yer vessel and all it contains, you admit that I got a legal claim against ya?"

"Why not?" asked Noah simply. "It's the truth."

"Well!" Mr. Bullwinkle collapsed into the nearest chair. "I'll be a hornswoggled son of a biscuit!"

Morning broke, with sunshine and clearing skies, but when Annie awakened, she was still depressed; nor were her spirits improved when, glancing out her cabin window, she saw that Noah's safe was being transferred from the Ark to the Salamander under Mr. Bullwinkle's self-important supervision. As the day wore on a couple of towing jobs blunted the sharpness of her resentment. Feeling some compunction about her brusqueness with Noah the night before, she determined that, when she had time, she would visit him in the hospital.

It was not until evening, however, that, with a bunch of wilting posies clutched in her fist, and riding grandly in a taxicab, she arrived at the hospital door. And then, to her astonishment, she saw Noah emerge from the hospital and descend the steps, his arm in a sling; while assisting him with what Annie regarded as sickening solicitude, and carrying a large suitcase, was Mr. Horatio Bullwinkle.

Hastily Annie ducked back inside the cab and watched while the patient was helped into an arthritic jalopy driven by Jake, the Salamander's unprepossessing mate.

"Quick!" snapped Annie to her startled driver as the other vehicle jolted away. "Foller that creep—heap—whatever ye call it!"

Unfortunately, the pursuit was short, for at the bottom of the hill Jake's venerable crate turned into heavy traffic, and Annie's cab was stopped by a red light. When the signal had changed, their quarry was gone.

Much time was wasted in futile effort to pick up the trail; so when at last Annie paid off her driver and clumped wearily back along the dock, it was dark.

But when she boarded the Narcissus and entered the messroom for supper, she instantly was greeted with the astounding news that Mr. Bullwinkle had paid three visits within the past hour, demanding to know when Annie would return.

"That horse's shenanigan!" she ejaculated scornfully, but her interest was now fired hotter than ever. "What'd he want?"

A thunderous knock and the flinging open of the door saved Peter the trouble of answering, for Mr. Bullwinkle himself was standing, glowering, in the doorway.

"Where you been all day, ya fat cow?" he demanded of Annie. "Here I bin, waiting to invite ya to a party tonight, an'——"

"A party?" said Annie, repressing her astonishment. "What kind o' party, Swole-Dome?"

"What do you care?" Mr. Bullwinkle growled. "It's a party, and I been sentenced to take ya. O' course"—he put one foot outside the door coaming—"if washing yer face is gonna be too hard on ya, that's a break for me."

"Hey, wait!" cried Annie, her inquisitiveness now unbearable. "Set down an' give yer brains a rest whiles I tumble into me Sunday dugs!" And she clattered up to her cabin.

When she returned ten minutes later, she revolved before Mr. Bullwinkle with pachydermous complacence. "How'm I doin'?" she asked coyly.

Mr. Bullwinkle surveyed her with jaundiced eyes. "As long as ya don't start walkin' on all fours," he commented, "ya'll do all right. Come on! I got a taxi waitin'!"

Mr. Bullwinkle entered the taxi first, and absentmindedly was closing the door when Annie forced it open and scrambled in. "Where we goin', huh?" she asked, bumping him to make room.

"What am I—an information desk?" he growled.

Annie's fists closed. "Well, wherever it is," she snapped back, "jest let one o' your pals make a pass at me——"

"They ain't blind!" He grinned suddenly. "And look, Annie, when we get there, do me one little favor, will ya?"

"What's that?"

"Keep yer shoes on!"

Furious, she crammed him hard into a corner, and they rode on in silence, but when they arrived at their destination, Annie's resentment switched quickly to astonished awe, for they had stopped in front of the Rainier, Secoma's swankiest hotel.

"Hey, we ain't goin' in here, are we?" she muttered uneasily.

"It's O.K.," Bullwinkle told her kindly. "If anybody stops ya, just tell 'em ya forgot yer mop an' pail."

Dumb with apprehension, she followed him across the lobby, but when Mr. Bullwinkle led her to a polished twelfth-floor door, Annie panicked. "Listen, Pie Puss," she said hoarsely. "What goes on in there?"

"I don't wanna spoil it for ya. An' look, Annie." His tone was earnest now, almost conciliatory. "No matter who ya meet in there, no matter what he says, don't show no surprise, will ya? Just string along with it. O.K.?"

"No, it ain't!" she said vehemently. "Not 'less ye tell me."

"I'll explain it later," he said hurriedly, and pushed the button.

The door opened and Annie shrank back a little; then she reacted in openmouthed stupefaction, for there stepped forward to greet them, clad in impeccable dinner jacket, black tie and gleaming shirt front, her old and smiling friend, Noah.

"Well, Annie! And, Horatio!" he beamed, and extended his hand, the other arm suspended in a black-silk sling. "Come in, come in!"—and he ushered them into a large, luxurious suite, with a food-and-drink-laden buffet attended by hotel waiters, and conducted them across the room toward a group of expectantly smiling people. "Folks," he announced with wistful pride, "here are my good friends and fellow workers, Captain Annie Brennan, senior master of my tugboat fleet——"

"Huh? Wass that?" ejaculated Annie, but Mr. Bullwinkle's prompting elbow jabbed into her ribs.

"——and Mr. Horatio Bullwinkle," Noah continued, "general superintendent of my other interests."

Mr. Bullwinkle made with his special, butt-sprung bow. "Pleased to meetcha," he mumbled, and grinned widely.

"And now, Annie," their host went on, "I want you and Horace to know my late dear wife's sister, Jane Temple, and her husband John, from Pittsburgh . . . their daughters, Anne and Grace . . . and my wife's Allentown cousins, Mr. and Mrs. David Armour."

They were plain, friendly folk, easy to know, and obviously holding Noah in high, affectionate esteem. And before long, thawing in the atmosphere of their warmth and obvious sincerity, Annie began to enjoy herself, while food was served and Noah himself handed her a slender-stemmed crystal glass, filled with liquid of pale and bubbling gold.

"Would you drink with me, Annie," he said benignly, "to our family reunion?"

Annie sipped. "My!" she exclaimed, the bubbles tickling her nose. "This sure is nice pop, ain't it?"

"It's champagne, ye silly old scut," the scandalized Mr. Bullwinkle whispered in her ear.

But Annie ignored him and held out her glass for more, and in this intriguing fashion an hour had passed before she was able to corner him alone. "Now, me good man—spill!" she demanded cheerfully. "What is this cockeyed deal?"

"Deal?" He stared at her owlishly.

Her tone hardened. "How come you an' Noah's so palsy, after you gyppin' him outta his boat?"

"What do ya mean?" he replied indignantly. "He's still got it!"

"Sa-ay, what are you givin' me? How about that salvage claim?"

For a moment he regarded her speculatively, then shook his head. "You ain't gonna get this, Annie," he said virtuously, "on account of you don't appreciate honesty like I do. I'll admit I did pull kind of a fast one last night. But when you tried to help him out and he wouldn't let you, and said he had no case, it—it's funny, Annie, I got to like the old guy. So today I told him to forget the salvage. I washed it right out."

"Ye're lyin', ye thief!" rasped Annie. "I seen ye take that safe outta the Ark!"

"Oh, that!" Mr. Bullwinkle coughed. "That was before I called the salvage deal off. Because, Annie, when I got that safe open"—he lowered his voice—"ya'll never guess what was in it."

"What?" breathed Annie, rigid with suspense.

"Nothin'," whispered Mr. Bullwinkle. "Not one solitary thing, except——" He gestured slightly. "See Noah over there? Them fancy drapes he's wearin'? Well, that's what he kept in the safe. Them clothes. And that's all."

"Ye're still lyin'," said Annie flatly.

"It's true," he protested. "An' because he appreciated me bein' so bighearted about the salvage, he told me why, and said I could tell you. That's the reason we was invited here tonight. Why he wanted us to pretend——"

"Yeah, I wondered about that too," she said. "What's the dope?"

"I'll tell you later," said Mr. Bullwinkle.

Much later, after profuse farewells, and loaded down with a bottle of champagne, they crawled into a cruising night-owl cab. Annie rolled down the window and took several gulps of sharp night air. "O.K.!" she croaked. "Give! Afore I start thumpin'!"

"Wha-wha's that?" asked Mr. Bullwinkle, struggling back to consciousness. "Give what?"

"You heerd me!" said Annie grimly. "Why he throwed the party.

Why he pertended to be a hot-pot industrial typhoon when we come in. An' why he's runnin' a skimpy little caffy, wid all that dough."

"What dough?" said Mr. Bullwinkle. "All he's got is what he makes out o' the Ark. He's as poor as we are."

"Then how in the heck——" Annie said, confused.

"O.K.," said Mr. Bullwinkle. "I'll tell ya. Gimme that bottle."

And having refreshed his faculties, he gradually revealed the story of gentle Noah Svenson, the orphan who had made good in the intricate field of admiralty law. Of how, with no kin of his own, he had taken into his care the family of his Eastern-born wife, at whose loving behest, each year, he would treat them all to a holiday in Secoma, all expenses paid.

"Then his wife died and it broke him up, and he lost all his money," Mr. Bullwinkle went on. "But he prob'ly figgered that if he could keep her family coming out, like before, it'd be a kind of a monument to her. Took every cent he could bank. But he figgered it was worth it."

"And they never found out he'd lost his money?"

"Never did. He don't want 'em to know."

"He's right," said Annie. "It wouldn't be the same."

They rode in silence for a while, and presently the taxi dropped them, across the tracks from the wharf; and, strangely at peace, they walked together under a canopy of stars, then came to a halt at the head of the slip, from where they could view their sleeping vessels and, astern of the Salamander, the dark shape of Noah's Ark.

After a moment, Annie pointed. "What about her?"

"I'm havin' her repainted and fixed up for him," said Mr. Bullwinkle huskily, as if ashamed. "Then I'll provision her from the Salamander's stores an' tow her across to Weyant Island. She'll be waitin' there for him when he gets back."

Annie looked at him. "I still can't credit it," she said slowly.

"Credit what?" he asked.

"You!" she told him, her voice unsteady. "Actin' like a human bean!" Vigorously she shook her head. "There's somethin' wrong," she muttered. "So I'm goin' ashore tomorrer to——"

"Annie!" The night dispatcher's voice came to them from the second-floor landing of the outside office steps. "That you?"

"Yeah, it's me," she bawled. "What ye want, Fred?"

"Sorry to bother you this late, but I knew you wasn't home yet. It's about this here bill the hospital sent down today. A bill for fixin' Noah Svenson's arm."

Mr. Bullwinkle started moving quietly away toward his Salamander, gradually increasing his pace.

"What bill ye talkin' about?" Annie yelled. "We ain't responsible fer that! Bullwinkle was s'posed to——"

"But they said Bullwinkle told 'em to send it to us!" cried Fred. "He claimed that since we was towing Noah's vessel, it was up to us to——"

"Why, that dirty, cheatin' no-good——Hey! Where is he? . . . Hey, come back here, you robber, you thief, till I belt the livin' daylights outta ye!"

But Mr. Bullwinkle was galloping down his own side of the slip, and Annie knew that pursuit now was useless.

"Oh, brother!" she exploded, and her exclamation was almost a shudder, but whether motivated by a need for violent physical action or relief from a narrow escape, it would be extremely difficult to tell.

TUGBOAT ANNIE'S LONG SHOT

Having demolished her second huge stack of crisp-edged hotcakes, dripping with butter and syrup, Tugboat Annie Brennan, master of the big deep-water tug Narcissus, of Secoma, sat back with a grunt of repletion and beamed around at her heartily eating crew.

"Say, Hank," she said to the second deckhand, blue eyes twinkling with fun, "did ye hear about the rich Scotchman what axed his daughter's boyfriend whether he'd love her as much if she had no money?"

"Sure," said Hank. "And the boyfriend said he would. So the old man kicked him out. Said he didn't want a fool in the family."

"Oh, ye knew that one, huh?" muttered Annie, disappointed, and turned with a hopeful titter to Big Sam, the engineer, who was stolidly munching. "Sam, what'd the miser leave to the orphan asylum?"

"Ten kids," replied Big Sam promptly, not even looking up; and instantly Annie's mastiff face purpled.

"Cuss you fellers! One o' ye's stole me joke book!" she bellowed accusingly. "Who's got it?"

"I have, Annie," said Hank with a grin, and handed it to her. "You were getting so clever it worried us. So——"

"Posh-pish! It's gittin' so's a pusson can't have no fun around here no more!" Annie grumbled. "What did the feller do," she fired at him suddenly, "when his pal found a five-dollar bill on the sidewalk?"

"Why, I don't know," Hank admitted. "What did he——"

"He borrered it," cried Annie triumphantly, "to visit a octupus an' have his eyes tested! Ye see?" She chuckled, her good humor restored. "I skunked ye, 'cause that one was in a book I ain't even finished readin' yet!" And heaving her massive frame upright, she waddled happily out on deck.

The air was clean and fresh after the night's rain, glittering snow pinnacles of the Olympic Range far to port reflected the early sun, and a brisk wind chased whitecaps over the sparkling blue water; and as Annie shot an expert glance at the two deep-laden fuel-oil barges wallowing lazily at the end of a towing wire astern, her big chest filled.

"Oh-h-h, happy days is here some more!" she roared contentedly, and clumped up the ladder to relieve Peter at the wheel.

"Say, Peter," she said as her big, calloused hands took over the spokes, "what's the difference atween a leddy takin' a bath an'——"

"Oh, for gosh sakes, Annie!" growled the usually phlegmatic Peter. "You been on that kick for two weeks now! Will ya quit?"

"O.K.! O.K.! But when ye hear the answer," said Annie indignantly as he went out the door, "ye'll be sorry ye missed it! An' listen!" she yelled after his rapidly retreating footsteps. "Tell Big Sam that as soon as I git the receipt fer them two barges at Port Haskins, we're headin' fer home!"

Then, hooking one big knee over a wheel spoke, Annie produced her joke book and proceeded to enjoy herself until the lighthouse on Speak Reef was abeam and the tug was running between the channel buoys of the bustling little lumber and fishing town of Port Haskins.

The Narcissus pushed her unwieldy charges alongside the oil dock, where they quickly were secured. Then, as Annie was about to climb ashore and obtain her receipt, a clipped and vinegary voice addressed her from the wharf.

"Hi there, cook!" said the voice. "Tell your skipper Mr. Triptoe's here, so he can get underway now! And the quicker the better!" And there jumped down onto the Narcissus's deck a small, dapper man with an alert manner and needle-sharp eyes. And as Annie stared at him he removed his headgear, carefully smoothed a few black strings of hair across his shiny pate and clapped it on again.

"Yeah?" replied Annie. "An' who the heck do you happen to be?"

"I've just told you," he said impatiently. "Name's Triptoe! Widdiken S. Triptoe! Now go and tell the master that——"

"I'm the master," said Annie pugnaciously.

"You—you're wha-at?" said the little man.

"Ye heerd me, Tanglefoot!" Annie rasped.

"Triptoe!" he corrected her sharply.

"Whatever it is. Anyways, me name's Annie Brennan, an' I'm master o' this tug. So state yer business an' git, because I jest don't like the cut o' yer jib!"

"Captain—Brennan?" The brisk gentleman seemed a trifle uncertain now. "Yes, that was the name Severn gave me. But——"

"Alec Severn?" Annie asked, surprised in turn.

"Yes! President of your company! You ought to know him if you're what you claim! But he said nothing to me"—and little Mr. Triptoe's disapproval was emphatic—"about the vessel's master being a woman! And that's something I don't like!"

Annie glared at him. "That makes it anonymous!"

"And you didn't get a wire from Severn about me when you picked up those barges at Port Townsend? What kind of a sloppy outfit is this?"

"Hey, wait a minute." Suddenly, with a guilty flush, Annie had recollected receiving a telegram at the Port Townsend oil depot the previous evening, but, deep in her latest joke book, she had thrust it into the pocket of her shirt, said shirt now reposing in a laundry bag in her cabin.

"Look, mister. Wait here," she said hastily, "whiles I go topside an' read me shirt—I mean—well, wait here!"

Hastily she pounded up the ladder, and seconds later was perusing, red-faced and perspiring, a lengthy message from her boss. It read:

WHITE WATER LOGGING COMPANY OF MINNESOTA HAS BOUGHT OUT GLACIER LUMBER COMPANY INTERESTS IN NORTHWEST WITH VIEW ENLARGING OPERATIONS. WHITE WATER VICE-PRESIDENT W.S. TRIPTOE IN CHARGE NEW OPERATIONS JOINS YOU PORT HASKINS FROM WHERE PROCEED SIWASH COVE MILL AND TOW TWENTY SECTION LOG RAFT TO SECOMA. THIS IS TRYOUT PENDING EXCLUSIVE WHITE WATER TOWING BUSINESS. GIVE TRIPTOE FULL V.I.P. TREATMENT. BULLWINKLE IN VICINITY SO USE CAUTION CASE HE BEATS US TO IT. DO GOOD JOB IN THIS ANNIE. ACKNOWLEDGE.

ALEC SEVERN.

"Oh, brother! Full V.I.P. treatment, huh?" Annie groaned as she got the impact. "I sure pulled a gin-dandy this time!"

Sheepishly she turned to Mr. Triptoe. "Seems to me now," she said with forced affability, "I must 'a' heerd o' ye someplace afore. So step aboard——"

"I am aboard!" he pointed out astringently. "Let's go!"

Ten minutes later the Narcissus was headed at top speed for Siwash Cove, and in order to avoid the censorious regard of Mr.

Triptoe, who, critically appraising, was prowling the tug, Annie took the wheel. And to her, presently, reported Clem, the Narcissus's radio operator, looking worried.

"Got news for you, Annie," he said. "And none of it's good. First, the boss called over the radiophone. After he stopped cursing, he asked why you hadn't acknowledged his wire about the passenger, and about picking up that million board feet of logs at Siwash Cove."

"Call him back!" said Annie hastily. "Say the queer feller's on board an' we're headin' fer Siwash—— But no! We can't do that, case Bullwinkle picks up the message an' snatches the tow! Let Alec wait! I'll straighten it out!"

"You're too late, Annie," said Clem somberly. "Alec just phoned back—and this time he really flipped his wig! Because he'd had a radiophone message from Bullwinkle thanking him for the tip, and saying he was heading for Siwash Cove in his Salamander to pick up that log boom as of now—immediately!"

"Oh, oh!" groaned Annie in deep despair. "Oh, oh! Listen, Clem. Phone the mill people at the Cove! Tell 'em we're on our way an' not to let——"

"Think I didn't, Annie? But the Salamander'd already tied onto the boom and left. What I can't understand, though—and the mill people couldn't either—instead of starting on the ordinary course to Secoma around Gull Island, Bullwinkle was heading for Suicide Narrows."

"Suicide Narrows?" Annie stared at him incredulously. "Why, that's crazy! Not even Bullwinkle's fool enough to try an' take that big log raft through there! Even at slack tide it's murder, an' he's got plenty o' time to go the safe way!"

For a few seconds she stood silent, deep in troubled thought. Then energetically, she started swinging the big wheel hard over.

"Where you going, Annie?" Clem asked, puzzled.

"After Bullwinkle, o' course!" grated Annie. "There's somethin' funny goin' on here, an' I'm gonna find out what it is!"

It was almost two hours before the Narcissus, under the impetus of every last revolution that the skill and experience of Big Sam could squeeze out of her pounding engines, overhauled, first, the long, sluggishly moving log raft, then the big, black-hulled, capable-looking Salamander. And as Annie put the Narcissus, under a slow bell, abeam and within hailing distance, Peter took over the wheel while Annie stepped out on deck, her face grim as she stared across; and Mr. Triptoe, eyes and ears alert, climbed to the upper deck to observe events.

For a few minutes, however, the arrival of the Narcissus was ignored; for within the Salamander's pilothouse a violent argument appeared in progress, though no words were audible, among three huddled figures. It terminated suddenly when the door was flung open and the Salamander's grease-stained engineer burst out and clattered down the ladder, his smudged face livid with rage. And immediately afterward there emerged, on bandy legs, the powerfully built Mr. Horatio Bullwinkle, owner and master of the vessel and Tugboat Annie's most bitterly cherished business rival.

Pausing for a moment to give some further instructions to Jake, his paunchy mate, who was at the wheel, Mr. Bullwinkle, pretending not to notice the Narcissus, leaned his broad back against the pilothouse, raised his eyes in artless admiration of the cloudless sky and started to whistle.

"Hey there, ye bristle-pussed lump o' dead shark!" roared Annie. "What the blue-starred hell ye mean by stealin' my tow?"

Mr. Bullwinkle's expression of bovine innocence intensified while, with cupped hand, he lent a listening ear.

"A dickeybird?" he speculated guilelessly. "No, dickeybirds don't drink! A dodo? H'm'm'm—could be!" Slowly his twinkling little black eyes swiveled until they met Annie's fury-congested face. "Well, bless me soul if it ain't the fugitive from the booby hatch!" he cried ingenuously, and shook his head. "Times sure must be hard when the bait's chasin' the fish."

"Thought ye'd dodge me by sneakin' through Suicide Narrows, didn't you, ye robber, ye thief? Well, lemme tell ye——"

"I didn't have to hide from you, Annie," countered Mr. Bullwinkle virtuously. "The mill gave me the raft without no fuss. And they ain't a thing ya can do about it. So too-ra-loo!"

With a gallant, butt-sprung bow, he was about to retire when Jake stuck his uncouth head out the door and said something, quick and low; whereupon, after a second or two of intensive thought, Mr. Bullwinkle nodded; then turned back to the Narcissus.

"Jake just reminded me, Annie," he said carelessly. "We got another big towin' job waiting. So if ya want to tow this boom to Secoma for me, I'll split the fee."

"What? Split a fee on me own job?" yelled Annie, outraged. Then suddenly: "Wa-ait a minute! You never split a fee in all yer mis'rable, rat-bitten life, 'less ye was forced to! What's the matter"—and Annie's eyes narrowed shrewdly—"you in trouble?"

"Like I said, it's gonna be hard to handle both jobs, is all," he said, elaborately offhand. "So think it over, will ya?"

"I sure will!" Annie replied emphatically. "An' when I come up wid the right answer——"

"Where'll you get it, missus?" interrupted Mr. Triptoe's acid voice at her elbow. "Out of a joke book?"

"Wass that?" Annie swung around, surprised; for she had completely forgotten that he was on board.

"You had your nose stuck in one the moment we left Port Haskins!" he snapped. "Meanwhile that fellow came along and outsmarted you—which, I judge, would be no great trick at any time."

"He stole the job! He knowed it was mine!" said Annie heatedly.

"He got it! And it's results that count with me! So he's the one who should handle my company's towing business!"

"Listen, Mr.—er—Slew-heel——" began Annie desperately.

"Triptoe!" he snapped, and gestured toward the Salamander. "Who is he? What's his name?"

"Nobody you'd care to know," Annie replied earnestly. "Why, he don't draw no more water around these parts than a yachtin' cap. An'——"

Suddenly she broke off, and it seemed that her casual scrutiny of the Salamander's long black hull intensified. Then: "H'm'm," she murmured speculatively, half to herself. "The missin' link."

"Don't you call me——" he began hotly, but Annie shook her head, still preoccupied.

"Unh-uh! Not you!" she grunted, her gaze still on the Salamander's hull. "I wondered why he was takin' a chance on runnin' through Suicide Narrows an' why he was willin' fer us to take over the tow. Now, mebbe I know!" She turned to him, grinning. "An' if I got the right answer, this time it didn't come outta no joke book! Excuse me a minute!"

Energetically Annie waddled into the wheelhouse, where, after glancing at the chronometer, she hastily consulted a tide table. Then she returned to the deck and addressed Mr. Triptoe once more.

"I'll make ye a preposition, mister," she said. "If I git that log boom o' yours delivered at Secoma free o' charge, will ye give us yer towin' business?"

"Don't be silly! The man's got it, and naturally he'll get paid! So run alongside and put me on board!"

"Who do you think ye're givin' orders to, ye little squit!" roared Annie. "If we ain't doin' business you don't draw no more water wid me"—she jerked her thumb at the busily chugging Salamander—"than he does! So there"—she yanked her joke book out of her pocket and jammed it into his hand—"find yerself some nice quiet spot—in the bilges fer preference!—an' study this to improve yer mind!"

She stamped back into the wheelhouse, where Peter stared at her.

"Ya sure blew our last chance o' getting his business that time, Annie," he observed.

"Yeah?" said Annie. "Mebbe! Mebbe not! Now look, Peter; let's shake our tail fer Suicide Narrows. We'll wait fer Bullwinkle there."

"S'pose he don't show up, Annie? S'pose all this stuff was just to throw ya off the track?"

"Look, pal," said Annie patiently, "you tryin' to think fer me is on'y gonna give ye varicose brains. So jest do what I telled ye, huh?"

"Sure, Annie. But——"

"If he don't show up—jest afore the tide changes too!—I'm wrong an' we'll skulk home an' eat bumble pie. But he will! He will!"

"What makes ya so sure?"

"Somethin' I think I seen, what ye don't l'arn in any business-efficiency school," said Annie with a sudden grin. "An' if I'm right, it'll show Mr. Traptop an' that ape Bullwinkle exackly how smart they reely are!"

There arose before the Narcissus, an hour later, a high and heavily wooded island, about fifteen miles long and divided across its mile-wide waist by a narrow, rock-strewn channel bordered with precipitous cliffs, between which raced, at tidal peak, a nine-to-ten-mile-an-hour current. Used mainly by commercial fishermen eager to beat a falling market, and even by them with trepidation and only when slack water at the change of tide nullified the deadly current, its pinched foreshores were strewn with enormous boulders. And even at brightest noonday the twisting, treacherous passage was sinister and dank.

The entrance was a gloomy cleft between the high and thickly forested walls, and it was here, a quarter of a mile offshore, that the Narcissus, awaiting the arrival of the Salamander, cruised idly off and on. And while they waited Annie paced the narrow deck, anxiously consulting her watch, while the last of the flood tide poured tumultuously out of the gap.

Then, from behind another island that blocked their vision to the north, appeared the Salamander with her tow. Slowly they straightened out and headed for the entrance, and again, worried, Annie glanced at her watch.

"It's almost slack water," she confided to Peter, who was standing in the open wheelhouse doorway. "He'd better put a bur beneath his starn if he expects that boom to git through the gut afore slack water ends an' the tide starts to ebb agin him!"

Her concern was justified, for Mr. Bullwinkle, gambling with time, only just made it; and even before the last section of the enormous log boom had disappeared into the gap, slack water already was well advanced.

A few hundred yards inside, the channel expanded to form a fairly wide lagoon before narrowing again to the most difficult and dangerous leg of the passage; and when the Narcissus, following now, rounded a long turn, Annie saw that, a hundred yards ahead, the Salamander and her tow had drifted to a stop and lay idle in the middle of the lagoon.

"Now what?" Annie rapped. "Here, Peter, take the wheel an' run her close till we find out what's goin' on!"

The Narcissus's bow wave creamed high as the tug surged forward; then, as they drew closer, they observed that the Salamander's engineer, staring upward, was once again engaged in furious altercation with Mr. Bullwinkle.

Simultaneously, Mr. Triptoe appeared at the top of the Narcissus's bridge ladder. "What goes on up there?" he asked, pointing. "What are they stopped for?"

"I got a pretty good idea," said Annie grimly. "Look, the engineer's goin' below again—an' is he mad!"

"He better make up his mind quick," rasped Peter. "If he don't, that ebb tide's gonna catch him in here and spill, strew and smash that log boom from hell to breakfast! ... Shall I take her in, Annie?"—and without waiting for her reply Peter jingled the engine room, and seconds later they were within speaking distance, with Mr. Bullwinkle owlishly watching their approach.

Annie stepped to the rail. "What's yer tale, snail?" she inquired. "What did ye stop fer—to admire the scenery or comb the knots outta yer head?"

Mr. Bullwinkle peered from under his palm. "Is that reely me old friend Annie?" he said. "Or have I got the d.t.'s again?"

"Whatever ye got'll be cured the hard way if ye don't git movin'," said Annie promptly. "What's yer trouble, asides from the creepin' rot?"

"Nothin' much, friend Annie, except a teentsy piece of dirt in my fuel line. It'll be cleared pronto, but meantime, how about passing me a line and steadying me through the pass? I hate to put ya to the trouble, but——"

"Don't let that decompose ye, friend Horatio," Annie responded politely. "Jest bend a shot line to that new steel hawser on yer bow an' we'll take it aboard an' have ye movin' in no time."

"On second thought, friend Annie," he replied, after a moment of hesitation, "this new line of mine being worth a lot of hard-earned dough, what about using a beat-up but serviceable hawser of yours?"

"No, friend Horatio. An' you know why. So shake the anchor outta yer tail. An' wid yer hawser send over a note, readin': 'Captain Annie Brennan, tug Narcissus: My tug Salamander wid log raft in tow is broke down in Suicide Narrows. Request immediate assistance.' An' sign it wid yer name, a X mark an' yer thumbprint."

While Mr. Bullwinkle digested this, his face underwent several interesting changes in color. And when he replied, his voice seemed a trifle hoarse. "About that note, friend Annie," he said; "after all, we've known each other for a long, long time——"

"Friend Horatio," interrupted Annie gaily, "that's eggsackly what I'm thinkin' of. So git busy wid the pencil."

Mr. Bullwinkle gazed at her very hard, and there was a curious throbbing in his jaw. "O.K., friend Annie," he acceded at length. "But I ain't never gonna forget this!"

"No, friend Horatio," agreed Annie; "I don't figger ye ever will!"

Abruptly, Mr. Bullwinkle spun on his heel and while delivering the orders to his deckhands he used a number of colorful words.

Presently the Salamander's shot line parabolaed over the Narcissus's stern, and attached was Mr. Bullwinkle's appeal for help.

"Fine, boys!" said Annie complacently, when the news was relayed up to her. "Make his hawser fast an' let's go!"

Slowly at first, then more rapidly, Annie's big tug straightened out the Salamander and her tow, and the little convoy resumed its voyage through the Narrows. But since much time had been lost, they were not more than halfway through before the tide turned, and from then on it was a grim and desperate battle against giant eddies and clutching whirlpools, and the peril of suddenly appearing outcrops of rock in midchannel, as the tide swiftly ebbed and the lethal current glided over them like molten green glass. Even the Narcissus's powerful engines were taxed to make headway against the rush and swirl of water, for she was dragging not only the dead weight of the huge and sluggish log raft but also the inert, deep-draft weight of the Salamander.

But gradually, fighting wildly for every inch gained, the Narcissus emerged into the broad waters and flooding sunlight of the farther end.

"Whoosh!" gasped Annie, wiping her sweating brow as she relinquished the wheel to Peter; for in the passage she had taken it over, trusting the lives of her crew to no hands but her own. "Sure was a close one!"

"Yep!" Peter said shakily, his own flabby, ashen face reflecting the strain. "Gosh, Annie, looka that current suckin' through there now!"

"Another ten minutes an' that would ha' bin it!" Annie agreed somberly. "Wonder how the queer feller took it? Last I seen of him he was up in the bows there, hangin' on like grim death! . . . Oh, here he is!" as Mr. Triptoe suddenly appeared at the top of the ladder. "Where was you—listenin' to the angels whisper?"

Mr. Triptoe stared at her with peculiar intensity, but he did not reply; and Annie, shrugging, went along to the radio cabin.

"Any news over the talky-talk?" she asked Clem.

"What you expected and told me to listen for," he grinned. "Bullwinkle started radiophoning before he entered the Narrows."

"Who'd he call—the Port Richmond oil depot?"

"You said he would, so why ask?"

Annie grunted. "Anythin' else?"

"Only the boss, raising tarnation again all over the sound, trying to locate us."

"Let him sweat!" Annie growled. "It'll pay him back fer wishin' Flatfoot on us." She paused suddenly, listening to the staccato hooting of a tug's air whistle. "Me friend Horatio! I wonder what kinda bilge the big goony's dreamed up this time?"

When she regained the deck, Mr. Bullwinkle was still tooting, supplemented by energetic beckonings from outside his wheelhouse. But before acknowledging, Annie picked up the wheelhouse glasses and trained them briefly on the waterfront of Port Richmond, a few miles ahead. What she observed apparently satisfied her.

"O.K., Peter. Slow down till we see what he wants—as if I didn't know!" she said with a grin. "An' keep the propeller clear o' that nice new steel hawser o' his." And as she leaned over the rail outside, staring astern at the approaching Salamander, she was again conscious of the presence nearby of a strangely subdued Mr. Triptoe.

When the distance between the tugs had closed to hailing distance, Mr. Bullwinkle, his knobby countenance radiating bonhomie, cupped his hands to his mouth.

"Thanks a million fer standing by, friend Annie!" he yelled. "Ya can let go our towin' hawser now!"

Before Annie could reply, her passenger said something violent beneath his breath, and she turned on him, Mr. Bullwinkle temporarily forgotten. "Who you tellin' to go to hell, ye cocky little squirt?" she indignantly demanded.

His sharp eyes met hers for a fleeting instant, then dropped. "Not you, anyway," he mumbled. "Go ahead, tell him! I won't butt in again."

Annie stared at him hostilely for a moment longer, then returned her attention to the grateful Mr. Bullwinkle.

"Friend Horatio," she bellowed, "think nothin' of it! I'm allus glad to do a nice piece of business wid a pal! But as fer lettin' go yer hawser——"

"Business?" yelped Mr. Bullwinkle, aggrieved. "What business? Surely," he continued reproachfully, "you ain't gonna hold me up over a little friendly turn, are ya? I'd do as much and more for you anytime!"

"To me, ye mean!" corrected Annie. "An' charge me ten times what I'm gonna stick you! So spit that sugar an' honey outta yer chops, friend Horatio, an' le's talk about my bill!"

"Why, you old fat-pot!" yelled Mr. Bullwinkle, all fences down. "What bill?"

"Fer savin' yer Salamander an' that log raft back in Suicide Narrows! That's salvage, friend, but I'll let ye off easy an' on'y charge ye two thousand bucks!"

"You're crazy!" he bellowed back. "We had a speck o' dirt in our fuel line, is all! And according to maritime law that's covered by the 'act o' God' clause, so I ain't liable!"

"Speck o' dirt in yer fuel line, huh?" countered Annie scornfully. "Then why did ye radiophone the Port Richmond oil depot to meet ye here wid a bargeload o' fuel oil?"

"I did no such a thing!" he roared. "So leggo my line right now!"

"Fine!" said Annie, and pointed ahead to where a motorized tank barge steadily was approaching. "Tell him to go home! An' let go your end o' yer hawser. I'll reel it aboard here. Then, if you kin tow that log boom down to Secoma under yer own power widout refuelin', ye'll git your hawser back an' collect the towin' fee, and I won't claim a red cent! Fair enough? O.K., then, friend Horatio! How about it?"

"I wouldn't trust ya!" returned Mr. Bullwinkle weakly.

"Ye don't dare to!" Annie told him triumphantly. "Because ye was so greedy to snatch that tow away from me that ye didn't even stop to fuel up—or forgot to—I dunno which! Anyways, leavin' port widout enough fuel makes yer vessel unseaworthy—an' that sure does leave ye open to a claim for salvage! An' right this minute you ain't got enough fuel in yer tanks to grease a gimlet! Well, what about it? Do ye send over a check for two thousand bucks an' git yer hawser back or does it git sold at a U.S. marshal's sale—an' mebbe the Salamander, too!—to satisfy the lien I'll slap on her, soon as we git in?"

There was a long pause, during which Mr. Bullwinkle performed quite a creditable fandango outside his wheelhouse. But when the

Port Richmond oil barge made a wide U-turn and ran alongside the Salamander, evidence enough of his duplicity, he surrendered.

"All right! I'll send over your ding-dong check!" he raged. "But if it takes me the rest of me natural life——"

"If your life was natural," Annie pointed out complacently, "ye'd be livin' on coconuts an' bananas! . . . O.K., Peter; turn his hawser adrift an' take her home. I'm goin' in me cabin fer a while to relapse."

A half hour later, with her shoes off Annie was propped up in her bunk, happily immersed in a brand-new joke book, when there was a tap at the door.

"Come in!" she yelled, hastily stowing the joke book beneath her capacious beam.

Slowly the door opened and Mr. Triptoe entered. "Hi, Annie," he said, and sat, uninvited, on the edge of a chair.

"Hi yerself, ye nasty little widget!" replied Annie promptly.

"Go ahead. Say the rest," replied Mr. Triptoe sullenly. "I've got it coming all right. Because, don't think," he snapped with a sudden return to acerbity, "that I missed what you pulled off today! Because, I'm not so dumb as you've a right to suppose!"

"Sa-ay." Annie sat upright, eyes wide with surprise. "Mebbe you got somethin' on the ball after all!"

"Enough to recognize ability if it slugs me over the head hard enough! Oh, I'm not trying to get out from under the salvage claim you've got against my company's log raft. We'll pay your award—within reason, that is."

"Ferget it!" said Annie. "Whatever I done was for the purpose o' gittin' yer towin' contract an'——"

"That you've got," he told her quietly. "Five minutes of watching you pull Bullwinkle out of that mess today settled that. But there's something else I wanted to talk to you about."

"Yeah?" said Annie, her eyes narrowing again. "Go on."

"It's about those joke books you read—like that one I see peeking out from under your—er"—he coughed modestly—"your stern right now. Why do you read them?"

"I dunno reely," said Annie, interested. "Mebbe because they're simple, an' make folks laff. An' they ain't too much left to laff at in the world today."

"I—I'm glad you said that, Annie," he said earnestly, "because—well—because maybe that's why I—I'm kind of addicted to 'em too."

"Ye're wha-at?" cried Annie, entranced; and like an agile pachyderm she bounded from her bunk.

"Yep," he admitted diffidently. "I read them all the time. After a hard day in the business world I find them quite relaxing."

"Why, ye wonderful little stinker!" she crowed excitedly. "I dunno whether to kiss ye or rub ye in me hair! Listen, pal, what'd the feller say when he was run over wid a brewery truck?"

" 'The drinks are on me!' " quoted Mr. Triptoe instantly. "That's an oldie! But before we go further, tell me, Annie, what first put you wise to the fact that Bullwinkle was short of fuel oil today? That's one I haven't been able to figure yet."

"Nothin' to it," said Annie. "I was sayin' somethin' to you about him not drawin' no more water than a yachtin' cap or somethin'—an' I happened to be lookin' at the Salamander an' seen how high outta the water she was. Hardly no draft at all, an' if she'd had fuel in her tanks she'd ha' been settin' deep. That's how I knew! But le's talk about somethin' important, like jokes."

"Suits me. By the way, when do we get into Secoma?"

"'Bout six p.m. Why?"

"What's the difference between a seven-course dinner and a bottle of beer?" he shot at her.

Annie was nonplused. "I ain't read that one yet," she admitted reluctantly. "I—I dunno."

"You don't know the difference?" chortled little Mr. Triptoe triumphantly. "Great! Let's go ashore together tonight, Annie—and I'll buy you a beer!"

TUGBOAT ANNIE LOSES COMMAND

Vicious rain squalls lashed the tumbling waters of Secoma harbor, and outside the rattling windows of the Deep-Sea Towing and Salvage Company offices, Puget Sound was an obscurity of gray swirling mist from the depths of which came the mournful barnyard hoots of moving shipping. But within the big main office, radiators hissed companionably and the aroma of freshly made coffee drifted from the hot plate in the corner.

This inner coziness was not, however, reflected in the rugged and spectacularly contused features of Tugboat Annie Brennan, master of the big tug Narcissus, nor upon the equally battered face of Captain Horatio Bullwinkle, skipper and owner of the rival tug Salamander, for they eyed each other with the hackle-rising hostility of a couple of angry bulldogs, while planted before a closed inner-office door, which bore the painted legend: A. SEVERN, PRES.

"O.K. Go ahead an' stare, fat-pot," Mr. Bullwinkle muttered as, momentarily, his little black shoe-button eyes met her bright blue ones. "I ain't workin' for Alec Severn. I'm my own boss. So what have I got to worry about? I'm only here outta—outta curiosity."

"Ye're here because Captain Price, o' the Navy Procurement Office, telled ye ye'd better be or else!" Annie growled. She added virtuously, "An' I ain't did nothin', either, 'cept larrup ye around a leetle to l'arn ye some manners."

"Well, ya needn't ha' slugged me wi' that two-by-four," objected Mr. Bullwinkle heatedly, "just because we had a little tiff!"

"No?" replied Annie complacently. "Well, then, next time I flatten ye wid me fist, stay flat!"

"Next time, eh?" roared Mr. Bullwinkle, and as their voices rose, Fred, the dispatcher, moved toward them, and Olive, the boss's secretary, looked alarmed. "There'll be no next time! Because if you ever punch me again 'cept in self-defense, I'll——"

"Great!" cried Annie, promptly assuming one of the more classic postures of the manly art. "Come on!"

Fred thrust himself between them. "Are you two crazy?" he demanded. "When the judge released you to Captain Price today, he said he'd give you ninety days if you came up before him for fighting again. And——"

"That fer the judge!" With a swooshing upsweep, her fingers snapped like a pistol shot under Mr. Bullwinkle's swollen proboscis. "All I ax is jest put me in the same cell wid this big ugly hippopotamouse!"

Further action abruptly was suspended, however, by the buzz of the intercom summoning them into Severn's office. Uneasily now, hostilities laid aside, they complied, although Mr. Bullwinkle, with unaccustomed gallantry and after a slight scuffle, made Annie precede him through the doorway.

Behind his desk, Alec Severn, plump and normally placidly good-humored, was pink with irritation. With him, standing at the window, was Captain Price, U.S.N., tall, lean, with shrewd blue eyes in a tanned, intelligent face.

"Hi, ye ol' gafoozler!" Annie greeted her boss with false joviality. "Hi, Cap'n Price. How's beans in the Navy these——"

"Shut up!" Severn ordered. "And close that door! What was that racket out there just now? You two been at it again?"

"'Twas him," said Annie promptly, jerking her thumb at Mr. Bullwinkle. "Somethin' he et, no doubt."

Quickly taking his cue, Mr. Bullwinkle emitted a genteel eructation behind his hamlike hand.

"It'd better have been only that!" Severn continued grimly, "because if you brawl again you're going straight back to the hoosegow..... That right, Captain Price?"

"That's right," said Price, unsmiling. "I intervened at court today only because the Navy needs your two big tugs to move that heavy equipment we want so badly up north. That, and the fact that you're both familiar with navigation in Alaskan waters."

"Navigation?" said Annie, with a disparaging glance at Mr. Bullwinkle. "He l'arned his, ridin' the hurricane deck of a jackass!"

"That's better," yelped Mr. Bullwinkle indignantly, "than learnin' it in a revolvin' door. If," he added with a significant stare, "ya could get that pot in a revolvin' door."

"Take that back!" yelled Annie, eyes blazing, but Captain Price coldly intervened.

"That's enough!" he said curtly. "You two are hopeless! . . . I'm sorry, Severn; I can't jeopardize important sea deliveries by this kind of nonsense. We'll take our towing business elsewhere."

"Aw, cap'n!" Annie instantly was remorseful. "We didn't mean nothin', did we, Horatio? Fack is, we're reely as close as two clams in one shell. Ain't that so?"

"No," said Mr. Bullwinkle. "It ain't. But I'm sorry too. . . . Honest, sir! I'll do a good job if she'll lemme alone! O.K., cap?"

Price eyed them for a long, appraising pause. Then: "All right, then. But to make certain that you stay in line, you're now going to have to post personal bonds."

"Bonds?" Abruptly, Severn straightened. "You didn't mention——"

"I know. But the season's already late, and since the stuff we're shipping is vital to those new radar stations for use in early spring, I've got to have a guarantee that it'll get there before the winter freeze-up. But this pair——" He broke off, shrugged.

"How much, then?" Severn asked quickly.

"Fifteen thousand each. To be forfeited for nonperformance."

"That scuppers me," said Mr. Bullwinkle unhappily. "I ain't got it."

"You own your Salamander, don't you?"

"Yeah. But it takes time to arrange a loan and——"

"I'll advance it," said Severn, "since one of my own employees"—he shot a hard look at Annie—"is partly responsible. I'll post bond for us and for Bullwinkle. He can give me his note, with the Salamander as security. . . . All right, captain?"

"I have no choice, right now," Price returned soberly. "And if things go well, we'll have business enough next season to keep you all profitably employed for months. But I'll take no excuses." He addressed Annie and Mr. Bullwinkle directly, "Any slip-up on this deal and the Navy's towing goes elsewhere! Got that?"

"Don't worry, cap!" said Mr. Bullwinkle briskly. "I'll keep her in her place."

Price ignored this. "And you?" he asked Annie.

"Yes, sir," said Annie, trying to sound meek. "I'll do me best."

"Pick up your barges at Pier Three in the Naval Stores Depot. They're big ones, and already loaded with equipment and supplies for Port Ragloff. That's the new Air Force and Radar Base on Ragloff Island in the Gulf of Alaska."

"What's the delivery date?" asked Mr. Bullwinkle.

"No specified date. Just get them there before the freeze-up starts, but in plenty of time for you to get out yourselves before you're iced in. Oh, one thing more! There'll be another barge, full of equipment to be repaired, waiting at Port Ragloff. You tow that back down here."

"Who does?" asked Annie quickly.

"Settle that between yourselves. It'll be a nice bit of extra profit. And don't forget," Price warned sharply. "Deviations or unnecessary delay in delivering up there will cost one or both of you fifteen thousand dollars apiece! Good luck"—he shook hands with them—"and good weather!"

They watched him go; then, as Annie and Mr. Bullwinkle were about to follow, Severn halted them. "Bullwinkle," he said, "if you'll stop in the outer office, Olive will fix up that note for you to sign. . . . Annie, I want to talk to you privately."

Uneasily Annie waited, while the door closed behind the now-swaggering Mr. Bullwinkle.

"Go ahead; say it!" said Annie defiantly, at length. "If I git in anymore shenanigoats wid Bullwinkle, ye're gonna fire me when I git back. But I already promised——"

"No, Annie," said Severn quietly. "I won't wait till you get back. Because I'm sending a substitute skipper with you. And if—in his opinion alone, mind!—you do anything connected with Bullwinkle that fouls up these deliveries on time, he will take over command of the Narcissus, and you're through!"

"Guess I can't blame ye, Alec," Annie said dully. "Who ye sendin'?"

"Well," Severn replied, "the Daisy's in dry dock for extensive overhaul. So——"

"Oh, no!" Annie exclaimed, aghast. "Not Truthful Tomkins! Why, he's the biggest gasbag——"

"He's a first-rate, reliable towboat man, Annie. Furthermore, he's wanted—and deserved a bigger tug for a long time. So perhaps here's his chance."

"Yeah, a chance like a shrimp in a lobster vat!" said Annie, suddenly furious again. "I'll make darn sure o' that!"

She blew out of his office like a departing gale, slamming the door behind her; and not until Severn heard her heavy, indignant footsteps clattering down the outside stairs to the wharf did he relax and permit himself a tiny, satisfied smile.

The tiered, rain-blurred lights of Secoma faded astern in darkness and swirling mist, as the Narcissus and the equally large and powerful Salamander, each towing a huge, heavily laden barge, left the harbor at suppertime and headed north in the teeth of the steadily increasing gale. Forty-eight hours later they were still bucking it, but they managed to move steadily abeam on the long reach Alaska-ward, among the islands of the Inside Passage. And in the Narcissus's darkened wheelhouse Annie was at the wheel, waiting for Peter to relieve her while she went down for supper.

Presently he appeared.

"Bro-ther!" he grunted. "Better start the whistle, Annie. Fog's so thick out there, we'd be better off closer inshore where we'd hafta part the trees to see where we was goin'."

"Yeah." Annie handed over the wheel and pulled the whistle lanyard, and when the hoarse, blaring note had died away she continued, "An' if the wind keeps up we're gonna hafta put in someplace till it blows over. It's too rough to go outside the islands right now. What's fer supper?"

"Steak. And ya'd better get below quick, before Truthful Tomkins eats his way clear down to the bilges. I dunno where he stows it all." Peter looked at Annie curiously. "I hear tell he was sent along on this trip in case he has to take over."

"Posh-pish!" said Annie quickly. "That's on'y if Bullwinkle starts pickin' on me again. An' that," she added virtuously, "ain't gonna happen no more. I promised Alec——"

Peter tittered. "Beg podden?" he said.

"Don't be so smart!" Annie rapped. "I'm takin' no chance on anybody runnin' the old Narcissus, 'cept me."

In the protected warmth of the wheelhouse Annie had not realized how strong the wind had grown, but as she descended the steel ladder to the lower deck it filled her throat and made breathing difficult, while the rain lashed like birdshot into her weathered face. While she fought it, her mind jumped to when they would have to leave the comparative shelter of the islands and battle the full fury of the stormy ocean outside, with the dead weight of the sluggish barges wallowing at the end of the long towing wire astern. And so thinking, she staggered aft to the fantail to try to ascertain how her own barge was making out.

She could see nothing of it, however, in the rain and fog. Off to starboard she noted automatically, however, that the lights of the Salamander were faintly visible; and somehow, watching the other tug's steady progress despite the turmoil, Annie felt the sharp edge of her dislike of Mr. Bullwinkle dulling. The Salamander, like her own Narcissus, was something solid, dependable, in a stormy world, and she had not ever underestimated her rival's professional skill.

"Might almost like the big loghead, if he was a human bean," she muttered as she went forward again toward the messroom. "Long as he keeps his ugly snout outta my affairs."

As she stepped into the light and warmth of the messroom, Annie beamed with pleasurable anticipation.

"Them combustibles sure sniffs good," she began enthusiastically to Pinto, the cook; and it was a second or two before she realized that no one was listening to her. Instead, her grinning crew were intent upon the words of Truthful Tomkins, a tall, emaciated-looking man with pipestem arms, and skinny legs encased in faded dungarees. His face, above a scrawny, weather-lozenged neck, was pale and bony, flanked by prominent ears, but his small brown eyes were exceedingly bright, darting and inquisitive, giving him the appearance of a raffish old crow.

"Hi, Annie!" He had glanced up and seen her. "Take yore things off an' hear this! . . . Well, as I was sayin', boys——"

"Would ye please mind," Annie interrupted with ponderous sarcasm, "if I axed Pinto to fetch me some grub whiles you're yakkin'?"

"Course not," he said hospitably. "Jist make yoreself to home. Well, like I said, I was up for my mate's certificate in front o' this mean, hard-boiled ole steamboat inspector. Now, up to then I'd done putty good, which made him mad; so the next thing he asks is: 'It's night and a port and a stabboard light is approachin' rapidly. But the port light's to stabboard and the stabboard light's to port. What's the situation? Ya got ten seconds to answer.' "

Truthful paused to take a gulp of coffee, then started working on a huge slab of pie, pretending to have finished his story.

"Fer Pete's sake, give 'em the score, afore I do!" snapped Annie, exasperated. "I've heerd ye tell it forty——"

"I'll tell 'em," said Truthful. "It was an airplane, flyin' low and upside down. . . . But even you don't know what happened next, Annie."

"Whatever it was, ye jest thunk it up," said Annie. Then, intrigued in spite of herself, she asked, "What did?"

"Old gimlet-puss give me another chance. 'One of me eyes is made o' glass,' he says, staring right at me, 'made by the best glass-eye maker in the world. Tell me which is the phony one an' you'll get yore certificate.' So I told him. . . . Pinto, more coffee!"

"Don't be stupid!" said Annie scornfully. "If the fake was as good as he said, how could you tell?"

"Nothin' to it, Annie. When I looked reel close I seen that one had the teeniest softer, kinder glint in it. So that was the glass one, o' course. . . . Pinto, where the heck's that jamoke?"

"Ye're pretty observant, ain't ye?" Annie said, after quite a pause.

"Ain't much I miss," said Truthful.

"Goody-goody-glumdrop!" said Annie. "Shif'less is on lookout, top o' the wheelhouse, an' the fog's so thick he can't see a dum thing. So, end of his watch, you'll relieve him."

"Wait a minute!" said Truthful. "I wasn't sent on board here to——"

"You ain't in command yet neither," Annie told him forcefully. "So ye don't draw no more water than a toothpick, an' ye'll do as I say! 'Sides, it's doin' ye a favor, reely."

"How so?" demanded Truthful.

"Think o' the fun ye'll have tellin' folks later, how it was so freezin' cold up there that ye grabbed a yard or two o' fog an' wrapped it around yer neck to keep warm. . . . Pinto, more coffee!"

Slowly, Truthful got to his feet and put on his oilskins, his bright gaze, now deeply speculative, fixed on Annie. "I can see," he drawled, "we're apt to have quite a time this trip."

"Me an' us both, pal!" said Annie. "I kin see right now, ye're gonna be more fun than a barrel o' donkeys!"

When Annie, her capacious innards comfortably stuffed, returned to the wheelhouse a half hour later, the wind had risen to almost full gale force.

"Where are we?" she asked Peter. "Clear o' Malcolm Island yet?"

"We passed it. And Fort Rupert's ahead, off to port. But in this stuff tonight we'll never see it. Annie, we gotta make up our minds——"

"I know," said Annie, worried. "Whether to take a chance through Queen Charlotte Sound to the open sea or keep on up the Inland Passage. It's shorter outside, to Port Ragloff, o' course."

"We'll take a terrible washin' out there," Peter warned gravely.

"We're gonna have to take cover somewheres right here inside, if this gits much wuss!" said Annie. "An' what bothers me is the time element. Every day counts now, in case we git froze in someplace. I wonder what Bullwinkle's gonna do. Mebbe I better find out, Peter. Hold that fog whistle till I git through."

She staggered aft to the radio shack, and had Clem, the radio operator, tune in on the other tug's radiophone frequency.

"Tug Narcissus to tug Salamander!" said Annie, when the connection was made. "Kin ye read me? Lemme talk to Bullwinkle if he's sober enough."

"This is him," said Mr. Bullwinkle's well-known rasp. "And I can read ya like a book. A comic book. What ya want?"

Quickly Annie outlined the problem. "The glass is still droppin'," she said, "an' if it ain't eased up before long, we oughta keep on fer the lee o' them islands north o' Cape Caution. It'll take us a coupla days longer to reach Port Ragloff, but——"

"You do that, dear!" interrupted Mr. Bullwinkle enthusiastically. "You take that calm, safe Inside Passage!"

Instantly Annie was suspicious. "Yeah?" she yelled. "Whiles you sneak out through Queen Charlotte Sound, so's ye kin be first at Port Ragloff an' grab that tow home, huh? Well, listen, ye big dumskull! I ain't lettin' you outta me sight!"

"Why, sweetheart!" he cried dulcetly. "I didn't know ya cared! Well, stick around, an', inside or outside, we'll slug it out together."

Troubled, Annie remained with Clem for a while, discussing the situation, and dictating a progress report to be relayed to Severn at Secoma. Then, half blinded by sheets of driving rain and spray, she returned to the wheelhouse, where she saw, to her annoyance, that Peter had been joined by Truthful Tomkins.

"Thought I telled you to relieve Shif'less on lookout?" she said shortly.

"At the end of his watch, you said," Truthful reminded her.

Annie turned to Peter and gave him a quick rundown on her conversation with Mr. Bullwinkle, while Truthful, clearing the moisture from one of the side windows, attempted, morosely, to stare out.

"But I don't get it, Annie," Peter protested as Annie finished her account. "Bullwinkle's a crackajack towboat man—let's face it!—and I just can't see him bein' fool enough to risk his tug an' tow outside, unless he had a very special reason."

"There's two," said Annie. "Port Ragloff has on'y one small loadin' dock an' whoever gits there first not on'y grabs that southbound towin' job but he kin hold up the other from goin' alongside till the freeze starts. Ye kin smell the frost right in that wind tonight, an' he'd like nothin' better'n to see me froze up in there fer the winter!"

"Possibly," agreed Peter dubiously. "But I still can't believe he'd take a chance outside. There's a hundred and fifty mile of open water; and that's plain murder!"

"Mebbe. Mebbe so," said Annie reflectively. "Anyways, if he does go out, we'll have to take a chance too. Meantime, we'll stick close to him. I seen his lights from the deck a while back, so he's still abeam. An' if he can take it out there——"

"Annie." Truthful, who had continued to stare out the window, but whose stuns'l ears had missed nothing, turned and interrupted her. "Ever meet a snake called a sidewinder?"

"Look," said Annie, "I ain't in no mood fer any more o' your cockeyed antidotes. So git outta here an' relieve——"

"No, this'll kill ya!" he said, with relish. "I a'most got et by one, once, but I'll tell ya about that another time. Point right now is, when a sidewinder wants to move ahead, he does it by snakin' from side to side, to fool ya about what direction he's gonna take."

"Listen," said Annie. "Why don't you go an' git yerself a job as a skeleton's shadder, an' quit annoyin' me?"

"Because," Truthful replied, after quickly peering out the window again and back, "I thought perhaps this sidewinder I told ya of might remind ya of somebody ya know."

"You poppin' yer buttons?" she demanded; then, sensing a deeper meaning, she asked sharply, "What ye gittin' at?"

"Ya said Bullwinkle's lights was right abeam of us a while ago?"

"Sartinly! Over to starboard there."

Truthful once more peered out the window. He said innocently, without turning: "I don't see no lights."

With a pachydermous bound, Annie reached the door, flung it open to a blast of screaming, freezing wetness and rushed to the rail. When she could clear her eyes of the stinging brine, she stared outboard, but all she could see was wind-tortured darkness and wreaths of billowing fog.

Annie rushed back to the wheelhouse. "Truthful was right, Peter!" she gasped. "Bullwinkle's switched out his lights an' took off!"

Grabbing the searchlight handle suspended from the deckhead, she switched on the beam. But of the Salamander and her tow there was no sign.

After a time Annie switched off the searchlight. "We gotta find out where he's headed!" she said desperately. "We jest gotta!"

"He ain't headed outside, Annie," commented Peter. "Otherwise he wouldn't ha' bothered to shake ya."

"He wanted you to head out like he said he was doin', though," Truthful said. "He tried to shame ya into that."

"Yeah! Knowin' I'd never make it, an' lose a lot o' time havin' to turn back! Lemme see, now. Where could he hole up that's big enough to take that barge an' hisself in, where they'd be safe?"

"He sure wouldn't waste any time down here," said Peter. "He'll prob'ly keep right on——"

"——up the Inside Passage, and makin' as much northin' as he can," put in Truthful eagerly, "hopin' that by the time he fetched Dixon Entrance the gale would be blowed out. Then he'd cut straight across the Gulf of Alaska."

"But after makin' that long detour he'd hafta fuel up again an' take fresh water aboard, afore he could risk the gulf. Didn't ye think o' that too?"

"I would have," said Truthful modestly.

"Sure gittin' in practice to take over, ain't ye?" said Annie bitterly.

"I aim to, if it's necessary. And I don't need no practice. Furthermore," Truthful added softly, "maybe this wouldn't ha' happened if you hadn't scrapped wi' Bullwinkle over the radiophone tonight. Severn ain't gonna like that. So if I was you——"

"I didn't scrap wid him!" Annie rasped. "An' you ain't me! Ye're nothin' but a imaginary line drawed through a suit o' dungarees. So go git lost!" She turned back to Peter. "O.K., Peter. Swing over toward FitzHugh Sound. We'll go up the Inside Passage too."

On the long beat north among the islands parallel with the British Columbia mainland coast, Annie sought incessantly for news of Mr. Bullwinkle's Salamander. Then, finally, early one evening amid the maze of islands south of Dixon Entrance, she got it.

"I dunno if it was the right one," bawled the grizzled, moon-faced Eskimo skipper of a big purse seiner as it paused, rolling gunwales under, to answer her hail, "because the weather was pretty thick. But a big tug and barge appeared to be headin' in out of the fog as we was coming out o' Sawmill Harbor."

"Ye sure he wasn't goin' toward Dixon Entrance?" asked Annie anxiously.

"Dixon Entrance? You crazy? Even the seals is seasick outside, in this blow, and she's good for another two-three days!" he shouted.

Annie waved her thanks, and the Narcissus dipped and plunged in the gathering night toward the distant, rain-dimmed beacons of Sawmill Harbor, a small logging, lumber and fish-cannery town at the end of a narrow bay set between stupendous cliffs.

It was dark and bitterly cold, with light snow flurries replacing the clearing rain, by the time the Narcissus had entered the port. And it was with dour satisfaction that Annie saw Mr. Bullwinkle's Salamander and her barge made fast in the adjoining berth.

She stood with Peter on the Narcissus's upper deck, and, as they watched, a door on the Salamander's salt-rimed main deck opened.

"There he is, the horse's rudder!" growled Annie. "Look, he's gittin' on the dock! I've a mind to go over an' kick——OO-oof!" For Peter's elbow had jabbed her violently in the ribs.

Annie, unable for the moment to speak, glared at him with angry astonishment, until his eyes flicked significantly downward to the deck immediately beneath the rail. Then, following his glance, Annie understood; for turned innocently upward and avidly eavesdropping was the face of Truthful Tomkins.

"Well, as I was sayin', Peter," remarked Annie loudly, and with instant presence of mind, "mebbe I'll sashay over after a while an'—ho-ho!—scold dear Horatio a leetle fer worryin' us about if he was safe or not.... An' as fer you"—she looked over the rail again and blasted wrathfully into Truthful's still-upturned countenance—"ye'd better keep that ugly old bag o' teeth, hair an' bones ye call a face outta my business, afore I stomp right in the middle of it!"

"It's for yore own good, Annie," he pointed out sadly. "After all, Severn instructed me that if you was to tangle wi' Bullwinkle again, I was to take——"

"You was to—what, friend?" said the kindly, amused voice of the Salamander's master, who, attracted by Annie's explosion, quietly had crossed the dock. "Oh, I remember you!" he said, affecting artless surprise. "You're Tomkins, skipper o' the Daisy! But she's on the repair ways in Secoma, an' you're here, and Mrs. Blimp doesn't like that. I wonder why? Could it add up"—he turned to Annie with a grin—"that Severn sent him along to take over, 'case you started bein' disrespeckful to me again?"

"Look, Bullwinkle," said Annie hurriedly, "I ain't got no beef wid you. So ye double-crossed us the other night. O.K.! But kin you help yer sneaky nature? Or mebbe it was jest a prank."

"It was no prank!" interrupted Mr. Bullwinkle warmly. "In our dealings, Fatso, I've learned to play fer keeps!"

"I don't blame ye," said Annie, resolutely unclenching her fists. "It must git tiresome bein' beat all the time. But look; le's make a deal right now. You leave me alone, an' I don't take nothin' from you. How's that fer bein' fair?"

"Suits me!" said Mr. Bullwinkle heartily. "An' to prove it"—he turned to put a comradely arm across Truthful Tomkins's shoulder—"how's about us goin' uptown together an' killin' a coupla fifths o' bait. We'll be here for a day or two, so let's me an' you get better acquainted!"

Grimly, Annie watched while they splashed joyously away together, coattails flying in the wind as they headed for the lights of the town.

"Ever smell trouble comin', Peter?" she asked as he stood silently beside her. "Well, take a good sniff right now."

"I know. They'll gang up all right. But all of us on the Narcissus are for you, Annie. So just watch yourself. You can take it."

"I'll hafta!" said Annie hoarsely. "Wid that kind of a setup I won't dare thump him now, if it kills him!"

Her resolution was not easy to keep, however, for during the ensuing two days, during which the gale continued to blow, but the sky cleared and a skin of ice began to form along the shore, Truthful Tomkins and the loudly gregarious Mr. Bullwinkle were inseparable. And when Annie encountered them they made it obvious that a close alliance had been reached; for the Salamander's master did his skillful best to goad her to violence while Truthful stood expectantly by, waiting for the explosion that would project him into her job. But with the obstinacy born of desperation, Annie refused to be drawn and either would stand, shaken with helpless fury, or, with a derisive twitch of her massive stern, waddle rapidly away.

Meanwhile, the enforced delay in the voyage, during which both tugs had been refueled and provisioned, was thoroughly enjoyed by their crews. Sawmill Harbor's shops and taverns were crowded, with many an enjoyable brawl to flavor the tedium of waiting, while the more venturesome found excitement by last-minute dodging of the logging trains that, day and night, whistled and rattled along the middle of the wide main street.

At first Annie had accompanied her shipmates ashore, for she dearly loved a crowd. Particularly, she was drawn to the noise and conviviality of the Mother Lode, but since this was also the favorite oasis of the now openly and insultingly belligerent Mr. Bullwinkle and his bosom chum, Truthful Tomkins, she formed the bitter resolution to stay away, and thereafter confined her walks to the vicinity of the wharves.

On these, her invariable companion was Big Sam, the engineer, whose lumbago sharply restricted his visits to the town; and their favorite goal was a large but ancient steam tug, Cascade, at the shoreward end of the wharf. Annie remembered her from years ago on the Yukon, and this recognition was a passport to the friendship of her caretaker and part owner, Olaf Torgesen, a gnarled, towheaded old philosopher with childlike, mild blue eyes, whose sole remaining ambition was to save enough money for a visit to his daughter in Skagway.

Realization of this devolved, however, upon the sale of his share of the Cascade—a most unlikely event, as Big Sam, after a professionally competent inspection, had discovered; for while the hull was sound, and the powerful engine, tail shaft and propeller remained in good working order, her tubes and boiler plates were corroded through and replacement costs prohibitive.

Despite the pleasantness of her visits with old Torgesen, however, and the calming influence they spread, Annie was impatient, anxious to get to sea; and by the third evening in port this possibility strengthened, for the government weather forecast prophesied a slackening of the gale by midnight, with snow and probable icing conditions to follow.

To celebrate their prospective sailing, the tug crews enthusiastically had planned a last few carefree hours ashore, with Peter and the others of the Narcissus urging Annie to share their final fling. But reluctantly she had refused to take a chance.

"I've did good so far," she said, pardonably proud. "But if I was to go up there to the Mother Lode an' happen to take a cargo o' kelp squeezin's aboard, then run into Bullwinkle, I'd be li'ble to skin him alive an' use his pelt fer a toopay. No, I'll stop here. You boys go up an' have a good time."

Nevertheless, it was with utter dejection that Annie watched them go, envying their high spirits as they hitched a ride on a string of empty flats that the shrieking little logging locomotive was taking back to the sawmill on the edge of the town.

Restless and lonely as the early arctic darkness closed in, and chilled through by the bitter and still-high wind, she entered the messroom, where Big Sam was writing letters, and flopped in the seat opposite. He looked up.

"Maybe you should ha' gone ashore wi' the crew, after all, Annie," he remarked sympathetically. "You look as lost as a porcupine without its quills."

Annie shrugged dispiritedly. "I got this far widout tanglin' wid Bullwinkle," she mumbled, "in spite o' his prize monkey, Tomkins. If I stay away from them I'll keep both me temper an' me job."

"Yeah, guess you're right. We'll be gettin' under way in a few hours anyhow, and——" He broke off abruptly, listening. "You hear somethin'?" he asked, puzzled.

"Sure do!" said Annie quickly. "Some boat's tootin' an air whistle out in the harbor! Come on, quick!"

Hastily Big Sam followed her to the rail and they stared seaward toward where, under the clear, star-hung and windy night, angry surf outside the harbor entrance still spouted and boiled.

Presently they again heard the series of distant, staccato hoots, and after a time there materialized, moving slowly toward them, a small diesel-powered fishing boat without lights.

"Put the searchlight on her, Sam," Annie directed, and a few seconds later the Narcissus's dazzling white shaft was cutting through the darkness.

"Has she taken a beatin'!" grunted Annie, who had followed Big Sam to the wheelhouse. "No small boats, no nets, most of her rail tore away! Must 'a' bin caught out in that blow."

TUGBOAT ANNIE LOSES COMMAND

"But look, Annie!" Big Sam replied tensely. "She shouldn't carry a crew o' more'n three-four hands, but there's over a dozen men on her deck!"

A few minutes later Annie and Big Sam were helping the small crowd of unshaven, haggard and exhausted men in wrinkled, brine-soaked clothing over the stringpiece of the wharf. They were, besides the fisherman's crew of four, as Annie's quick, solicitous questions brought out, the eleven-man ship's company of a coastal cargo and trading steamer, the Chilkoot, of Nome, Captain Burdett, master.

"We were southbound from Sitka when that gale hit," said Burdett, a tall, wide-shouldered man, with a strong, but drawn face and weary eyes. "It was too strong for us, so I cut across the south end of Horseshoe Island to get into that deep, protected bay there. The wind blew us too far inshore, though, and she stripped her propeller on the rocks."

"She sank?" asked Annie quickly.

"No, thank God! She scraped over and had enough momentum to pile up on the beach. It's a sand-and-gravel foreshore," he went on, anticipating their question, "completely protected by those high cliffs all around. That's where she's resting now, with practically no damage except the propeller and shaft and maybe a few sprung plates under her stem. And if it hadn't been for Captain Johanssen here, we'd be there yet."

"How'd the seiner find ya?" asked Big Sam. "Radio SOS?"

"Naw," volunteered Johanssen, broad and squat in his fisherman's torn oilskins, with tobacco-stained teeth, and eyes like chips of blue glass stuck in his leathery face. "His vireless vent out ven he hit. But ve vass coming down de channel soon after, looking for shelter, yust like him. He had his boat ofer by den, so ve picked dem oop."

"But why didn't ye stay up there where it was sheltered till the gale blowed itself out," Annie asked, "'stead o' takin' the poundin' ye must 'a' got, comin' here?"

"I offered him a thousand dollars to risk it," said the steamer captain. "My vessel's only two thousand tons, but she's crammed full of valuable cargo and she's got to be moved out pretty quick, before she freezes in and gets pounded to bits in the winter gales. What about this big tug of yours?" he asked Big Sam. "She could do it easy, and including the ship, there's over eight hundred thousand dollars at stake."

"I'm her engineer," Big Sam explained. "Tugboat Annie Brennan here's her master."

"That so?" asked Burdett with interest. "I've heard of you! Well, what about it? The underwriters'll pay big, and——"

"Wish I could," said Annie with deep regret. "But I'm under contrack, doin' a towin' job fer the Navy. So's the Salamander along the way. An' since there's no lives bein' risked——"

"Have to figure something else, then," Burdett said tiredly. "Well, captain." He turned to Johanssen, shook hands. "Thanks, more than I can tell you! See you in the morning."

"Where all o' ye gonna sleep?" said Annie. "I could ha' put ye up, but we're sailin'——"

"We'll go over to the lumber mill. I know the superintendent, and he'll fix us up. Thanks anyway. Good night. . . . Come on, boys!"

They watched as, at the head of his weary men, Captain Burdett plodded along the wharf toward the town. Then Annie turned back to the fishermen. "Anythin' I kin do fer you fellers?" she asked. "Hot grub? Blankets?"

Johanssen shook his head. "Ve'll tie up at de cannery across de vay, dere. I deal vit dem." He stared after the retreating ship's company of the Chilkoot. "Too bad nottin' can be done for Captain Burdett. He ban nice falla, und dat ship o' his is big, rich plum."

"Yeah," said Annie, feigning casualness. "Sure is a shame. Good night."

A few minutes later the seiner was a slow-moving blob as it moved across the channel toward the cannery dock. Then Annie grabbed Big Sam's arm, hard.

"Let's git back to the messroom!" she said urgently. "We gotta find a way, quick, to do somethin' about this!"

In the messroom, with cups of steaming coffee putting warmth back in their veins, they discussed the glittering prize so tantalizingly out of reach. "It ain't total salvage, because her master came back here to git help. That means she ain't legally abandoned," Annie said. "But if she ain't pulled off soon, like Burdett said, she's sure a goner." She put her face in her hands. "A deal like this, what I could walk off wid right under Bullwinkle's fat nose—an' we're tied to that Navy barge! It would hafta happen to me!"

"He's in the same fix, Annie."

"I know. Not that he wouldn't knock off his Navy barge in a second if he got a smell o' this! Still, come to think of it, it wouldn't do either of us any good if we ditched the barges an' grabbed the Chilkoot. An' now that I can't have it, I almost wish he'd try."

"Why wouldn't it do any good, Annie? Look at that big profit! The underwriters'll give ten times what this job's payin' us!"

"So?" And suddenly Annie grinned wanly. "Well, Number One, we'd forfeit that fifteen thousand that Alec had to put up. Right?"

"The other'd be worth it."

"Number Two, the Navy's contracted both our time an' our sarvices. So if either or both of us salvaged the Chilkoot afore we fulfilled the Navy contrack, the gov'ment'd be entitled to the award because it was earned in their time. An' that's what Bullwinkle's gonna find out if he tries to glom onto this!" She left her chair and paced heavily. "Sam, there's jest got to be a way to solve this!"

"For you?"

"Fer Alec. He's still me boss, ain't he? Listen"—she bent over the table, her heavy face close to his—"are you sure the tubes an' b'iler on that old Cascade of Olaf's can't be fixed up?"

"I told ya the other day, Annie. I could put her propellin' machinery in good runnin' shape in a few hours. But without tubes and a boiler to feed her steam, she's just no good! Why, old Torgesen even took the coal outta her and sold it. That shows ya how hopeless it is!"

"Yeah, guess ye're right, Sam." She sighed resignedly; started pacing again, then stopped. "Look, pal," she said morosely, "this whole deal's got me so beat down that I gotta relax somehow, afore I blow me topper. So mebbe I will sashay into town fer a while. Will ya come wid me?"

"Sure, Annie," said Big Sam cheerfully. "We'll go up to the Mother Lode and make big ones out o' little ones for a while. But remember," he warned, "no matter how much swamp juice you lap up, ya still gotta stay clear o' you-know-who."

When Annie and Big Sam entered the hospitable, smoke-thick interior of the Mother Lode, Annie's volatile spirits instantly soared. Feeling exceedingly jolly and benevolent, she even sought out Mr. Bullwinkle and the perfidious Mr. Tomkins, to bestow upon them her forgiveness and some wassail.

They were not hard to find, for around them were the noisiest and most hilarious of the bar customers, including crew members from both tugs; and if Mr. Bullwinkle's florid countenance was turned with fatuous admiration upon his buddy, it was with some reason. Truthful Tomkins, as a raconteur, was having a huge success.

"So there I was, gents," he was declaiming with a grin, "fishin' from that little boat. Cold, soakin' wet, an' not a bite from a sardine, even, all day. Then, just as I gave up, a big gray cod jumped into the boat!" He paused impressively. "So, know what I done?"

"Rubbed it in yer hair?" asked Annie genially.

Truthful Tomkins's eyes, first startled, then bitter, rested on her for a second or two. But he recovered quickly. "No, Mrs. Buttinski, I did not!" he snapped. "I just told that codfish, 'Oh, no, ya don't!' I said. 'If ya don't bite, ya don't ride!' An' I throwed it back."

"Pooh!" scoffed Annie, her good-humored disparagement so loud and prompt that the delighted audience forgot to applaud Mr. Tomkins's effort. "Somethin' better'n that happened to me an' Carl Hansen o' the tug Dupont, when we was fishin' one day. Jest like in that lie o' yours, Truthful, we'd had no luck neither. Well, Carl had just spit his chaw o' tobacco over the side, when all of a sudden the biggest sea lion bull I ever seen surfaced alongside, wid a thirty-pound salmon in his jaws. An' he was so grateful when he seen that chaw that he throwed the salmon right into Carl's lap, then went after the quid. An' would you believe me——"

"Aw, nuts!" cried the frustrated Mr. Tomkins. "I suppose ya throwed the salmon back in too?"

"Nothin' as silly as that," replied Annie complacently. "All that happened was, seein' we had hold of a good thing, me an' Carl give up towboatin' fer a spell, an' us an' that sea lion fished on fifty-fifty shares—an' a lay fer the boat, o' course—all the rest o' that season! An' if you kin top that one, my pilin'-bustin' friend," she shouted delightedly over the roaring laughter of the crowd, "I'll pay ye ten bucks!"

While she waited for the offer to be acted on, Mr. Bullwinkle had pushed himself angrily forward. "Listen, you old dugong," he growled to Annie. "Scram outta here before I bat ya one!"

But Truthful Tomkins, to whose face wounded pride had lent the color of an astringent tomato, quickly intervened. "Let her alone till I get her money, Bullwinkle," he said loudly, and the augmented crowd, sensing a contest, cheered, then quieted.

"Well, a good many tides ago," began Truthful, "when I was just a sprout pickin' up odd towin' jobs, I bought me one o' these little steam gigs, or tenders, they used to have in the Navy. Remember them? So one day on the way home after pickin' up hemlock deadheads to make a dollar, I was passin' Suicide Narrows with a flood tide pourin' in, when suddenly my engine quit. I was out of fuel!"

"Oh, man," someone murmured. "That current's about fourteen knots!"

"Sixteen," said Truthful quickly. "There'd been a earthquake the day before an' the channel got tilted a mite. Anyways, I was bein' sucked right into it. An' nothin' to feed the fire and work up steam with. So what did I do?"

"Survived—I guess," ventured Annie. "Though, lookin' at ye, it's hard to tell. How'd ye do it—stuff the firebox wid a few shavin's offa yer skull?"

"What I done," said Truthful, elaborately ignoring her, "I reached over the side an' got hold of a passin' dogfish and tickled its belly to make it bark. Then I grabbed the bark an' threw it on the fire, and in ten seconds I had enough steam to run a——"

At that moment Truthful's voice was drowned out by the ear-piercing whistle of a passing logging engine with its train of rattling flats, and in that brief pause Tugboat Annie's expression changed swiftly from reluctantly admiring attention to Truthful's yarn, to a sudden tense alertness in her snapping blue eyes and an access of supercharged jubilation that, like a flash of inspiration, raced through her now-fast-clicking brain. What were his final words again? And what had happened just as he said them?

Mentally fighting for the connection that she felt would herald the birth of a brilliant idea, she was oblivious of the roar of appreciation that had awarded Truthful's effort. Then, suddenly, she had it! She knew! And, wildly eager, she looked around for Big Sam.

Before she could reach him, however, Mr. Bullwinkle blocked her way, his fingers digging into her arm.

"What's the matter, ya fat welsher?" he rasped. "Truthful won, didn't he? Well, where's his ten bucks?"

"Eh? What's that? Oh—yeah, yeah!" Quickly she dug into her wallet and fished out a ten-dollar bill. "Here, give him this! Buy him a drink! Here's one fer you too!" She stuffed more bills into his hand. "Buy everybody a drink!"

Thrusting him roughly aside, not even noticing his stupefied stare, she went again in urgent search of Big Sam and, when she had located him again, dragged him, nonplused, off to the comparatively quiet rest-room passage at the back of the noisy room.

"Have you went loco?" he demanded uneasily, but after a quick, cautious look about her, she brought her lips close to his hairy ear.

"I'm gonna ax ye one quick question," she croaked in a half whisper, "an' I want a fast, true answer, yes or no. Listen."

Big Sam listened, and as he did his broad face spread in an astonished, triumphant grin. Then he nodded, suddenly solemn. "Why, yes, Annie," he said. "That's easy done."

"If ye'd said no, I'd ha' slewed ye!" she grinned in quick relief. "Now listen hard again, because here's what we gotta do. I'm goin' back in there an' bandy a few verbs with Bullwinkle. He won't like it—or mebbe he will—an' Truthful too. Anyways, there might be a lot o' noise. But whatever happens, Sam, I kin look after meself, so you're to stay right here! Got that?"

"If you're gonna start somethin', Annie," objected Big Sam stoutly, "I want to be right alongside. An' besides, it'll lose ya your job. An' Truthful will take over the Narcissus!"

"I figger that. But you'll do what I tell ye!" she said fiercely. "An' there's Peter an' the rest in there if I need help—which I won't. Now then, after things quiets down, you go in—I'll be gone by then—an' tell both Bullwinkle an' Truthful all about the Chilkoot—where she's lyin', how easy she'll be to drag off—the whole works, except the fact that her crew an' them fishermen is back here. They fell right into their bunks, prob'ly, or the word would ha' spread."

"But if I tell 'em about the Chilkoot they'll both leave the Navy barges here an' make a beeline for Horseshoe Island!"

"Remember what I telled ye earlier, about the fifteen thousand dollars they forfeit, an' no towin' fee, an' the Gov'ment grabbin' the salvage money? Tell 'em that too. That'll stop 'em! From then on, it'll be a race atween 'em to dump their barges at Port Ragloff an' see who gits back fastest to the Chilkoot. An' it won't be Truthful. I'll make darn sure o' that."

"Ye mean ye want Bullwinkle to win over the Narcissus, Annie?" asked Big Sam uneasily.

"I wanna make sure Truthful will be last into Port Ragloff, to pick up that home-goin' barge, Sam," Annie grinned suddenly. "Because, if Bullwinkle gits there first, he sure ain't gonna stop to hook onto it—not wid the smell o' that Chilkoot salvage in his puss. That way he'll cheat hisself outta the towin' fee an' Truthful will earn it. An' somebody's gotta earn dough fer the boss, 'stead o' horsin' around like me. All set now?"

"One thing more, Annie: If you're stayin' here in Sawmill Harbor after they sail, I am too. Tim, my oiler, has his chief's ticket. He can handle things below."

"If things goes wrong, Sam, it'll cost ye your job too."

"O.K. There's other jobs."

"That, God bless ye," said Annie huskily, "is what I hoped ye'd say. An' I'm sure gonna need ye. Well"—she moved toward the crowded bar again—"here goes!"

Back in the bar, Mr. Bullwinkle and Truthful Tomkins were toasting each other in vast bonhomie with the beer that Annie had bought, and neither noticed her approach until she was standing quietly beside them. Then, ignoring their quickly hostile stares, she quickly plucked the glass from Truthful's fingers and dashed the contents full in Mr. Bullwinkle's face. And before he could clear his streaming eyes, she landed a roundhouse swing that knocked him flat on his back a dozen feet away.

Instant pandemonium broke out, it being the pleasurable impression that this was anybody's fight. Truthful Tomkins went down in the brawl.

"That's done it!" he yelled. "Yo're fired! Severn said if ya beat up on him again you was through!"

"So I'm fired!" Annie bellowed back with vast enjoyment. "I'm through! An' you're takin' over my Narcissus! Well, glory be! Both you an' Bullwinkle kin go plumb to——"

The melee swept between them, but in the ensuing confusion another of Annie's piledrivers—inadvertently, no doubt—connected glancingly with the cadaverous, rage-distorted visage of Mr. Tomkins, who promptly disappeared underfoot, but his panicky voice rose high above the tumult.

"Ya hit me!" he yelled. "I'm bleeding! I——"

"Don't be silly!" Annie chortled happily back. "Bones don't bleed!" And with a quick glance at the still-recumbent Mr. Bullwinkle, she butted her way through the furor and scuttled contentedly out the door.

Outside, the night was clear; cold and star-bright, with the last of the gale dying amid the pines and snows of the higher peaks; and in the frosty, invigorating air Annie proceeded at an elephantine trot back to the Narcissus, where she packed a couple of suitcases for herself and one for Big Sam and set them in the shadow of a lumber pile on the wharf. Then, by hearty cuffing, she awakened Shiftless, who was doing his watchman's stint in the warmth of the galley, and chivvied him, shivering, out onto the wharf, where she made him assist her in crowbarring a considerable pile of the adjacent stacked lumber over the edge of the wharf, from which it tumbled, with a tremendous clatter, down on the Narcissus's fantail.

"There!" she said, viewing with deep satisfaction the confusion of heavy, criss-crossed planks. "That'll make sure the Salamander gits the start she needs."

Then suddenly came the pound of running feet along the wharf in what seemed to be a hotly contested foot race, and there rapidly appeared the respective crews, bearing assorted lumps and abrasions, of the Narcissus and the Salamander, with Mr. Bullwinkle and Mr. Tomkins sprinting valiantly in the lead. And last of all, panting heavily, came Big Sam.

Annie stepped from the shadow of a concealing lumber pile, while the tugs' crews poured on board their vessels and made frenzied preparations for immediate departure, and it became continuingly evident that the race to get away first was still at full blast. And as Big Sam came abreast of the Narcissus, Annie intercepted him.

"It worked, huh?" she grinned.

"Perfect!" he panted. "I told them about the wreck, and they was all for streakin' right out to it and to hell wi' these barges, till I told them about havin' to forfeit the bond money and such. That cooled 'em all right, but they couldn't wait to get down here and underway. Still looks like a close race to me, though."

"Won't be," said Annie, beaming, and she pointed to the huge jumble of lumber on the Narcissus's fantail. "Time Tomkins has had all that lifted off, the Salamander will have a nice head start."

"Who dumped that there?" asked Big Sam, startled.

"I did," said Annie. "Wid Shif'less's help."

"Oh! Ya did, eh?" snarled Truthful's voice beside her. "Wait till Severn hears o' this! Takin' yore cheap revenge for gettin' fired, by fixin' it for Bullwinkle to get to that salvage deal before me! First thing I do when we get underway is get a message off to Alec about you! An' time ya get back to Secoma you won't be able to get a job as deck hand on a garbage scow!"

Annie ignored him. "Looka Bullwinkle castin' off an' hookin' onto that barge fer Port Ragloff, Sam," she commented softly.

This was enough, and soon Mr. Tomkins's hoarse exhortations were urging the Narcissus's crew to greater speed in getting the lumber back on the wharf. But long before they had finished, the Salamander and her charge had drawn away from the dock and were proceeding at a steady six knots toward the open sea.

Finally, and long after the Salamander's lights had disappeared, the Narcissus also got underway. It was the first time in many years that Annie's tug had sailed without her; and, as they stood watching, Big Sam's heart went out to her as she stood, massive, silent, staring.

"Don't take it too tough, Annie," he said gently. "It'll all work out O.K., maybe. And if it don't, well——"

"What's that?" said Annie abstractedly. "Oh—sorry, Sam! I was jest tryin' to figger how much to pay to Olaf Torgesen. More'n enough to send him on that trip to visit his daughter, anyway, if all goes well. Then there's the small barge to hire, an' what to offer the loggin' company. An' I wonder, too, how much of a deadline we got, afore we try to make this deal pay off?"

"There's one important thing ya haven't mentioned, Annie," said Big Sam, and his eyes were worried.

"What's that?"

"How many hours it'll be before Alec Severn planes in here with his hair afire, after he gets that message from Truthful Tomkins. Now there's somethin', sweetheart, that'll really bear stewin' about!"

A few snowflakes drifted down from the oyster-gray sky and the air was bitter cold, presage of the deadly arctic freeze which, almost in a matter of hours now, would wrap the coast in the relentless ice of the long, dark winter, when, four days later, Mr. Bullwinkle stood on the Salamander's deck as she surged fast over the calm, flat sea. Ahead loomed the black, precipitous crags of Horseshoe Island; and as he raised his glasses he paused for a moment to reflect amusedly back on the spectacle, a few days ago, of the Narcissus moving slowly into Port Ragloff with that big Navy barge in tow, and nothing to anticipate but a dreary run back to Secoma with a similar one at her tail, while his Salamander surged triumphantly past, bound for an incredible salvage prize.

Equally ludicrous were the blistering curses that the red-nosed Tomkins had hurled at him as the two tugs passed close aboard. Well, let him learn something! Get smart!

Even Annie had received a comeuppance long past due, and in future she'd show him a little more respect—although about her, he had to admit, you never could tell. Still, let her show a proper submission, and he might even put in a plug for her with Severn—another stupid old coot.

Yes, the world was a wonderful place this morning and—But what was that creeping out into the open sea from a fold in Horseshoe Island's frowning cliffs? Instantly professionally alert, Mr. Bullwinkle expertly trained his glasses. He lowered them, looking puzzled; shook his head in sharp bewilderment; then looked through them again.

This time, when he lowered them, he did it slowly, as though in acute pain. Then he turned and in anguished tones yelped at his paunchy, pimpled mate, who was at the wheel.

"Jake! Jake, get out here!"

Alarmed, Jake left the wheel and took his turn with the glasses, and when he, in turn, lowered them, his mottled brow, in spite of the intense cold, was beaded with sweat. Wordlessly, he handed the glasses back, shook his head and morosely reentered the wheelhouse.

Mr. Bullwinkle followed him. "It ain't!" he said hoarsely, desperately. "It can't be!"

"So go ahead, be a stupe!" said Jake unfeelingly. "But if that ain't the Chilkoot bein' towed by that old wooden steam tug we seen alongside at Sawmill Harbor, I'll——An' she's pushin' a barge alongside herself at the same time, with a smokin' locomotive on it."

"Locomotive? Did you say a loco——"

"Look fer yourself! You've got the glasses!" said Jake indifferently. "It's one of them little fifteen-ton, direct-connected loggin'-train jobs—they're small, but plenty powerful!—that Sawmill Harbor's full of. They burn hog fuel—which that barge is prob'ly full of——"

"And she's spittin' steam!" cried Mr. Bullwinkle incredulously. "Steam as well as smoke! I kin see it!"

"Sure is," agreed Jake, after he had taken another turn with the glasses. "And she's feedin' the steam to the steam lines on that old beat-up tug while she tows the coaster." He took a deep breath. "And if that ain't the damnedest contraption I ever seen at sea, I'm a monkey's sitty-down!"

"But—the Chilkoot! It's the Chilkoot they're towin'!" Mr. Bullwinkle wailed. "Now who in damnation would ever think of a screwball thing like that?"

"A smart cooky," pronounced Jake, after another prolonged scrutiny through the glasses.

"Not—not——Oh, no; not her!"

"Ye guessed right," said Jake succinctly. "There she is, large as life an' twice as ugly, standin' outside the wheelhouse o' that old Cascade. Wanna say hello?"

Within a half hour the Salamander was making an expert U-turn and, on the same course now, running abeam and within hailing distance of the cascade, while, on the latter's opposite side, the barge-borne locomotive puffed and rumbled with the utmost efficiency while it compressed the life-giving steam into the old tug's innards through Big Sam's skillfully improvised connections. And astern, at the end of a long towing hawser, manned by a skeleton crew of her own ship's company and with Captian Burdett on his bridge, was Mr. Bullwinkle's rich, cargo-fat lost prize, the S.S. Chilkoot.

Mr. Bullwinkle stood on his bridge surveying this scene of prosperous, happy activity, while his numbed brain sought feebly to cope with the bitter magnitude of his disappointment. Nor did his spirits improve when there floated across the water the amused accents of his so recently discounted rival.

"Well, as I live an' breed," said Annie roguishly, "if it ain't the old monkey grinder hisself! Where's yer hurly-burly, chum?"

Slowly Mr. Bullwinkle forced himself to turn and face her. "Who'd ya hire to do yer thinkin' for ya, Fatso?" he rasped. "All this ain't your work."

"That's right," admitted Annie cheerfully. "It was Big Sam what figgered how to pipe the locomotive steam to the Cascade's engines. An' once I knowed that, all I done, I hired that dinky little lump o' pig iron from the loggin' company, an' rented the barge. An' ol' Cap'n Olaf Torgesen, what owns this tug—that's him at the wheel now, lookin' so proud 'cause she's at sea again—he wanted to lemme use her fer nothin'. An' all in all——"

"Why don't yer wear yer other head—the one that don't talk so much?" he said sourly.

"An' all in all, it on'y cost Alec five hundred bucks."

"Cost Alec! Hah!" exploded Mr. Bullwinkle. "Wait till he gets a load o' the way ya used me an' Tomkins as goats so's you could grab a salvage job o' yer own!"

"Tell him yerself," said Annie hospitably. "He took a flyin' machine up here soon as he got that squawk from your pet louse, Tomkins. . . . Alec! Come on out here! There's a case o' cute rigor mentis wants to see ye!"

Alec Severn, bundled in a heavy overcoat and a muffler over which his pink cheeks and little cherry nose peeked with the utmost cheer, appeared from behind the warm lee of the pilothouse, and stared with well-simulated surprise at the Salamander's master.

"Well, bless my soul," he cried, "if it isn't——"

"Watch yer langridge, Alec," said Annie warningly. "He thinks," she supplemented, "wid that hundred-ant-power brain o' his, that all this is a trick I played on him."

"A trick? . . . Why, my dear fellow, you were hired, same as a tug of my company was, to perform a simple little Navy towing job. And just because Annie was astute enough to pick up some salvage on the side——"

"Astute? There's guys in the pen for bein' astute! Why, she even cheated me outta that return towin' job!"

"You mean the one that Tomkins picked up with the Narcissus after you turned it down? He's joining us with it at Sawmill Harbor, where Annie will, of course, resume her old command. She's one of my most valued employees, you know."

"Yeah," crowed Annie, with only a sidewise glance at her employer, "I sure am! 'Specially when I promised to turn the salvage award over to the company kitty after Alec promised me me job back. . . . That right, Alec? I could ha' kept it all fer meself. I wasn't workin' fer you right then, remember?"

Severn coughed delicately. "I remember," he said. "Anyway, you're really happier this way, aren't you?"

"Yeah, Alec, I am," said Annie deeply. "In fack," she concluded, staring meaningfully across the water at the glowering Mr. Bullwinkle, "if I could on'y git a certain nasty black spot outta me eyes, I wouldn't be no happier if I was a queen wid a diamond tarara!"

TUGBOAT ANNIE AND THE DANGEROUS CHEAPSKATE

It was a blustery spring day, with the white-flecked waters of the Puget Sound port of Secoma patterned by cold sunshine and the shadows of fast-moving rain clouds, and the air alive with the high, wild piping of gulls. But in the private office of Alec Severn, the plump and amiable little owner of the Deep Sea Towing and Salvage Company, the atmosphere was heavy as he sat behind his desk and stared morosely at the weather-beaten, mastiff face of his senior skipper, Tugboat Annie Brennan.

"Well, that's the jam I'm in," he said unhappily. "And there's not a cussed thing I can do, without outside help."

"But, Alec, all yer tugs has been workin', an' fer months me own Narcissus was haulin' big supply barges up to them new arctic bases," Annie protested. "Gov'ment contracks pays good, an'——"

"That work has slacked off now!" he said irritably. "You know that! And as a result of being in constant service, my whole tug fleet needs a complete overhaul. But I just can't swing it."

"So along comes this San Francisco feller, Bulger——"

"Bolzer, Annie! B-o-l-z-e-r! And he'll finance me, yes—provided he approves our operation methods."

"Does he know the towboatin' business?"

"No, but he's a business-administration expert. And since he tells me he has many contacts with shipping companies, he might steer some jobs our way."

"Ye check his financial standin'?"

"Naturally! I'm not a fool, Annie!" he snapped testily. "But I do wish I didn't have to leave tonight for that Sea Freight Carriers' Convention in New York. It's important, though, for business."

"Don't worry, Alec," said Annie, promptly reassuring. "I'll run things here fer ye like I've allus done."

Severn looked uncomfortable. "Not—not this time, Annie, I'm afraid," he said placatingly. "You see, Bolzer insists on coming in to supervise while I'm gone. It'll give him a chance to study——"

"Ye mean ye're hirin' him?"

"I asked him about that, but he doesn't care one way or the other, as long as I give him authority to appoint himself in an emergency where he'd have to commit the company. So he'll come in as an adviser only, at present. But mind, Annie" —and Severn's tone hardened—"whatever he says here goes!"

"It won't work!" said Annie abruptly. "Unless his job's official, he could git us in a jam, then duck out an' leave you holdin' the sack. No, sir! Put him on the payroll. Then you're his boss."

"What's wrong with your thinking today, Annie?" he said impatiently. "A tugboat owner's always liable for the mistakes of his employees! But this way, if he was at fault, I could sue him! Anyway," he ended in sudden appeal, "quit arguing, will you? I need his money—and I need it soon!"

"O.K., ye ol' gafoozler," she replied quietly and stood up. "When's the financial blizzard takin' over?"

"Before I leave. I'll want you to meet him. So come back——"

"Can't," said Annie. "I got that tow fer Foss Harbor right away."

"That's right; I forgot. Well"—he held out his hand—"see you when I come back. And please don't tangle with Bolzer! I'm already committed for dockyard space and new supplies for overhauling the tugs, and if you foul me up with him, Annie, I'll be out of business and you'll be out of a job!"

"I won't let ye down, Alec," she assured him.

From Foss Harbor the Narcissus was dispatched to other jobs, so a few days elapsed before she was headed once more toward her home port. Meanwhile, however, Fred, the office dispatcher, had kept Annie informed by radiophone of the radical and, to her, alarming changes and innovations which Mr. Bolzer, upon taking charge, swiftly had effected. Puzzled and worried, she had said nothing of this to her crew, but now, with their return so imminent, she could no longer keep still.

"I don't like it! Not wuth a cuss!" she exploded suddenly to Peter, the Narcissus's bovinely phlegmatic mate, who was at the wheel, with the tiered lights of Secoma rising out of the windy darkness ahead. "I'll bet Alec never figgered on this crazy stuff when he put him in charge!"

Peter stared. "Who you talkin' about, Annie?" he rumbled.

TUGBOAT ANNIE AND THE DANGEROUS CHEAPSKATE

"That Bulger character! Fust thing he done, Fred told me, was put box lunches aboard the tugs on short hauls to economize on galley fuel oil an' cook's wages."

"Oh-oh! That won't last long!" said Peter deeply. "The crews'll quit!"

"An' how! But wuss than that, he's replacin' all the serviceable gear what's on the tugs, wid ol' wore-out stuff that he's dug up from God knows where! An'——"

"Wha-a-at's that?" Even the lethargic Peter now was startled. "Why, in towboatin' ya gotta use the best, regardless o' cost! Because not just ships and cargoes but even lives sometimes has to depend on it! Why's he doin' that, Annie?"

"Fred says he's makin' us use up the old stuff afore the tugs is overhauled, to save buyin' new when they're in service again. But lemme tell ye, Peter," Annie growled, her big face grim, "he ain't gonna play no such battledore an' cockleshell wid me!"

"What's he like?" Peter asked. "You met him yet?"

"No. But way he's actin' he's prob'ly got a extra head he uses jest fer thinkin' up fool idears. Well, anyways"—she peered forward through the window—"there's the channel lights openin' up. So we'll soon find out."

A half hour later, as the Narcissus came alongside her wharf, the door off the office landing was flung open, silhouetting a short, slight, narrow-shouldered man in a neat, dark business suit. He leaned over the rail, peering intently down at the tug. Then, quick as a rabbit, he scuttled down the steps, bounded across the wharf and jumped on board, and in seconds was greeting Annie, who stood, face expressionless, outside the pilothouse door.

"Hello, there! Hello, there!" he said briskly and thrust out his hand. "I'm Bolzer, and I guess you're Tugboat Annie Brennan. Glad to see you, Annie!"

"Hi!" said Annie without enthusiasm. "So you're Bulger, huh?"

"Bolzer!" he said. "Spelled with a 'z'!"

"That's yer privilege," she told him stolidly. "Middle name's Thrifty, though, ain't it? Least, that's what I hear."

"What's that? Oh—thrifty! Ha-ha-ha! Ve-e-ry funny," he chuckled, but his lively brown eyes sharpened a bit. "You're right too! I'm all for economy. All for it. When it makes sense. But never mind. There's lots to do, so let's get at it! First, I've got a good job lined up for the Narcissus here, and——"

"What is it?"

"One I dug up myself. Never let the grass grow when I run things," he said complacently. "I've got a lot of fine shipping leads——"

"The job—what is it?" Annie rasped.

"Ever hear of the steamer Chesil Bank?"

"Yeah. Big old coaster what's rottin' on Seal Reef, where she piled up a year ago."

"You're right, Annie! Absolutely right!" cried Mr. Bolzer, happy as a quizmaster. "Only she's afloat again. She was bought for peanuts, as is; then a Canadian salvage outfit was hired and got her off the reef."

"What was she bought fer—scrap?"

"Far from it! Beyond a few sprung plates and a cracked propeller shaft, she's still a valuable ship. So you'll bring her down here for repairs."

"Who bought her?"

"Some people I know. She's at Nanaimo, B.C., now, taking a cargo of lumber aboard. Her new owners figured she might as well earn some freight on the way here. And as bait for their future towing business, we're quoting 'em twenty percent off our regular fee."

"That ain't good!" said Annie quickly. "Alec never cut rates—an' they'll expect it every time now! Look, why should you favor——"

"Isn't that my business?" he suggested briskly.

Annie stared at him; then she shrugged. "When do we leave?"

"In the morning, after you turn in your good gear. And since there's no use wearing out a valuable, nearly new towing wire on just a——"

"Hold it!" said Annie harshly. "The Weather Bureau's predictin' a heavy sou'west gale widin a week! An' up among them islands we'll need the best equipment we got. So——"

"Let me finish, please! The substitute hawser you'll ship will do this job in any weather. I—we got it cheap along with some other equipment that's plenty good enough for work like this."

"So?" Annie replied, and for a long pause she eyed him. Then, "Where is this—this substitute hawser?" she demanded.

He gestured. "Over in the supply shed there."

"I'll inspect it right now. An' if it ain't good enough," she ended doggedly, "I don't take it."

"You'll take it, missus," replied Mr. Bolzer softly, and he clattered agilely back down the ladder, and seconds later the office door banged behind him.

"Come on ashore wid me," she muttered to Peter. "We're gonna have a look at that rope."

Twenty minutes later Annie barged, unannounced, into the office where behind Severn's big desk, Mr. Bolzer was checking a list. He looked up, then glanced significantly at the door. "Knock-knock!" he said playfully.

"On'y thing I'm gonna knock," said Annie heavily, "is that beat-up, wore-out old hawser! It'd mebbe do fer haulin' scows across the harbor. But in the weather we might meet haulin' the Chesil Bank down here through them islands? Unh-uh!" Emphatically she shook her head. "I ain't takin' it!"

He said furiously, his face livid, "I'm in charge here, and you'll do what I tell you! Otherwise you're fired! Right now!"

"Not by you, I ain't!" Annie roared back. "Sure, Alec said you'd be runnin' things, but he also telled me you wasn't a reggaler employee! So hirin' an' firin' ain't up to you! Not yet, mister! An' the on'y way ye'll make me take that rotted-out lump o' hemp is to gimme a written order on a company letterhead, signed by you as official manager o' this company! So stick that in yer hat an' smoke it!"

"Don't be stupid! I'll appoint another skipper and tell your crew to——"

"They'll walk off! Because you're a outsider—an' where a tow's safety is consarned ye don't draw no water!"

Tensely he glared at her. "All right, you asked for this!" he said metallically. "My orders—my official ones, mind!—will reach you in the morning!"

Boiling with rage, Annie steamed out of the office and back to the tug, where Peter was sitting on the rail, waiting for her. And as she stormed on board he gestured with his thumb across the slip.

"Look who's just come in," he commented.

Annie looked across and saw, making fast alongside the opposite wharf, the big, powerful, black-hulled deep-water tug Salamander, owned and commanded by her bitter archenemy and business rival, Mr. Horatio Bullwinkle, to whose proximity she normally reacted with bristling hostility. But now she barely flicked it an indifferent glance. "Yeah," she grunted, and turned away.

Early next morning—a morning gray with rain and leaden, low-scudding clouds—a notice was issued to all personnel that Mr. Bolzer, as per previous agreement with Mr. Severn, was, as of now, official superintendent of the Deep-Sea Towing and Salvage Company, whose orders must be obeyed on pain of instant dismissal.

To the notice a rider was attached, announcing the appointment of Captain Peewee Jorgenson, formerly of the tug Crocus, as commander of the Narcissus to replace Captain Annie Brennan, who was hereby and forthwith discharged from the company's employ.

Stony-faced, Annie read it, and a half hour later, while she was

TUGBOAT ANNIE AND THE DANGEROUS CHEAPSKATE

cramming her clothes into a battered old suitcase, there appeared at her cabin door the rebellious, angry-eyed crew of the Narcissus, including the hemp-thatched, gigantic-framed Peewee Jorgenson.

"So that fathom o' shark's gut fired ya, Annie!" Peter growled. "Well, tell him to go to hell. Ain't a man in the company won't back ya—includin' Peewee!"

"Yust yeu say de vord, An-nie," supplemented Peewee, "und Ay kick his teeth in."

Later in the morning, with the substitute hawser on board, the Narcissus surged away into the rain and mist along the slip, while Annie stood forlornly on the wharf in the heavy downpour and watched, for the first time in many years, her beloved old tug sail without her. Then, as the rain-blurred Narcissus disappeared, she blew her nose violently into a huge blue bandanna.

"Dang me!" she muttered. "Must 'a' ketched ammonia! Oh, well"—she picked up her suitcase—"now I better go find me a fleabag ashore, an'——Oof! Why in tarnation don't ye watch where ye're goin'!" For, in turning, she had collided violently with the powerful frame of Mr. Horatio Bullwinkle, who had come up, unobserved, behind her.

"Hel-lo, dear," he said dulcetly, and grinned. "What ya doin'—skipping off wi' the boodle? Or did they kick ya ashore to get fumigated?"

Instantly Annie's big fists bunched. "Don't you start nothin', ye ugly ape!" she roared. "I've took all I'm gonna take today! So bungle off whiles ye kin still live an' breathe!"

At once Mr. Bullwinkle's manner changed, for in her strained, unhappy face was a desperation he could not mistake. "O.K., O.K., ya old fat-pot," he said soothingly. "What's the trouble? Mebbe I can help."

"If I telled ye," Annie mumbled, disarmed by this unexpected sympathy, "ye'd prob'ly git drunk to celebrate."

"Could be," he admitted. "But anyway, come on over to the Salamander out o' the rain and we'll sort it out. Now, then, what's been gripin' ya?"

Their long-standing business and personal antagonism, often bitterly fought, had at least taught them respect for each other's professional competence; so, on this common ground, Annie told him what had occurred. And, listening, Mr. Bullwinkle's anger blazed.

"Why, that dog belly!" he rasped. "And he ain't even a towboatman! If they's anything at all I can do, Annie——"

"Thanks, Horatio. But what worries me is this gale that's blowin' up. If the Chesil Bank gits caught in it an' that stinkin' hawser parts, what about the skeleton crew she'll have on board to handle the lines? The worst danger spot, o' course, is that rough open water atween Mission Island an' Ship Head. If they kin git past that——"

"And if they don't," he interrupted somberly, "that steamer'll drive ashore sure as blazes, and ain't nothin' your Narcissus can do!"

"But my boys'll take some awful risks tryin'. Because they know that by me goadin' Bulger into bein' Alec's employee, it'll be Alec that damages'll fall on if that steamer an' her cargo's lost! An' if anythin' happened to 'em, through tryin' to pull me an' Alec out of a hole——"In fast-rising tension Annie leaned forward. "Look, Bullwinkle, we can't jest sit here on our fat starns an' wish 'em safe home. We gotta do somethin'."

"What about the Coast Guard? Ya could alert them."

"Yeah," Annie snorted. "An' if that hawser did hold, which it might, they'd think the nutpeckers had drilled holes in me nuggin. No—I got a better idear. I got near three thousand dollars saved outta me wages. An' wid that I'll hire yer Salamander here an' go up to meet 'em! Then if the steamer gits in trouble, we'll put yer towin' wire on her an' take over!"

Mr. Bullwinkle stared. "Are you nuts?" he asked. "Out of a job, and riskin' your hard-earned savin's?"

"Peewee an' the boys was willin' to risk their jobs to stand by me!" she retorted. "An' now I—well, I can't explain it, but——"

"You've explained it, Annie," he said quietly. "And you've got yerself a deal."

"A straight hirin' job, mind. An' no chiselin'."

"Straight hirin' job. Ya can have it in writing, if ya like. Furthermore, I'll skip me profit and only charge ya straight operating expenses."

Instantly Annie's eyes narrowed. "What's the ketch?"

"There's no ketch, ya stupid jerk!" Mr. Bullwinkle roared, and his virtuous indignation for once was real. "I want to do my part too! This time I'm on the level."

"On'y time you're on the level," Annie replied, grinning, "is when ye're drunk or asleep. But come on"—she got energetically to her feet—"le's git our John Monikers on that paper afore ye change yer greedy mind!"

In his cabin the transaction was completed and, since they did not plan to leave until the following night, Mr. Bullwinkle offered Annie the hospitality of his tug and occupancy of his cabin.

"No, thanks," she declined with a grin, "there's somethin' pretty important I gotta look up ashore."

"Somethin' that's hooked up wi' this deal?" he asked curiously.

For a moment she did not reply. Then she said abruptly, her blue eyes hard and bright, "Ever know a leopard to change its spot? Well, somethin' Bulger said last night jest didn't fit in wid his skimflint business methods. So I'm gonna check around wid the customs house an' some ships' agents an' marine-insurance people I know. An' mebbe they kin come up wid the answer. Well, be seein' ye, Bullwinkle. Thanks a lot."

Three nights later, buffeted by a vicious southwest gale and beset by treacherous crosscurrents and powerful tide rips, the steamer Chesil Bank was threading slowly southward in rain and utter darkness, through the narrow but fairly well-protected channels between the islands. Deep-laden with her cargo of heavy timbers, she plunged and wallowed, sending explosions of spray over the fo'c'slehead.

Here the brine-soaked, shivering members of her scanty crew kept close watch upon the dripping hemp towline which stretched through the deep blackness to the straining Narcissus, fifteen hundred feet ahead.

Inside the Narcissus's wheelhouse Peewee Jorgenson's huge calloused hands expertly gentled the kicking wheel, his keen eyes striving to pierce the darkness ahead of the sea-washed window. He turned sharply, as the door swung open and Peter staggered in with a bottle of coffee.

"Whoosh!" Peter gasped. "Sure takin' a beating, ain't we?" He poured the scalding coffee into a thick mug and offered it to Peewee. "Want this while I take the wheel?" he asked.

Peewee shook his head. "No, t'anks, Peter. Ay keep it till ve cross dat open vater yust ahead. Next half hour vill be pooty rough going, so better you hang on good."

"You ain't kiddin'!" grunted Peter, and he stared through the side window to where the running lights of the Salamander, a hundred yards abeam, wildly pitched and rolled. "I sure feel better since Annie and Bullwinkle showed up!"

"Ya. So, better get 'em on radiophone und say dat if ve cross here hokay, dat hawser vill hold anyt'ing, und dey can go home."

On the Salamander a similar conclusion had been reached, and even as Peter was making the sputtering radiophone connection the tug's powerful bow smacked a green sea away as she swung around, then ran back, to be usefully nearer the Chesil Bank when she was towed clear of the shelter of Mission Island.

The full force of the gale leaped to meet them as the crucial trip across the three miles of wild, open water commenced, and all three vessels, for minutes at a time, disappeared under the impact of giant, smoking seas.

On the Salamander, with Mr. Bullwinkle at the wheel, Annie fought her way aft along the upper deck, and there, stunned and half blinded by the driving spindrift, she clung to the rail, watching the rolling, plunging bulk of the Chesil Bank only fifty yards away while, in the shelter of the house on the fantail below, two deckhands crouched, shot line coiled, ready to put the tug's heavy towing wire on the steamer's fo'c'slehead if need arose.

Yard by yard, the little convoy battered its way across the maelstrom of the gap; then, after forty critical minutes, there appeared out of the welter, close ahead, the dark, precipitous loom of Ship Head, beyond which was comparatively sheltered sailing. Annie realized that the Narcissus already had progressed beyond the Head and that, in a matter of minutes now, Mr. Bolzer's hawser would have passed the test, with the Chesil Bank drawn to safety.

Jubilantly Annie returned to the wheelhouse. "She done it, Horatio!" she yelled. "Soon as me Narcissus gits her past the Head, we kin turn tailcoat an' make fer home! An' when we git in, pal, I'll buy ye a fifth o' kelp squeezin's what'll set yer hair afire!"

"If I get to open the bottle before you do," he replied with a grin. "Anyway, what are you celebratin'? You're still out of a job, and this little trick has shot yer savin's all to hell! So——"

He was stopped dead by a sharp crack that rose above the tumult of wind and sea. And instantly they knew what had happened.

"There she goes!" Annie yelled despairingly. "Git the searchlight on her, quick!"

The Salamander heeled sickeningly and shuddered throughout her length as Mr. Bullwinkle jammed the wheel hard over and she came hard about, while the searchlight's dazzling beam cut through the wild, wet night. Then it focused on the Chesil Bank, and Annie, who had rushed out to the rail, saw that, with the parted hawser trailing from her bow, the steamer was being blown inexorably back toward the murderous, surf-exploding base of towering Ship Head.

Slamming at full revolutions into the solid green seas, the Salamander drew closer; but now, caught in the deadly grip of a flood-tide current whose velocity was trebled by the force of the gale behind it, the Chesil Bank was drifting with incredible swiftness toward the foot of the cliff, where the enormous combers detonated with terrifying force against black-fanged rocks among which, within minutes, she would meet complete destruction.

Without hesitation Mr. Bullwinkle took a desperate gamble and, by superb seamanship, ran his Salamander razor-edge close across the steamer's plunging bow. And in that split second of imminent death, Tugboat Annie, who trusted no hand but her own, had snatched the shot line from a deckhand's terror-paralyzed grip and sent it whizzing with unerring aim across the Chesil Bank's rail and into the desperation-eager hands of the seamen on her fo'c'slehead.

The Salamander kicked forward and, when the heavy towing wire was hauled up and made fast to the steamer's bitts, Mr. Bullwinkle came about, his tug slugging it out with the assaulting seas, her powerful towing engine paying out wire and slowly taking up the strain. For a few heart-stopping seconds no progress could be made; then, with agonizing slowness, the Chesil Bank's head began to swing until, with her stern scant feet from the thunderous battleground of reef and surf, she was hauled clear and safely towed into the sheltered island channel beyond Ship Head.

The wind still was blowing strong, but the sky was blue, the sea sparkling when, early next morning, the Chesil Bank was secured alongside a Secoma cargo shed and the Salamander surged across the harbor toward her home slip.

"Well, Annie," remarked Mr. Bullwinkle complacently, "that hunch o' yours sure paid off!"

"Ye're wrong," Annie replied, her heavy face grim. "The payoff don't come till I meet Bulger an' Alec Severn when we git in."

"Severn?" Mr. Bullwinkle stared. "Ya said he was in New York."

"I wired him afore we sailed that he'd better sashay home fast. Know what he wired back?"

She produced a crumpled, brine-stained telegram and handed it to him. It read:

FLYING BACK IMMEDIATELY. IF YOU AT FAULT WILL MAKE FIRING FINAL.

"That's sure definite, ain't it?" Mr. Bullwinkle rasped. "Damn dirty shame after what you done!"

"Mebbe it ain't so definite," she said cryptically. "Better stick wid me an' see what I mean."

The Salamander entered the slip and, as she moved toward her berth, Annie glanced across. The Narcissus already was alongside; and on the wharf, staring at the Salamander, were Mr. Bolzer and the choleric and angry-eyed Alec Severn, who, while the Salamander was being made fast, stepped on the stringpiece.

"Annie," he bawled, "get over here at once!"

"Give yer orders to a coupla other suckers, Alec!" she shot back. "I ain't workin' fer you now—remember?"

After a quick, startled exchange of glances, he and Bolzer started around the slip, and Annie and Mr. Bullwinkle descended to the wharf to meet them. And, not by accident, Annie planted her solid bulk between Mr. Bolzer and retreat toward the shore end.

"Now, then——" Severn began, but Annie quickly interrupted.

"I'll say it, since I know the full score," she said calmly. "Uglypuss Bulger here fired me fer refusin' to use a rotten hawser in bad weather." She turned to him. "That right?"

"It wasn't rotten!" he snapped. "It would have done the job fine, except for that extra strong gale. I couldn't foresee that!"

"It was rotten an' ye knowed it! Yet, like the horse's tail ye are, ye was willing to risk men's lives on it—because ye did know about that comin' gale! I telled ye that, meself!"

"All this is nonsense, Annie," Severn put in heatedly. "What would Bolzer gain by taking a risk like that?"

"I'll git to that," said Annie, grimly now. "So listen good! The rotten hawser what Bulger provided snapped, off Ship Head. An' if it hadn't been fer Bullwinkle an' the fine job he done wid his Salamander, the Chesil Bank would ha' bin a total loss! An' more important, so would seven human lives!"

"What—what do you mean, seven lives, Annie?" Severn gasped.

"Her crew! An' since it was your tug what used that defective hawser, Alec, it's you who'd have had to pay."

"You know better than that!" Severn protested shakily. "All our towing contracts contain a disclaimer-of-damage-liability clause!"

"When you handle 'em, yes. But you was in New York, so Bulger drawed up the Chesil Bank contrack. When I got through nosin' around ashore the other day, I had Olive show it to me. An' sure enough, the disclaimer clause had bin struck out. Ax Bulger who done that!"

Slowly, Severn stared at the scarlet face of Mr. Bolzer. "But—but why?" he asked incredulously.

"I had to, Severn," he cried, "or we mightn't have got the job! It was taking a chance, perhaps, but——"

"Yeah! A chance," said Annie, "that on'y came off because the Chesil Bank was saved. Except that it could still leave Alec liable fer the thumpin' big salvage award the Salamander earned by savin' her!" She turned to Severn. "Did Peewee tell ye all what happened last night? I axed him not to 'til I saw ye."

"No," Severn replied, white-faced. "He just said Bullwinkle was handy when the line parted, and you'd explain the rest."

"Well, here it is!" And briefly but pungently she told him. "So wid ship an' cargo wuth about three hundred thousand," she ended complacently, "an' the danger we run, the award'll be at least a third

TUGBOAT ANNIE AND THE DANGEROUS CHEAPSKATE

o' that. Insurance won't cover it because there ain't none. A friend o' mine ashore telled me her owner's reputation fer sharp dealin' is so bad that no underwriter would cover her. So it'll come out o' ship an' cargo. I'm givin' twenty-five percent of it to Bullwinkle, o'course——"

"You? You're giving it, Annie?" Severn asked, astonished.

"Sure. As a well-earned bonus," she said, affecting not to notice Mr. Bullwinkle's astounded gratification. "Ye see, I pledged me savin's to hire the Salamander, figgerin' she'd be needed if that hawser parted."

"So her owner will sue me to recover!" said Severn wildly. "And I didn't even supply it!" Angrily he turned on Mr. Bolzer. "You did!"

"Don't blow off at me!" that gentleman snapped. "I'm only your employee. This fat hag made sure of that! And as my employer you're responsible, not me. That's the law!"

"That's right, Alec," affirmed Annie quietly. "If I hadn't ha' riled him into makin' hisself manager, you'd ha' bin in the clear. So if ye want to make his firin' me stick, now's yer time to do it."

For a long moment Severn's eyes, hot with anger, met her steady gaze. Then, suddenly, his face sagged and he shook his head.

"No, Annie," he said dully. "Whatever your damn-fool reason was, you must have figured it was helping me. So——"

"Thanks, Alec," she said huskily. "That's what I hoped ye'd say. An' it sure lifts you offa the hook. Because I paid a few bucks to a admiralty lawyer ashore, an' he telled me that if a tug-company employee—meanin' you, Bulger!—knowin'ly supplies defective equipment an' don't tell his boss his real interest—which, in this case, is sole ownership o' ship an' cargo—he can't secure his loss at his employer's expense. Whew! Ain't that a jawful?"

"You mean," Severn gasped incredulously, "that Bolzer here owns the Chesil Bank?"

"An' her cargo. Through a dummy company, o'course. The customs folks dug that up fer me. An' look! Look at the guilty puss of him! The setup was, that——"

"I see the setup!" Severn rasped, and furiously he grasped Mr. Bolzer's shirt front. "You couldn't get insurance, so casting your ship away was no good! But this way, if she was lost, the damages I'd have to pay you, you skunk, you'd lend back to me to get control of my business!"

"Instead o' which," Annie grinned, "he'll hafta sell ship an' cargo to pay the salvage claim! Ain't that swellegant? An' fer attempted barratry they'll stuff him in the hokey-pokey fer the next ten—— Hey! Grab him, Bullwinkle!"

TUGBOAT ANNIE AND THE DANGEROUS CHEAPSKATE

For Mr. Bolzer, wrenching free of Severn's grip, had started to run. But Mr. Bullwinkle's long arm shot out and grabbed the seat of his pants. The fabric parted, however; and with his unexpectedly renewed momentum Mr. Bolzer shot like a projectile into the dock.

Dodging the splash, Annie turned complacently back to Severn. "That'll cool him off. Now, what was you about to say?"

"I was trying to figure how you first got onto Bolzer."

"Simple as mud," she replied. "When a miser like him telled me he voluntarily cut a towin' fee, me self-conscious warned me there must be somethin' phony. So, after he fired me, I started snoopin' fer it ashore. An' now, o'course, ye won't git any financin' from him. But——"

"I'll manage, Annie!" he said stoutly. "As long as you and I are together——"

"Ye interrupted me. I was gonna say, ye don't need his dirty money now. Even after payin' off Bullwinkle an' givin' the boys on the tugs the bonus I promised 'em, ye'll still have more'n enough to put the company back in shape. That salvage award——"

"What do you mean, I'll have enough?" he protested quickly. "Why, Annie, that salvage money will be yours! You can quit working and buy yourself a nice little home ashore, and——"

"I like workin'!" she cut in roughly. "An' the old Narcissus is me home! It's all I'll ever want!"

"But I'm not entitled to one cent! You weren't even working for me at the time! Bolzer had fired you!"

"When I git fired," Annie said irascibly, "you'll do it! Nobody else! So poof an' fiddlesticks! Asides——" She looked off to where Mr. Bullwinkle was helping to pull the sodden, terrified Mr. Bolzer back on the wharf. "Come over here, stupid, an' tell Alec in whose name I hired yer Salamander fer that salvage job!"

"Severn's Deep-Sea Towin' and Salvage Company, o'course," said Mr. Bullwinkle, joining them. "I told ya not to be a fool—'specially when ya guaranteed payment outta your own savin's. But——"

"That satisfy ye, ye ol' gafoozler?" said Annie to her boss, with a triumphant grin. "You'll have the dough ye need, I've still got me job, an' that lump o' crab bait"—she pointed to the subdued and shivering Mr. Bolzer—"will git his lumps in court. So now, since I didn't have no sleep last night," she concluded with a prodigious yawn, "I'm gonna scuffle back to me Narcissus an' knock off a few hours' fiesta!"

TUGBOAT ANNIE AND THE SUNKEN GOLD

With her wake spinning jeweled arabesques over moonlit water, the big salvage tug Narcissus of Secoma, homeward bound, rolled placidly down the Inside Passage of Alaska. In her tiny cabin abaft the wheelhouse, Tugboat Annie Brennan, the vessel's master, roused from sleep by some subtle warning of danger, levered her big body upright, and sniffed; then, still uneasy, she padded to the door, opened it and sniffed again. Now it was unmistakable; hastily donning a slicker over her old flannel nightgown, she entered the wheelhouse.

"Somethin's burnin' someplace, Peter!" she said to the tug's large, phlegmatic mate. "Can't ye smell it?"

Peter leaned out of the doorway and vigorously inhaled. "Forest fire," he said. "Prob'ly on the mainland."

"This early in the year?" said Annie quickly. "That ain't good! Some o' these little settlements is still pretty isolated. An' remember them hunters what was trapped up Pack Rat Inlet last year? What was left o' them wouldn't make a pinch o' snoose for a Swede midget!"

As she spoke, quick footsteps sounded along the deck, and Clem, the radio operator, appeared. "We've got a fast rescue job on our hands, Annie!" he said abruptly. "Just had a radiophone call from Barney Hogan, woods boss for the Forest King Logging Company at the Cougar Landing camp. Know where it is?"

"'Course I do!" Annie snapped. "It's at the south end o' Lost Pass acrost from Whiskey Island. What's the deal?"

"There's a big forest fire on the mountain behind their camp. It's eating down toward 'em, and they've got to be snatched out o' there fast!"

"Ain't they got no boats?"

"A couple of putt-putts. Nothing to handle this deal. There's twenty of 'em and their gear. Their winter-cut log boom's made up, and Bullwinkle's due there today to tow 'em out."

"Bullwinkle?" At mention of her rival, Horatio Bullwinkle, master and owner of the big bluewater tug Salamander, Annie's rugged face suffused. "How'd that hambone come to be——"

"Ya know damn well, Annie," Peter cut in. "He's on that five-year Forest King Company towin' contract he beat you outta."

"Oh, yeah. I did slip on me ta-ra-ra on that one. Go on, Clem."

"Hogan tried to call Bullwinkle for help, but couldn't connect. Then while I was calling the weather stations Hogan cut in, and——"

"O.K. Phone Hogan to git his boys out on the boom wid their gear an' cast off! The current'll carry 'em away from the shore, an' we'll pick 'em up afore they've drifted too far."

Following Clem out, Annie clattered down the ladder, yelled to Big Sam, the engineer, for top speed, rousted out her startled crew, crackled an order for Pinto to shake up a quick breakfast, and, with the big tug shaking from keel to masthead from the accelerated propeller thrust, she puffed up the ladder to check again with Clem.

"What's the scoop?" she demanded. "They cast the boom off yet?"

"They can't," he said tensely. "Hogan says the tide would spill the boom all over Whiskey Reef. So they'll burn or drown if we're too late! Bullwinkle's hours away—I just talked to him. The jerk said this was just a trick of yours to skunk him out of Hogan's tow."

"Nuts!" Annie said. "Tell Hogan to hang on!"

Through the maze of islands and risky short-cut channels the Narcissus sped until, at daybreak, a sinister red glow waned and flared under the loom of the land. Soon Whiskey Island slid past the port beam, and the tug surged across the Lost Pass entrance, toward the mouth of the Cougar River a quarter mile away, while Annie's smoke-stung eyes sought to locate the landing. Then a sudden flare-up of waterfront shacks revealed the cluster of loggers, desperately waving from a big, chain-bound log boom at the water's edge. Swiftly the tug surged alongside and made fast; but the loggers were staring anxiously along the fore shore of the pass. "Cast off that shore line, you brushcats!" Annie bellowed.

"Wait! We can't!" someone said. "Hogan an' Ole ain't back. They're tryin' to find the——"

"Here they come!" a shout went up, and two running figures

pounded back along the narrow beach, plunged through a fiercely burning patch of brush and leaped out onto the boom. And with the shore line cast off and Hogan and his crew safely on board, tug and boom moved out into the strait.

Topside, Annie instructed Peter to head for Port Klootchman, a modern, fair-sized fishing and cannery harbor on Kupreanof Island, about sixty miles away. "They's a marine hospital there if Hogan an' his boys needs it. An' Clem's told Bullwinkle we got 'em aboard, an' he kin pick up the boom from there." Then she went in search of Hogan.

He was on the fantail staring back at the still blazing ruins of Cougar Landing; on Annie's approach his fire-seared face managed a painful grin. "Golly, chum!" she gasped. "Better rub some lard on that——"

"It'll wait, Annie. We're plumb lucky to be here at all. And my boys shore are grateful!"

"'Twas nothin'," she disclaimed, abashed. "Anyways, what was you an' Ole doin' back along the pass—practicin' fire eatin'?"

"N-no," he said slowly, and his gaze went to the smoking mountainside behind the landing. "We was looking for the Snowman. It was him started that blasted fire."

"What was that ye called him?" Annie said.

"The Snowman. The Abominable Snowman. Least, that's what our camp belly robber named him when he first seen them big footprints in the snow by the cookhouse last winter. He's just a crazy old hermit that's lived on the mountain, God knows how many years, and doesn't want no strangers around."

"Ye mean that's why he set that forest fire? To drive ye out," she asked incredulously, "if it killed ye or not?"

"Yeah, but anybody as crazy as him, Annie, they ain't responsible. That's why Ole an' me wanted to make sure he—well, wasn't hurt, maybe. But that fire! There wasn't time."

"Ye done what ye could, Barney," Annie said quietly. "Had this—this Snow Bum ever bothered ye afore? Other years, I mean."

"There was no other years, Annie. The company owned just one small stand o' big trees—a one-season cut—back o' the first ridge. So last year we built our headquarters camp at the landing, then moved back in and started cutting. Then, when we'd floated the winter cut down the river on this spring's flood and made up the boom, we was through. Ready for Bullwinkle to tow us out."

"Well, if ye was leavin' fer good why'd the—the Snow Bum try an' burn ye out?"

Hogan shook his head. "Like I told you, he's cracked. After the cook saw snow tracks back in the early winter, we'd notice somethin' watching us from between the trees. Looked like some big animal. A bear, maybe. It was him, in clothes he'd made outta raw pelts."

"An' he never come close?"

"No. We'd leave food out nights and watch. Nobody'd see him; but by mornin' the grub was gone. Well, about a mile along the pass from Cougar Landing is acres o' bare rock an' boulders—bed of an old glacier, maybe—full o' cracks and holes. An' one day after the snow was gone a coupla my boys was crossin' this stony patch looking for deer, an' they damn near stomped on him, lyin' asleep under a ledge o' shale. He leaps up—a huge guy in them stinkin' furs! Long white hair and whiskers an' wild, crazy eyes, an' took off up them big rocks like a mountain goat! An' him eighty years old if he's a day!"

"Did they go after him?" asked Annie.

"You kidding? They high-tailed back to camp with him following! Screamin' like a banshee! Pitchin' rocks! Cussin' and yelling a lot o' senseless babble about claims an' gold pokes, an' how they couldn't prove nothing, and they'd never take him alive, and so on!"

"Sounds like a old-time Yukon sourdough what's lost his migs," commented Annie. "Then what happened?"

"Nothing. We left him strictly alone, because whoever went near that big bald space above the pass would get a shower o' rocks at their head. But here's somethin' curious, Annie. Every evening, in good weather and bad, he'd sit on top o' the cliff, just starin', for hours on end, into Lost Pass directly below!"

"An' then prob'ly creep back into whatever hole in the rocks he lived in, to sleep," Annie muttered, and suddenly her eyes filled. "Pore ol' guy. Barney, ye sure he set that blasted fire?"

"It figures," Hogan replied somberly. "Couple o' days ago we had our boom all made up an' ready to be towed out. But it just didn't seem right to take off an'—an', well, leave him here alone. So me and the boys starts scoutin' that rock area, hoping maybe we could sweet-talk him into comin' along, when *Boom!*—a rock knocked Frenchy Gagnon cold; and there's this crazy old monkey scrabblin' up the slope an' peltin' us as he goes. That night he was up on the mountain behind the landing, yelling curses at us out o' the dark. Next morning a drum o' kerosene was missing—remember, the woods are still wet—and last night all hell rolled over that mountaintop."

"Guess ye're right then, Barney. Still, I sure hope the pore ol' coot——" Annie began, but sharply was interrupted by strident and odiously familiar siren blasts from Mr. Bullwinkle's Salamander. And a few minutes later she was accompanying the Narcissus on a parallel course, close abeam, while her powerfully built and bandy-legged commander gazed bovinely across from his upper deck.

"Hi, Barney. What'd that fat thief there kick ya in the face for?" he asked solicitously. "Ya catch her pickin' yer pockets, mebbe? She would, mind, like right now she's tryin' to grab this boom-towin' job o' mine."

"Ye're a liar!" said Annie hotly. "Clem telled ye we'd meet ye at Port Klootchman!"

"Ya can keep that slop, dear, for them that would swaller it," he said kindly. "I'm here to pick up that boom. So——"

"Git on wid it then, ye—ye public inconvenience!" Annie roared. "But mind ye take Barney an' his boys to the Port Klootchman hospital fust."

The Salamander moved alongside and, with both tugs under a slow bell, the loggers were transferred; Annie watched, the Narcissus rolling in the long swell, until the Salamander and her tow were headed for Port Klootchman. Then she turned away and entered her wheelhouse.

"O.K. I'll take the wheel now, Peter," she said.

"Where to now, Annie—home?" Peter asked as she jingled for "full ahead." Annie did not answer, but when the tug picked up speed she wrenched the wheel hard over, and Peter stared.

"That cussed Snowman!" she said grimly. "I keep thinkin' o' the pore loony, mebbe hurt an' needin' help, like Barney said, an' dyin' alone wid' no help around! So go tell Clem to notify the office we're headin' back fer Cougar Landin'."

When the Narcissus arrived, the fire had burned itself out; an onshore breeze, blowing back the heat and smoke, showed only a desolation of charred stumps and a carpet of gray ash. Here and there, however, embers still glowed; so until evening the tug patrolled Lost Pass while Annie and the crew minutely scrutinized the area of rock, boulders and shale. But beyond occasional spirals of soot and ashes swirling across it, nothing moved.

Then, in the long Alaskan twilight, with the Narcissus anchored in Lost Pass below the cliff and Pinto left as shipkeeper, Annie and the others lowered the workboat and went ashore. The rock area above the beach was inaccessible on foot, so they approached from the direction of the landing through clouds of choking, eye-stinging soot and still warm ash dust until, racked with coughing and half-blinded, they struggled through to the bare, formidably contorted detritus of a long-vanished glacier.

"If he's still livin'," said Annie, wiping her streaming eyes, "it's gotta be here someplace! So spread out an' start lookin' for the old coot."

But after nearly two hours of grueling, meticulous search, they arrived, sore-muscled and exhausted, back at their starting point and flopped down to rest.

"It's no use, Annie," said Clem wearily. "We've covered it all."

Annie rubbed her blackened, sweat-stained face, grunted morosely, creaked to her feet and then stood motionless—an earthy, solid figure, alone with her private thoughts in the eerie silence of a ruined wasteland.

"Well, le's go," she said dully. But instead of moving, her big body tensed, and she turned, listening, in the direction of the cliff's edge, invisible behind the intervening rocks. "I hear——"

"So do I!" Hank cried, and scrambling over the granite shelf behind them he dropped to the other side. After a difficult, shin-bruising pursuit over the confusion of upthrust shale and giant boulders, and guided now by Hank's urgent, summoning shout, the others reached, almost at the cliff's brink, a ten-foot-deep crevice formed by two slanting rock slabs.

Hank, down in the crevice, looked up at their approach. "He's here, Annie," he said quietly. "But he's hurt. Hurt bad."

He stepped to one side, and they stared down, horrified, at a large, grotesquely contorted bundle of what looked like a mangy, fire-scorched animal fur topped by a tangled mop of once-white but now singed-and-blood-soaked hair and whiskers. In the gaunt, pinched old face, faded blue eyes held a glazed stare; the withered lips moved constantly in a babble of unconnected words and phrases which rose, at times, to a defiant shout, then subsided and finally ceased. But their theme was, as Hogan had said, of mining claims, the Klondike, gold dust and pursuit.

"Same crazy ravin' Barney told me about, pore guy," said Annie sympathetically. "But we'd sure never ha' found him widout him yellin' out like he done. Well, let's git him outta there right away an' down to the tug."

"Down to the tug? How?" asked Shiftless. "We sure can't carry him out the way we come. That trip over the rocks alone——"

"Our Lyle gun, o' course!" said Annie impatiently. "We've took people offa wrecked ships wid it plenty times."

With tremendous effort, but gently, the injured man was hoisted from the crevice; now there was only an occasional shallow sigh to indicate that he was still alive. And with Annie and Hank left to watch him, the others set out on the return trip to the Narcissus.

Twilight slowly deepened into night; then, finally, came a hail from the darkness of the pass, followed, when Hank acknowledged it, by the report of the Lyle gun and the hiss of the soaring line. Shortly afterward the unconscious "Snowman," securely lashed into a hammock-like canvas sling, was on his way down to the tensely waiting and anxious group on the Narcissus's deck.

Annie, staring anxiously down, was relieved when reaching hands guided the sling expertly on board. Then suddenly Hank gripped her arm. "Look who's here," he said. Following his gaze, her soot-stained, sweat-streaked face hardened; approaching the Narcissus along the darkened pass, running lights shining like gems, was Mr. Bullwinkle's fast-moving Salamander.

Instantly Annie hailed her crew. "Run that gear back up here fast!" she roared. "We're comin' down!"

But when Annie, followed by Hank, had reached her deck, the Salamander already was made fast alongside, while Mr. Bullwinkle, outside the Narcissus's galley, was listening with flattering interest to Shiftless's graphic account of the finding of the Snowman.

"An' he was still ravin' about gold-dust pokes and so on, eh, Shiftless?" he said sorrowfully. "Hogan told us about that, on the way to Port Klootchman. Tch, tch, tch! Too bad! . . . Oh, hello, Annie!" he greeted archly. "Ya look like ya stuck yore head up a chimbley! Shiftless here was jest——"

"I heerd him!" she snapped. "Shif'less, go tell Peter to git underway. Now, then"—she turned back to Mr. Bullwinkle—"how'd ye know we was here?"

"We just accidentally happened," he said innocently, "to overhear Clem's message to yer office. Then, too, when Hogan said you was worryin' about the poor old coot maybe bein' still alive—an' you with a heart like a cow, dear—I come to help."

"Ye come, ye lyin' thief," she told him harshly, "to see if I'd found his poke—if any—or got a tip, mebbe, from his ravin', about where it was! Otherwise ye'd ha' skulked back by yerself! Anyways, they ain't no poke. It's all in his pore crazy nuggin. It's not real."

"How d'ya know?" he asked quickly.

"Stands to reason. If he'd struck it rich he'd ha' took it out an' spent it years ago, same as the rest. Look at all them gold-rush ships what come back to Puget Sound ports loaded to the gunnels wid miners an' their pokes—millions o' dollars' wuth of gold dust."

"O.K. An' look at all the ships that didn't get back!" Mr. Bullwinkle countered eagerly. "Every rotten old tub that could float was in that trade. Scores o' them was lost up-an'-down the Inside Passage here, bringin' men back from the gold fields. Some of 'em was drownded, and their pokes went down with 'em! Others swum ashore with or without their pokes. An' know what my guess is?"

"That the Snowman's one o' them?"

"That's right! I think his ship went down right in this pass, an' his gold dust with it. He got ashore O.K., but thinkin' about what he'd lost must have drove him offa his rocker!"

"Yeah, could be," Annie admitted.

"Sure it could! I'll bet there's even records, someplace, o' some o' them missin' ships! An' if I knew where to look——Annie! Ain't ya listenin'?"

"I'm thinkin'," she said, and as she spoke, the clatter of rising anchor cable sounded along the deck. "Look, tell yer mate to cast off. We're gittin' underway. He kin pick ye up again when we git outta the pass. Then come back here, an' we'll mebbe talk a deal."

With alacrity Mr. Bullwinkle obeyed; when he had disappeared around a corner of the house, she entered the galley. Mr. Bullwinkle returned and found her in the messroom.

"Set down if yer pants is clean, Bullwinkle," Annie invited, affable now. "Fust thing, what about Hogan's log boom? Ye was s'posed to tow——"

"Hogan's still in hospital. Him an' his boys want to go down with it, so I'll pick it up later. Now what's yore deal?"

"Somethin' we talked about gave me the wrinklin' of a idear. If it pays off—an' it could—whatever we find goes to the Snow Bum if he's still alive. It's his. All we detract is expenses. If he dies, we try an' trace his kin——"

"How can ya when nobody even knows the old boy's name?"

"—an' if we do," Annie continued, "same deal, plus mebbe ten percent fer our trouble. Leave it or lump it."

"I got a choice?" Mr. Bullwinkle snarled. "What if he croaks, an' they ain't no kin that we can find?"

"Then we divvy it, hurly-burly an' tit fer tat. Meanwhile, you wait here till I git the Snow Bum to the hospital at Post Klootchman, an' talk to a old pal o' mine what's watchman at a cannery there. Then I'll be back. Now, then, is it a firm deal?"

"Yeah, guess so," he said dubiously.

"Well, say it!" Annie demanded, rising.

"O.K., it's a firm deal!" yelled Mr. Bullwinkle. "Ya sure as hell don't trust me, do ya?"

"'Course I trust ye, Horatio," said Annie soothingly.... "Don't I, boys?" Whereupon the sliding door to the serving shelf between messroom and galley shot wide open, revealing the grinning faces of Pinto and Clem.

"Sure you do! Everybody does!" they assured her. And the door closed.

When an ambulance—waiting by prearrangement at the Port Klootchman wharf—had sped the Snowman to the hospital, Peter headed the Narcissus for the fish cannery across the harbor, while Annie and Clem stood outside the open wheelhouse door.

"Who is this Potlatch Murphy you're going to see now, Annie?" asked Clem curiously. "Seems to me like I've heard the name up here."

"Who ain't?" said Annie, grinning. "He's the oldest livin' fossil in Alaska. An' when it comes to local shippin' history, he's a walkin' velocipede."

"Cyclopedia, Annie," corrected Peter mildly with a smile.

"Same thing, ye dope! But most important, right now, he served in the old U.S. revenue cutter Bear all through the gold-rush days on this coast, and ain't a ship loss or sinkin' he don't know about. That's his shack on the dock there, Peter. Head in alongside."

Even before the Narcissus had tied up, there stepped agilely out to greet them a small, sinewy, completely bald old man with a merry, wizened little face and lively brown eyes.

"Well, by the Seven Virgins o' Noorvik! Annie!" he cackled.

"Come on aboard, ye old gooey duck till we see what still nails ye together!" yelled Annie, delighted.

But first Potlatch darted into his shack for a bottle. "Fifth o' kelp extract," he piped. "This we gotta celebrate!"—and jumping nimbly to the tug's deck, he rattled up the ladder and vigorously shook hands. "To stay as old as me, Annie," he advised, "ye gotta have a passion—wimmen or likker! Mine's likker! Now then," he whooped, "why don't we all get stinkin' and have some fun?"

"Hey, slow down, ye old hellion!" Annie grinned. "I want to ax ye some questions fust! So come along to me cabin. They're important."

Potlatch listened with alert attention while she briefed him on the happenings at Cougar Landing involving the Snowman. "So kin ye tell me," she concluded, "of any vessel what sunk in Lost Pass durin' the gold-rush years?"

"Yep," he said promptly. "There was two. Mind ye, I couldn't swear either of 'em was lost in the pass itself; but they went down either there or the waters around Whiskey Island. One, I remember particular, because it also concerned the revenue cutter Bear I was servin' in at the time. She was the steamer Quinault, on a reg'lar run between Norton Sound, Skagway an' Secoma, and her master was a fat Dutchman name o' Captain Van Ronkel."

And, with the relish of all old-timers reliving the past, Potlatch described in detail the story of the Quinault. How the Bear, on coast patrol, had received urgent orders from Washington to intercept the Quinault in the Inland Passage and remove a passenger wanted on a serious Federal charge. The Quinault at the time, according to her schedule, would be approaching the vicinity of Lost Pass; so, intending to intercept her at the north end of the pass, the Bear sailed at top speed south from Petersburg——

"Hold it," said Annie suddenly. "She's not——"

"——but we missed her in the fog, and she was never seen again," said Potlatch, intent on finishing his story. "What was that you said, Annie?"

"I said she ain't the one! If the Bear was headin' south to intercept her, the Quinault musta bin headin' north! The one I'm tryin' to trace was bound south, and it was full o' miners from the Yukon, wid their pokes. What was the other one, Potlatch?"

"The Kenbarra, Annie. Captain Andrews was her master. And she *was* southbound, carryin' miners and about $460,000 in gold dust, it was figgered later. Last seen o' her, accordin' to the report the Bear got, she was goin' at a fast clip through Frederick Sound. But if she kept straight on through Lost Pass or hit a reef on the west side o' Whiskey Island, nobody ever knew. But outside o' them two, Annie, no ship was ever lost within seventy mile o' Lost Pass."

"She's the one. The Kenbarra, I mean," said Annie happily and flung open the door. "Clem," she bawled. "Fetch yer fiddle. What me an' Potlatch is gonna do to the turtle trot'll kill ye!"

It was many hours later when Potlatch, fighting briskly, was tossed out onto the wharf from which—after ardently embracing a mooring bollard—he hurled a boisterous farewell after the rapidly departing Narcissus.

"I knowed," said Annie with a rueful grin as she set the tug's course for Lost Pass, "when he started coaxin' the ventilator cowl to blow Reveille that it was time to send him home. But he sure liked you, Clem, else he wouldn'ta hit ye. Look, did ye send the message to the office tellin' 'em to lemme have all the dope they kin get about the Kenbarra?" He nodded. "O.K. Now git in touch wid that no-good Horatio Bullwinkle that we got good news about our deal."

Minutes later Clem returned. Mr. Bullwinkle's reply was brief. To the point. It said simply, "What deal?"

Annie looked at Clem. Then, granite-faced, she jingled Big Sam for flank speed. The chips were down.

The extent of Mr. Bullwinkle's perfidy amply was demonstrated when, in late afternoon, the Narcissus again entered Lost Pass. The

Salamander was anchored just below the bluff, and alongside her was a small but well-equipped and self-propelled salvage barge from Port Klootchman. And emerging from the water up the side of the barge was a diver, carrying the heavy, barnacle-encrusted rim of a ship's porthole, which his helper took from him and tossed on the top of a heap of other minor salvaged articles on the barge's deck.

"He's found the Kenbarra!" Annie croaked, dumfounded, to Peter, who had taken over the wheel. "Put us alongside!"

As she waited, her knuckles white with tension on the rail, Clem approached and handed her a radiogram. "From the office," he said, "Better read it right away." But the Narcissus was now nudging the Salamander's rail, and she impatiently crammed the message into her pocket, jumped over to the rival tug and presently was glaring at Mr. Bullwinkle's broad back as he addressed the diver.

"How'd ya make out this time, Mac?" he asked genially.

"Duck soup, cap'n! When she went down, her boilers exploded and opened her up like a busted sardine can. And that safe was right where we figured. The derrick can hoist it up anytime."

"Anythin' else down there that looks promisin'?"

"Can't tell yet. Too much muck's stirred up. There's lots more o' that junk, though," and he pointed to a sodden heap of what seemed to be scraps of black, withered leather and corroded chain. "Whole big case of it. When do you want your safe up?"

"After supper. You'll hafta have some rest. O.K.?"

The diver waved assent, and Mr. Bullwinkle turned to meet Annie's menacing glare. "Why it's Fatso!" he cried in artless wonder. "Kinda thought I smelt somebody behind me." He indicated the barge. "Ain't this the limit? Poor today an' rich tomorra!"

"How'd ye locate the Kenbarra so fast?" she gasped, big fist closing.

"The—oh, the ship? Be glad to tell ya, Annie," said Mr. Bullwinkle benevolently. "After ye left I missed ya; so I went up to where ya found the old guy, to try an' forget. An' while——"

"Oh, yeah? That I kin believe!" said Annie bitterly.

"An' while strollin' around," he continued, "lo an' behold if I didn't find the stinkin' cave he lived in, right under the overhang o' that cliff! An' in a heap of old rags was a wallet holdin' two waterstained pieces o' paper. One was a sketch o' the pass below the cliff marked with an X. Later I trawled a drag where he'd marked, then radioed fer the barge quick—because there she was!"

"Well, I come back," said Annie roughly, "wid almost the same inf——"

"Wait, lemme finish. The other piece o' paper," he resumed

triumphantly, "was a receipt from the captain to a passenger—the old loony, prob'ly—fer $200,000, in currency what he'd had put in the ship's safe!"

"Wha—at?" Annie gasped incredulously. "Are you sure?"

"Ready to be brang up! An' all done wi' no help whatsoever from you!"

"I was workin' on it!" Annie countered desperately. "The ship's name is the Kenbarra, Cap'n Andrews, master, out o'——"

"My, my, how wrong can we get?" said Bullwinkle mildly.

"I even had our office check, an' by golly," she cried, suddenly remembering, "I got their report right here! So, ye skunk-faced lump o' petty larceny," she trumpeted, thrusting the message in his hand, "read *that*!"

Mr. Bullwinkle did, then looked at her peculiarly. "You seen this yoreself yet, Fatso?"

Alarmed, she snatched it. It read:

WRECK OF S.S. KENBARRA FOUND OFF WHISKEY REEF 1932. DESTROYED AS MENACE TO NAVIGATION. BOSS SAYS QUIT HORSING AROUND UP THERE. GET BACK PRONTO OR NO JOB.

Dumbly Annie stared at it, high hopes punctured, ego utterly deflated; and, keeping her head down to avoid Bullwinkle's amused regard, she did not even resent the solicitude in his voice as he murmured, "Why don't ya step over the side, dear, an' take a nice long walk?"

Presently he was gone, jauntily climbing the ladder toward his cabin; but Annie remained by the Salamander's rail while, slowly recovering, she flogged her unresponding brain for a plan to force her triumphant rival to share the wealth without litigation. Then, too tired and discouraged even to think, she became aware that two of the salvage-barge hands, but a few feet away, were discussing the disposal of some of the salvaged rubbish on their deck.

"Shorty says this goes overboard," said one, pausing at the heap of brine-pickled leather and rusty chain. "What the hell is it?"

"Dog-team harness," said the other, a swarthy, flat-faced Aleut. "One time long ago," he pointed north, "gold miners pay weight in dust to buy. This never got there and now is junk. Too bad."

Stolidly they heaved it over the side, but a fuse in Annie's brain was lit; presently she straightened, blue eyes snapping, and climbed to Mr. Bullwinkle's cabin. After pausing to restrain her exuberance, she gave a subdued knock on the door; then, unbidden, she entered.

"I didn't come to fight wid ye," she said almost humbly. "I come to—to—— Well, since ye read that message from the office, I better speak plunk an' plain. Alec wasn't foolin' about firin' me, Bullwinkle. An' if I don't go back wid some kinda deal——"

"Look, don't start that again!" he rasped. "I told ya the score!"

"It ain't that one-sided," she replied. "No vessel's name was in our deal, an' wid my witnesses we could hang ye up in the courts fer years. An' somehow I still think this ship ye found is the Kenbarra. But if ye're able to prove it ain't, I'll let ye offa the hook on the old deal an' make another that'll be easy on you an' save me me job. So what do ye say?"

Mr. Bullwinkle's consideration was brief, for he well knew that her threat to sue had teeth. "O.K.," he said, "I'll prove it!" And, producing a faded, soiled and brine-stained oblong of paper, obviously genuine, he showed it to her.

"There it is," he said. "Ship's name, shipmaster's name, amount, master's signature! An' now," he asked, "what's yore offer?"

"You give us yer thirty-day note fer five thousand dollars, plus turnin' over to our company, as of today, yer towin' contract wid Hogan's outfit."

"And in return, what?"

"In return we give up any an' all claims, present or future, on whatever ye take out o' this wreck. O.K.?"

"You win," he said.

"Git yer pen an' spellin' book then, an' start writin'," Annie said, suddenly impatient. "I want this thing cut-an'-dried in a hurry so's I kin git back to me job o' just plain towin'!"

The agreement was executed in duplicate, with Jake, the *Salamander*'s mate, and Peter, called over from the Narcissus, as witnesses. When Annie left, tucking her copy in her capacious shirt front, Mr. Bullwinkle gallantly accompanied her to the deck.

"Why don't ya wait around an' see us bring the safe up later?" he suggested, still euphoric inwardly over what he considered the best deal he had ever made. "Wouldn't ya like to see what's in it?"

"I know what's in it," said Annie. "A soggy mess o' paper money what sea water's ruined years ago."

"Don't be silly," said Mr. Bullwinkle. "Ships' safes are always made watertight. You know that. And anyways, no matter how bad a condition money's in, or how old it is, the gov'ment will repay ya in full. . . . That right, Peter?"

"That's right," Peter agreed and gave Annie a curious look. "But she knows that as well as you do."

"Ye figger on recoverin' any gold pokes, Bullwinkle?" Annie then asked. "Because I'll tell ye now, they ain't any."

"How the hell do you know?" Mr. Bullwinkle demanded scornfully.

"Because she's the S.S. Quinault, Van Ronkel, master——"

"Ya read that on the receipt I showed ya!"

"—an' she sank in March o' 1902—which I didn't read on no receipt! An' that date alone should tell ye why there'll be no gold pokes, because whoever heard of a gold ship comin' south that time o' year when the Yukon's bin locked in the sea fer months! No, Bullwinkle, she was bound north, not south!"

"By dad, she's right!" Peter exclaimed, "She sure is right!"

"So what?" Mr. Bullwinkle demanded. "She still had $200,000 in her. Has, rather, as it belongs to me!"

"Ain't arguin' that, Horatio. But afore that it belonged to Herman Slager, the Snow Bum's right name, that is! An' the night she sank, the revenue cutter Bear was lookin' to stop her an' arrest Slager. He was a international crook, wanted in the Africa an' Australia gold fields an' the Kimberley diamond fields!"

"Look," said Mr. Bullwinkle violently, "are you nuts too? Where'd you get all that claptrap? Or ya just bein' smart, or what?"

"From Potlatch Murphy, over to Port Klootchman," said Annie equably. "An' even a windbag like you's gotta admit that Potlatch Murphy, the old devil, knows what he's talkin' about."

"So what was this Slager's racket?" Mr. Bullwinkle asked.

"He'd go into gold fields or diamond fields whenever a new one opened up, like he had headed fer the Klondike. Then he'd buy the dust or nuggets or whatever from the miners at goin' rates. They'd be glad to sell, o' course, because it saved 'em comin' out an' losin' time on their claims. Then, by the time they started lookin' fer him, it'd be months too late, because he'd skip as soon as he'd made his killin'!"

"Well, what was illegal about it if he paid 'em goin' rates? Look, Fatso, this don't make sense! So I ask ya again, what was Slager's racket?"

"If I telled ye that, Horatio," said Annie with a grin, "ye'd know what makes the time bomb tick. Well," she moved toward the rail, "pommy de terre, as the Frenchies say. . . . C'mon, Peter," and with Mr. Bullwinkle staring after her in utter distrust, she clambered back onto the Narcissus and got rapidly under way.

But in the Narcissus's wheelhouse, as they headed back for Port Klootchman to pick up Hogan's boom, Peter's normally placid face was grim. And when Annie asked him what was wrong, his reply was prompt.

"You!" he exploded. "That's what! Lettin' a tin-plated eight-ball like Bullwinkle diddle ya outta a hundred thousand dollars on a stupid deal fer five thousand an' a towin' contract! An' that silly talk about what a crook Slager was, then not provin' it! An' that yak-yak about a time bomb! What's got into ya? You crazy, Annie?"

"Peter," said Annie softly. "Today, when I found out in front o' Bullwinkle that the ship he'd found wasn't the Kenbarra, I dumm near died! An' I didn't know who or what the other one was. Not till I discovered that she'd bin bound north, not south. Then——"

"How in the world did ya discover that?" Peter grunted.

"Them dog-team harnesses the diver had brought up. Because what would they be doin' on a ship comin' out o' the North? I figgered, but couldn't make sure, she was the Quinault till I skunked Bullwinkle into showin' me that receipt. An' knowin' then, from what Potlatch had telled me about Slager, that Bullwinkle's money plus Hogan's towin' contrack was the on'y real deal, I talked him into makin' it."

"Guess I'm stupid, Annie; but I still don't understand what Slager done that made him a crook!"

"Ye don't know because I ain't telled ye yet. As fer the time bomb—know what it is? It's anything ye've had around fer a while what explodes in yer puss when ye least expect it. An' that's what Bullwinkle is haulin' up outta Lost Pass tonight. An' it's right in that safe!"

"But that ain't right, Annie!" Peter protested angrily. "If it's somethin' really dangerous ya should ha' warned——"

"Hunh-unh!" Annie grinned. "It ain't dangerous that way. An' it won't explode till Bullwinkle axes the gov'ment to change his $200,000 into clean new bills. Meantime, he'll have scallions o' fun spendin' it in his mind. But when he does—*Boom*! Because ye see, pal, Slager—that cheatin' old Snow Bum—used to pay off his suckers wherever he operated, wid counterfeit dough!"